Alone and Wrestling

An Anthology

For Elaine + Kirk,
Enjoy a bit
Many blessings

5/23/23

Alone and Wrestling

An Anthology

Seymour Rossel

Rossel Books
Dallas, Texas

Published by:

Rossel Books
6523 Genstar Lane
Dallas, Texas 75252
https://RosselBooks.com

First Edition

ISBN:
978-0-940646-78-0 hardcover
978-0-940646-79-7 paperback
978-0-940646-80-3 eBook / Kindle
Library of Congress Control Number: 2022933642

I extend my grateful appreciation to **Lorna Keating** *for her insightful and incisive copy-editing. Particular thanks go to* **Deborah Rossel Bradford** *for her suggestions and attention to detail. And the child in me would not be satisfied without mentioning the abiding debt I owe to my first writing teacher* **Siddie Joe Johnson** *(1905-1977). She was the face and spirit of the children's department of the Dallas Public Library from 1938 to 1965. She began reading my poetry and fiction before anyone should have, led me to books by authors who had authentic style, encouraged me to join her weekly Young Writers' Circle, taught me how to be critical without being cruel, and made me a true disciple of libraries and librarians. Her own published books and poetry modeled what she taught. It hardly repays my debt but it is pleasing to have this opportunity to pay homage to Siddie Joe in print. —* **SR**

Dedicated to
Cary K. Rossel

You live the teaching of Hillel.
Most of us ask, "If I am not for
myself, who will be for me?" Some are
better and go on to ask, "If I am
only for myself, what am I?"
Only the rare few like you don't
stop by asking but go on to
answer the final question,
"If not now, when?"

Alone and Wrestling

*That same night he arose, and taking his two wives, his two maidservants, and his eleven children, he crossed the ford of the Jabbok. After taking them across the stream, he sent across all his possessions. **Jacob was left alone. And a man wrestled with him until the break of dawn.*** — Gen. 32:23-25

Contents

Essays in Education

Foreword

Seymour Rossel and I have interacted directly and indirectly throughout my career. Around 1972, when I was active in the Westchester branch of the National Federation of Temple Youth, Seymour was the Director of Education at Temple Beth El of Chappaqua, NY, where several of my close friends (even to this day) were active, and students of his. In 1973, I recall encountering Seymour when he visited a class taught by our "mentor-in-common" Rabbi Manuel Gold (of blessed memory) in Manny's elite education program for high-school students at the Hebrew Union College-Jewish Institute of Religion's New York Campus. Seymour was then Executive Vice-President at Behrman House Publishers helping Jewish education take a welcome turn towards serious scholarship. Later, in his work as Dean of the School of Education at the New York Campus of Hebrew Union College-Jewish Institute of Religion and in our frequent interchanges at early Coalition for Alternatives in Jewish Education conferences, my regard for Seymour as a gifted scholar and teacher deepened. Shortly after I left my position as Associate Director of the Commission on Jewish Education for the Reform movement of North America, Seymour became the Director of that Commission, and I watched our common interest in Jewish education flourish under his guidance. As Publisher of the Union of Reform Judaism Press, Seymour brought forth texts that demonstrated the serious nature of liberal Jewish scholarship. And under his own imprimatur, Rossel Books, Seymour has published works that cover the wisdom from Chelm, texts on the Shoah, introducing Biblical stories to children, a guide to the weekly Torah portions, and master works from scholars such as Rabbi Chaim Stern and Dr. Jacob Neusner. Certainly, subsequent interactions solidified our friendship, and deepened my respect and awe of Seymour's learning, and ability to make that learning accessible and interesting.

You now hold in your hands Rabbi Seymour Rossel's latest opus, *Alone and Wrestling*. This anthology of Seymour's many stories, articles, essays, and sermons, is also a retrospective, as it spans the entirety of his career (thus far, thankfully). While each piece is thought provoking and challenging, taken as a whole, the book shows an organic development of thought, and a life-long love of everything Jewish.

Some of the pieces herein are haunting—in a good way. Echoes of Seymour's thought spring up long after the article has been read. "Isaac: God's Special Child" is one such example. On the surface (*p'shat*), the biblical text offers very little as to the character, and characteristics, of our second Patriarch. Through serious scholarship and intellectual creativity, Rabbi Rossel offers a shocking analysis of Isaac—and forces us to see people who we might think of as "other" because of different learning modalities as part of God's plan.

"When Two and Two Make Three" is a serious explication of the importance of magic and demonology, dreams and amulets, in the life of our religious antecedents. While we like to think that such things should have no place in the pursuit of knowledge, our ancestors relied heavily on such "sciences" to explain their world. And such ideas persist today. That will make one scratch one's head and roll the idea around, while walking down the street and spying "a lucky penny." Hmmmm ....

"Our Dialogue with Buber" brings an intimacy to the pursuit of knowledge. I wish I was in the office when Seymour and his friend probed the remarkable Martin Buber, who was as inscrutable in person as he can be in his writing. And I, too, want to know if "Yes" was an answer or an affirmation.

And if you want to know the power of a single book and how it can change history and a people, "The Purity of Piety" will provide all the insight you need. The selection of Rabbi Rossel's sermons will make you think, and his essays on education should be read by every teacher and teacher-to-be.

You don't need me to give a precis of each precious gem in this compendium. As Hillel said (quoted in Talmud Bavli Shabbat 31a): "*Zil g'mor*—Go and learn." The great thinker Ahad haAm (in a letter to Rabbi Judah Magnus) wrote: "Learning—learning—learning: that is the secret to Jewish survival."

Rabbi Seymour Rossel's life has been dedicated to learning and teaching. With this book, and the lives Seymour has touched through his writing, publishing, and teaching, I have no doubt that we will not be searching for the last Jew anytime soon.

From the 1970s on, I have sharp memories of a cowboy hat and boots (long before they were fashionable in New York City and its environs), a pipe, a rich and raucous laugh, and incisive wit and wisdom—all of these on or in the person of Seymour Rossel. Those memories remain in focus. To this day, with a tip of his cowboy hat, a shuffle of his cowboy boots, a wave of his hand holding a now-unused pipe, and a hearty laugh, I see Seymour riding off to work on his next project. And I know we will all continue to learn from a master teacher, for which I am ever grateful to the Holy One.

Rabbi **Gary M. Bretton-Granatoor**
Rabbi of Congregation Shirat HaYam,
Nantucket
Written in Brooklyn, NY
April 2022 / Nisan 5782

"The Last Jew
in America"
& Other Fictions

The Last Jew in America

Jewish philosopher and educator, Henry Slonimsky (1884-1970), believed that being a member of a great people bestowed "grandeur on the self." Individually, our lives are brief; identity imbues us with near immortality. "A people is itself a person with definite distinctive features, and, if carried by a sense of power, is the creator of history and of spiritual reality" (Essays, p.141). This short story (hopefully humorous) explores the cloverleaf-like intersection of on-again, off-again identity and assimilation.

Albert Einstein was a Jew; Albert Schweitzer was not. I keep this truism in mind because I grew up with a Jewish kid named Steven Schweitzer, but I never met a Jewish kid named Einstein. If you think about it, Albert Schweitzer could have been a Jew. If he had even hinted that he was Jewish, people would have believed it. He looked Jewish enough. He behaved in ways my Hebrew School teachers always spoke of as "Jewish." As far as I can tell, he and Einstein were equally righteous fellows, but Schweitzer was more religiously inclined than Einstein. Einstein eschewed organized religion; Schweitzer wanted to reorganize it. But everyone knew Einstein was a Jew, and Jews claimed him as their own. Mind you, if we Jews thought we had a chance of getting away with it, we might have claimed Schweitzer, too.

Someone—it might have been my brother, of whom we have always been a bit suspicious because he is an accountant and he voluntarily teaches at a Temple on Sunday mornings— told me about a Jewish population study that determined that fifty-five percent of America's Jews are assimilating. "Disappearing," he said.

"Dropping out" was the expression we would have used in high school. In college, we would have said that they were so "laid back" that we couldn't "reach" them anymore. However you express it, a few days after I heard this news, I noticed that my hair, which up to then had been only graying slightly, was beginning to accumulate on my comb in the mornings.

"Don't take it so personally," I thought, staring into the mirror. But I noticed that it continued to bother me on a daily basis. It was an image that haunted me as I sat behind my computer. Fifty-five percent! And what if the rate of assimilation had accelerated since the study was published? Were we hurtling downhill like a skier out of control? One day I wondered, "What would the last Jew in America do to assimilate? Was it humanly possible for the last Jew to assimilate entirely? Would only fifty-five percent of him assimilate? Would the Jews in the rest of the world come to look for him? How would the *National Enquirer* report the story?"

FOUND! THE LAST JEW!

DATELINE: MIAMI. The last Jew in America was located two days ago by an expedition of Jewish sociologists from Tel Aviv. Jewish American, Daniel Moskowitz, was discovered living peacefully in a condominium he had purchased in 2004 from another assimilated Jew. The identification was made entirely through extraordinary luck. Moskowitz had evidently forgotten to remove the talisman from his doorpost when the old tenant left. For the past six years, Moskowitz has been escaping notice by living as a bachelor under an assumed name, calling himself Albert Schweitzer.

Schweitzer/Moskowitz's neighbors claimed no knowledge of his waning Jewishness. "He seemed such a likable person," said Mrs. Wendel Tecumseh of North Dade, who has known Moskowitz for nearly five years. "Who would have thought that a person named Schweitzer could be a Jew?" Mr. Tecumseh added: "A person should not be judged by heritage, you know. There are traces of tradition everywhere in America." Jonathan Siegel, an Episcopalian who lives next door to Moskowitz, was far more vociferous. In an angry mood, he said, "All things considered, I am thinking of selling instead of living in a changing neighborhood."

The sociologists from Tel Aviv University asked Schweitzer/Moskowitz if he would participate in their survey on the Vanishing

American Jew. At last report, the subject had not yet agreed to do so. In a telephone conversation exclusive to this reporter, we asked Schweitzer/Moskowitz if he would, in the end, submit to the Tel Aviv study. His reply was, "I have half a mind to."

The Memorial Jewish Welfare Federation of Greater Miami, now a division of the March of Dimes, has already publicly stated that they would conclude their yearly campaign by sending Schweitzer/Moskowitz a pledge card. When asked if this would be efficacious, the executive director of MJWFGM would only comment, "It couldn't hurt..."

But I digress. Let's get back to the hair accumulating on my comb. Was it logical to assume that the Jews of America would vanish without a trace? If Einstein was theoretically correct, things don't just disappear. Of course, whole civilizations have vanished in America before. It is a well-known fact that America is a kind of cultural black hole. Even so, it wouldn't seem to those living inside the black hole that things have disappeared. To Americans themselves, even living in the very vortex, things which had already disappeared would still seem present, even if nothing and no one outside of America could see them. Take, for example, literature. To those of us in America, there would still seem to be writers. We'd be singing the praises of Kings who wrote macabre works and Clancys who penned techno-thrillers and Browns who concocted pseudo-historical eschatology. But to those outside the black hole, all that could be seen would be one gaping mother lacuna.

But assuming that Einstein was right (and things don't just disappear) and assuming that America was not a black hole (and things were not being sucked into an enveloping eddy), where were the vanishing Jews going? They certainly were not disappearing from Monsey, though some might say that being in Monsey was like being in a Star Wars parody where everyone dressed like Darth Vader. That might be true (for it is well known that you can count the number of holes it takes to fill the Albert Hall), but on the other hand, the Jews might be disappearing to Florida, to Arizona, to North Carolina, to Texas. If they were disappearing *to* those places, were they disappearing *from* those places, too? Miami, Phoenix, and Houston seemed like good candidates for places where one might fall off the world with few, if any, taking any particular notice. That was what passed through my mind as my comb passed through my hair, and the hair fell off my comb, and the stray strands floated gently down the drain. I just kept telling myself, "Don't take it so personally."

But while we are speaking personally and of things disappearing, our family legend has it that we once kept kosher. When my great-grandfather died, my mother declared her independence of organized religion by bringing a package of bacon into the house and placing it on the bottom shelf of the refrigerator. (Grandmother, who was living with us at that time, had escaped two bad marriages, both to Jewish men. The first husband was abusive; the other was lazy. The first she divorced; the other she abandoned.) Family legend doesn't say how Grandmother felt about finding the refrigerated package of bacon.

I imagine her opening the big white door and confronting the package staring up at her from the bottom shelf. Hormel. *Trafe.* Like a virus waiting to spread. She probably frowned and raised her eyes to look at the bread. She had kept the bread in the refrigerator ever since my mother threw out the old tin breadbox. One more piece of tradition gone. One more small hair running down the drain. One more moment of doubt each day. Of course, family legend doesn't say whether Mother ever actually used the bacon she brought into the house. It is understood that Mother never went so far as to actually bring ham into the house. Bacon was a symbol; ham was no doubt a sin. I seem to recall the same package of bacon from when I was nine; the same package from when I was eleven; and it might have been the selfsame package that I stumbled upon when I returned home from college at twenty. The package of bacon always exuded a faint smell redolent of forbidden meat and symbolic erosion.

When it came time for me to study for my Bar Mitzvah, there was further attrition. I was sent to a Conservative synagogue three blocks farther from the house than the Orthodox synagogue. My mother had some careful plan in mind. Was she consciously attempting to vanish? "On a stairway to hell," my grandmother murmured as she walked my brother and me to Hebrew school past the Orthodox shul on those icy Chicago afternoons. But Grandmother continued to live with us even when one of her ex-husbands, the lazy one, showed up. She merely moved him in and asked us to call him "Gramps."

"Gramps" would read from the Bible. He would sit in the reddish-orange easy chair with me on his lap on one side and the Bible on his lap on the other, blowing smoke rings from his pipe and reciting the deeds of King Solomon. He was a lot like Solomon: He never worked a day in his life, and he intended to do nothing more than consume food, pass along sacred stories, and blow perfectly formed smoke rings. One afternoon, after a stormy day and a withering rain of words, Mother tossed him out. Discounting my younger brother, I wondered if I were doomed forever to live in a house of women.

I don't remember my father at all. Mother tossed him out when I was a little less than two. I can't say with any certainty whether he went before or after the tin breadbox. It was probably before because I have a visual memory of the breadbox covered with a calico pattern with little pink strawberries scattered through red latticework. It had a Rockwellish quality and had once seemed utilitarian like all good American things should be, but the refrigerator had rendered it extinct, so it vanished like my father had before it.

It was just after "Gramps" was dethroned that Mother made her next bold move. This I remember quite well because of all the bickering it caused. Mother somehow took it into her head to begin lighting the *Shabbos* candles with the silver cigarette lighter from the table in the living room. My grandmother objected strenuously to this breach of Jewish tradition.

According to the history of Jews in America, Grandmother should have worked in a sweatshop making ready-to-wear garments. She never did. Before Mother's divorce, Grandmother had worked in a match factory making safety matches. She must have been good at her job, too. She was ever reminding us to be careful with fire. And she despised the idea of using anything besides a match to light the *Shabbos* candles. Matches were good enough for her mother and good enough for her grandmother. Where did my mother get the *chutzpah* to use a bulbous gleaming cigarette lighter? As Friday evening approached, Grandmother would prepare the food, go to the kosher bakery for the *challah*, set the table, and place the brass candlesticks in the center. Then, to make her point, and even though my mother would refuse to use them, my grandmother would place a box of safety matches prominently between the candlesticks.

When Mother came home, she would smell the food and praise my grandmother for it. Then she would look at the table, see the box of matches, and glare. Grandmother would glare back. Glares went forth in thrusts and parries. In this art, they were evenly matched. When we were all gathered around the table, Mother would go off to the living room to grab the silver lighter from the coffee table where it sat on a little silver tray between a matching silver cigarette server, a matching silver ashtray, and a strange silver contraption for collecting ashes that looked like a cross between a nautilus shell and a jug and was called (for some inscrutable reason) a silent butler. Mother brought the lighter into the dining room. Calling up reserves of pomp and circumstance, she utterly ignored the safety matches and lit the *Shabbos* candles with the blessing and the cigarette lighter.

In time, Grandmother grew canny. She endeavored to hide the cigarette lighter. Once she placed it on the end table beside the sofa, secreting it behind the lamp with the Chinese woman base. Mother found it. Once she placed it on top of the television set. Who would think to look for a cigarette lighter there? No one, not even the television repairman, ever looked at the top of the television set. All that was atop the television cabinet was a yellowing lace doily. Of course, if I were hiding the lighter, I would have hidden it where the television repairman always hid things. He would go straight to the television, remove the back cover, and crawl almost altogether inside. I looked inside once when he had the back of the television removed. There was a good shelf filled with little glass tubes on a little tin base. You could easily hide a cigarette lighter on that shelf beside the tin base. Nevertheless, though no one else might have thought to look at the top of the television cabinet for a cigarette lighter, to my grandmother's chagrin, Mother did.

Then came the Friday that my grandmother tried her most elegant trick. She left the cigarette lighter in plain view, right on the coffee table, right on the silver tray, directly between the ash tray and the cigarettes. Mother found it at once. She brought it to the table and went to light the candles with it. She triggered the top with her thumb. The lighter sputtered a few sparks but refused to light. Grandmother glared. She had burned out all the fuel. Mother glared. She was not to be overcome so easily. She marched to the kitchen, opened the cabinet where the lighter fluid was kept, opened the screw at the bottom of the cigarette lighter, and turned them both upside down, the tin of lighter fluid above the cigarette lighter. She smiled and squeezed. Nothing came out. Grandmother glared. She had emptied the lighter fluid tin. Mother tossed out the brass candlesticks. It was the last time candles were lit at our house. Every Friday night, Grandmother prepared the food, went to the kosher bakery, and set the table. Every Friday night, we waited at the table for my mother to come home. Every Friday night, dinner began, and Grandmother would murmur under her breath, "Another nail in my coffin."

I didn't really miss the *Shabbos* candles. For me, their presence was never a question of identity. I was just glad that my mother and grandmother didn't get a divorce. There had already been too much divorce in my family. Whatever it took for them to get along, that was fine with me. If not lighting the *Shabbos* candles meant that everything would remain peaceful at home, I was in favor.

I moved in with this Jewish girl a few years later, and she lit *Shabbos* candles in brass candlesticks. I always wondered if they were the candlesticks my mother had discarded. I never insisted on her lighting the candles with a cigarette lighter. Once, I mentioned it as an idea, asking, "What makes the matches traditional? Even candles are an innovation." But my girlfriend resisted the idea of using anything besides matches for lighting her candles. When I divorced her fourteen years later, I had twins, both girls, who had grown up thinking that matches were an essential part of their Jewish heritage. As for me, tradition was the smell of *challah* in the refrigerator, the memory of a calico breadbox, and the package of Hormel bacon that remained forever unopened.

For most of our marriage, my wife and I lived in the suburbs. One day, our twins were ready for preschool. The moment had come. There was a Conservative synagogue not far away. It was convenient. But we were better Jews than that, so we went "shul shopping." Or "shuls hopping." My wife called it something like that. We kept at it until my wife smiled approvingly in one rabbi's study. We joined a Reform Temple. My mother came to visit, and we all went to the Temple for Friday evening services. When the organ started playing, I think my mother mumbled something under her breath. It might have been, "Another nail in the coffin."

We didn't think that way. My wife thought the rabbi was wonderful. He really understood what it meant to be an American Jew. He kept talking about it in his sermons. I might have appreciated what he meant, but frankly I never quite understood his sermons. In the end, I nicknamed him "Holocaust Harry." No matter where his sermon began, it always ended with something about the Holocaust and not giving Hitler "a posthumous victory." This seemed very distant from the everyday life of a computer programmer. Like the other men in the congregation—all of whom commuted at least an hour to get to work in the morning and another hour to get home in the evening—I slept through most of the sermons.

One night, my wife said, "Maybe we should go to Temple, and you should stay home and get some sleep."

"What's wrong with sleeping at the Temple?" I wanted to know. "Isn't *Shabbos* supposed to be a day of rest?"

"You snore," she answered. She was right. We had reached another milestone. I stayed home and fell asleep in front of the television. The television had gone from being a lot larger than I to being the size of the old breadbox in my grandmother's kitchen. It also never complained about my snoring.

I did attend Temple on the day that my twins celebrated their Bat Mitzvah. The part that I didn't sleep through was wonderful to see. Of course, the divorce had come a few years before, but even spending a lot of time with my ex-wife at the Bat Mitzvah could not ruin the occasion. For one thing, with the amount of money I was spending, I was determined to have a good time. It was then I began to contemplate whether divorce had become a Jewish tradition like the Holocaust and the *challah* and the matches. I also wondered if other American Jews were wondering this, too. I asked my brother, but he wasn't wondering. He was accounting. He could account for everything that happened in the family. I could account for none of it. To me, it seemed buggy, like a bad segment of program code.

I was at a low point in my existence. I began to watch late night television. You could tune in to any talk show or any sitcom and know that Judaism was good for a laugh. Do people joke about things that are disappearing? If so, why weren't they making blue whale jokes or trading jibes about horned owls? Why was it only funny that Jews were going extinct? Both my daughters had solemnly promised to marry Jewish boys. Both dated only non-Jews. What would be the end of it? My hair kept getting caught in the comb, and I kept growing older.

I went to see my optometrist. "I can't quite get the world in focus anymore," I told him.

"You're getting older," he said.

I confessed to being confused. "Does getting older mean that I can't have spectacles like I've always had?"

He laughed. "You misunderstand," he said.

"Most things," I replied.

"See here," he said, "as you get older, your eyes get better. You aren't nearly as short-sighted as you used to be."

"Are you Jewish?" I asked him.

"I used to be," he said. "Now I am Methodist. I live in Westchester, and there are no Jews in my town. I would have fought, but my wife said 'Switch' so I did."

"You talk like a Jew," I said.

"It's a hard habit to break," he answered.

He made me glasses, bifocals. "You'll get used to them," he said. "You have to look through the upper part to see things far away. You have to look through the lower part for reading."

But I couldn't get used to the bifocals. To watch TV, I had to practically get on top of it. To take a close look at my daughters, I had to lower my head. None of this seemed to make sense. It is all a matter of perspective, I told myself.

Like the Jewish question. In the distance, they tell me, we are vanishing. Right now, I see us thriving everywhere. What difference whether the synagogue is Orthodox or Conservative or Reform? That nice distinction makes more sense to the rabbis and cantors than it does to the people sleeping through the sermons. Everyone eats bagels. Non-Jews included. When I hear American leaders speaking, they are saying things I was taught were Jewish. Priests don't seem to care so much anymore about the reality of Jesus. I even heard once that a priest was speaking of the Holocaust as a human tragedy. Everyone eats lox. It may even be that the Scots invented it. It doesn't really seem to matter. If you look closely, you might think we Jews were the only real Americans and that everyone else was just trying to be Jewish.

Rabbi Holocaust Harry had gotten through to me on one score. He once said that "Jews are short-term pessimists and long-term optimists." Maybe my optometrist was right. The real answer is to stare through the bottom part of the lenses only if you want to watch us disappear. If you look through the top of the lenses, you will see us out there being Jewish. It is all a matter of perspective, I tell myself.

All this notwithstanding, I worry. They say that already fifty-five percent of us are gone. Whenever I look in the mirror now, I check to see that I am still all there—not my hair, of course, that is as lost as the Ten Tribes—but the rest of me. If I am vanishing, I wonder which part of me will go first? Will I start to fade from my feet up or from my head down? Or will the fading occur only on the inside until at last there will be only forty-five percent of me remaining, and it will all be on the surface like an exoskeleton? Or is all this just as symbolic as the bacon in Mother's refrigerator. Maybe American Jews are developing new symbols while the pundits conduct polls centered on old ones. I must check with my brother. He will be able to account for it all.

And I spend a lot of time worrying about my old friend, Steve Schweitzer. Has he disappeared? Has he succumbed to assimilation? Or is he in some distant jungle planting a new strain of Jewish life? One day soon, I'll friend him on Facebook.

The
Demonstration

*In my Senior year at Southern Methodist University,
my Creative Writing professor and good friend, Dr.
Marshall Terry (1931-2016), submitted this story and
a sample of an unfinished novel I was writing to a na-
tionwide competition. I was the Southwest Region Win-
ner of the Book-of-the-Month Club Writing Fellowship
for 1968. This distinction came with no cash whatso-
ever. Three national finalists came away with all the
prizes. But one of the competition's judges was assem-
bling an anthology to portray youth in the late 60s. He
thought my story captured "an important vibe" of that
counterculture and so, in 1969, this story was included
in* Growing Up in America, *edited by Robert A.
Rosenbaum, and published by Doubleday Press.*

The cold chill of the outside air seeped in through every un-
sealed seam and through the loose slats in the brown wooden
walls covered with chipping paint. Bill was playing guitar, half
sitting, half lying on a mattress spread out on the floor a few
feet from the record player. The bookcase beside him was
stuffed with the unreal worlds of Ferlinghetti, the dingy blue-
jean morality of Kerouac, the frenzied genius of Nietzsche, and
the twisted imagination of Miller. Hot-water pipes, strung hap-
hazard along the gray-brown ceiling, knocked intermittently,
punctuating the constant hum of the secondhand refrigerator.

The smell of heavy, flat beer pervaded our single room
apartment, settling all around us. Bill's guitar underscored everything: its unreal, untuned sound clinging to the dirty needle-

crafted throw rug and hanging from the walls like a thousand balloons rubbed against a pants leg—friction, static friction.

Staring at the wall, I flexed my fist just to feel my body move. If I came out of sleep too quickly, the balloons might come crashing to the floor with a leaden thud. So I lay back, watching Bill—long, low, sleek, and black—stroking the guitar. The wooden walls turned vomit color, holding back a tide of effervescent motion careening from balloon to balloon. It was my merry-go-round for one, with extra seats that never got filled and a short, fat, black man who spun the wheel with the instep of his clubfoot.

When the guitar was gone there was only Bill, humming softly as he lay staring at the bookcase. The refrigerator noise and the knocking in the pipes were his percussion. His concert hall reeked of bad beer. The humming itself was a soft under-the-breath moan that Bill meant for himself alone to hear although he knew that I could hear it. I pulled the covers up and pushed the pillow down closer to my stomach. Even as I tried to sleep, I knew that I was already awake. The wall was dirty. I carelessly scraped one hand across it sending chips of paint spiraling to the wooden floor. The guitar sounds still lingered in my ears as I stretched out on the bed and began remembering everything that I was trying to forget.

I finally drifted off—sleep was my escape. When I woke again, Brenda was there. In the hazy half-world between waking and sleeping, I could feel the pressure of her kiss, the hand poised above my stomach, and the taste of her lips. Her soft whispering made airy sounds in my head; my mind still gently reclined. How long had I been asleep? The sound of rain outside tapped against my forehead. Time was like the painted chips spiraling slowly to the floor. I drew her down, my hands in her black hair, to kiss her wet pink tongue. Bill was gone, his guitar resting face down on a crumpled sheet beside the mattress. Rain tapped against the window.

Brenda went into the kitchen to put on coffee. I slipped out of bed and lit a cigarette, then climbed into my clothes. The night was wearing off and the reality of a tomorrow that was today just beginning to ache. In the washroom I took two aspirin and sat down on the stool. The smell of coffee was pungent black, staining and pouring, hot and wet, down my throat. Brenda opened a window shade to the muted sun.

"It's a sun shower."

I walked past her and looked through the dirty window-pane. Rain blocked my vision; I couldn't think; I couldn't see the clock above the old bank. A hundred thoughts hung loose. It was good that Brenda had come. She was resting on my bed, looking up at the ceiling, thinking, perhaps, or waiting for me. I came back and stretched out beside her, feeling her warmth all along my body, feeling the searing heat where my face rested against her sweater. Brenda was gentle.

She held my hand beside her cheek. "There's going to be a demonstration." Short and clipped, she could hide the length of meaning in her precision—my thoughts began to flow like a torrential rain.

First was the feeling of pulsating action. It was what I had been urging them to do. Something to wake this city up, to stir the students a little, to make people sit up and take notice.

"Baby ..." she said, raising my face with her hand. "Stay out of it. It won't just be our group that's in it."

Stay out of it? When I had helped to bring it along? When I had nurtured it and watched it grow in Bill's mind and in John's and in Ed's? I stared at Brenda, tried to find a wrinkle to interpret somewhere in that serious face. "You know that this is what we've been working for."

"Yes."

I felt warm, the glow of summer magic—the heat of thought, the thought of action. As if it were an old silent film, I watched the little guy holding a crushed straw hat wearing a Hitler mustache, hitting away at an old fat man who just kept laughing. Action. Suddenly the old man was gone—burnt fat, sizzling and smoking, popping in little bristling bubbles. All gone, fat man. Burnt black by little man.

"Stay out of it, baby."

Brenda's eyebrows were lowered, her forehead had knitted in determination. Up there was exhilaration, the thought of long-needed action. The other end was someplace in the present, somewhere close to Brenda.

"If you won't stay out of it ... Don't let me know. Just don't tell me." Slowly I sank back into calmness, my lips resting against her and my mind filled with fiery furnaces. There was quiet in the black of her skin.

I was alone when Bill came back. He gave me a smile, lifted the four records on the turntable and set the machine in motion. The first record dropped like a stone on ice. The arm came to rest at its edge and began its inexorable trip toward the center.

These were the only records they had. This was the drum record: bongos, cymbals—just that and flutes. This was Bill's "real art, man, real." Drums unrelenting, flute shrill and unsettling. The drums disrupted my thoughts. I went into the bathroom and looked in the mirror.

My eyes were set deep in sockets that looked scooped out as if something had gouged out flesh to set them. They were blue, darker than I remembered, with flecks of green. My nose fell from a jutting forehead like snow between two sled tracks— straight, narrow, and imposing. My countenance could be stretched, might be expanded grotesquely by the unknown. Feelings I couldn't understand might turn the color to pure white.

I lit a cigarette. My thoughts were on a trip, concentrating on the world, seeing balloons hanging from every wall. One of the balloons had a Bill-face with two huge ice-cream scoops for eyes. There were merry-go-rounds and short guys with clubfeet. There was the lonely sound of the guitar and rattling drumbeats under shrill flutes.

"Damn it, man, open a window when you smoke those."

Bill reached into the room with half his looming black body and pushed the window up. I watched him through the smoke haze. He struck a match—thousands of dancing colors playing at the tip (how many angels?)—and lit a stick of incense in the brown ceramic holder. The smell was orange blossom pink rose.

It was simple, really. I just went to school and told all my white friends what a great liberal I was. I even had a Negro roommate, a fine fellow, a regular guy. "Just like us," I might say. And a black girl friend, too. And then one day I was on the black side of a demonstration against the school, and then it was different. After that, I would wonder about the doubt in their frozen little faces, look twice at the ice-cream scoop eyes that revealed their minds, work to regain their favor, their friendship. Or would I?

It was like a bad trip. Maybe it was one already. It was like coming down from a high without knowing where it would stop coming down. The incense burned bright for a second—green, yellow, black, red white and blue. I reached out to the flame with my hand and felt no heat as it neared the smoldering end of the stick. No heat. No cold. Pure being and nonreality. I was up.

When the orange blossom pink rose smell and the sunflower look and the spectrum touch were all complete and the cigarette had been dredged to the last bit of elastic smoke and the room seemed like a firefly of bristling being, I settled down on the mattress and waited. Slowly the impressions failed, the morning light was afternoon brilliance, and the sun had moved beyond the top of the window frame. I had watched its quick progress in the morning sky through smoke rings around the deep insets of my eyes.

The only food left was a little cheese and a bag of potato chips. The chips were stale, and the cheese had to be cut away from its mold. I split the cheese into two halves and ate one, washing it down with the flat yellow beer that tasted of age. Food was a second beginning for me, a stimulant only slightly less potent than the first. I immediately felt the need for more, the biting, fixated connection between stomach and brain that pressed me to do something.

I was already into the grocery man for four dollars. There was the ten I owed at the bakery (Brenda's birthday cake included) and four more at the vegetable stand.

The grocer sat behind his waist-high counter on a high stool. On his right was his cash register. Beneath his left hand was a thick black book filled with oversized scrawlings. I had seen enough of the powerful inscriptions. Indelicate accountings, serious, somber calculations telling how much people owed him. My name was there and Bill's and the names of a thousand others, mostly Negroes, mostly poor.

Like an emperor he decided with a nod of his head—its face scarred in the war—which families would be extended credit and which would be refused. He watched me through tiger eyes knowing that soon he would either have my cash or have to decide my case.

Here was the enigma: the cash register was often the quietest thing in the store. Credit was the medium of exchange here—often backed only by an honest face and a solemn promise. Although the grocer could stop anyone from buying, he didn't. It was the feel of power that fascinated him.

Usually he stretched out his left arm with its dead hand dangling at its end and pushed a yellow slip of paper at me. A quickly penned note we both knew was worthless; his long, inexorable scrawl in the book and I would be deeper in debt. There were a few cans of tuna, a can of sardines, some beef sticks, a fresh bag of potato chips, and a soda.

The maimed left hand always rested on that book as if administering an oath by its contents. The other hand counted groceries and punched cash register keys. The grocer's agile hand had five fingers; the left hand had been hit by shrapnel in the war. I signed the paper quickly, saw the scrawl in the book, and came away feeling like Esau—that I had sold my birthright for a meal. As I emerged from the dark little store, the sun was remorseless, and I was right in its oppressive rays.

The tuna tasted good. Afterwards I tried to go back to sleep.

But the boredom I suffered lying in bed and staring pointblank at the vomit-green wall was too much to bear while there was still sunlight. Back on the street again, I tapped a newspaper holder at the end of the block for a few dollars in nickels and dimes. A bus was coming, and the little white box was hanging open like a broken alligator snout. I grabbed a newspaper, then boarded the bus, stuffing the change deep in my pocket.

White marble banks stood at rigid attention on either side of the street as I passed in my regally outfitted (all the latest in advertisements) bus. Between the banks there were bookstores, clothing shops, candy stores. People swarmed in clumps. Billboards shot past in a profusion of smoking, liquor, automobiles: red, green, yellow, and aqua. The bus was becoming crowded, too. I got off.

I walked toward the smell of salt and the heavy air of the seaside. I watched the waves clipping the shore and unbuttoned my shirt to let the sun soak through my skin, tanning me, burning me, baking me. The morning showers were long forgotten in the heat of the afternoon. The Pacific was an azure jewel set squarely beneath powdery clouds. Like small freckles, swimmers, clad in a myriad of bright suits, stood out against the ocean. I felt the weight of the obsession in my mind.

Cars flashed by me, never slowing, setting my mind—already ajar—whirling. There comes a time, some point in space, when a man must think, plan, evaluate, decide. The cars spinning past, the heady salt-air smell, the heat welling up through my hair, the faint jingle of pilfered change in my pocket, my mind was spinning like a great fortune wheel. How big a demonstration? I deferred thinking.

We were younger then, Brenda and I. Did we really know? Bill wanted it to be a controlled exercise. It was not. Ed warned them that peace was the best response. Who had brought guns? A rally? Who called the police? It was just a question of rights, student rights. We weren't looking, weren't asking for anything else. Someone had fired, but who? Night sticks swinging, the unsnapping of the leather belts that held pistols in their holsters, the sound of terror as a man was hit over the head, the cries that stifled logic and purpose. The afternoon sun beat down on the campus. If we had known that there would be burning, would we have been there? The crowd moved, running. If we had thought that the grocery and the vegetable stand and the rest would be robbed and burned, would we have demonstrated? Was this what I had nurtured? Was this the thought that I had put in Bill's mind, in John's?

There was the Esau striking back, there was the white lady who refused to sit next to a Negro on the bus, there was the innocent grocer who had only wanted a little thrill of power. In the confusion, I stood still. Bill pulled at my arm, screamed to me to get down. I remember the blur of motion, the sound of the policemen crying through their bull horns. I remember the true-blue stuffing me into the back of a truck. I remember pounding at the walls of that truck with my hands until they gave out, then with my head.

In a way, I guess, we did know.

I used an average step as measurement. The walls were six feet apart and formed an almost perfect square. The whole cell could have been a cube, except for the distance from the floor to the ceiling. On one side of the cell was a platform made of wooden slats which served as a bed. The slats were nailed at intervals of four inches to a frame which was, in turn, bolted to the floor. The bed was two and a half feet wide and stretched the full length of the wall. This left a total area of three and one half by six feet of iron floor.

The clear area was lessened by the only plumbing fixture, a trough four inches wide—the length of my thumb from the knuckle to the joint is about an inch—and six inches deep which hung suspended some three inches from the wall and six inches from the floor. And a small basin of porcelain which fed the trough.

The walls themselves were iron sheeting, broken only by a small window about six and three-quarters feet from the floor on the wall opposite the door, and by the door itself. The door (except for strips of iron reinforcement at the three-inch square peephole and around the door's edges) seemed to have been cut from the sheet of iron in which it was now hung. While there was a window in the iron sheeting opposite the door, there was no window in the brick wall just beyond it. The only light entered in a square ray through the peephole. It cut through the dark cell to form a diamond shape on the slats of the bed. After taking all the measurements, I played with the dust as it filtered through the solitary stream of light.

Lament for the Kibbutz

In 1963, I was welcomed along with other members of the Young Judaea youth group on Kibbutz Hatzerim, seven kilometers west of Beersheba. Over a few weeks, I worked many tasks—in the kitchen as a dishwasher, in the fields moving irrigation pipe, around the outskirts framing wooden ceilings for new residences, laying underground plumbing for a watering system in the commons, pruning peach trees in a new orchard, and helping corral an escaped bull. On this small kibbutz, the spirit of self-sufficiency and pioneering was dominant. The economics of Israel has changed drastically. Utopian ideals of earlier generations no longer attract the young. Computers, factories, and entrepreneurial opportunities have moved most kibbutz settlements away from agriculture. Young people often leave the kibbutz and never return. I am not nostalgic, but I am appreciative of the critical role the kibbutz played in forging the positive values of modern Israel.

The children watched the campfire being lit. A few formed a line to pass wood from the nearby trailer to adults tending the fire. Some played and others chatted as they waited for the kibbutz to gather. The class of thirteen-year-olds sat side by side gazing at the whirling wisps of blue-gray smoke leaving hazy trails above the flames. Tonight, they were celebrating their *Bar Mitzvah*—tonight they would be welcomed as adults and become members of the kibbutz.

Tzvi sat on one of the rocks circling the firepit warming up his accordion. Quietly, as if to himself, he sang a pioneers' song,

> The sun brings up its light,
> The Hebrews' plow turns the earth,
> Plow straight out and return ...
> Song, O song, arise.
> With hammers ringing;
> With plowshares joyfully dancing;
> It's a song that's never ending;
> It's only just beginning.

As more grown-ups arrived, they sat on rocks and on the ground joining the song to reiterate the chorus, "It's a song that's never ending; it's only just beginning." Women covered themselves with blankets from their apartments. Evenings like this on the desert's edge were brisk and nights were cold.

Some now recalled fireside evenings before battles, the quiet mood of friends knowing they were soon to be parted—some to be lost forever. Others remembered childhood days in Russia or Poland or adolescent days in the *hachsharot*, the agricultural training camps of the Zionist youth movements in the Old Country. An evening fire for singing, dancing, and storytelling was their *kumsitz* (in Yiddish, the "coming and sitting"), an elemental component of life, the reward of their labors before the movies and the television were easy to find. Before there were elaborate coffee makers and dining halls with snacks and cakes laid out by the kitchen staff, and before there were lengthy meetings with hundreds of decisions to make, and before there were traveling troupes who went from kibbutz to kibbutz to perform—before all of this was the *kumsitz*, the sitting together and sharing of self.

The sound of the singing intensified. The melodies changed to rousing tunes of the *Palmach* generation—songs of the War of Liberation, songs of enthusiasm and endeavor, marches born of work and battle. Even now, twenty years later, some rose to dance the *hora*, to let hearts beat faster and souls rise breathless from within. Others clapped out the rhythm or beat it out on a thigh or on the sole of a boot. The children sensed an undercurrent of adventure. It was clear the adults were sharing feelings beyond discussion, emblems of the past and promises of tomorrow, ample hopes of home and homeland.

Even the mechanical noise of the jeep's arrival did not break the mood. The accordion played on, the singing did not cease, and the dancing did not end as Dodick cut the jeep's engine and two kibbutzniks helped an elderly man alight from the passenger seat. Only when the song was sung to its end did the accordionist strap his instrument closed and, removing it from his shoulders, place it on the ground before him. Then all attention was given to Dodick—tall and commanding, the very image of a pioneer—who stood facing them, silhouetted by the glow of the fire.

"*Haverim*, friends," he began, "I see that we have been successful in keeping one secret. I am glad of it. Besides, it may be a first for Kibbutz Yad HaShoah—an actual surprise.

"Tonight, we know, is very special. Not only is there abundant food waiting ..." He pointed to decorated trailer wagons laden with lamb cubes skewered to be cooked over the open fire; trays of chickens already barbecued; piles of flat, round Middle Eastern *pita* bread; huge bowls of diced salad vegetables; dishes decorated with olives and pickles in abundance; and shining aluminum canteens of water and punch. "We are celebrating the eve of *Shavuot*, the day they say the Ten Commandments were given at Mount Sinai.

"And what could be more fitting than for us to single out our class of thirteen-year-olds, those who have come of legal age, on this occasion of their *Bar Mitzvah*? Normally, we ask each member of the class to stand and tell us his or her feelings and to tell us about the *mitzvah* he or she performed this last month. But not tonight. Instead, we bring a gift to our new adults. We are honored by our distinguished visitor. Thanks to David Bin Nun, whose son Mordechai ..."

Irit, one of the thirteen-year-old girls interrupted. "You mean *Moimoi*!" she blurted out. Moimoi blushed, of course, and everyone laughed.

"Excuse me. *Moimoi*!" Dodick corrected himself, "who is about to become a *Bar Mitzvah*. Thanks to Moimoi and his father David, who is our representative on the national kibbutz movement board, we have imported one of the founding members of Degania, the very first kibbutz. Meet Mr. Yitzhak Barsky, a *halutz* of the first generation of kibbutzniks, a true pioneer!"

The kibbutzniks responded warmly. In a country where history was constantly remade, even the recent past seemed distant. Now, here before them was a man born in the last century, a man who had seen the resettlement of the Jewish homeland nearly from its Zionist inception, a man whose life was literally the living dream of one hundred and fifty generations of the Jewish people.

Through his wrinkled brows shone the gleam of experience, and the vigor of his youth was still apparent like an aura around his slightly-stooped figure. The hallmark of a generation, his white shirt open at the collar and his loose, dark-colored trousers fit about him as simple robes of state must have rested on the shoulders of Saul the farmer king. And the kibbutzniks sat reverently, a willing audience.

"*Bar Mitzvah*—" Barsky began, his voice thin and brittle as the crackling flames. "It is good that your kibbutz celebrates it the same way for boys and for girls. When we started working the fields at Degania, the women would stay behind all day to cook. It was hard labor, harder than we ever imagined. They had to cook on open fires—there was no gas, and, of course, no electricity. They cooked on two stones turned upright in the ground, and the food was either half-done or mostly burnt.

"Then one day they came and said, 'It is not right for you to labor in the fields and we at the fire. We wish to work in the fields, too.'

"We laughed. Women in the fields! Our mothers had never worked; they had always stayed behind to tend the household. But now our women wished to change that. It took us a while to adjust to the idea.

"Then we thought, perhaps it is better after all. We turned a few fields for vegetables and the women began tending these. Soon, some women were working in the fields beside us. But when we lifted the heavy crates, they slowed us down and the men would call out to them, 'For God's sake, woman, hurry and let's be done with it.'

"But at night, when we were worn and tired, we would sit and marvel as they pressed on with the cooking. 'Where do you get the strength to keep on working?' we would ask. And when we climbed wearily into bed at night, the women would chide us: 'A little more strength, man. After all, a farmer must plow.'"

The adult kibbutzniks laughed; some of the young ones also understood.

"Slowly, over the course of time, we redivided the work and the women returned to be nurses for the young or to tend the kibbutz laundry or to work in the dining hall, the clothing center, the kibbutz store, or the offices. Some still worked in the fields and the orchards. And, at harvest time, everyone—man, woman, and child—was in the fields. But what we had learned was that it is not doing the *same* job that makes man and woman equal. It is the dignity of labor itself."

The kibbutzniks spoke quietly among themselves as the old man paused to drink a glass of water. He waited a moment, then looked again at the class of thirteen-year-olds sitting conspicuously to themselves.

"Some would say those were exciting times," he went on. "They were, in a way. There was hope, too. And while some things looked worse then, other things seemed very good, indeed. We lived in peace with our Arab neighbors in those days. Well, let us say, a kind of peace.

"I remember one Arab, a youth named Mahmoud. The first time I saw him, he was in chains being led by a British army posse to trial in Haifa. He had stolen some army horses, and the posse apprehended him before the horses could be sold. Stealing was a way of life in his family. Only the year before, one of our members had shot his brother, Ahmed, when his family staged a night raid against our kibbutz.

"I can still see Mahmoud, his black hair, thick and glossy, combed down on his high forehead. He sat proudly on the horse, but on his face was the shadow of wounded pride. I do not think he was sorry for what he had done, but he was awfully sorry that he had been caught.

"Days later, I heard about his trial from one of the Zionist officials in Tiberius. He was charged with the murder of several Jews and an Indian soldier. But the only charge on which he was convicted was stealing the British army horses. At the trial he answered every charge with the same words, 'Do you have a witness? Did you catch me?'

"He was soon freed, that Mahmoud, and soon causing us more trouble. He went to call on the Zionist Organization in Tiberius and warned the officials that we would have to pay for what we had done to his brother, Ahmed. He wanted compensation. He mentioned a large sum of money. In those days, peace could be purchased.

"The kibbutz discussed the threat, and in the end we decided that we could not afford to pay that kind of money. Besides, it did not seem right for us to pay when Ahmed had been trying to break in and rob us.

"But the threats continued. Sometimes they were delivered to us by officials of the Zionist Organization and sometimes by neighboring Arab chieftains. And slowly, as time passed and we ignored his warnings, the amount of money he wanted went down and down until it was only a matter of fifty pounds or so. Now it seemed that it was better to have peace and save everybody's face. They sent me with the money.

"I met Mahmoud again in the fields outside of Degania. He climbed down from his steed to greet me though we did not exchange kisses as friends would do. But he put his arm around my back and drew me aside and for a while we two walked together. We talked about the weather at first and the cows and the land. I told him that I admired his horse, and he reminded me of our first meeting when he had been in chains. He asked me if I thought then that he was afraid, and I answered that I had not thought so.

"Time is a wearisome thing, he told me. It passes on and on and on and on and wears out the best of men. But you, he said, you are old and yet you look young and quick. And I am young and feel ancient. I am like an old woman, he said to me, and I stared at him. To me, at the time, it seemed the opposite.

"He was tall and handsome, I thought, and in the full prime of his youth. His words surprised me; his attitude and his bearing were at such odds with them. He pointed to a rock by the side of the road. It was a formidable stone, a landmark. Do you remember when one of your men was wounded on this road and his donkey killed? he asked. I nodded and said that I remembered. I was with a friend hiding behind that rock, he said. We wanted the donkey, but when we asked your friend to dismount, he cocked his rifle instead. So we shot. One shot wounded him, and the other brought down the donkey. He shook his head. A shame, he said.

"And do you remember the night that my brother Ahmed was killed? I was with him on that raid, he said. You had good cows. Beirut and Damascus cows you had. And we came close to getting them, too. But the watchman was too quick for us, he said. Then he paused, thoughtfully. We could have sold those cows ...

"And do you remember when an Arab coach was held up along this road? It was a grand coach with four horses. I lay down in the roadbed and waited. My brother and three others were there by the roadside. He pointed to a small ditch near where we were walking. When the coach stopped, he said, they came up from the ditch. He smiled. It was Mahmoud's plan.

"Then he held out his hand, and I gave him the fifty pounds. You have changed us, you know, he said to me. That was the last time I saw him. Later he was hanged for murder by the British. That time there were witnesses."

The darkness had all but absorbed the old man's last words. Dodick brought him a chair and he sat. A thoughtful mood descended on his listeners, and Barsky paused a while before beginning again.

"Sometimes," he said, clearing his throat, "we forget how hard it is to be young. Perhaps it is even harder to be young than to be old. A young boy came to us from Kishinev. His name was Avi, and his father had sent him with a note asking us to watch over him. But he did not seem to want much watching. He worked hard and seldom spoke to anyone. Once he took sick with malaria, but it was a light case, and we paid little attention.

"Then, one night we found him dead in the fields. He had slashed his wrist with a knife, and in his hand we found a note. It said, 'There is a future for you. I leave you my share in it. Tell my father that we have failed. Even here, they have overcome us.'

"Such things happened—they were times when such things happened. The young cannot always change by leaving what they know behind. But the collective, the *kibbutz*, is something new, and it means finding strength in one another.

"When you take up tender roots and transplant them, you hope. But hope and care are not always enough. The roots must be strong, else the plant cannot survive. And even in the last moments of its dying, the young plant seems green and strong above the ground. Who can tell? If it is true of plants and of young people, too, perhaps it is true of nations which come up in a night and perish in a night. For what are nations but the work of people, most of whom cannot discern their right hand from their left hand?

"Degania was fortunate. Always we survived the crises. And good fortune sent us a prophet, too—the gifted writer and thinker, Aaron David Gordon—some called him 'A. D. Gordon'; he liked us to call him just 'Gordon.' He came to us in his early sixties when we were still in our teens and twenties. He brought his ideas to test them out, to work, and to sing among us."

There was a reverent stir among the kibbutzniks. The name of Gordon was well-known, his ideas were known and taught, and now before them stood a man who knew Gordon face to face. Barsky took another glass of water, cleared his throat, and coughed. Then he continued.

"Gordon was old and bent by comparison with most of us, but his eyes burned like flames. It was as if inside of him he carried the eternal light they keep in synagogues. He was aglow with energy and vitality. They say he created the religion of labor, but he claimed we need no more religion. We need to make the land our friend and the garden our temple.

"Once we were hired by the Jewish National Fund to plant trees to help dry the swamps. We were paid by the number of trees we could plant, and we planted as quickly as we could—digging the holes, moistening the soil, putting the seedlings in the ground, and packing the loose earth around them. But Gordon did not hurry. He planted each tree as if the totality of creation were dependent on its survival. Each placing of each seedling was a work of love for him, each plant a symbol of the nation's future. He took little heed of how long it took him to accomplish each planting. And when he had done with one, he stood back from it for a while to contemplate it. It was not to admire his work but more as if to say a prayer over it, to bless it, or perhaps to prophesy its destiny.

"Working the fields, when the rest of us were exhausted from our labors, he was still strong, ready to sing and dance around the evening campfire. When we were spent, he was invigorated. Long after the campfire died to embers glowing, he sat over the table in his room and wrote by candlelight the essays of his philosophy, telling of the joy of labor and the dignity of common work on God's earth.

"He was a blessing to us. To all of us, save one teenage girl, Bathsheba. Bathsheba came to us through Gordon. He found her one day wandering alone in Tiberias, and he told her about Degania and the way we lived, shared whatever we had, and worked together. He promised to speak to the members to have her admitted. Naturally, we all agreed. Whatever Gordon wanted was good enough for us. And Bathsheba came to stay.

"All day long she worked beside Gordon, watching him, copying him. From morning 'til night like a shadow she kept by him. Wherever his eyes came to rest, she was there; wherever his feet trod, she passed that way.

"One night there was a meeting around the campfire, and Gordon spoke to us, reading from his writing white hot from the night before. They were words of love for the country, words of admiration for simple toil. Suddenly we heard a shot and we all ran to see what had happened.

"We found Bathsheba in the graveyard, her body slumped across one of the tombstones, the gun still in her hand. She was not quite dead, but her wound was severe. She had shot herself in the head. We went for the doctor from Tiberias, and when he came, he told us that it was no use. She would soon die.

"I was angry. 'Send for another doctor,' I said. 'Do not give up so easily. We are her family, and we must do what a family would do for its own daughter.' So we sent to Jerusalem, and after pleading with the hospital there, a doctor finally came to look at her. He merely shook his head. I sat beside her for many days, but it was no good. She raised her head near midnight one night, opened her eyes for the last time, and looked around—maybe she was trying to find Gordon—but as I reached out to her, she fell back dead.

"I sometimes wonder when these children lost their hope. I wonder what was in their heads when they took their own lives. Were we so far from their homes? Were we lacking in some human way? But I think I know the answer.

"We gave life to so many, but the life we made was so raw and open that it sometimes festered the way a wound will fester. Or perhaps the wound was in them and the healing could not be perfected in time. But they died, and we buried them with our children and placed inscriptions on their gravestones which said that they took their own lives. And when visitors are shocked by seeing these inscriptions, we do not apologize. That was the way it was, and who are we to conceal it from those who follow?

"I speak about Gordon as if he were with us forever. In truth, he was ours for only three years before he died. It just seemed so much longer. Have you ever been with a person who made you forget time? Can you imagine how it felt just working beside him and what we learned? He was full of contradictions. In his twenties, Gordon managed a great estate; by his forties, he was working as a common laborer. He loved philosophy and Tolstoy, but he also loved the stories told by uneducated *Hasidim* of their wonder-working *rebbes,* and he also loved the kabbalists who wove alchemical tales and thought they would redeem the world by their piety. Only if you can imagine someone who is at home anywhere and who could make you a true believer by working beside you—only then could you know how intense were those years. Gordon lived with us at Degania, true, but his 'religion of labor' rubbed off on all the Jews of Palestine.

"And now, you are part of our kibbutz movement. This is something new in the world and something new for our people. Before, for two thousand years, we Jews were either imprisoned in cities or impoverished in backwater towns. We Jews were accustomed to every kind of life except the life of labor—of reaping and sowing done for our own benefit and for its own sake. But that is what you, especially you children of the kibbutz, have changed.

"Now you thirteen-year-olds are adults, and the class of twelve-year-olds is right behind you, and the classes of elevens and tens and nines are behind them. What will be your future? You will need to find it as we did. You will need to work, dance, and sing; you will need to love your neighbor and to discover your place within your people. You possess a young land with an ancient history. I only think that if you leave the land, if you stop tilling the soil and sowing the crops, in the end you will have to find it again."

The Box

My ambition to become a writer began when I was nine years old. I took a pencil and a little spiral notebook that my aunt had given me and retreated under a table in our living room (possibly the least-used room in our house). Hidden from view, I composed my first story and added a truly underwhelming full-page illustration. Even before my tenth birthday, I gave up illustrating my stories, but creating and telling them became a way of life.

The new ball was already scratched. He had been bouncing it against the concrete house near the lattice gate. He stopped bouncing it when he heard the whispering inside and walked along beside the wrought iron fence looking for the people who were talking. Finally, he saw them and pressed his face, warm with the afternoon sun, against the cool white painted rails.

With one rail at either cheek, he stared at the gathering inside. The men and women, dressed in black, stood in two small groups, their backs to him. One of the groups was almost completely hidden behind a grey stone statue. The other group gathered together like the living room draperies. Someone in the front was speaking, but he couldn't hear the words though they echoed on the steep sides of the engraved monuments.

Suddenly the speech was over, and he heard a sound of iron handles snapping against the side of the wooden casket as the men lifted it and slid it carefully into the side of the white cement block. Slowly they swung the side closed and then turned away. His hands closed around the pink rubber ball and squeezed it tightly. He had watched something he was not supposed to have seen. As the men turned away from the huge white stone, he ran to recover his position by the gate.

Too late he saw the white paint smudge on the ball and stared open-mouthed at the two stripes running down the jacket of his new black suit. Then the smell of paint came to his nose, and a guilty lump began to form in his throat. They would know what he had done. Now what could he do?

She came through the gate dabbing lace against her eyes and took his hand and walked to the big black car, pushing him in before her. He sat very still, crossing his arms in front of the white stripes on his jacket, still holding the ball in one hand. It was the biggest car he had ever been in. He lay back against the grey cloth seats and tried to make himself small. Looking down, he pulled up his crossed arms for just a moment to see if the stripes were still there, then he closed on them again, covering them, and looking at her to see if she had noticed what he had done.

Her eyes were closed, and her hand was on his knee. Outside the car, a few people stopped to look in at her, shook their heads, and turned to walk away. She pressed the handkerchief to her eyes again and the car began moving, pushing him deep into the grey seat. There were two men in the front. One was driving and the other, a younger man, had spun halfway around in his seat and was looking at her. He had grey eyes. It was the first time he had ever seen a man with grey eyes. He sat back in the grey seat and stopped fighting the force pulling at him and watched the grey eyes watching her.

Then he looked at her, too. Did she see them? Did she know that the young man had grey eyes? Had she ever seen anyone with grey eyes before? He carefully placed the ball next to his side and reached up to tap her on the shoulder, but the white smudge of paint on his thumb cautioned him and he settled back in the seat instead, still watching the grey eyes.

He crossed his arms across his chest and felt the car slowing down to make a turn. The young man in front turned to speak in whispers with the driver. He looked up at her again and saw that her eyes were open now, that she was watching the road. She stuffed the handkerchief into her purse and adjusted her skirt as she lifted one leg across the other. With one hand, she brushed a wisp of hair back from her forehead.

Surely, she will see the white stripes, he thought, holding his folded arms to his chest. The car moved slowly readying for another turn, and her eyes left him to watch the road. She had still not seen the damage. How long could he hide it from her? The grey eyes were toward him now, staring at him. He felt the lump in his throat thickening.

There was a small throbbing in his head. What was the man staring at? Did he see the paint? Did he know? Suddenly the man's hand whipped into the air, extended toward him, holding a yellow box. Candy. "Would you like these?" It was almost not a question. He started to reach for the candy, then felt her eyes on him and held his arms tightly crossed as he eyed the yellow box.

"Go ahead, Danny, take the candy, and thank the nice man."

"Thank you. I don't think I want any." He pressed his arms closer to his chest.

"Go ahead, son, it's for you," said the man, watching Danny carefully. Could he take the candy without showing the paint smears? He wriggled a little in his seat, then reached out a hand and snatched the box of candy.

"Danny!" Her cold stare was on him. "Apologize to the man. You know better than to grab things."

"It's all right, ma'am. I'm sure he didn't mean to grab it."

"Thank you," she said, her voice very soft, and she adjusted her skirt again. Did she feel the grey eyes looking at her? Danny watched as the man turned around, then quickly opened the box and took out a piece of candy and put it in his mouth.

Soon, the car was stopping, and the man got out first and held the door as they climbed out. Then the man walked them to the green door and opened it for them. He even went through the courtyard and held open the door to their apartment as they went inside. She said "thank you" again, and Danny slipped inside and into the washroom.

As he ran the hot water over his hands, he heard them talking. "Maybe I shouldn't have taken him at all." Her voice was clear through the thin wall. His voice was muffled because he was standing in the hall. Danny stopped listening to them and turned to scrubbing the white from the new black jacket, but it wouldn't come out. At least he had gotten his hands clean. Maybe he could hide the jacket somewhere. He ran the water over his hands once more, listening to the sound of it against the white enameled sink; then he left the bathroom and went to the bedroom where he folded the jacket so that the stripes were not visible and stuffed it into a drawer.

People began to arrive. He could hear the voices in the living room. It seemed like everyone was talking in whispers. The quiet bothered him. He slipped into his blue jeans and pulled on an old sweatshirt and went into the kitchen. Some old lady was in there making something. When she saw him, her face constricted. Was there something wrong with him? He looked at his hands. They were clean. Was it his face? He slipped out of the kitchen, still under her gaze, and walked quickly into the washroom. He examined everything there: sweatshirt, jeans, hands, face—everything seemed all right. Finally, he came out and found her in the living room surrounded by people. He felt hungry, wanted to go outside in the courtyard to bounce the new pink ball. The pink ball! He had forgotten it.

He quickly went to the bedroom and found it on the dresser. Then he took it to the bathroom and scrubbed until all the paint disappeared in the white enameled sink. Then he took the towel and dried it and stuffed it into one pocket admiring the bulge that it made. Again, he went in and sat by her side. The conversation was still going on in whispers, but he was too tired to listen. He leaned his head on her lap and fell asleep listening to the echoed rumblings when she spoke.

She woke him up to come to the table. Someone had put him in his bed while he was sleeping. There were still people in the house, and he began to wonder how long they would stay. A couple left as they sat down to eat. The rest sat in the living room and continued talking lowly. The old lady from the kitchen was serving the meal, and afterward she brought in a piece of cake for him. The cake was very good, and he noticed that instead of milk, they were giving him orange soda. It was a strange day, he decided. Nothing was going the way it usually did. There was something wrong with her. Or maybe it was just a strange day.

He chewed the cake readily, washing it down with the orange soda and thought about the yellow box of candy. He must have left it in his jacket. He could get it right after supper. Her eyes were on him as the old lady cleared the table.

"Are you tired, Danny?" she asked.

"Yes, kinda."

She just nodded and didn't say anything else. Pretty soon they were back in the living room, and the whispering was starting again. He wanted to slip away and have some candy, but she had one hand on his knee. When she finally moved it, he slid away from her along the divan and went after the box.

Carefully he opened the drawer and pulled out the jacket. The yellow box was in the pocket, he thought, but all the pockets were empty. Had he taken it out? Where had he put it? He looked around the room. It wasn't anywhere. He pulled the pants off their hanger. The pants pockets were empty too. He pulled the pink ball out of his blue jeans and went through those pockets. No, it wasn't in any of them. He closed his eyes and tried to remember what he had done with it. Had someone taken it? He looked under the dresser, but it hadn't fallen there. He looked under the bed. No, it wasn't there either.

Finally, he gave up. Subdued now, he came back into the living room and sat next to her mourning the loss of his yellow box of candy. He went over and over it in his mind, but he couldn't remember where he had put it. Now it was gone, and there wasn't anything he could do about it.

The old lady came into the living room and asked if anybody wanted something to eat. No one wanted anything. One lady asked for some coffee. Then the old lady leaned over toward him, the constricted look back in her eyes. "Would you like some more cake?" At first, he didn't understand. His mind was more focused on the candy he had lost. "Would you like some more cake, Danny?"

"Yes, ma'am," he answered, starting to hop down from the divan. "All right. You may sit there, and I will bring it to you."

He looked up at her and nodded. In a minute, the old lady had returned with some cake and another glass of orange soda. It really was a strange night. He ate the cake with his fingers, oblivious to the eyes watching him and the constricted face of the old lady serving coffee to one of the guests.

Sitting on the divan, he had dozed off several times, awakening with a start as his chin snapped forward against his chest. All the people were gone now except for the old lady who was rinsing a few dishes in the kitchen sink. When she was done, she left, too, without saying anything. He was alone with her again, sitting next to her on the divan, his head propped against her arm.

"Want to go to bed?"

He nodded and followed her to his bedroom. She pulled the covers back, and he slipped between them, turned on his side, and was asleep in a moment.

The noise of the laughter stirred him. At first, he wasn't sure what it was. He turned over and tried to go back to sleep, but he had slept too long during the day; he was not tired. So he listened and the voices seemed to be laughing. His room was a shadowbox—shapes moving up and down and back and forth as he moved his eyes. The shadow he cast on the wall was a giant tiger, its tail the blanket that lay twisted near his feet. The dresser was an elephant, its trunk—the lamp—raised high in the air. He crawled under the sheet and decided to be a big game hunter, but the noises came through the sheet.

Finally, he threw the sheet off and got off the bed. He moved carefully, planting each foot as he walked through his shadow jungle. Stealthily, he peeked around the corner to see if anything were there. The voices were muffled now and reminded him of the day's whispers. He turned to look back into his room and saw the jungle shadows move. Then he turned the corner and stepped out into the living room.

The light from above the dining table flashed in his eyes. The rest of the room was dark. The noises were coming from the darkness, but up on the table he saw a yellow reflection. Like a crafty hunter, he crouched low to the ground and started into the dark. It was a new jungle now, built of moving shadows and short sharp noises. He moved rapidly behind the table. Had they seen him? His heart beat so that he could hear it. In his mind, he remembered the run from the painted white iron fence to the gate that morning. There was something forbidden about this, too.

He came up at eye level to the table and saw the yellow box. Quickly he put his hand out to grab it, but as he touched it, he felt it moving away from him. He had hit the box. Like a yellow dart it slid over the edge of the table and dropped to the floor with a sudden thud. The noise stopped, only his heart beat like a primitive drum. With desperate precision, he flattened against the solid wooden center leg of the table. Then slowly he peered around the thick leg and saw the grey eyes looking toward him. The shadows were gone. They had turned the light on. Did they see him? He darted back behind the heavy wood.

"Where's the kid?" the young man said as he flipped the light off. She giggled a little. "Be careful. I'm ticklish."

Danny carefully peered at them from behind the table. They were both stretched out on the couch. Maybe they wouldn't see him now. He inched over to the spot where the yellow box had landed and picked it up carefully. He had left it in the big car. The grey-eyed man must have come to return it. Danny started to crawl toward the hallway, but he heard a clicking and then the light was turned on again. Danny pressed against the big wooden leg.

They were talking again.

"He was an auto parts salesman. Traveled a lot."

"He left you at home? If I had a wife like you, I wouldn't leave her home alone to go traveling."

"That's why we adopted the kid."

Danny wondered what "adopted" meant.

"What?"

"That's why we adopted the kid. To save the marriage. That's why we adopted him."

Danny wondered if they would ever turn out the light again. What would the man with the grey eyes do to him if they found him here? His heart was pounding hard and heavy.

She was talking again. "Of course, now that he's dead, I don't want any chains on my feet." She brought her feet up to show him. The man crushed his cigarette in the crystal ashtray, then reached for the light switch. The shadows came alive as the glow of light died in the air. Finally, Danny thought he was safe. Crouching low on all fours, the candy box in his hand, he moved to his bedroom, taking one sidelong glance at the couch to see if there were any danger.

Then he was back in bed, under the sheet, and settling his head against the foam rubber pillow. The word "dead" was echoing in his forehead. Who was dead? He put his arm up in the air and watched his shadow against the wall. He fell asleep then, the yellow box buried safe beneath his pillow.

❋

Derech

A Path Between the Worlds

American Jews belong to a chain of tradition which is in constant need of updating. To create a path for our future, we need to reckon with our past. Yet, holding the past as sacred can be nothing less than idolatrous. We need instead to compare our path to that of a sailboat. There is no straight way when sailing into the wind, but tacking back and forth with effort and skill can succeed. I like to think that this story works on several levels, and I like to hope it points forward.

Winter. Grey winter: sea mirrors the color of the sky. Grey winter: the sea never ends; the sky never ends. Standing on the shore. Inside a vast, clouded crystal ball. No shadows fall; light diffused comes from everywhere at once but does not penetrate. Atmosphere hangs suspended and apparent. Forward and back equidistant; past and future equipresent. History and prophecy equally obscured. All within becomes a metaphor. All within apprehends the metaphor; it lingers in passage between. A morning fog along the seashore.

The wilderness was like this for my people. No shadows for forty years. A generation suspended between history and prophecy. Forward and back. Equidistant. Perhaps they read the metaphor as it was happening. Forty days and forty nights before the mountain. Forty years. Forty heartbeats in forty brave soldiers and forty made famous by being rich enough to give the money to buy the forty guns that stopped the forty hearts but saved the nation they built in the wilderness and made a desert bloom.

His father's study was his favorite room. Imma, his mother, seldom entered it. She could not bear the crowded feeling of the oversized desk piled high with papers, the room stuffed with furniture, the green chair so much in need of repair. She could not forgive the books stuffed into bookshelves 'til every space was filled, the bookshelves like Lower East Side tenements piled high, story upon story of immigrants. But Abie slipped soundlessly into this Lower East Side of the mind just to run his finger along the uneven rows of spines.

To disturb Imma, he struck sudden dissonant chords on the upright in the corner. Now stop and listen. Her voice came echoing down the length of the house. But she would not come into the study. Not even to clean it as she did her daily rounds of dusting and mumbling, singing snatches of pioneering songs. Not even to place the flowers in it that she placed so carefully in every other room when spring and summer made them abundant in the bed she planted by the back porch where sunlight fell full each afternoon.

In the study on the wall opposite the desk was the painting of the old man, a woolen prayer shawl across his shoulder, his head banded by leather strap, mounted by a phylactery box, a prayer book in hand, left arm throbbing beneath the sevenfold wrapping of ribboned leather. What spirit danced immobile in that face? How it seemed to study Abie as he sat considering it from the green armchair. How it stared as Abie held a book close beside him, now drifting off to sleep, dreaming stories of magic rings, of cobblers, farmers, and Polish lords, of birthrights traded for thick brown lentil soup—stories his father told.

Three times a week the tutor came and sat with Abie in the study and drilled Hebrew syllables into Abie with paid distraction. On occasion the tutor, Mr. Jacobs, was animated, punctuating the words on the page with tales of how the *Alef Bet* came to be. Once he sketched letter after letter with a stubby pencil on a clean white sheet of paper calling for their names.

As Abie pronounced a letter—*alef* or *lamed* or *yod*—Mr. Jacobs etched a few lines around the letter and a face appeared. If it smiled, the answer was correct—a frown, a mistake. Later Abie tried, but the faces refused to appear though the letter *tet* managed to become a majestic battleship with a slight frown around its stern.

But most of the time Mr. Jacobs read passages carefully, bulbous red nose pressed closely to the page. With this improvised pointer nobly marking his place in the text, his hand was free to worry a lock of hair above his ear. Then Abie repeated the passage, his recitation dotted with corrections from Mr. Jacobs. Abie's half-brother, Doug, dubbed Mr. Jacobs "The Nose."

Imma sometimes listened to the lessons from the doorway. She would, ever and again, cluck her tongue disapprovingly. Sometimes she held Abie close at night and, in her equable way, would say, "This is not Hebrew you learn. When my little man grows up, I will teach him Hebrew." In the bed across the room Doug would coyly snort through his nose as if it were an involuntary noise and communicate to Abie a disposition toward the tutor, toward Hebrew, and toward Imma, too. When the lights were out, Doug would turn to the wall and hiss out a sarcastic whisper, "My little *man*."

Imma was from Israel. Doug's mother had been American. Abie knew that she would not gather Doug in, breathe a heavy odor at him intimately, call him "my little *man*." Doug, it seemed, was free of that. Soon, of course, Abie would be a man. Soon, perhaps, he would be free of it, too.

The Thursday before the weekend of his Bar Mitzvah, Abie sat in the study, behind the desk, between his father and Mr. Jacobs. The doorbell rang. Abie's father answered the door.

"Mr. Trachson?" came the voice at the door with an official intonation. "New York Police Department. Detective Richards. May I come in, sir?"

A shuffling of feet.

"Of course," Abie's father answered. The door closed; his father reappeared. Would Mr. Jacobs take Abie to the kitchen table and continue the lesson there? But though they went, books in hand, to the back of the house, both Abie and the tutor listened.

"Not very serious," the policeman was saying in a voice loud enough so that each word rang distinctly through the hall. "You see, they have a sort of 'club' ... well, a gang. And in order to belong, well, each boy steals, pilfers, 'swipes' something as they call it. A magazine, or a comic book, or anything he fancies, you see. The mother of one of the boys found a couple of radios and a set of walkie-talkies in her son's possession, you see. She called us."

Abie could hear his father clearing his throat, or perhaps it was the policeman.

"We normally throw a scare into the boy. Shake him up a bit, you see, and return the merchandise and all is well. But when the Ashman boy was scared, he told us about this 'club' and gave us a list of names. Now it seems that Douglas, your son, you see, is a member. Of course, I don't know if he has stolen anything yet, but I felt it was my position to tell you, well, to warn you. Now, I'll be on my way."

There was a sound of shoes setting the hallway floorboards creaking and some soft speaking. Mr. Jacobs looked self-consciously at Abie, then down at the page, slowly reciting a passage of the Hebrew. Abie followed the nose that marked the place and repeated the text in pensive tones, but it was clear that the lesson was over.

Later, Abie sat in the front room and tried to watch television. Instead, he thought—about Doug, about Imma, about Mr. Jacobs, about his father. It began to seem to him, as he deliberated, that he was more like his father on the inside than Doug was. Doug looked like their father, but inside Doug was a thief. His father—their father—on the other hand, was a professor. Abie was like his father on the inside; Doug was like Imma; and they were none of them like Mr. Jacobs. Doug and Imma disliked Mr. Jacobs, so it was Abie and his father who liked him. And it was Abie and his father who used the study; Doug and Imma who stayed away from it. And it was Abie and his father who liked the green chair.

Abie stood on the couch eyeing his reflection in the mirror above the mantlepiece. His eyes were like his father's—two white pools with brown islands surmounted by two black mountaintops.

That night, after the hugging and after the lights were switched off, Abie asked Doug how he could join the club. Doug had been crying, his face turned toward the wall. "You're not man enough, 'my little *man.*'"

"Saturday," Abie said, "I'll be a Bar Mitzvah. Then I'm a man."

Doug still faced the wall. Abie imagined he could see the reflection of his brother's face in the cream-colored plaster across the room. "Sunday, then ... Sunday, I'll tell you how."

Abie fell asleep thinking there must be such a thing as a good thief and dreaming of a birthright afloat in a thick lentil sea.

He awoke more troubled than rested and saw that Doug was already out of bed. He tried to think out what was on his mind. He was not worried about the Bar Mitzvah. He was ready even though Mr. Jacobs still fussed over each minor error in pronunciation and each slightly misplaced accent. He was not worried about the club. Face that later, he advised his inner voice in another, more certain inner voice. It was about Doug that he worried.

He dressed slowly, savoring the chance to look at himself in the mirror again, now frowning at the rounded chin, the straight nose, the hair that fell precariously near his eyelashes. All his mother's features. Oriental, like his Imma. Making him somehow half-Israeli. They could never be hard deep lines.

Half-dressed, he reached into his dresser's top drawer. Beneath the schoolbooks was the bound green ledger his father had once given him. His personal history. Now, he turned to an empty page and recorded the date clearly across the top. *I am impressed by my eyes*, he wrote. *The rest of my face is terrible, but my eyes show what is inside me. I feel light today like the sun coming up.*

He tapped the pencil against his teeth.

Doug is a thief. What else should he write? *Tonight, I will begin to be a man.* Ledger closed and safely hidden, he finished dressing. Smells of baking bread came up from the kitchen.

The day passed in measured rhythm. Mr. Jacobs arrived in the early afternoon to finish the interrupted final review. Abie's father spent the day in the study, the door closed. Imma baked and cooked and sang Hebrew songs for herself beneath her breath. Doug was sent on errand after errand until, exasperated, he stormed out of the house and was not seen again until late in the afternoon.

Imma laid new suits on the beds in the boys' room. She inspected the boys before she left them alone to dress. "Ready?" Doug asked.

Abie paid no attention. His suit was made of silk. He felt the cool, shiny lining, the sleek fabric of the jacket. It felt like his father's. He smiled.

"Think you're a *man* now?" Doug asked.

Abie nodded.

"Want to Indian wrestle?"

Abie shook his head.

"What's wrong? You afraid that I'll beat you?"

"Don't feel like it."

"Come on. Two-out-of-three," Doug said.

Abie moved half-heartedly toward his brother. Doug was stronger. There was no doubt of that. The two boys faced one another, squared their shoulders, set their feet, and grasped hands. For a moment, Abie felt the advantage was with him this day. He pushed his shoulder against Doug's arm and caught Doug's knee with his own. But Doug changed the angle of his body and with a jerk, pulled Abie in the direction that Abie was pressing. Before Abie could stop, his feet had slipped out from beneath him.

"That's one for me. Want to try again? Or would you rather just give up?"

The smile on Doug's face was close to angelic; Abie felt he must try again. Grasping hands, the boys squared off. Doug counted to three and then jerked Abie's arm backward and pulled. Abie countered, moving forward; Doug leaned backward. Abie fell to the floor across his own foot.

"Okay," Doug said. "You can get up now. I won." Abie did not answer. He looked up at Doug through a haze and saw the half-smile on his brother's face fading.

"Come on," Doug said. He put a foot in Abie's ribs. "Wake up, fake. Come on."

Abie shut his eyes. He wished that Doug would talk louder. He could barely hear his name being called through the ringing.

"Abie. Come on. For Christ's sake, come on. I didn't hit you that hard." Abie listened to his brother's footsteps echo. "Imma! Dad!"

Abie was beginning to recover even as his father appeared. "Some cold compresses," his father snapped as he carried Abie to the bed.

He leaned across Abie's body and whispered in his ear. "Abraham. Be still. Keep your eyes closed. Look deep inside. Can you feel yourself coming back? Slowly now, open your eyes a little. The light is warm. The light is life. Can you feel it?"

Imma came and pressed a cold washcloth to Abie's forehead and left it there. "He has just had the breath knocked out of him," she said.

Abie opened his eyes and felt the dizziness leaving him. The light felt warm. He looked at Doug, who turned away. Abie's hand was lost between his father's hands. Imma stood behind Doug.

"I'm all right," Abie said. In his mind's eye, he could still hear his father's whisper.

His father looked at Doug. "We'll talk later." Doug nodded. Abie felt guilty.

Imma handed Doug his new suit. "Change in the other room," she said.

Slowly, Abie stood. The others left him alone. He took stock of himself. The dizziness was gone. There was just a tenderness in one ankle, perhaps he would limp for a while. He dressed in silence, retying the knot in his necktie three times. Finally, he took out the ledger and wrote, *Light is life.*

Doug came back to the room as Abie slipped the precious book back into its resting place.

"I'm sorry," Doug said.

Abie nodded. They were brothers.

❀

The study was empty. The house was filled with the scent of bread and cake freshly baked, the smell of the approaching Sabbath. Abie sat in the green chair and inhaled the sweetish aroma. Precious moments of life confound the memory with fullness of emotion, sensation, color, smell, sight, and sound. Sabbath bread; this day in a lifetime of days, weeks, years; the closeness of family; the comfort of ritual.

His father entered into the study. On the desk, the Bible was open to the page Abie would read in the morning.

"Abie, are you feeling better?" his father asked, settling in the leather desk chair. "Most people are afraid of life, Abie. Afraid to seize it, afraid to shake loose its fruit." The white-haired man eased himself back in the chair. His eyes closed beneath heavy eyelids. "I had my Bar Mitzvah in November of 1930. That's ancient history to you, I know." Abie fingered the frayed upholstery of the old green chair. "A lot of people came to my Bar Mitzvah. People I didn't know; people who didn't know me; people my father did not wish to see. They were good people, simple and reverent, like the old man in the picture there. Synagogue Jews.

"They were disillusioned, too. They had lived through a war without understanding it. They had been followers of my grandfather, your great-grandfather. He was a great *rebbe*, Eliyahu Tzadik. Some of the stories I tell you were his stories. Telling stories was his way of teaching people about life. He would tell them a tale, and they would understand.

"While he was alive, people came from long distances just to be near him. Some came with questions to be answered or arguments to be settled. Rebbe Eliyahu had united under his leadership three separate groups of *Hasidim*, 'Pious Ones.' He sometimes said that he had a thousand followers. There may have been twice that many. He was a very great man, Abie. That's why his followers called him *Tzadik*, 'Righteous One.'

"He had a special *derech*, a path, his personal way of dealing with God—through prayers and melodies and teachings. Before each holiday he would create a new song. Sometimes it had words; often, it had no words at all. He would teach it to everyone in his court—all the followers who had come to spend that holy day with him. And they would sing it until the whole courtyard was filled with music. Eliyahu was a strong man. Constantly he spoke with hope of a joyful life. His God was full of compassion and love. His court was a palace full of life.

"That is where my father grew up. Sitting in the Tzadik's study, listening to stories and teachings. Eliyahu's followers believed that their *rebbe* could work miracles. In the court, they whispered that the Tzadik knew God's secret name to call on Him and talk to Him the way that I am talking to you. He did work a kind of miracle. Once a man brought his retarded child to Eliyahu for a cure. No. He could not cure the child. But he taught that man to feel a child's pain, to love the child; and that was very difficult. Do you understand?"

Abie nodded. "Yes, sir. Could he really talk with God?"

"Wait. We'll come to that part." Abie's father closed his eyes again. The leather chair squeaked beneath his weight. Abie waited.

"Suddenly, everything was torn away from my father. The life of the court, the gardens, the hothouse, the great Sabbath table, the women crying because they had no children or because the children they had refused to study, the men who wished a blessing from the Tzadik for their businesses, the young men who listened carefully to each *toyreh*, each teaching of the *rebbe*. With a crying in the bedroom, a limp cold hand, a memory of long side-whiskers and earlocks, and the quenching of the fire of life that had burned so brightly, Eliyahu died.

"Immediately, his followers wished to raise my father, your grandfather, to the *rebbe*'s place. The *Hasidim* who mourned Eliyahu's passing truly believed that the divine fire had passed into his son, your grandfather. But your grandfather did not feel it. He stubbornly refused to take Eliyahu's place. At last, he locked himself in a small room for three days and would not eat. On the third day, haggard and very pale, he came out of that room. Before he could talk, my mother had to give him a glass of tea. Finally, he turned to the followers who had gathered, and said, 'I do not believe in God.'

"The *Hasidim* were convinced that a *dybbuk*, an evil spirit, had entered his body and was possessing him. Even mother thought that he was ill.

"That night, my father rose up at midnight and told his wife to dress. Then, like thieves in the dark, like Jacob fleeing Laban with Rachel and Leah, they gathered their few belongings and left the court of Eliyahu.

"As they passed through the *shtetl*, the Jewish section of town, it seemed to my mother that the whole village was weeping. And it was true. The Tzadik had been the heart of the *shtetl*. All the business of life depended on him. The bakers, the smiths, the carpenters, the innkeepers, they were all dependent on Eliyahu's followers and Eliyahu's court. Nor was the heart unaware as it tore itself from the body. My father wept, too, and left his tears to dry to salt on the wounded cobblestone.

"My father had to travel under a new name, for it was known far and wide that he was the son of the great *rebbe*, Eliyahu Tzadik. Remembering what he had said to the *Hasidim* about not believing in God, he felt closest to another in Jewish tradition, the father of Abraham, Terach. The ancient rabbis believed that Terach was a maker of idols. So my father chose to be called by Terach's name. But to be called Ben Terach, the son of Terach, would bring him too much attention. So he invented the name Trachson. All this happened before I was born.

"When I was old enough to understand, when I was just turning thirteen, I heard this from my father. I asked him if it were true that he did not believe in God. He told me this story: There was once a great *rebbe* who lay dying. His students gathered around his bedside and asked if there were anything they could do to comfort him. 'Yes,' the *rebbe* said. 'Tell me again that there is truly a God in Heaven.' 'But, Rebbe,' they said, 'all your life you have told us that there is a God. How is it that now you wish us to tell you?' 'I have lived to help others learn that God exists,' the old *rebbe* said, 'and now, when I die, I must learn this for myself; but now you must live to help others understand. As I have been your assurance, you must now be mine.'

"Abie, this is very important. The Bible does not command us to believe in God. No. It commands us to fear the Lord, to honor the Lord, and to love Him. Even so, most people when they honor the Lord and obey His laws, come to believe in Him, also. But Grandfather, who had always obeyed the Lord and feared Him, had never learned to know the Lord, so he thought he was unworthy to take the place of the great Eliyahu, his own father.

"Grandfather would have been a very great *rebbe*, Abie. But he did not believe that he had a *derech*, a way to deal with God. In truth, he knew a better *derech* than most of us, but I will tell you about that tomorrow. Now it is time for supper. Are you hungry?"

Abie nodded. In imaginings, he was far away. He was a prince, a *rebbe*. Men gathered around him to hear him speak for he knew a special way of talking with God. Women whispered that he could cure their illnesses, but he could not hear them for he was deep in prayer. Then, suddenly, came a chill Northern wind; the people began to fade. In an instant he was alone like the old Jew in the portrait clinging to his prayer book and his shawl.

❋

The large loaves of challah, the Sabbath bread, were on the table covered with an embroidered white cloth. Beside them was the long silver knife with its jagged edge. The smell of the bread was more pungent tonight than usual, and the knife seemed to offer up a special gleam. Abie headed for his usual seat opposite Doug.

"Not this Sabbath, Abie. This Sabbath you must sit at the head of the table. And you will lead the *kiddush* prayer over the wine and say the blessing for the bread."

So Abie took his father's place and began to recite the prayers. Imma, Doug, and his father joined in his imagination with Grandfather Trachson and Rebbe Eliyahu Tzadik. Together the family sang the responses until it seemed the room was filled with song. Abie's Sabbath had begun.

That night, Abie tossed in bed, unable to rest. Finally, exhausted, he slept toward dawn. Through the drawn curtain, the morning light bathed his face and taunted him to wakefulness. Doug still slumbered. From the chest of drawers, Abie removed the ledger. He wrote: *Morning of my Bar Mitzvah. On this morning I woke early, hardly slept. The sun is a sign God has sent me, a Bar Mitzvah present, an omen for the great-grandson of Eliyahu Tzadik.*

He crawled back beneath the covers and tried to imagine an Eliyahu Tzadik with a rounded chin, a straight nose, and brown hair falling across his forehead. He fell back to sleep painting images, seeing visions of gardens and courtyards, of people by the hundreds moving like waves in great patterns, and flowers blooming in profusions of lilac, crimson, and emerald.

This time his Imma awakened him, her breath both close and pungent as she kissed his cheek. Could she ever lose that difference that separated her from being an American mother, Abie wondered. For it made him love her in a most uncomfortable way. Doug was already awake and dressing. Abie dressed quickly, washed his face and brushed his teeth, ran a comb through his hair, paused to think whether there was something else he had forgotten to do in the bathroom, then rushed downstairs. Breakfast was dry cereal, toast, and milk. He ate hurriedly and waited for the rest of his family to eat. Father was the last one to come to the table. Abie was impatient.

"Abie," his father said at last, "come with me into the study."

Abie sat in the green chair again, but now his father sat on the edge of the desk, one leg planted firmly on the floor and the other dangling.

"Do you understand why we are having your Bar Mitzvah at home instead of in a synagogue?"

Abie nodded.

"Why?"

"Because this is the right way—" Abie began.

"No. There is no 'right way,' only a feeling. I did not want you to think this Bar Mitzvah was a show, or that it was any better than any other Bar Mitzvah either. It is not something you are doing to please me or your Imma. What you do will be for your own sake. When a Jewish boy reaches the age of thirteen, he becomes a man, a member of the Jewish people."

"Even without a Bar Mitzvah?" Abie asked.

"That's right. Even without the ceremony. The ceremony is only a way of speaking with God and a way of showing your people that you are ready to be a man. It is not a law. The law is that a child becomes an adult at thirteen, with or without the ceremony."

Abie watched as his father walked around the desk, then sat placing the palms of his hands flat on his knees and closing his eyes. Abie closed his eyes, too.

"No. I had better start where I left off last night," he said. "Do you remember the story I was telling you about your grandfather?"

Abie nodded, then remembered that his father's eyes were closed. He opened his eyes to check, then closed them again. "I remember," he said.

"Your grandfather settled in a *shtetl*, a small Jewish village, in Poland and became a tailor. He called himself Yusef Trachson. All day he worked on coats and pants and shirts. His hands grew rough from handling the coarse materials that were all the

Jews could afford. When I was ten, I began working with him. I learned to cut material along a soap-marked line; I learned to stitch a seam and sew a button.

"At night we studied together, my father and I. He was getting me ready for my Bar Mitzvah. But as we studied, he would remember a particularly good expounding of this passage or that verse which his father, the great Tzadik, had taught to him. He would teach it to me just as his father had taught it to him. And he would excuse himself and go to his room. Sometimes I stood outside the door and listened to him weeping. You understand, he was not a happy man. Once he told me that he was 'chosen to suffer' and told me to remember that when all other memories faded away—you see, I still remember it.

"When he would recite to me one of the expoundings, a *toyreh*, he learned from his father, he would have me memorize it. When we worked together cutting and mending, he would ask me to repeat these *toyrehs*. He would listen. On the Sabbath, we went to shul and prayed for blessings in the coming week. There was no *rebbe* in this small *shtetl*, but there were two small houses of meeting because there were two different groups of *Hasidim* living cheek by jowl, each following the teachings of a different distant *rebbe*.

"My father did not believe in either of the two *rebbes* that the shuls represented. He felt keenly the distance of the *rebbes* and how it separated not only the followers from their leaders but the two factions from each other. Yet he knew that many of his father's *Hasidim* had come from many distant cities while the Tzadik was alive. So we alternated, taking turns going now to one shul and again to the other.

That was how it happened that when I was thirteen, a visitor passed through the *shtetl* and recognized my father. The visitor was an old man, a devoted follower of Eliyahu. He did not speak to my father and told no one in our *shtetl* who my father was. Until the Sabbath came.

"That Saturday morning, we went to the small shul on the eastern end of the *shtetl*. After the service, the visitor was asked to give a *toyreh*, a teaching. He smiled and began one of Eliyahu's greatest *toyrehs*, but at the end he purposely made many mistakes and confused the whole teaching so that none of it was intelligible. The *Hasidim* murmured in wonder. Could such a fine beginning truly lead to such an ignoble and confounded conclusion?

"My father, who did not recognize the man after all those years, could not abide the twisting of the *toyreh*. The color rose to his face. He sprang to his feet and he retold the entire teaching in front of the whole congregation. Then the visitor asked how he knew the *toyreh* so well. 'I was a disciple of Eliyahu Tzadik,' my father replied. 'Or perhaps his son?' the visitor said with a smile. Every *shtetl* is a small place. Sometimes the world is a small place. And that is how it came to pass that there were so many of Eliyahu's followers at my Bar Mitzvah. They came to honor the grandson of their Tzadik. True, a new *rebbe* had been chosen to replace Eliyahu. But he also came. I remember him especially, for he had gentle eyes and hands as soft as Merino wool.

"My father had me read the whole Torah portion in honor of the *Hasidim* who gathered in the *shtetl* that Shabbat. And that is the same portion which I chose for you to read today, Abie. The portion named *Vayeitzei*, 'And he left …' Here, I will read the English for you:

> And Jacob left Beersheva bound for Haran. He encountered a certain place; and he slept there because the sun had set. Of the stones of the place, he took one for his pillow; and he rested in that place.
>
> And he dreamed, and there was a ladder implanted on the earth, with its top reaching heaven. And behold there were angels of God ascending and descending on it. And, behold, the Lord stood above it and said, "I am the Lord, God of Abraham your father, and God of Isaac. The land on which you lie, I shall give to you and to your descendants. And your descendants shall be like the dust of the earth and you will spread out westward, eastward, to the north, and to the south. Through you and your descendants, all the nations of the earth shall be blessed."

"And this is the *toyreh*, the expounding, the teaching, of Eliyahu Tzadik that my father made me memorize. *And behold the angels of God ascending and descending…* Why ascending and descending? Why not the opposite? We think of angels as God's messengers. Should they not come down from God first and then return to the heavens? But, no! The messengers of God ascend the ladder before they descend. There can be but one explanation. Jacob in his dream has discovered a *derech*, a way of dealing with God.

"This is the ladder, the *derech*. It is for us to reach out to God. God is always above the ladder, waiting, listening, compassionate and loving. We have only to speak first to Him and God is sure to answer, for just as the angels go up, they surely descend again. It is always ascending and descending, never the opposite.

"And more: it is not enough for Jacob to speak with God through words, for words alone are not strong enough to ascend the ladder. Only through the three-fold path of words, actions, and intent can the ladder be scaled. Jacob and his descendants must constantly scale the ladder anew. This is the reason more than one messenger is on the ladder ready to carry our message up. Do you understand?"

Abie nodded.

"A little, I think," his father said. "But your world is much farther from it than my world was. When I came for college to New York, I saw that America is far from Europe in many ways. American Jews are not the Jews of the Old World. In Europe, in the synagogue, Jews sought God; in America, they seek community. So much is the New World path the *derech* of community that they speak the prayers of their fathers and grandfathers in the language of their Israeli brothers and sisters. Perhaps, in the end, this will be your path, too. Surely, many of the old paths are lost and some rightly so.

"All the same, your Bar Mitzvah is also my act of faith. You will take an oath of action; you will set out on your quest. And I will fulfill an oath I have taken."

Abie shifted in the green chair.

"This is why your Bar Mitzvah will he here at home. In the synagogue, the witnesses would be those who seek meaning at the base of the ladder, those who pass the ladder never seeing it. For some, community may be enough; for many, it is all they can master. But here in this study, today, you are the *rebbe*."

❀

The leather chair was moved out from behind the desk. The desk was cleared. Slowly, the room took on a new shape. Imma and Doug entered as if it were natural for them to do so, as if it were a part of the order of things. Abie stood behind the desk and in the accents of the East European courtyards, read the morning prayers. Then came the story of the ladder with words that seemed to echo in a room that should not have reflected sound, where the spines of the books should have absorbed the letters, the vowels, and even the decorative melody of the even Hebrew cadence, as if language could be food for stories and not vice versa, as if phrases and sentences were laden enough with meaning as they were spoken to slake the dry thirst of cloth glued to cardboard and wrapped around paper and stacked upon shelves so that the shelves groaned beneath the weight of the memories they had to support.

"Ascending."

"Descending."

Words spoken cannot be recalled. They are sustained in the ripples of the air just as pebbles dropped in ponds cause the water's surface to vibrate to infinity if we could but see it. Would ears deceive so? Did it not seem that he was hearing the words just before speaking them as if they were just now coming to rest in this room after wandering in some forty-year echo? Were these the words his father spoke that now he heard and that guided him to say them well, to say them truly as they should be said?

And as he set out to teach the *toyreh* that Eliyahu Tzadik taught to his son Yusef, known as Trachson, who taught it to his son who taught it to him, did he not hear the words in his own silent voice—or in some silent voice—within him—before he said them aloud? Oh, yes, Abie thought, there is a mystery here: a link between what may have been before and what might follow, in the inclination of the ear, or in the pitch of the voice, or in the hollow of the throat where sounds begin, or perhaps in the common air, in the atmosphere that may be more dense than ever we imagine as we move through it—as the fish swim through the ocean without perceiving the sea. And is not our region of the atmospheric heavens merely a thinner ocean permitting us more easily the illusion that it is not there, while actually carrying to us the reverberating accumulation of eras of sound, the shapes of myriads of generations of beings passing and leaving their impressions eternally palpable so that we could reach out and trace their hazy images and follow the courses of their lives engraved in ever-receding motions of the air with a surety and faith that could not be shaken even by the skeptic, even by the cynic, even by the sea where the fog runs dense and the whole may seem a fishbowl carved in grey or the inside of an opaque crystal ball if we could but imagine ourselves within?

So, too, the presence of Eliyahu Tzadik descended to that study to bear witness in the name of heaven to a holy act, in answer to an angel that ascended even according to Eliyahu's own teaching. Compared to this, miracles need not exist.

Master of Wood

This story first appeared in the Spring 1966 issue of Espejo ("The Mirror"), the student literary magazine of S.M.U. In 1967, I moved up the ranks from Editorial Assistant of Espejo to Editor. Before entering college, I spent a year in Israel during which I did some dabbling in archaeology, studied Hebrew and Judaic subjects, and worked on a kibbutz. Three great urges—writing, publishing, and teaching—ended up pursuing me as much as I pursued them. Thus, a career.

There was a man with tongue of wood
Who essayed to sing,
And in truth it was lamentable.
But there was one who heard
The clip-clopper of this tongue of wood
And knew what the man
Wished to sing,
And with that the singer was content.
— Stephen Crane

The chill wind blew across desolate ground carrying dust as the river carries silt—plucking particles from loose topsoil, sucking them into its stream, spewing them earthward at random. At the desert's edge, sand, caught in the swirling turbulence, fell into jet-sprays of water and spun to the ground. Cold and heat commingled as the sun tossed fiery light carelessly above the horizon. Slowly the wind settled as uneasy as a river before a dam. All the time, sprinkler heads twisted side to side sending precious water into even rows of plants. Where the water reached, the green spread like verdant velvet; at the ends of the field, the desert rose and fell in a giant sea of cinnamon.

The bulbous blue and white bus pulled to a halt before the settlement gates. A small disfigured man stepped down and squinted in the morning sun. One hand he raised to shadow his scarred face, the other hand swept grey hair from his forehead. The driver, a gaunt fellow with eyes like two pearl insets, lowered two suitcases to the dusty ground. The man nodded to the inlaid eyes and lifted the suitcases. Quietly he turned to walk toward the buildings on the hill.

He moved slowly upwards stopping frequently to rest the cases on the ground as he passed fields of cotton and sugar beet. At the top, he came to a ring of large buildings. In the middle, an iron-grey tower stood like a quiet sentry, its small platform empty. At its base, flowers grew in wild profusion—reds and yellows and whites in roses, gardenias, and poppies.

He raised one hand to shield his eyes and slowly turned around. The sun was inching its way up into the cloudless sky while the blue and white bus rumbled into the distance where the brown hills and the clear sky closed in around the winding black road. Then, turning and retrieving his suitcases from the ground, he headed for the largest building. The brilliant sounds of metal tinkling against metal and the hurried sounds of muffled voices filled his ears while the smell of cooked eggs flared his nostrils. A small group of people passed him as he stepped aside to give them room.

Entering the building he brushed several men in the hall and walked past the large glass doors leading to the dining hall. Inside, people were busily eating while the waiters moved from table to table pushing little handcarts of food in front of them. Beyond, the short hall ended in another door. He knocked and heard no response and no movement inside. Finally, he tried the knob and finding the door open he stepped inside. Across the entire wall opposite him books were stretched end to end on long shelves. Next to him was a small table piled high with correspondence and loose papers. There were two chairs around another small table surrounded by boxes of unused mimeograph paper in neat packages.

For a while he walked around the small room glancing at the scratchings on the scattered papers and studying the spines of the shelved books. When he was finished, he sat in one of the chairs. He was up again in an instant crossing the room to his suitcases. He picked them up and set them closer to the chair.

Sitting down again, he folded his arms across his chest and closed his eyes.

A young man stood looking down at his worn face as his eyes slowly opened. The young man smiled. "*Shalom.*"

He looked into the young man's eyes. "I'm afraid," he replied in English, "that I don't speak Hebrew. Do you speak any English?"

Without any hesitation, the young man picked up the conversation in a fluent English.

A moment later, they were introducing themselves and shaking hands. The young man was the *Mazkir* of the settlement. "That is," he explained to his visitor, "I am the one that people blame when something does not go right."

"Where did you learn your English? It's very good."

"I studied in an American college, Mr. Stein." But even as he finished this sentence, he had begun to speak again in Hebrew. The Hebrew was one uninterrupted flow until the young man looked up at Stein and suddenly realized that something was wrong. He paused and waited for a moment.

"I could understand it better in English."

"I am sorry. Please forgive me. I didn't realize what I was doing. It has been a long time since I spoke English. I said that we received a letter from the Israeli ambassador in England and another from the Old Vic Company. We were expecting you. Will you be here long?"

"I'm not sure."

"What did you do at Old Vic?"

"I was the stage manager and a carpenter."

"How long were you there?"

"Twelve years."

The young man paused and looked at his bookcase. When he turned back to Stein, one eyebrow was slightly raised. "What made you leave?"

Stein glanced quickly at his suitcases, then held one hand outstretched before him. He opened the hand and spread the fingers out fanlike on the table. When he tried to bring the fingers together, they would not form a fist. The young man nodded and turned his face away, flexing his hand beneath the table—forming a fist, releasing it, stretching the fingers, and forming the fist again.

"I am sorry. We were expecting you, though, and we prepared a room for you. If you will follow me, I will take you to it."

They walked out of the building, each man holding one of the suitcases. "Over there, Mr. Stein, is the dairy. We produce milk for the hospital in town and for our own use. The large building next to the dairy is the carpenter's shop. That might be of some interest to you. Over there are the nurseries and the children's houses. You see, we don't provide room for parents to keep their own children. All the children stay together. And this is your house. There are five rooms in each house. The bathroom is the third door. This one is your room." The young man opened a door. "Shall I come for you at lunchtime?"

"No. What time will that be?"

"Lunch is at noon and lasts until two o'clock. Supper begins at six and lasts until eight."

When the young man was gone, Stein sat on the bed and stared at the small room. Something was missing in it, that unknown spark which converts a room into a living thing so that when it is there, the room seems to have some reality. But this room was unreal. Stein crossed the room and walked outside. He turned and looked for a lock on the door, but there was none so he went back inside and carefully slipped the cases under the bed. Then he pulled the bedcovers to the floor. Satisfied, he started off again.

He walked to the east, to a side of the kibbutz he had not seen before, and found the orchards. Walking through the rows of peaches where the small fresh fruit was still too young and hard to be good, he came to the pomegranate trees. The pomegranates were yellow and turning red or red and turning brown. They reminded him of gourds he had dried to use in creating sound effects. As he passed, he saw that some of them were already rotting on the tree and wondered why they had not been harvested.

Beyond the orchards was another field, the vineyards. The vineyards of Israel were legendary, producing the fine grape which had produced the ritual wine of the Jews for thousands of years. But these vines were naked, standing like brown skeletons on the cinnamon soil, their spines supported by stakes driven into the ground. Wire was strung from stake to stake and held the arms of the skeleton straight out at its sides. From the arms the sun-dried twigs extended like useless fingers. At the far end of the vineyard men were swinging axes, cutting the vines where they touched the golden soil. Behind the men, a tractor turned the soil throwing the roots into the air with a stuttering thud as the blade encountered each twisted root.

Looking down, Stein realized the difference in the ground beneath him. While the soil in the orchards had been turned so that the soil was loose and yielding to the step, and while he had constantly dodged the jets of water from the sprinkler heads between the trees, the soil here in the vineyard was parched and cracked, dried by the sun until it contracted and formed a thick upper crust where there was once topsoil.

He started toward the group of workers but stopped midway to watch them swinging their axes. One slash where the skeletal form met the dead soil was enough to kill a vine which had taken many years of cultivation to develop. Stein pushed back the grey hair from his forehead, then looked down at his hands and saw his fingers silhouetted against the lifeless vines.

One of the workers looked at Stein, seeing the figure of a small graying man, his body bent and arms dangling at his side. Then, whether it was Stein's gaunt body or the picture he presented against the field of skeletal forms was hard to tell, the worker looked up again, following Stein's retreat with his eyes before catching up with three quick swings of his axe.

Stein walked around the bottom of the hill into the valley on the northern side where he found the remnants of what was once a house and what was now four short walls being slowly eaten by the eroding sands. He could have jumped the wall or stepped over it at some low point, but searching for the remains of the doorway Stein entered where the door had been.

Sand was piled high in the corners of the ruin. Eventually, the sand would cover it completely and the only remains would be a hill of sand, a *tel*, the Israelis call it. As he stood staring at the small heaps of sand, a gust of wind came up and blew around his face, raising grains of sand all around him. Quickly he stepped over the wall and started to climb up the hill.

The hill was steep above the deserted house, and at the top was a wooden fence. Inside, the cows lay in the shade of metal shelters. All around them the ground was heated by their enormous brown and white bodies and the afternoon sun. The air above the ground steamed like an open fire on a wet night.

As he walked away from the cows, Stein was drawn to the western side of the kibbutz. Leaving behind him the fields and the orchards and the sight of men working in the graveyard of vines, his brown skin creased on his forehead, and he lowered his heavy brown eyebrows. His thumbs rubbed against his fingers where the callouses of constant use were already softening. He came to a large metal shed. From within, the smell of sawdust came to him like a confidential whisper, opening his ears and eyes until sights and sounds became opaque and only the familiar odor penetrated to his senses with its inaudible buzz-saw mumbling. His eyes closed and his muscles tensed. The skin of his arms tightened around his joints. Opening his eyes, he felt himself moving toward the shed, his feet brushing reluctantly against the ground.

Lumber lined the inner walls of the shed, stacked and arranged in neat piles. Only the middle of the floor provided working space, and it was crowded with machines—big, silver, and humming. His eyes scanned the shop with a knowledgeable glitter, resting finally at the floor covered with sawdust and wood shavings. His hand reached for the metal lathe and, turning the movable end, he loosened the clamps and slid his hand along the shining steel surface.

"*Comment allez-vous?*"

Stein wheeled around, facing a tall young man with a wide blonde moustache turned up at either end. "Excuse me?" The man stared at him. "Do you speak any English?"

"*Anglais?*" The young man shook his head from side to side.

Stein muttered something and nodded. The young man smiled uncomfortably and went back to his work. Stein took his hand from the lathe and began to leave. He brought one hand to his head and was about to run it through his hair when the sound of the buzz-saw stopped him. Wood shavings were flying toward him, bouncing against the black knit of his sweater. For a moment he stood, feeling the curlicues of waste bouncing away from him, then he bent and picked up a block of wood. Carrying it with him, he walked back toward his room.

Near the watchtower, he paused to sit on the grass next to the red and green garden. He fingered the piece of wood, turning it around and around, holding it in one hand, and tracing its grain with the other. His face was frozen in hard creases as he carefully changed the angles of the wood, seeing it from every possible side.

The little girl had seen the scar which ran from his ear to the end of his left eye. He said, "Hello," but it was too late. With a little cry, she was gone, running away from him. He looked again at the piece of wood and lifted it to throw it away from him. Somehow, the wood and the arm had been made of the same grain, and he could not separate them; when he stopped trying, the wood was still in his hand.

He took it to his room and put it on his bed. Looking at a watch, he felt an emptiness in the pit of his stomach. Carefully, he withdrew the suitcase from beneath the bedcover and opened it. Every tool was carefully placed and anchored in the case, and each blade was oiled and sheathed. He drew one long-bladed knife and ran the end of one broken thumbnail against the blade collecting the oil and testing the edge. Gripping it firmly, he picked up the wood. Suddenly, his hand opened, and the knife slid to the floor with the metallic sound of silent thrust as it landed embedded in the wood, handle up. He pulled his fingers together and brought them into a fist feeling the strain across the back of his neck, the muscles in his cheeks quivering. Slowly, he released the fist and spread his fingers fanlike pressing them against his knee.

With the same hand. he traced the scar from his eye to his ear where it faded in the memory of his fingertips. He touched his hands together and then pulled the knife from the floor. Slowly, at first, his hands began to work, pressing the blade against the unformed wood splaying splinters, shavings, and dust into the stagnant air.

When he was finished, his eyes turned to the bed. He looked at his watch and realized the time. Grabbing the wood, he started for the dining hall. The hall was already emptying as he approached it, but he fought against the crowd as if he were swimming against a strong current. The dining hall was empty. He moved quickly, pushing through the people again as they stood massed in the door.

A few yards in front of him, a little girl was walking away. He ran to catch up with her and, turning her around, he drew in his breath. "I'm sorry. I thought …"

Quickly he searched for other little girls, looking carefully as he passed through the people, walking one way and then another. Finally, he saw her long black hair, bobbing up and down beside a young woman, who held her hand. They were across the field already, near the children's quarters. "Wait," he called, but they only kept walking. He ran behind them into the small building where all around him parents were saying goodnight to their children.

He saw the black-haired girl and leaned down in front of her. She pressed her face deep into the folds of the young woman's skirt. Stein held out the wooden figurine. Carefully, she stared at him, then slowly she put her hand out. Still she did not take the doll. Stein bent lower, sitting on one knee, offering her the doll in one outstretched palm.

Still her hand reached beyond it. Suddenly, he understood and bent forward so that his face was closer to her. He felt her fingers tracing the soft scar, and then she smiled. She smiled until she laughed, and he was laughing with her. Then he opened himself to her and felt her young body next to his and felt her warmth as he closed his arms around her. The world spun around him, its bright lights blinding him, and then there was no world but only the little girl and Stein and silent laughter in the air all around them. He was spinning faster than the tiny wheels inside his watch. He was far beyond time and moving faster than any man could move. When the laughing stopped and the girl stepped away again, it had been only an instant. Stein offered her the doll. She took it and stared at it. Then she turned it around in her hands and felt the sanded finish.

She handed it back to him.

He nodded a little sadly as she spoke to him in Hebrew. "*Todah.*" Then he stood and stared at the doll as if he had never seen it before. He gave it to the young woman. She, too, spoke to him.

Not knowing what they had said or what to answer, he turned and walked out of the children's house and into the green field. He stared at the outline of the dark metal tower and straightened his back slightly as he ran his hand through his thick gray hair.

"Isaac: God's
Special Child"
& Other Fascinations

Isaac: God's
Special Child

Can a special needs child become a patriarch of God's chosen people? Is this the reason God asks Abraham, "Is anything too wondrous for the Eternal?" (Gen. 18:14). My inquiry opens with clues regarding Isaac's idiosyncratic name and proceeds to examine evidence that can dramatically alter the way we read the biblical story of the son of Abraham, the father of Jacob.

Legends claimed that Zarathustra's birth was foretold from the beginning of time, that he emerged from the womb laughing, and that the whole universe delighted with him. Even so, Zarathustra's name means something like "camel herder." Isaac's birth was also foretold by heaven even before he was born; God had commanded that the baby be named *Yitzchak*—Isaac—which means something like "(he) laughs." The name is not assigned because Isaac emerged from the womb laughing. He did not.

The Bible attempts three times to supply an origin for Isaac's name—three times in three different ways in three incidents in three chapters of Genesis.

In Chapter 17, between Verses 1 and 19, a) God changes Abram's name to Abraham; b) God changes Sarai's name to Sarah; c) God makes a covenant with Abraham that includes obedience and circumcision in exchange for fertility, nobility, and the land of Canaan; d) God promises Abraham a son through Sarah; e) God commands that the son be named *Yitzchak*; and f) God promises to continue the God-Abraham covenant with *Yitzchak* as "an everlasting covenant for his offspring to come." God does almost all the speaking in Chapter 17, but in Verse

17, "Abraham threw himself on his face and laughed as he said to himself, 'Can a child be born to a man a hundred years old, or can Sarah bear a child at ninety?'"

Imagine that! Abraham is bowing to God—"threw himself on his face" is the idiom used for this worship position—and laughing and asking himself if what God is promising is even remotely possible.

Wisely, no doubt, Abraham does not express his inner misgivings to God. Instead, in his only spoken words in Chapter 17, Abraham gently suggests that God need not do the impossible because God has already given him a first-born son, "Abraham said to God, 'O that Ishmael might live by Your favor!'" (18).

God responds to Abraham's laughter, not Abraham's words. In Verse 19, God says, "Nevertheless, Sarah your wife shall bear you a son, and you shall name him *Yitzchak* ['(he) laughs'], and I will maintain My covenant with him...." It is not explicit, but the text implies that God named the promised son *Yitzchak* based on Abraham's laughter.

The second incident comes in Chapter 18. This time, Sarah laughs at the idea of having a child at her age. It begins when Abraham welcomes and feeds three men. They turn out to be more than simple wayfarers. In fact, one is either YHWH or the angel spokesman of YHWH and the other two are angel servants of YHWH. Abraham only learns this by stages as the chapter proceeds.

> They said to him, "Where is your wife, Sarah?" And he replied, "There, in the tent." Then one said, "I will return to you next year, and your wife Sarah shall have a son!" Sarah was listening at the entrance of the tent, which was behind him. Now Abraham and Sarah were old, advanced in years; Sarah had stopped having the periods of women. And Sarah laughed to herself, saying, "Now that I am withered, am I to have enjoyment—with my husband so old?" Then YHWH said to Abraham, "Why did Sarah laugh, saying, 'Shall I in truth bear a child, old as I am?' Is anything too wondrous for YHWH? I will return to you at the same season next year, and Sarah shall have a son." Sarah lied, saying, "I did not laugh," for she was frightened. But [YHWH] replied, "You did laugh" (Gen. 18:9-14).

The passage ends with YHWH confronting Sarah directly, "You *did* laugh." The implication this time is that Sarah's laughter, noticed by YHWH, resulted in the name *Yitzchak*.
The third incident occurs in Chapter 21.

YHWH took note of Sarah as promised, and YHWH did for Sarah as declared. Sarah conceived and bore a son to Abraham in his old age, at the set time of which God had spoken. Abraham gave his newborn son, whom Sarah had borne him, the name of *Yitzchak*. And when his son *Yitzchak* was eight days old, Abraham circumcised him, as God had commanded him. Now Abraham was a hundred years old when his son *Yitzchak* was born to him. Sarah said, "God has brought me laughter; everyone who hears will laugh (*yitzchak*) [with] me." And she added, "Who would have said to Abraham that Sarah would suckle children! Yet I have borne a son to him in his old age."

This time, Sarah explains the name, saying, "God has brought me laughter." And for the third time, much is made of the issue of old age. In fact, Isaac literally is the child of parents in their advanced years.

The Jewish sages, reading the stories of the birth of Isaac hundreds of years later, felt compelled to account for this. In the Talmud they observed that Sarai had always been infertile, but once God changed her name to Sarah, her youth must have been restored (*Rosh HaShanah* 16b). The sages also imagined that people roundabout refused to believe that the child was born of Abraham and Sarah. Rumors spread that the old couple had adopted a foundling. Sarah put an end to those rumors, the sages said. She made a party and invited all the women around to attend. Many had their infants with them and Sarah's breasts gave forth "like two fountains" and she proceeded to give milk to every infant. So the women were convinced of the miracle (*Bava Metzia* 87a). The sages thus zeroed in on one hinge of the enigma of Isaac—the old age of both parents.

Modern scholars suggest that the name *Yitzchak* (Isaac) is a shortened form of a more probable name, *Yitzchak-El*. The longer name forms a parallel to *Yishma-El* (Ishmael), Abraham's first son. The name *Yishma-El* means "God hearkens," and the name is attested in other ancient sources. The name *Yitzchak-El*, then, should mean "God laughs," and this name is not attested outside the Bible. The biblical editors may have been purposeful in omitting *El* here, but even without the *El*, *Yitzchak* means "(He) laughs" and the *He* refers not to Abraham or Sarah but to God. Other references to God laughing in the Bible all occur when human beings attempt to defy or act independently of God (Psalms 2:4; 37:13; 59:9). Likewise, here in Genesis, Abraham and Sarah both believe they "know better" and God reminds them, "Is anything too wondrous for YHWH?" (18:14).

There is another proof in the text. In Genesis 21:5, Sarah says, "God has brought me laughter; everyone who hears *yitzchak* me." Nearly every translation inserts a word to explain the unusual Hebrew of the last half of the sentence. Often it is "everyone who hears will laugh [with] me." The sentence translates very nicely if reading *yitzchak* as a simple verb with God as the subject. We can read either "God has brought me laughter; everyone hears! God laughs at me," or better, "God has played a joke on me; everyone hears! God laughs at me." This is the second hinge of the Isaac enigma. It is the presumed joke or laughter that God has wrought.

Ironically, after all their waiting and all God's promises, the child finally born to Abraham and Sarah is a child of their combined old age. Intended by God to inherit the leadership of Abraham's people, their child's name clearly states that Isaac is somehow laughable, somehow "God's joke." The obvious supposition is that the child is deficient or handicapped in some respect. The suggestion has often been made that Isaac suffered from Down syndrome, a condition in which extra genetic material causes delays in the way a child develops physically and/or mentally. But whether it is Down syndrome or some other deficiency, it is apparent from the text that the narrator considers Isaac's defect God's doing, God's will.

The Torah text as we have received it is the end product of much editorial work. Editing was continuous—first in oral form and then in written form—possibly right up to the time of the destruction of the Temple. Scholars take many paths to understanding the text and all the paths bear fruit of one kind or another and enrich our understandings. One of my teachers,

Professor Cyrus Gordon—extraordinary linguist, archaeologist, and Bible scholar—often reminded us that, setting aside various sources and influences, the narrative we now have is the end product, and there is always much to be learned by reading it as a unified entity just as its final redactor intended it to be read.

Another of my teachers, Dr. Joseph Campbell—disciple of Jung, distinguished lecturer, and master of world mythology—proposed that the enduring nature of scriptures lies in their "renewability" (my term), that is, their propensity to continually inspire new interpretations and insights. New inspirations in turn produce new myths for us to live by. The scriptures do not change, but the way they are viewed shifts constantly according to who is reading and when. In the following, I propose to apply these two principles to the narratives relating to Isaac, son of Abraham and Sarah.

Of course, the biography of Isaac has been examined intensely throughout the ages by commentators, critical scholars, and learned laypersons resulting in a veritable mountain of religious and secular data. What is already known is important. Most of what I suggest has been suggested before. I only hope to arrange these insights (and a few of my own) in a startling way. Reading these narratives together we may climb to a place that, at first, can only be glimpsed from afar.

❄

The child is named "[God] laughs." Isaac is somehow different, somehow laughable. No wonder Sarah wishes to expel Ishmael, Abraham's first son born of Sarah's maidservant, from the camp. The narrative points to this directly: In Genesis 21:9, Sarah's decision to exile Hagar and her child is foreshadowed by the statement that "Sarah saw the son whom Hagar the Egyptian had borne to Abraham *playing*," and the word for "playing" comes from the selfsame root as Isaac's name, "laughing." Indeed, we might translate the verse to say that Sarah saw Ishmael *laughing*—laughing in a normal childlike way, laughing at play—and this vision was a total affront to her matriarchal pride. Put plainly, Hagar's child laughs like a normal child while Sarah's child is laughable.

This is not to imply that in ancient times infants born with defects, whether obvious at birth or subsequently discovered in early childhood, were necessarily the butt of jokes. No, I have a far more sinister suggestion to make a little later. Here, we need only say that the narrator has made a case, through three careful repetitions (the classic two clues and a clincher), for Isaac to be "God's jest." If God truly intends Isaac to become the next leader of the Hebrews, then the words of Genesis 18:14—"Is anything too wondrous for YHWH?"—attain a richer, deeper meaning as if to say, "Do you not think that God can take a child who seems defective and make him the next link in the patriarchal chain?" Stick around. The story really gets interesting from here.

The next sequence featuring Isaac is the story of the binding found in Genesis Chapter 22. Since so much commentary already exists on this passage, since it is so familiar to readers of the Bible, and since my interpretation of it differs so radically, you can "raise up your eyes" to envision the story in a new way if you approach Genesis 22 with what philosopher Paul Ricœur calls "a second naïveté." In other words, it is best to set it aside until we have gathered a little more evidence. Pertinent information and new understandings appear if we turn at this juncture to the search for a suitable wife for Isaac.

Sarah's death is briefly related. In Genesis 23:2-3a, we are told that "Abraham proceeded to mourn for Sarah and to bewail her. Then Abraham rose from beside his dead...." It is noteworthy that no mention is made of Isaac mourning his mother despite the fact that, as we soon discover, he has not departed the scene. Meanwhile, Abraham rises with new vigor to make all the necessary preparations for the burial of Sarah and the continuance of his people. Through the remainder of Chapter 23, Abraham succeeds in purchasing a plot of land and a burial cave from Ephron the Hittite.

Abraham's next endeavor, undertaken in Genesis 24, is introduced by the oft-repeated verity, "Abraham was now old, advanced in years." He adjures his servant to take a solemn oath (of the kind taken on a deathbed, see 47:29) not to take a wife for Isaac from among the Canaanites (24:4): "Go to the land of my birth and get a wife for my son Isaac." The servant responds in an interesting and somewhat unexpected way (24:6), "What if the woman does not consent to follow me to this land, shall I then take your son back to the land from which you came?" This introduces for the first, but not the only, time an intriguing possibility, namely, that a woman whose bride price is agreed to and who is sold by her family might even then have the last word and "not consent" to leaving home. Was it customary in some places for men who married to leave their own homes and become part of the household into which they married (compare Gen. 2:24: "Hence a man leaves his father and mother and clings to his wife, so that they become one flesh")? Yet, before we conclude this, we should see how the story develops. This query on the part of the servant foreshadows a central theme.

Abraham replies prophetically, saying, God will send an angel to prepare the way and provide a suitable wife for Isaac. If not, the servant is released from his oath. In no event is Isaac to be taken to Haran. Abraham may be speaking metaphorically, while at the same time the narrator may be hinting that Isaac would be severely disoriented by being removed from familiar surroundings. Similarly, the rest of the Isaac story gives us the sense that the best course of action in dealing with Isaac was always to keep him close to home. He is the only patriarch who is forbidden, by Abraham and by God, to leave Canaan—and this even at a time of great famine, the very kind of exigency which drove his father to Egypt.

We need not go verse by verse here. The servant is obviously a trusted steward, faithful and reliable, probably Abraham's right-hand man. He prepares a caravan of ten camels laden with treasure. We know that what is intended is a purchase of a bride at a generous bride price. After a long journey, the servant has the camels kneel by the well but does not water them. Instead, he sets up a test in the form of a bargain with the God of Abraham (24:14): "Let the maiden to whom I say, 'Please, lower your jar that I may drink,' and who replies, 'Drink, and I will also water your camels'—let her be the one whom You have decreed for Your servant Isaac."

Without further ado, the perfect maiden appears. On the surface, she has all the appropriate qualifications; she is of Abraham's own family, she is beautiful, and she is a virgin. Moreover, when the servant asks her for water from her jug, she bends down to give him water and immediately offers to water the ten camels until they are sated. And that is one large amount of water to draw and a great deal of work to volunteer!

One would expect that the servant would be entirely satisfied at her performance. She has acted unerringly in accord with the test he set. But instead of simply rejoicing, he wonders (21) "whether the Lord had made his errand successful or not." Obviously, there is still some other hurdle to overcome. The servant presents the maiden with gifts so valuable that their specific weight in gold is mentioned. And he asks for a place to stay for the night.

She runs ahead to tell her (28) "mother's household." Her brother, Laban, runs out to meet and greet Abraham's servant. After the camels and the men who traveled in the caravan have been fed and bedded, and after the servant's feet have been washed as a sign of hospitality, food is brought to him. But the servant's mission is urgent. He refuses to eat before relating his story. He says he has been sent by the rich chieftain Abraham to find a wife for his son (36) because a) Sarah has died after giving Abraham a son "in her old age"; b) Abraham has designated Isaac as his heir and promised him everything Abraham owns; and c) the pledge is dependent on the maiden returning with the servant to Canaan which Abraham has said would be no problem since an angel of God would ensure the mission's success—but which the servant again notes remains dependent on the woman's willingness without which his oath is null and void.

The narrator presents us with several clear-cut impressions: The servant's quest must be important, and much must depend on it; otherwise why repeat it at such great length? Also, there is no false start; God's hand is clearly indicated. Rebekah is the first and the only maiden the servant encounters at the well. Rebekah's lineage is given here and repeated three times in detail. Even before speaking with her family, the servant signals his intention by giving her expensive gifts, arm bracelets, and a nose ring. And the servant thanks the God of Abraham profusely.

It is also noteworthy that in telling his story to the family of Rebekah the servant stresses only the positive—the great wealth and blessings enjoyed by Abraham. He omits saying Isaac's name and speaking of Isaac directly except to say (24:36) that the prospective groom a) is a son of Sarah and Abraham's old age; and b) all his master's wealth has been promised to his son. When he completes telling his story, the servant asks if Rebekah's family intends to comply with Abraham's wishes. They answer:

> The matter was decreed by the Lord; we cannot speak to you bad or good. Here is Rebekah before you; take her and go, and let her be a wife to your master's son, as the Lord has spoken. (50)

The servant bows low to the ground and pays over Abraham's fine gifts of silver and gold to Rebekah and to Laban and his mother.

The idea that far from Abraham and Canaan, back in the city of Nahor, Abraham's relatives, Laban and Rebekah and their family, worship the same YHWH ("the Lord") known to Abraham, and would automatically accede to a "matter decreed by the Lord" is incredible. More likely, considering what next transpires, the reply is intended to set the servant's mind at ease while giving the family a chance to consider their bargaining position. A large treasure is at stake. (If this is, indeed, a negotiation, we should compare it to the negotiation between Abraham and Ephron, the Hittite, when Abraham wished to purchase the cave at Machpelah (23:11). Ephron began that negotiation by offering the burial site to Abraham at no price. Nevertheless, as seen in the continuing negotiation, Ephron's initial statement was obviously not meant to be taken literally—it was a ploy, probably no more than an indication that Ephron was willing to sell.) It is likely that the same is true here. Laban may speak of "the Lord" and fate but only as an indication of his willingness to contract for Rebekah's marriage: "... we cannot speak to you bad or good" is what we would call "a positive maybe." In response, the servant proceeds, as Abraham did with Ephron, not to haggle but to immediately pay out what represents the highest price (53), "The servant brought out objects of silver and gold, and garments, and gave them to Rebekah; and he gave presents to her brother and her mother."

Negotiation apparently complete, the servant rises in the morning, ready to take Rebekah and depart for Canaan. The mother and brother say (55), "Stay with us for a day or ten," obviously an idiom meaning something like "for some indeterminate time." The servant insists on leaving at once. The mother and brother then call Rebekah and ask her to make her final decision (58), "'Will you go with this man?' And she replies, 'I will.'"

As we know from ancient marriage contracts and from the fact that Abraham sent an impressive treasure as a bride price, marriages were generally arranged between parents. (Laban, in the text, is certainly acting *in loco parentis* though we are offered no clue as to where his father might be.) In such matters, maidens were either too young to consent or had no say. But at every turn since the initial exchange (24:5a), when the servant asked Abraham, "What if the woman does not consent to follow me to this land...?" the narrator has reminded us that Rebekah does have the ultimate say in this particular contract. This is not entirely unknown in marriage contracts from Nuzi, Ugarit, and other ancient sources, but it is the rare exception and usually signals some extenuating circumstance.

Why is Rebekah in charge here? To answer that, we need only glance back at the test that the servant set up at the well. It was intentionally a test to discover a maiden who exhibited exceeding kindness—kindness to human beings and kindness to animals, too! It was also a test of patience, endurance, and determination. These are precisely the qualities the maiden would need to deal with Isaac since Isaac was incapable of functioning in the world as a healthy tribal chieftain, a healthy merchant prince, or the next patriarch of the Hebrews. With these qualities, Rebekah could live with a husband who had been born to the old age of his parents, who would always behave like a child and think like a child and be as willful as a child. That is what the servant evidently conveyed when he stressed that Isaac was a child of the old age of Abraham and Sarah (24:36). Passing the test proved that Rebekah was the predestined woman. All the same, because of the exigent circumstances of Isaac's disability, it was still *her* choice.

Remember, too, that not once during his lengthy narration and negotiation does Abraham's servant mention the name

Yitzchak. It is always "my master's son" or "Abraham's son." Surely, this is no coincidence. The servant knows that Isaac's best defense in the getting of a wife is to go nameless and be known only as one who will soon inherit great wealth. A name like "[He] laughs" could hardly be a strong point in any negotiation.

With the final decision in hand, the family bids Rebekah goodbye with good wishes. Her departure from the place of her birth, her homeland, echoes in every way Abraham's own departure from Haran. As she departs, her family blesses her with a prediction of her future (60b):

> O sister! May you grow into thousands of myriads;
> May your offspring *seize the gates of their foes*. [Italics added.]

This compares nicely with the words of God to Abraham as he left Haran (12:2-3a):

> I will make of you a great nation, and I will bless you;
> I will make your name great, and you shall be a blessing.
> I will bless those who bless you and curse him that curses you...

And it corresponds, even more precisely, with the blessing extended by God to Abraham just after he sacrificed the ram instead of Isaac (22:16b-17):

> Because you have done this and have not withheld your son, your favored one, I will bestow My blessing upon you and make your descendants as numerous as the stars of heaven and the sands on the seashore; and your descendants shall *seize the gates of their foes*. [Italics added.]

Rebekah is departing just as Abraham departed and with the same promise on her horizon as Abraham was given. Her destiny awaits as she and her entourage join the caravan of Abraham's servant and his men.

The narrator abruptly jumps to the end of the journey (24:63-67):

> Isaac went out strolling in the field toward evening and, lifting his eyes, he saw camels approaching. Lifting her eyes, Rebekah saw Isaac. She alighted from the camel and said to the servant, "Who

is that man walking in the field toward us?" And the servant said, "That is my master." So she took her veil and covered herself. The servant told Isaac all the things that he had done. Isaac then brought her into the tent of his mother Sarah, and he took Rebekah as his wife. Isaac loved her, and thus found comfort after his mother's death.

When the servant says, "That is my master," we might automatically assume that he has had news of Abraham's death, but the narrator knows this is not the case. Yet, there is a sense in which Isaac has become the servant's "master." In Abraham's time, if a powerful man died with no apparent heir, his chief steward often became his heir. When the servant asked Abraham what would transpire if the maiden refused to return with him, the patriarch made it a condition of the promise that the servant would be released from the necessity of seeking any wife for Isaac. The implication was that either the servant would be freed or possibly would become the new master of the household. By faithfully fulfilling his oath, as well as obtaining a wife for Isaac, the servant has actually ensured that everything Abraham has is now Isaac's and that includes the servant himself! He is, indeed, Isaac's servant.

The veiling of Rebekah may also artfully serve a double purpose. On the one hand, it seems from other instances to be a formal token of a marriage ceremony. On the other hand, it affords Rebekah a special anonymity here. Veiled, Isaac may perceive her as Sarah or even, generically, as the woman who has become his guardian and sponsor as his mother had been previously. Faceless, she is simply his destiny.

Yet the meeting between Isaac and Rebekah is unlike the detailed account the servant gave to Rebekah's family, unlike the elaborate account the narrator gives of the servant's journey, and even unlike the account of the covenant made between the servant and Abraham. One verse seems sufficient: "The servant told Isaac all the things that he had done." The sense seems to be that the servant made his mission understandable to Isaac, but not in any depth. All that Isaac needed to know was that he, Isaac, was secure. The rest was up to Rebekah.

What comes next is an obvious breach of the usual marriage customs. By rights, the bride would be taken into the tent of her husband to consummate the marriage. In the case of a dead father, the son might take his bride into the tent of his late father, thus taking possession both of the bride and of his father's property. Instead, Isaac takes his new guardian and bride into the tent of his late mother. Seemingly, this is the one place in the whole world where Isaac feels secure. And the narrator signals this by saying that Rebekah immediately replaces Sarah. "Isaac loved her, and thus found comfort after his mother's death." In this way, Isaac, who did not mourn his mother, instead finds comfort in her replacement.

We can now read afresh, with a "second naïveté," Chapter 22, the narrative of the binding of Isaac. At once, the redactor indicates that we should make no mistake about "the test." In the first verse, the word used for God is *Ha-Elohim*, "Sometime afterward, *God* put Abraham to the test." Later, when the angel appears to stop Abraham's hand, it is an angel of YHWH (22:11). "Then an angel of YHWH called to him from heaven: 'Abraham! Abraham!'" Commentators often observe this difference and note that it signifies that some later hand inserted YHWH into the script. But we are not concerned with "a later hand" since we are approaching the narrative only as it was finally composed. It is precisely the meaning of the last hand to touch it that interests us. Therefore, we must assume that the narrator has something specific in mind when he or she notes the specific identity of the God testing Abraham as being different from YHWH, the God who stays Abraham's hand. And perhaps this becomes self-explanatory once the tale is told.

God instructs Abraham to go "to the land of Moriah" and sacrifice Isaac on one of the heights there (2). Although later Jewish tradition associated Moriah with the hill in Jerusalem on which the Temple was built (see 2 Chron. 3:1)—and similarly, the Samaritans associated it with Mt. Gerizim, the site of their Temple—the narration in Genesis would seem to preclude any such possibility. For one thing, if Abraham were traveling to Jerusalem (or to Shechem), there would be no reason to split wood or carry wood to the top of the mount. Wood was plentiful in the hills of Judea. Moreover, the location is never specified in

Genesis as "Mount Moriah," only as a "height" in the land called Moriah. And no "land of Moriah" has ever been adequately identified so any mountainous region with a possible tradition of human sacrifice would serve. Three days distance from Beersheba, the place would most likely be in the wilderness where wood was scarce.

More in keeping with exceptional storytelling, though, the name Moriah may be intended as a word play on the root r-a-h, "to see" (from which it cannot be etymologically derived— never a problem in biblical narrative where sound is as important as sense) as with the "terebinth of Moreh" (12:6). In both cases, God's call included an implied *vision*. In 12:1, "YHWH said to Abram, "Go forth from your native land and from your father's house *to the land that I will show you.*" In 22:2, "... go to the land of Moriah and offer [Isaac] there as a burnt offering on one of the heights *that I will indicate to you.*" If we accept the name Moriah as a play on words, the "land of Moriah" is also "the land of visioning." As the chapter progresses, the word play on "vision," "sight," and "visioning" builds as a kind of subplot until it eventually provides its own elegant dénouement.

> So early next morning, Abraham saddled his ass and took with him two of his servants and his son Isaac. He split the wood for the burnt offering, and he set out for the place of which God had told him. On the third day Abraham lifted his eyes and saw the place from afar. Then Abraham said to his servants, "You stay here with the ass. The youth and I will go up there; we will worship, and we will return to you." Abraham took the wood for the burnt offering and put it on his son Isaac. He himself took the fire and the knife; and the two walked off together. (3-6)

The actual site of the binding of Isaac is spoken of as "the place"—repeated in both Verses 3 and 4 as a *specific* place "of which God had told him." Abraham "sees" the place when he "lifts up his eyes," a distinctive Hebrew idiom. (As we have noted above, the selfsame idiom is used of both Isaac and Rebekah at the conclusion of the servant's tale (24:63-4)," ... *lifting his eyes*, [Isaac] saw camels approaching. *Lifting her eyes*, Rebekah saw Isaac." We could simply translate the idiom as "looking up." Nevertheless, the Hebrew "lifting the eyes" and the English "looking up" both carry multiple meanings implying not only a physical act but an attitude. In the case of "lifting the eyes," the underlying implication is insightful vision, a thing being seen in a new way.)

Isaac is described as a "youth" indicating that he was at least an adolescent, literally, a young unmarried man. There is no certainty and no way of establishing certainty in the matter of Isaac's age. He was no infant (he was capable of carrying the wood up the mountain). By logic, he could have been thirteen or fourteen, or just as easily, twenty years of age or more. The only evidence in the narrative is that this incident seems to have taken place before his mother died. Sarah died at the age of 127 (23:1) and Isaac was born to her when she was already past 90 (see 17:17), so placed just before her death, Isaac might even have been in his mid-thirties at the time of the binding!

> Then Isaac said to his father Abraham, "Father!" And he an-
> swered, "Yes, my son." And he said, "Here are the fire and the
> wood; but where is the sheep for the burnt offering?" And Abra-
> ham said, "God will see to the sheep for His burnt offering, my
> son." And the two of them walked on together. (7-8)

This is the only exchange between Isaac and Abraham and the only time that Isaac speaks in this epochal story. Essentially, the narrative of the binding of Isaac is Abraham-centric; Isaac's role is almost incidental. Yet, in this fleeting conversation, the narrator portrays an adult who speaks like a child, and like a child, is satisfied with a simplistic answer. Giving Isaac the benefit of the doubt, even if he were merely an adolescent, the question he asks is entirely too naïve. Moreover, the answer Abraham tenders is hardly the kind of discussion that would have passed between a father and his grown son. Without bela-boring the point, the narrator leads us to believe that Isaac is somehow ignorant or else innocent of what is in his father's mind.

Yet here is the crux of the matter: What *was* in Abraham's mind? The conditions of the "test" indicate that it was child sac-rifice. Hence, the tale of the binding of Isaac is often referenced as the proof-text that Israel's God does not demand or require the sacrifice of children but the need for a proof-text must pre-suppose that the sacrifice of children was practiced in Abra-ham's time.

❀

On the apparent evidence for child sacrifice, Bible scholars are sharply divided. In the Phoenician settlement of Carthage on the coast of North Africa, archaeologists unearthed what seems to be a ceremonial staging ground and cemetery in use from the tenth to the fourth centuries BCE. Burial urns in this cemetery are limited to the charred remains of children and young animals leading some experts to conclude that this was a place devoted to child sacrifice. Corroborating textual evidence comes from Roman sources which claim the Carthaginians were notorious for sacrificing their children. The archaeologists at Carthage called the place by a biblical name, "Tophet."

Tophet is mentioned in Isaiah (30:33), Jeremiah (7:31f., 19:11f.), and Job (17:6) where it is considered to be a place where idolaters practice abominations. It is said that King Josiah, as part of his reforms, "defiled Topheth, which is in the Valley of Ben-hinnom, so that no one might pass his son or daughter through the fire of Molech" (2 Kings 23:10). What this means is not entirely clear. Molech (sometimes called Milcom or Malcam) was a Canaanite god worshiped in idol form and associated with fire and warfare. Scholars debate what is meant by "passing a son or daughter through the fire ..."

The evidence in the Bible does not settle the case for child sacrifice at all. In Kings, Isaiah, and once in Jeremiah, it seems that child sacrifice *was* practiced in Tophet. In Jeremiah 19, Tophet is only called a place of idolatry. And the Book of Job seems to imply that Job will be given *an unearned bad reputation* like that of Tophet. Some scholars think that Israelite accusations against Molech worshipers, like Roman accusations against the Carthaginians, were mainly ancient mudslinging—verbal warfare—and no child sacrifice was actually practiced. But what could "passing a son or daughter through the fires of Molech" mean? It might refer to a kind of wave offering of a child over a fire in the presence of the idol—something akin to the widespread Indian practice of walking on a bed of fiery embers or stones.

Was child sacrifice ever a normative part of any ancient culture? There is no definitive answer thus far. We can admit, on the one hand, that child sacrifice may have been practiced on rare occasions throughout the ancient Near East throughout the entire period of the Bible. On the other hand, we can be reasonably certain that the practice was not widespread and was never the norm despite the fact that YHWH held a claim on the firstborn of humans and cattle (see Numbers 3:13, for example). More importantly for our study, sacrificing a child to gain merit with a god is not the only, or even the most common, form of child-killing.

A great deal of intentional child-killing, both ancient and modern, and mainly involving female children, is directly related to population control. In addition, there is one common kind of child sacrifice rarely mentioned in any literature: the calculated killing or abandonment of the defective child. Historically (and to this very day in some places) in almost every human society, children born too obviously weak to survive—misshapen, missing limbs, or otherwise defective—were regularly consigned to death, whether intentionally or benignly, by neglect, abandonment, or sacrifice.

Earlier I stated that I would proffer a sinister suggestion regarding the binding of Isaac, and this is the moment to put the cards on the table. Isaac was a special child in an era when special children were probably "sacrificed" in one way or another. Abraham had not been disappointed in Ishmael, but I believe he was terribly disappointed in the fruit of Sarah's womb. Although promising him great progeny, God had played a cruel joke on him by waiting until he and Sarah were too old to give birth to a healthy child, and only then presenting him with a laughable son. Ordinarily, in due course, he would have abandoned Isaac or neglected him to death, but Sarah would not be denied her child. She protected Isaac fiercely, maintaining him in her own tent, forcing Abraham to send away Ishmael, even forcing Abraham to name Isaac his sole heir. Abraham's reluctance in all this is noted in the narrative:

> The matter distressed Abraham greatly, for it concerned a son of his [Ishmael]. But God said to Abraham, "Do not be distressed over the boy or your slave; whatever Sarah tells you, do as she

says, for it is through Isaac that offspring shall be named after you. (20:11-12)

It is precisely in the story of what happened with Hagar and Ishmael that the binding of Isaac is foreshadowed. This is one of the rare cases in all of ancient literature in which child abandonment is documented.

When the water was gone from the skin, she [Hagar] left the child under one of the bushes, and went and sat down at a distance, a bowshot away; for she thought, "Let me not look on as the child dies." And sitting thus afar, she burst into tears. (15-16)

God spoke to Hagar through an angel, opened Hagar's eyes so that she saw a well of water, and promised to make Ishmael into a great nation (17-19). What we learn in these few verses is that a) a child that can no longer be maintained, for whatever reason, is sacrificed, however unwillingly; b) the ultimate fate of such a child is in the hand of God (here represented by God's angel); and c) in the case of God's chosen, God may provide a replacement for what is lacking. The binding of Isaac repeats these three lessons even more dramatically.

My contention is that the narrator is leading us to understand that as Sarah neared her death, she became too weak to continue to tend for and to protect her son Isaac. Abraham was placed in pretty much the same position as Hagar. He was alert enough to realize what he would have to do now and what, by all rights, he should have done when Isaac was an infant. The time had come to settle the matter of Isaac.

Isaac, though, could not simply be abandoned. He was, after all, a gift from God. Undoubtedly, the best procedure would be to return the gift. Perhaps God would provide a sound replacement in exchange for this sacrifice. This sentiment is attested at the Tophet in Carthage. Among the inscriptions from the second century BCE, a mother named Bissabaal thanks Baal Hammon and a goddess (probably Tanit) for giving her a baby "in exchange for a defective child," and a father named Tuscus states that he gave Baal "his mute son Bodastart, a defective child, in exchange for a healthy one." This kind of exchange may very well have been Abraham's motivation as he accompanied his son Isaac up the mountain.

It was, nevertheless, a "test." For Abraham, destroying Isaac was also an admission that Sarah was lost to him. Clearly, if Sarah recovered from whatever ailments she was suffering, Abraham knew she would not forgive him for the death of her only child. Abraham, himself, felt certain he was still capable of fathering other children, as evidenced by the fact that he married again after Sarah's death and sired six more sons (25:1-2). Ever faithful, Abraham counted on God to bring him through, to help him do the right thing in this extreme case: "God will see to the sheep for His burnt offering, my son."

❋

What happens atop the height seems unexpected to Abraham. Like Hagar, he goes out with one vision of what the future holds and discovers another, different vision of the future.

> They arrived at the place of which God had told him. Abraham built an altar there; he laid out the wood; he bound his son Isaac; he laid him on the altar, on top of the wood. And Abraham picked up the knife to slay his son. (20:9-10)

If Isaac were not somehow deficient, it is hard to imagine that at his age he would so readily submit to being bound and laid upon an altar. But the child was so tractable that Abraham had known from the outset that he would require no help in this effort. There was no reason for him to bring his two servants up to the mountaintop to restrain the youth. This youth would do as he was instructed. Of course, we could also argue that the narration is being told only from Abraham's point of view, meaning that we have no information about the motivation of Isaac—a fact that led to countless speculations and commentaries on Isaac's willingness to be sacrificed to God. But there is no indication given in the narrative of any kind of struggle, either through words or strength. In the narrative as it is composed, Isaac simply acquiesced to his father's will.

Again, as in the case of Hagar, it is an angel who steps in at the last moment. In Abraham's case, he recognizes this intervention as the angel of YHWH, his personal God, the God he knows by name.

> Then an angel of YHWH called to him from heaven: "Abraham! Abraham!" And he answered, "Here I am." And he said, "Do not raise your hand against the boy, or do anything to him. For now I know that you fear God, since you have not withheld your son, your favored one, from Me." (11-12)

This is the climax. God is satisfied that Abraham has done what was right in Abraham's sight. Nevertheless, God has more in mind for Isaac. It is surely a powerful message. It would be a less impressive message if Abraham had been unwilling or unable to carry out the sacrifice. If he had not raised the knife to slay his son, there could be grave doubts about his sincerity or his will-power. But Abraham is strong and steady, a man of purpose whose hand is stayed by nothing less than an epiphany at the very last moment of his test.

> When Abraham lifted his eyes, his eye fell upon a ram behind [him], caught in the thicket by its horns. So Abraham went and took the ram and offered it up as a burnt offering in place of his son. And Abraham named that site YHWH-*Yireh*, whence the present saying, "On the mount of YHWH there is vision." (13-14)

The narrator now provides the dénouement. Everything here is about vision and envisioning. Again, the idiom of "lifting the eyes" is crucial, surely not accidental. The knowledge that a ram would be a suitable substitute for Isaac was hardly self-apparent. Abraham realized it only at the last moment, lifting his eyes to see a higher purpose. As much as his son Isaac would continue to be a burden for him, he suddenly realizes that his burden is God's will. He would have to "see" his way out in some other manner. And as we have witnessed, his new vision led him to import strong stock from his own family to ensure the future of his people.

With this epiphany in mind, the final sentence is easily unraveled. Abraham calls the place "YHWH will see" or "YHWH sees." And the narrator makes sure you understand the meaning by referring to a current epigram. If you want to experience an epiphany, as Abraham did, there is a proper place provided by God: "On the mount of YHWH there is vision." The subtext is that what you see when you lift your eyes from afar (the place where a child sacrifice is appropriate) may be very different from what you see when you are at your destination (the mount of YHWH where a new vision may suddenly present itself). What an elegant metaphor for setting goals, reaching significant points along the way, and realizing that new goals without end always lay ahead.

> The angel of YHWH called to Abraham a second time from heaven, and said, "By Myself I swear, YHWH declares: Because you have done this and have not withheld your son, your favored one, I will bestow My blessing upon you and make your descendants as numerous as the stars of heaven and the sands on the seashore; and your descendants shall *seize the gates of their foes*. [Italics added.] All the nations of the earth shall bless themselves by your descendants, because you have obeyed My command." Abraham then returned to his servants, and they departed together for Beersheba; and Abraham stayed in Beersheba. (15-18)

Let there be no misunderstanding: The child Isaac will serve God's purposes. What seems defective to the human eye may be destiny in the realm of God's will. In the words of Genesis 18:14: "Is anything too wondrous for YHWH?"

It is through Isaac that God promises Abraham numerous descendants and that "your descendants shall *seize the gates of their foes*," an obvious foreshadowing of the same words spoken to Rebekah by her family as their hope for her (24:60b): "O sister! May you grow into thousands of myriads; May your offspring *seize the gates of their foes*." Thus, the narrator deftly shows that the choice of Rebekah is predestined, and the only way for this destiny to work itself out is for Abraham to stay his hand. The next patriarch will be Isaac, but the woman behind the man, the next "Abraham," the one who will truly fulfill the will of YHWH and ensure the destiny of the people of YHWH, is Rebekah.

It goes almost without saying that the story of the binding of Isaac ensured through the ages that Jews would eschew child sacrifice. But the narration goes far beyond that simple conclusion. It is Abraham's epiphany that every special child is God's will. Abraham's success on the mountain lies in this new vision. If so, he has learned a lesson that we still need desperately to learn: God creates all things with a purpose. It is up to us as human beings, as God's partners, to find meaning in all God's creations. No life, no matter how much it may seem accidental, deficient, or even laughable to us, is insignificant. Whatever God brings into this world comes to serve God's purpose in some significant way.

When Two and
Two Make Three

At one point, now nearly twenty years ago, I considered writing a popular history of Jewish magic and mysticism. I had just completed examining the role of dreams and dream incubation in biblical narratives in Bible Dreams: The Spiritual Quest. *I discovered that popular practices in ancient societies still held some exciting possibilities for us today. Why not examine the role played by our ancestors' sincere belief in demons and demon-control? The results never became a book, but there's some real fun and maybe some insights here for your delectation.*

A friend of mine, several tips into his cup, passed his hand through the air and confided to me that demons are everywhere. "For instance," he said in something close to a whisper, "it is a *demon*strable fact that a demon lurks in every door hinge. Just consider the evidence: At capricious intervals, door-hinge imps announce their presence by squeaking. You recognize them as demons because they take special pleasure in revealing themselves at the most inopportune moments—for example, when you are attempting to sneak into the house after a long night of drinking." Stirring his latest martini, he went on to explain that door-hinge demons seldom respond to either spells or incantations. Nor are they mollified by amulets or charms. Conspiratorially, he added, "You can propitiate them, however, through a simple anointing. Pouring oil on them leaves them as content and docile as the family dog."

On the surface, the Hebrew Bible does not seem too mindful of demons. Nevertheless, we might say there is more in the

Bible than what meets the eye. For example, many commentators suggest that the stranger with whom Jacob wrestled may have been demonic. They may even know who this particular demon was. Just call him the Demon of the Jabbok River. They base their intuition on several suppositions. First, river demons are well attested in mythology the world over. Second, river demons are generally described as more dangerous by night than by day—thereby accounting for the Jabbok demon's insistent demand to break off the wrestling match at daybreak. Third, since Jacob spent much of that biblical day crossing and re-crossing the Jabbok River, it is only reasonable that he might struggle with the river's demon that night. From a purely psychological point of view, if you spend the entire day doing some repetitive yet hazardous task, that task may easily haunt and trouble you by night.

Another example from the Bible is the suggestion of a demonic presence at the opening of the story of Cain and Abel. Here, God explains the human condition to Cain, saying,

> "Why are you distressed, and why is your face fallen? Surely, if you do right, there is uplift. But if you do not do right Sin crouches at the door; his urge is toward you, yet you can be his master."
> [Gen. 4:7]

The personification here may be merely a matter of translation. Modern Bibles often translate the verse impersonally as "*sin* crouches at the door; *its* urge is toward you, yet you can be *its* master," but the Hebrew is entirely ambiguous—you can have it either/or, even more to the point, *both* ways. In other words, there may or may not be a demon crouching at your door. These are two examples of demons lurking in the text. In a sense, though, it is striking that the Bible contains so little by way of demonology.

The same is not true of the great body of literature produced by the Jewish sages of the Talmud and the Midrash. You might say that they were cognizant of what we call "superstition" or what they would acknowledge as "popular opinion." In their work, spanning many centuries, demons and demonology often appear in conjunction with magical practices. Although they sometimes depict demons in benign contexts (much as we might mention a "muse" visiting an author), the predominant view seems to be that demons are active, evil forces in the world, forces that must be overcome through the use of magic and enchantments.

Formally, most sages accept demons as real and denounce magic as a remedy; most claim to prefer reason and logic to superstition and charms. Judah Ha-Nasi, the head of the academy (who is credited with bringing the Mishnah into its final form), is quoted as saying, "Only one who practices magic will be harassed by witchcraft" [Nedarim 37a]. In effect, the punishment he proposes for superstition is a matter of "measure for measure"; that is, one gets what one expects to get. The common deterrent to the practice of magic is thus the threat of falling prey to magic. Judah's argument is neat, if somewhat circular. Clearly, however, he is not saying that magic does not exist; only that it will plague the person who tampers with it.

This is typical of the way in which the sages deal with the problem. For example, to abate the influence of magic, the sages sometimes attempt to reward those who defer from using it.

> Ahabah the son of Rabbi Zera taught: The person who does not practice magic is brought inside a boundary [close to God] which not even the Ministering Angels may enter, as it is written (Num. 23:23): "For there is no magic in Jacob, neither is there any divination in Israel." [Nedarim 37a]

Here, Ahabah promises Jews who refrain from utilizing magic a secret of the highest order—one that even angels are excluded from knowing. But notice the way he phrases his promise: "inside a boundary which not even the Ministering Angels may enter." His explanation begs for clarification. The translator inserts "close to God" to make the reference clearer, but this seems a weak interpretation. More likely, Ahabah's words are directed toward those who already comprehend their meaning, that is, "insiders." One well-attested practical usage of both Jewish magic and mysticism is the creation of, or the crossing of, "boundaries." These boundaries are every bit as real to the magician and the mystic as borders drawn on a map are to cartographers, historians, and politicians.

It seems likely that Ahabah is specifically addressing sages who are mystics, those who sought heavenly secrets, the kind of

mysteries that might put them in the company of angels or ele-
vate them to the angelic status of an Enoch, a Jacob, or an Elijah. Ahabah is speaking directly to them—not to witches or
sorcerers—in the full knowledge that the early mystical tradition included enough practical magic to keep mystics safe on
their journeys. Possessing secrets such as the magical uses of
the various names of God, the mystics were no doubt tempted
on many occasions to use magic to combat demons as well.
Ahabah recommends against this as if to say, "Save your magic
for the real purpose for which it was intended."

Thus, the formal, "official" view of the rabbis during the
long talmudic period held that magic should not be used for
worldly things. Nevertheless, just as angels were proliferating in
the popular imagination, so, too, the world of demons was becoming ever more populous. And just as the mystic sages in
their pursuit of heaven studied the magic necessary to influence
angels, so, too, the magic for countering demons in the world
advanced among them to an ever more scientific level.

Popular belief—Jewish and non-Jewish—held that the science of warding off demons originated in Jewish magical wisdom. This view is often stated in Jewish stories and legends, but
it is also posed as fact in the writings of the credulous first-century CE historian, Josephus. In his masterwork, *The Antiquities
of the Jews*, Josephus recounts how he personally witnessed an
exorcism:

> Now the sagacity and wisdom which God had bestowed on Solo-
> mon was so great, that he exceeded the ancients; insomuch that
> he was no way inferior to the Egyptians, who are said to have
> been beyond all men in understanding ... God also enabled him
> to learn that skill which expels demons, which is a science useful
> and sanative to men. He composed such incantations also by
> which distempers are alleviated. And he left behind him the man-
> ner of using exorcisms, by which they drive away demons, so that
> they never return; and this method of cure is of great force unto
> this day; for I have seen a certain man of my own country, whose
> name was Eleazar, releasing people that were demoniacal in the
> presence of Vespasian, and his sons, and his captains, and the
> whole multitude of his soldiers. The manner of the cure was this:
> He put a ring that had a Foot of one of those sorts mentioned by
> Solomon to the nostrils of the demoniac, after which he drew out

the demon through his nostrils; and when the man fell down immediately, he abjured [the demon] to return into him no more, making still mention of Solomon, and reciting the incantations which he composed. And when Eleazar would persuade and demonstrate to the spectators that he had such a power, he set a little way off a cup or basin full of water, and commanded the demon, as he went out of the man, to overturn it, and thereby to let the spectators know that [the demon] had left the man; and when this was done, the skill and wisdom of Solomon was shown very manifestly: for which reason it is, that all men may know the vastness of Solomon's abilities, and how he was beloved of God, and that the extraordinary virtues of every kind with which this king was endowed may not be unknown to any people under the sun for this reason, I say, it is that we have proceeded to speak so largely of these matters. [*Antiquities*, 8, 2:5]

Josephus' colorful account is evidence that belief in the demon world was widespread wherever Jews lived in the opening centuries of the millennium. Sometimes magic formulae were ascribed to Moses (also considered a great Jewish magician) and at other times to Solomon. In first-century Alexandria, for example, Jewish magicians composed a recipe book called *The Key of Moses* (or, sometimes, *The Eighth Book of Moses*). Other Hebrew compositions providing bundles of magic formulae go by names such as *Moses' Sword* or *The Key of Solomon*. In first-century Rome the satirist, Juvenal, portrayed Jewish women (who had come to the capitol as prisoners) earning their living by practicing witchcraft.[1] In the third century, the Greek Church Father Origen described the use of Jewish names of God in the incantations of pagans practicing necromancy.[2] In Babylonia, jars and bowls were fashioned containing lists of the names of demons and spirits in Hebrew and Aramaic.

What was true in Rome, Egypt, and Babylonia was equally true in the Holy Land—everywhere, magic and demonology went hand in hand. The Talmud fairly abounds with such references, some in depth and some in passing. The preeminent sage, Yohanan ben Zakkai, for example, specified:

None are to be appointed members of the Sanhedrin, save for those of stature, of wisdom, of good appearance, of mature age, *possessing a knowledge of sorcery*, and conversant with all of the seventy languages of humankind—thereby, the court shall have no need of an interpreter. [Sanhedrin 17a, italics mine]

Sages of the high court are also portrayed putting theory into practice as in the following strange tale concerning cucumbers:

> The Sages, seeing that [Eliezer's] mind was clear [even as he lay on his death bed], entered his chamber and sat down at a distance of four cubits.[3] "Why have you come?" he asked them. "To study the Torah," they replied. "And why did you not come before?" he asked. They answered, "We had no time." ... He crossed his arms over his heart, and cried out to them, saying, "Woe to you, my two arms, for you have been like two parts of the Scroll of the Law when it is closed. Much Torah have I studied and much have I taught. Much Torah have I learned, yet I have barely skimmed the knowledge of my teachers—[gaining only] as much as a dog laps from the sea. Much Torah have I taught, yet my disciples have only drawn from me as much as a painting stick might draw from its container. Moreover, I have studied three hundred laws on the subject of a deep bright [leprous] spot, yet no one has ever asked me about them. Moreover, I have studied three hundred—some say, three thousand—laws regarding the planting of cucumbers [by magic] and no one, excepting Akiba ben Joseph, ever questioned me concerning this lore. Once, he and I were walking together on a road when he said to me, 'My master, teach me about the planting of cucumbers.' I pronounced a charm, and the whole field [beside us] was filled with cucumbers. Then he said, 'Master, you have taught me to plant them, now teach me how to harvest them.' I sent forth another incantation and all the cucumbers gathered themselves in one place." [Sanhedrin 68b]

Magic may have been strictly forbidden according to the law of the Torah (which had commanded that witches be put to death), and even according to the laws of the rabbis themselves (since they had extended the command to include males practicing magic), yet Yohanan mandates that sages should have a command of sorcery, and Eliezer demonstrates magic for Rabbi Akiba. The Talmud tries to reconcile this apparent discrepancy:

> By what reason was Rabbi Eliezer allowed to [perform this magic]? Did we not learn, "If one actually performs magic, one is liable [to be put to death]?"—However, if it is only to teach, it is different. For it has been said (Deut. 18:9), "You shall not learn to do after the abominations of these nations," meaning, you may not learn in order to practice, but you may learn in order to understand. [Sanhedrin 68b]

The tradition of magic as wisdom stretches back to time immemorial and was deeply embedded in the worldview of the talmudic period. It was popularly believed that the knowledge of demons and the art of controlling them stemmed from the wisdom of Solomon. The Talmud also praises Moses for his ability to control demons. And just as we would expect, it traces the knowledge of demon-control back to Abraham saying that Abraham passed this knowledge along as his gift to the (pagan) sons he bore through his concubine Keturah[4] toward the end of his life. Obviously, conventional Jewish opinion considered magic (1) equivalent to wisdom and (2) a special provenance of Jewish practice.

It is wonderful that faith makes room for illogical notions. Of course, all knowledge is imagination. What is fiction in one time and place may be fact in another. We may turn our scientifically trained noses up at the idea of flying carpets, for example. But if you sit on a small Oriental rug, enter into a deep state of meditation—smoke a hookah, ingest an hallucinogen, or just concentrate on the intricate woven patterns—you may soon experience a flying carpet. The human imagination is virtually boundless. Our capacity for accepting things on faith is equal to nearly any necessity.

Popular imagination accepted the presence of angels and demons for good reason. There is much that we cannot explain without resorting to something mysterious and beyond. Why are some people inexplicably fortunate? A guardian angel must be watching over them. Why are some people inexplicably wicked? A demon must have gotten into them. Why not ascribe good luck and evil fortune directly to God? One answer is that sometimes the evil person is consistently lucky while the good person suffers incessantly. If we were to say that God personally directed these things, then we would have to accept the kind of God who plays dice with the universe. To accept the presence of angels and demons is to avoid the necessity of agreeing with Ralph Waldo Emerson's evaluation: "The dice of God are always loaded."[5]

By the same token, accepting the presence of demons forces us to account for how the demonic can exist in a world created by a good God. (The existence of any evil in the world is, of course, one of the major concerns of theology.) In the time of the Talmud, which recorded the work of the rabbis and sages from the first century BCE to the sixth century CE, theories on the origin of demons varied. One view held that God intentionally created them in the last moment before God rested for the Sabbath.[6]

> Rabbi Hama... said: In speaking of [the creation of] souls, [the Torah] enumerates four [Genesis 1:24: *every kind of living thing, cattle, creeping things, and wild beasts*], but in speaking of [the creation of] bodies, [the Torah mentions] only three [1:25: *wild beasts of every kind, and cattle of every kind, and all kinds of creeping things*]! Rabbi [Judah the Prince] replied: This [fourth] soul refers to the demons whose soul the Holy One, the Blessed, created, but when God came to create their bodies the holiness of the Sabbath intervened and God could not create them. From this you learn a lesson in behavior from Scripture, namely, that if a person is holding a precious stone or a costly thing on the eve of the Sabbath at the moment of sunset, we tell him, "Discard it," for God at whose behest the world itself came into existence [did likewise]—engaged in the creation of the world, God had already created the souls [of demons], but when God came to create their bodies the holiness of the Sabbath intervened and God refrained from creating them. [Genesis Rabbah 7:5]

The theory Judah expounds is that God literally ran out of time, or more properly, God respected a self-imposed time limit. When the Sabbath began, the creation of their bodies was still incomplete, and demons thus became disembodied spirits existing in the world. The lesson Judah extracts from this may seem odd at first: "Throw away precious things you are holding when the Sabbath commences." Jewish law delineates the kinds of work not permitted on the Sabbath and these include creating (which God refrains from doing in the case of the bodies intended for demons) and carrying (which we should refrain from doing even if the thing we are carrying is priceless). The holiness of the Sabbath should take precedence over even the most precious things of creation (and Jewish law allows for the breaking of the Sabbath only in order to save a human life). Based on this and like theories, it became common Jewish wisdom that demons are more rambunctious, more dangerous, and more tenacious in moments of transition between the holy and the mundane. They are supposedly looking for the bodies that God should have given them, and so any bodies are fair game for them. Transitory times auspicious for demons include both the moments before the sun actually sets to separate ordinary weekdays from the Sabbath and other holy days, and also the moments following holy days when the ordinary weekdays are about to recommence. These are times, the sages advise, when human beings would do well to be particularly cautious.

Rabbi Jeremiah ben Eleazar speculated on a different origin for the demons. At the time of the building of the Tower of Babel, he taught, the people divided into three factions. One faction declared, "Let us ascend and dwell [in Heaven]." A second faction declared, "Let us ascend and serve idols." And a third faction declared, "Let us ascend and wage war [with God]." God punished the factions according to their declarations. Those who wished to dwell in heaven were scattered. Those who wished to serve idols had their language confounded. Those who wished to wage war with God, however, "were turned to apes, spirits, devils, and night-demons."[7] Rabbi Jeremiah's theory should make the most ardent Darwinist cringe and so should another evolutionist theory cited in the Talmud. According to one treatise, the male hyena turns into a bat after seven years, the bat after seven years turns into a vampire bat, the vampire bat after seven years becomes a nettle, the nettle after seven years becomes a thorn [some read the word for "thorn" as "snake"], and the thorn after seven years becomes a demon.[8] This theory allows for the constant creation of new demons.

Certainly, not least among theories, is the one that claims that demons, while initially created by God, were subsequently the descendants of illicit pairings of the first human beings.

Rabbi Simon taught: Throughout the entire one hundred and thirty years during which Adam held aloof from Eve, the male demons were enticed by her and she bore them children, while the female demons were inflamed by Adam and they bore him children ... This accounts for the view that house spirits are benevolent since they dwell with human beings. The view that house spirits are harmful derives from the fact that they understand the evil inclinations of human beings. As for those who maintain that demons of the field are benevolent, the reason is that they do not grow up among human beings. The view that field spirits are not harmful derives from the fact that they do not comprehend the evil inclinations of human beings. [Genesis Rabbah 20:11]

This model accounts for both the creation of demons and the inclination of demons to do harm to human beings. The sum of all these theories, or any one taken on its face, accounts for the presence of demons. Demons are disembodied spirits. They may be the spirit remains of those who, in their lifetimes, were enemies of God. They spring from our own evil inclinations. They were originally created in great abundance. They continue to be created from the things we dread.

According to another source, demons have the power to alter their appearance. They can see; yet they remain invisible.[9] A more elaborate description of this appears in the Talmud:

Demons resemble the ministering angels in three ways; and in three ways they resemble human beings. Like the angels they have wings, they fly from one end of the world to the other, and they know the future. Like human beings they eat and drink, they propagate, and they die. [Hagigah 16a]

The wonder of it all was how we managed to maneuver through a world so full of disembodied spirits. Just note:

Our sages taught: Abba Benjamin said, If the eye had the power to see them, no creature could endure the demons. Abaye said, They are more numerous than we are and surround us like a ridge around a field. Rabbi Huna said, Everyone has a thousand on his left hand and ten thousand on his right hand. Raba said, The crush during the academy lectures open to the public [in the months of Elul and Adar] comes from their presence. The fatigue of the knees comes from them. The clothes of the scholars wear out from their rubbing against them. Bruises on the feet are due to them. [Berachot 6a]

This is a starting point. Demons occupy an important place in Jewish magic practice, especially since one object of magic is to counter and, if possible, combat the fearful elements of the world. So the Talmud indicates that just to reveal the presence of demons requires the use of magic:

> To discover the footprints of demons, take sifted ashes and sprinkle them around a bed; and in the morning there will be the appearance of something like the footprints of a rooster. To see demons, take the after-birth of a black she-cat who is the off-spring of a black she-cat (the first-born of a first-born), roast it in the fire, grind it to a powder, and put it in the eye; they will then become apparent. Pour the mixture into an iron tube and seal it with an iron signet so the demons cannot steal it. Always close the mouth so as not to be harmed by them. Rabbi Bibi ben Abaye did these things, saw the demons, and came to harm. The scholars, however, prayed for him and he recovered. [Berachot 6a]

Demons were thought to be most menacing in certain specific places. These included ruins, wells, rivers, pools, and latrines. Dark places were said to be among their favorite haunts. We have already noted that moments of transition were considered times when demons could easily gain an upper hand over human beings. Such moments not only included twilight (especially the twilight on the eve of holy days and the twilight at the close of holy days), but also dawn; the solstices—summer and winter; the equinoxes—vernal and autumnal; the moment of childbirth; the instant before death; the first appearance of menstruation; even the first entry of a child into the study of Torah. Many Jewish folk customs now associated with the holy days and with life cycle events had their origins in magical formulae meant to ward off demons at critical moments of transition.

An entire volume would be needed to catalogue these folk customs and their possible magical origins. The following three examples provide a taste of anti-demonic magic and encompass many of its underlying concepts.

> Against a demon one should say thus: You were closed up, closed up were you. Cursed, broken, and destroyed be Bar Tit [*son of clay*], Bar Tame [*son of defilement*], and Bar Tina [*son of filth*] as were Shamgez, Mezigaz, and Istamai. [Shabbat 67a]

> Our sages taught: A person should not drink water from rivers or pools at night, and if he drinks, his blood is on his own head, because of the danger. What is the danger? The danger of Shabrire [the demon of blindness]. But if he is thirsty, what is his remedy?

> If someone else is present, he should say to him: "*So-and-so* [insert the name] son of *So-and-so* [insert the name], I am thirsty for water." But if he is alone, let him say to himself: "O *So-and so* [inserting his own name], my mother told me, 'Beware of Shabrire'— *Shabrire, Brire, Rire, Ire, Re*. I thirst for water in a white glass."
> [Pesachim 112a]
>
> Against a demon of the privy one should say thus: On the head of a lion and on the snout of a lioness did we find the demon Bar Shirika Panda; with a bed of leeks I hurled him down; with the jawbone of an ass I smote him. [Shabbat 67a]

In all three of the above formulae, words are portrayed as the most effective weapon against demons—provided they are the right words, spoken in the right sequence, sent forth with the right amount of faithful force. In the first formula, for instance, stating that a demon is "closed up" imprisons the demon. Once imprisoned or bound, the demon is then "cursed, broken, and destroyed"—again by means of performative language.

The second text points out the commonplace belief that demons are more likely to strike out against solitary individuals, so naming another person, thereby reminding a demon that you are not alone, may scare the demon off. If you *are* alone, you must resort to a stratagem. You first remind the demon that your mother (or, often, a recognized magician of whom the demon might be afraid—Moses or Solomon, for example) has instructed you in the ways of demons. Then, having deflected the demon's attention to another person, you surprise the demon by using its own name. In magic, calling a thing by its true name provides a degree of suasion or power over it. The formula, "*Shabrire, Brire, Rire, Ire, Re*," subsequently renders the demon harmless by reducing its name by one syllable with each utterance (effectively reducing the demon to nothing). Similar word patterns are common in magic. One more ploy is used in this instance: the mention of water in a "white glass." Demons—creatures of shadow and darkness—are thought to be frightened off by the color white. Scholars point to many similar uses of white: brides wear white to avert the envy of demons; Jews are buried in white shrouds to ward off demons; Jews wear a kittle, a white shroud-like garment, on Yom Kippur (the Day of

Repentance) possibly to convince demons they are already dead; and so on.

In the third formula, having named the demon, you call upon a remedy which often works (in this case, a plant: "a bed of leeks"), then, for good measure, you do battle against the demon directly—again, all by means of performative language. Here, saying that the demon has been found both on the head of a lion and the snout of a lioness may be intended as a way of splitting the demon's strength in two by forcing it to be in two places at one and the same time.

In general, three means of combating demons are 1) direct frontal combat, 2) compromise in the form of a treaty or agreement, and 3) the use of some stratagem which will cause the demon to be vanquished or to vanish. Two of these are clear in the examples above. The treaty or agreement is often employed in negotiating with benevolent demons, as in the following tale:

> Rabbi Berekiah ... said: It once happened in our village that Abba Jose of Zaythor was sitting and studying at the mouth of a fountain. A certain demon that dwelt there appeared to him and said: "You know that I have been dwelling here for many years and you and your wives used to come and go, evening and morning, and have never been harmed. But now you should know that a certain evil spirit desires to settle here and he will harm people."
>
> Abba asked the demon: "What shall we do?"
>
> It answered: "Go, warn the townspeople. Say to them that whoever has a hoe, a shovel, or a spade should appear here tomorrow at daybreak and watch the surface of the water. When they notice a disturbance on the surface, let them strike the iron [implements] together and cry out, 'Ours wins!' And do not let them depart this place until they notice a stain of blood on the surface of the water."
>
> So Abba went and warned the townspeople: "Whoever has a hoe, whoever has a shovel, whoever has a spade, let all of them come to the fountain tomorrow at daybreak and gaze upon the water." When they noticed a disturbance in the water, they struck their iron implements together and cried: "Ours wins! Ours wins!" And they did not depart until they noticed a kind of blood clot on the surface of the water. [Leviticus Rabbah 24:3]

Rabbi Berekiah concludes the tale by noting that demons sometimes require the help of human beings. Besides being an example of how a treaty or agreement may be struck with a demon, the story contains several interesting elements. For one, noisemaking is used partially to get the demon's attention and partially to harm the demon. Demons dwell in stillness and silence; hence, it is assumed that noise and music are effective against them. In the same vein, one Jewish tradition states that the ram's horn (*shofar*) is blown on Rosh HaShanah "to confuse Satan."[10] For another, almost all societies consider iron an effective weapon against demons since demons tend to make their homes in caves and beneath stones, and iron was the most effective tool for cutting rock. The noisemakers in this example are all iron implements. Similarly, metal objects—often knives or swords—were placed in the bed or under the pillow of a pregnant woman and even at times in the cradle of an infant. The title of the book of magical recipes, *Moses' Sword*, reflects the use of swords to ward off demons, and since keys were often made of metal, titles such as *The Key of Solomon* may be intended as double entendres to mean "key" both in its literal and figurative senses. It should also be remembered that the Kingdom of Judah grew up in the Iron Age when the control of this base metal was an indication of the human ability to control nature. All this notwithstanding, in this story, the verbalization of the formula "Ours wins!" appears to be the most important part of the magic.

Combat against demons is generally effected through language. Amulets or charms may serve as more or less permanent symbols of the verbal formulae. Particular plants and roots are often carried to ward off demons. At times, even bodily gestures may be employed. To achieve the greatest effect, however, bodily gestures are most often accompanied by specific words; amulets are inscribed, and even plants are often decorated with some magical formulae or symbol.

As often in logic and in magic, when it came to demons, the rabbis of the Talmud employed mathematics. It was widely held that demons were attracted by even numbers and repelled by odd numbers. The earlier sages of the Mishnah seem not to have considered this (or perhaps, to have been ignorant of it or indifferent to it[11]) when they ruled that four cups of wine were to be consumed by each person at the Seder table on the eve of Passover. This ruling, though, disturbed the rabbis of Babylonia who discussed the problem at some length. Their discourse on the matter is found in the Babylonian Talmud in pages related to the laws of Passover.[12]

> [Mishnah:] *And they should give a participant not less than four* [cups of wine]. [Gemara:] How could our rabbis enact a ruling which would lead one into danger? Surely, it has been taught that a person must not eat in pairs, nor drink in pairs, nor cleanse himself twice, nor perform his [sexual] requirements twice!
>
> Rabbi Nahman explained: Scripture (Exod. 12:42) calls this [Passover evening], "a night of guarding [unto God]"—a night that is always guarded from demons. Raba said: The cup offered with the Grace [after meals] combines [with the other three cups] for good but does not combine with them for evil. Rabina said: Our rabbis instituted four cups as symbolizing freedom—each one is a separate obligation.

Doing things in even numbers placed one in imminent danger from demons. The Babylonian Talmud, discussing the brief passage from the Mishnah, begins by summarizing things that should not be done in twos—and this apparently applies to all even numbers, especially two sets of twos. The problem is that the Mishnah specifically requires four cups of wine on the evening of Passover. Surely, the earlier sages must have realized the danger of four. Three rabbis offer explanations for the four-cup requirement. The first explanation, that of Rabbi Nahman, is that this particular night, the eve of Passover, is eternally safe from demons because of God's decree that it is "a night of guarding."[13] If this had been an entirely persuasive argument, the discussion might have ended here. But at least one serious objection can be raised against Nahman's argument. In the verse he quotes (Exod. 12:42), it is uncertain who is doing the guarding. If it is God, then all is well. But if it is "a night of guarding [unto God]"—that is, a night where human beings are doing the guarding in God's honor—then it is unclear whether the night is safe from demons.

Raba offers a more imaginative solution. He attempts to find a way to add two and two and come up with three instead of four. Since the danger only comes after the first two cups are complete, he focuses his attention on the third cup, the one that is offered with the Grace after Meals. This cup adds to the first two, making them an odd number, one that will not attract demons. But it "does not combine with them for evil." In other words, the next cup begins the count all over again, standing on its own as an odd number. Instead of a total of four cups for the evening, Raba counts three cups and one cup. Rabina's solution simplifies this suggestion. Since all four cups symbolize freedom, each one should be considered free and independent of the others. He counts four as one, one, one, and one.

It is implied that one may accept any of these three solutions or—since the matter is unresolved—any other solution which may present itself. Yet, this is hardly the end of the discussion. The Babylonian rabbis next turn to the Mishnah's prohibition against performing the sexual act twice.[14] Abaye reasons that the earlier authorities of the Mishnah who laid down this proscription could not have meant this literally. After all, each sexual performance is the result of a newly aroused decision so each must be counted on its own. Each sexual act is always singular: when it comes to intercourse, one and one never make two. Hence, there must be a different way of understanding the Mishnah's ruling: "… a person must not eat in pairs, nor drink in pairs, nor cleanse himself twice, nor perform his [sexual] requirements twice!"

> Abaye said: … This is what it means: A person must not eat in pairs and drink in pairs. Nor may he perform his [sexual] requirements even once [if he has eaten or drunk in pairs], lest he be weakened and become susceptible [to demons].

Apparently, Abaye takes the word "twice" after "his [sexual] requirements" to mean, "for two reasons." Eating two meals and drinking two drinks would leave a person in an already dangerous state—having intercourse even once after inviting the demons to attack would be unhealthy because it would 1) weaken a person and 2) render a person susceptible to harm. Abaye's message is: Have intercourse as often as you wish, but never after eating or drinking in pairs. Abaye never once mentions the matter of cleansing twice, so it is safe to conclude that the Babylonian rabbis were more concerned with matters of eating, drinking, and sex.

The discussion in the Talmud continues with another concern about pairs: How can a person best avoid drinking two drinks in a row? One rabbi, it is told, used to take a drink and before having a second, go out to look at the street (repeating this procedure as often as he wished). In this way, each drink counted as a new round of drinking. Another rabbi used to drink, then count a beam in the ceiling. In this way he was first drinking, then counting, then drinking anew. We are told that Abaye's mother hit upon a different stratagem. When Abaye finished drinking one cup, his mother would bring him two more cups, one in each hand, thus always raising the count to an odd number. The discussion goes on to speak of ten cups, eight cups, six cups, and so on—always returning to ways in which these may either be turned to odd numbers or accounted for in other clever ways.

Then, abruptly, the discussion takes an unexpected turn:

> Rabbi Joseph said: The demon Joseph told me that Ashmedai, king of the demons, is appointed over all "twos-in-a-row"; and a king is not designated as a harmful spirit.

Setting aside the strange coincidence that Rabbi Joseph had a talk with a demon named Joseph—or, rather, accepting this at its face value—the gist of the rabbi's statement is that "twos-in-a-row" are not dangerous after all, since a king (even the king of the demons) would find it beneath his dignity to do harm. You can guess the reaction that this statement would elicit, and here it is:

> Others explain this in the opposite sense: On the contrary, a king is quick-tempered, does whatever he wishes. Why, a king may break through a wall to make a pathway for himself and none may say him, "Nay."

The other rabbis take what we might consider a less naïve view of kings. If what Rabbi Joseph reports is correct, then the danger of "twos-in-a-row" is even greater than had at first been suspected! But Rabbi Joseph is not the only one who has had a conversation with the demon named Joseph:

> Rabbi Papa said: Joseph the demon told me, "For two we kill. For four we do not kill. For four we harm [the drinker]. For two [we strike] whether [the drinking of two has been] deliberate or accidental; for four [we strike] only if it has been deliberate and not

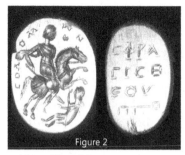

Figure 1   Figure 2

accidental." And if a person forgot himself and happened to go out [after drinking in pairs], what is his remedy?

Let him take his right-hand thumb in his left hand and his left-hand thumb in his right hand and say the following: "You [two thumbs] and I, surely that is three!" But if he hears a voice saying, "You and I, surely that makes four!" let him respond to the voice, "You and I are surely five!" And if he hears a voice saying, "You and I are six!" let him respond, "You and I are seven!" This once happened until [the count reached] one hundred and one, upon which the demon burst.

In other words, even if a person has put himself in danger, there may yet be magical remedies. It is possible to outsmart demons if you know what to do and how to do it. The gesture of placing opposing thumbs in opposing hands is a good example, and it is also employed by the rabbis of the Talmud as a remedy against the "evil eye." Having broached the issue of remedies, the Talmud now inserts an aside that is of special interest to our examination of the nexus between demons and magic:

Amemar said: The chief of the sorceresses told me: One who meets sorceresses should say to them, "Hot dung in perforated baskets for your mouths, O witches! May your heads be bald. May the wind carry off your crumbs. May your spices be scattered. You sorceresses, may the wind carry off the fresh saffron you hold. As long as God showed grace to me and to you, I had not chanced upon you. Now that I have chanced upon you, your grace and my grace have cooled!"

The Talmud's discussion continues for many a page of mathematical reckoning. We need not review the entire section, much of which serves to amplify what we have already heard. Two comments from the discourse, however, are worth adding: First, it is noted that "In the West [meaning, among the rabbis of the Land of Israel] they were not so concerned about 'twos-in-a-row'"—this may indicate that associating demons with the danger of pairs was especially a Babylonian, not Palestinian, concern. Second, the Talmud provides its own summation accompanied by an admonition:

> This is the position in general terms: When one is especially concerned [about "twos-in-a-row"], they [the demons] are especially concerned [to harm] him; while when one is not especially concerned, they are not especially concerned about him. Nevertheless, one should take heed.

The Jews living in the Land of Israel may have had less concern about doing things in pairs, but they were equally concerned with both magic and demons. A brief text, written in elegant Hebrew, was currently[15] circulating among the mystics. It was named, *Sefer HaRazim*, "The Book of Secrets," and was a primer on the angels of the six heavens. Nearly 700 angels are named; many are identified by function. But scattered through the book are formulae that are of more value to magicians than to mystics. Do you wish to have a conversation with the moon? There is a formula. Do you wish to know the future? There is a formula. Would you like to destroy an enemy? There is a formula. Would you like to have your dreams interpreted? There is a formula. There are also formulae for seeing the sun at night, for doing battle with wild beasts, for calling demons to your aid, and for warding off illness.

Beyond that, the Book of Secrets provides insight into the intellectual environment of Jews in the West (both Palestine and Egypt). It is evident, for example, that the sages who read this book were well versed in the classics. Though we know they spoke Aramaic in normal conversation, *Sefer HaRazim* includes almost no Aramaic—indicating that its readers were entirely conversant with Hebrew. Of course, Hebrew and Aramaic are closely related, so this is far less surprising than the fact that *Sefer HaRazim* is generously spiced with Greek terms (written in Hebrew letters) and even includes an entire prayer in Greek—indicating that its readers were influenced by, and somewhat conversant with, Greek (at a time when they were ruled by Rome). The Greek terms, moreover, are mainly technical, magical terms—indicating that the mystics were absorbing Greek magic (or at least the Greek names for magical practices) into their vocabulary. A blending of cultures was obviously underway, and this is further attested by the fact that the names of some angels are of Greek, not Hebrew, derivation.

In fact, the cultures were blending in both directions. Magical recipes on Egyptian papyri around this period typically invoked Jewish angels and included Jewish formulae. Amulets and charms written for pagans and Christians incorporated Jewish magical motifs. And Jewish magicians seem to have been writing charms and creating amulets for non-Jews especially in Egypt where Jews were much more assimilated into the general culture of the Roman Empire.

The blending can best be appreciated when it is represented visually, as in the bronze amulet in Figure 1.[16] The front depicts a rider spearing a female demon. The inscription engraved around the picture, along the side and top edges reads: "One God who conquers ev…" The last word clearly should be completed as "evil." Either the engraver neglected to complete the word, or else the engraver intentionally wished not to include the word "evil" on a charm meant to protect its wearer from evil. Either way, the reference to "One God" marks this as a charm created by a Jewish magician or influenced by Jewish magic.

This is also clear from the reverse side: a picture of a lion and a snake positioned beneath three names: *Iaô*, *Sabaôth*, and *Michaêl*. *Michaêl* is the guardian angel of the people of Israel. *Iaô* (misspelled on the amulet as *Iaôth*) is the Greek transliteration for "Yah," a shortened form of "YHWH," the name of God in Hebrew. *Sabaôth* is another Jewish name for God. The misspelling of God's name as *Iaôth* could indicate that the amulet was manufactured by a non-Jew but not necessarily. Magicians were typically scribes skilled in writing and unskilled in craftsmanship. A magician would likely commission a craftsman to create a bronze amulet. But the craftsmen were typically artists and not scribes. They would therefore copy letter-by-letter from texts provided by the magician. The misspelling here is telling since the craftsman seems to have copied the final letter of *Sabaôth* mistakenly to *Iaô*, thereby producing *Iaôth*. This may

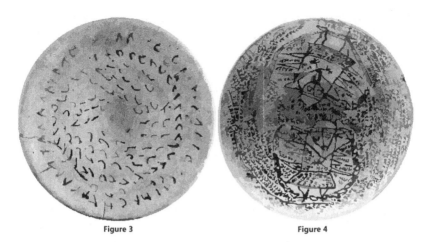

Figure 3   Figure 4

also account for the missing letter of the word "evil" on the other side. Today, we might reject a mistaken inscription, but the ancient magician would probably accept minor errors without much comment since most of the folk purchasing the amulets were themselves illiterate and could not be expected to notice any minor discrepancies.

Figure 1 is a typical amulet. If the picture of a rider slaying a prostrate demon tends to remind us of images of St. George and the dragon, there is no coincidence. Borrowings of artistic poses—particularly heroic poses—have been common throughout the ages. Figure 2[17] presents a beautifully crafted amulet of hematite and contains the same imagery of the rider spearing a prostrate female demon.

The inscription surrounding the rider here is "Solomon." King Solomon, of course, was known for his ability to subjugate demons, and his name as an inscription is known on amulets intended both for Jews and Christians. Solomon was also closely associated with horses. He maintained an enormous stable in Jerusalem though it is unlikely that he would have ridden horseback since his horses were trained for pulling chariots.

On the other side, there is a picture of a key, and above it are the words "Seal of God." Some scholars hold that the key symbolizes the power to shut demons in based on stories of Solomon's creation of "seals" that demons were powerless to break. Another possibility is the double entendre mentioned earlier—a reference both to Solomon's possessing the key to demon control (his wisdom) and the iron (as in an actual key) with which to control them. This amulet, now in the Kelsey Museum of Archaeology in Ann Arbor, MI, was crafted with great care and was probably far more expensive than the first example. Still, the wearers of both amulets expected much the same degree of protection.

In general, as the ancient world became the medieval world, the many strains of magic—Egyptian, Coptic, Greek, Babylonian, and Jewish—blended in a way that the cultures themselves resisted. An apt comparison can be made with modern science in the periods of World War II and the Cold War as scientists strained to share their evolving knowledge of atomic energy while political entities—the United States, Great Britain, Germany, France, the Soviet Union, China, etc.—attempted to secure scientific knowledge as a private preserve. The problem with scientific knowledge was much the same as that with magic; everyone, everywhere, needs to be able to control the forces of evil—whether those forces are atomic energy, harmful bacteria, or myriads of demons.

Toward the end of the talmudic period, "demon bowls," a unique approach to demon control, became common in Babylonia. Dating from the sixth to the eighth century, CE, these clay pottery bowls were inscribed with magical formulae intended to be read by the demons themselves. The vast majority of the bowls so far discovered are in one of three Aramaic dialects—Syriac, Mandaic, or Jewish-Aramaic. A very few of them are inscribed in Persian.

In most cases, the bowls are inscribed in a spiral that begins at the inside center and continues outward to the bowl's rim. Sometimes bowls are inscribed on both sides so that when the bowl is inverted the writing starts inside, spirals to the rim, and continues for a few lines on the outside.[18] Some are written in patterns other than spirals, and sometimes the writing itself is in no real language but is merely a psuedoscript. This may indicate that some manufacturers were simply illiterate (and so were clients), or it may mean that the formulae were actually less important than the pattern of the writing. Of course, it could also indicate that some folk thought the demons were illiterate or that demons would sap themselves trying to decipher anything written whether or not the language was comprehensible to human beings.

In the case of these bowls, the protective magic was intended to control, combat, and defend against demons. The bowl in Figure 3,[19] for example, contains a series of repeated characters without meaning, i.e., pseudoscript, executed in the typical spiral format.

The bowl in Figure 4[20] is also in pseudoscript but provides a vivid example of the kinds of drawings often worked into the text. This particular bowl was found inverted on top of another with an inscribed eggshell placed in the space between them. (Unfortunately, the eggshell did not survive long enough for its inscription to be recorded and translated, but likely enough the eggshell text was also done in pseudoscript.) What is salient is that the demons on the bowl have their hands tied and their feet chained. This is a vivid portrayal of what the bowl was meant to achieve.

Most of the demon bowls were discovered in excavations in Nippur where a large Jewish town existed from the beginning of the Arab period right down to the last century. The bowls were found placed face down in the ground. The owners seem to have believed that demons came from beneath the earth and would be attracted to buried objects, especially bowls, since they are normally used to contain food.[21] Sometimes, when two bowls were inverted on one another and buried together, they would be sealed with pitch, and often the enclosed space would contain an object such as the eggshell reported in the case of Figure 4 or even fragments of human skull. The idea that writing had magical properties is not difficult to extrapolate here. Though many of the purchasers and some of the artists might be illiterate, the efficacy of the bowls seems to rely on the demons themselves being literate. As the demons came up from below, it was thought, they would read and be lured, entangled, and driven off[22] by the writing and images on the bowls. Thus, if you buried the bowl under your home, it would protect your home from underworld demons; many bowls are found buried in the corners of homes presumably because this is where cracks might allow the demons easiest access.

Though the bowls above are in pseudoscript, most bowls were inscribed with performative language. One bowl, rendered in my own vernacular translation, reads:

> O wickedest of the wicked, I now conquer you and bind you with the bonds of your evil ones. You are bound and sealed in one of the four corners of his house, [prevented] from sinning. You shall not sin against Bar Cupita and all the members of his household and shall not damage things foolishly, not by night and not by day because we bind you with this strong bond of evil and again we bind you with this bond that you are bound by it, O brothers of Hanoch, the evil one.

Another (similarly rendered) reads:

> This charm is established for health, for the guarding and sealing of the house of Paroh bar Arznish and his entire dwelling even by the seal of King Solomon, son of David, against those not brought forth from this planet, against all that could not stand before him, against every devil … against devils and roof-dwellers and all howlers of the night, and all monsters and all satans, and against all idols and curses—all are excommunicated and banned.

The inscriptions may contain familiar magical words and formulae, sometimes repeat a single word three or seven times, sometimes elongate a single word by repeating consonants three or seven times each, and so on.

A few of the bowls were intended not so much for personal protection as for the harm of some enemy since it was a fair assumption that one's enemy was either a demon or possessed by a demon. They instructed other demons to visit the enemy's house or to attack him in the public way. These more "aggressive" bowls could be buried near the enemy's home or in a cemetery where one might expect that many demons would read them and be called to the cause. But the majority of the demon bowls unearthed to date were protective in nature.

From the fact that bowls were typically personalized for the head of a household, we might compare the protective magic implied in the bowls to the kind of protective magic implied in modern insurance policies. No insurance policy could possibly keep us from dying at our appointed time, yet there is a certain comfort in knowing that we are betting *with* the actuarial tables and that there is an insurance policy in a drawer somewhere. In the same way, there must have been comfort in knowing that there was a bowl buried in the corner.

Conceptions of demons and magic in talmudic times are indicative of social conditions. Demons occupied a relatively small place in the deliberations of the sages, but their frequent mention indicates that the sages did not take the presence of demons lightly. They shared with their laity a deep-seated belief in the ubiquity of evil spirits. Within the texts, we glimpse both the growth of a science and the proliferation of an industry.

Lest we think that, by now, we have risen above all such superstitions, consider the way in which the majority of people in our society think about and react to the ubiquity of bacteria and the dangers of viruses. Some rely on science as the new magic against these potentially harmful threats to our wellbeing. But both science and homeopathy are employed in the struggle against them, and a thriving industry of drugs and patent medicines fills the shelves of every local drugstore and grocery, not to mention machines and devices which are claimed to cleanse the air we breathe indoors.

In ancient times, the threat of demons and the everyday necessity of battling demonic threats became a fit discussion for even the most intelligent human beings. The more it was discussed, the greater the need seemed for practical measures to combat demons. Even today, if you do not need an aspirin or pain killer by the end of watching a Superbowl or a World Series game, it will not be because the drug companies have withheld their commercials. Since ancient times, there has been no end of the making of amulets, the writing of charms, the crafting of bowls, and the sale of potions and roots. If there had been a Wall Street before Wall Street, the bullish money would have been invested with magicians and sages. After all, anyone who can add two and two and make the sum equal three is obviously a talent worth courting.

❀ Endnotes

1 Juvenal, *Satires*, 6:542–7.

2 Origen, *Contra Celsum*, 4:520, end.

3 Traditionally, a distance of "four cubits" was required to remove one-self from any dangerous personal contact. It was necessary to remain four cubits away from anyone who had been excommunicated, anyone suspected of being possessed, anyone suspected of possessing an evil eye, and so on. In this case, though it is not spelled out, there may be some superstition regarding Eliezer's imminent death or his death bed—either of which might attract demons.

4 See Sanhedrin 91a.

5 Ralph Waldo Emerson (1803–82), *Essays*, "Compensation" (First Series, 1841).

6 See Mishnah, *Avot* 5:9.

7 Sanhedrin 109a.

8 Baba Kamma 16a.

9 *Avot deRabbi Nachman* 37.

10 Rosh HaShanah 9b.

11 The Mishnah was compiled in the Land of Israel (called "the West" by the sages of Babylonia) and it seems that Jews in the West were less concerned about the danger of pairs with regard to demons. The difference is considered a bit further on in the discussion.

12 The entire discussion is found in Pesachim 109b-110b.

13 Exodus 12:42: "It is a night of watchfulness to the Lord for bringing them out of the land of Egypt. This is *a night of watching* kept to the Lord by all the people of Israel throughout their generations" [italics mine].

14 Throughout this discussion, of course, "in pairs" must mean "two times in a row." Since the sexual act is normally performed by a pair of people, "two times" is clearly the intent of the rabbis. Please do not think of this footnote as condescending. I offer it only to confound the many sorts of demons who are constantly trying to confuse us as we read.

15 The date of composition is usually reckoned to the late third or early fourth century, CE

16 Kelsey Museum 26114. Purchased in Syria, exact date of manufacture unknown.

17 Kelsey Museum 26092. Purchased in Egypt, exact date of manufacture unknown.

18 The reason for text pouring over to the outside of a bowl is generally to accommodate the extra verbiage required when bowls are inscribed for an unusually large number of members of a family or household. When the text being written is too short to reach the rim on the inside of the bowl, lines of the text are often repeated until the rim is

reached. Manuel Gold suggested that some logic distinctive to the bowls precludes leaving any blank space on the inside.

19 Kelsey Museum 19501.

20 Kelsey Museum 33756.

21 Demons were known to gather wherever food was readily available as at festivals such as Passover or at the mourners' feast following funerals. In the case of the Passover Seder, at one point the door is opened, and a special Psalm is recited, as Manuel Gold suggests, to drive out any lingering demons. See his essays on Passover in Manuel Gold, *Renegade Rabbi* (Rossel Books, 2019).

22 As per Manuel Gold, who points out that "trapping demons" is a great hazard.

❄
Janusz Korczak
The Dilemma
of King Matt

*My close friend since adolescence, Dr. Marc Silverman
of the Hebrew University is the foremost expert on the
moral-educational thought and humanist philosophy of
Janusz Korczak. In a paper delivered in 2015, Dr.
Silverman explained, "In ways similar to those of Martin Buber, [Korczak] accepted on one hand, the necessity of 'I-It' relationships between human beings, other
human beings, and the world ... for the sake of con-
structing and sustaining human civilization. On the
other hand, Korczak was certain that without 'I-Thou'
relationships characterized by human beings lending
respect, care, and love to each other and to the world,
human civilization is doomed to ethical emptiness—the
absence of direction and of meaningfulness." This is a
fine insight to introduce my minor paean to Korczak, a
writer and educator I have always admired.*

Treblinka is a small railroad crossing about 62 miles northeast
of Warsaw. In the forest nearby, the Nazis set up a death camp.
During World War II, the Nazis murdered 750,000 Jews in
Treblinka. At the end of the war, the Nazis destroyed the camp
and tried to wipe out every trace of the killing they had done
there. But the Polish neighbors knew what the Nazis had done.
They came to the forest to dig up the mass graves. They rum-
maged through the skeletons of the dead Jews looking for gold
teeth or jewelry that the Nazis might have missed. When they
left, bones and skulls were scattered all over the grounds.

Some years later, the Polish government allowed the Jews
to rebury the bones. Much later, in the early 1960s, the Polish

government allowed the Jews to raise money to create a monument. Today, if you visit Treblinka, you pass through a forest path and come to a clearing. There are 16,000 broken tombstones in this clearing. 15,999 of them are inscribed with the names of cities, little towns, and villages whose Jews were murdered here. Only one broken tombstone has the name of an individual. The big letters on that stone spell out "Janusz Korczak." Beneath this, on the same stone, in smaller letters, is the name, "Henryk Goldszmit."

Inventing Korczak

Henryk Goldszmit was born in the city of Warsaw in 1878. He came from a wealthy Jewish family. His father was a lawyer and his grandfather was a doctor. He wasn't given much in the way of Jewish education. He did not study in a religious school. No one in the family cared much about Bar Mitzvah or synagogue. Little Henryk thought school was pretty easy. He was one of those lucky people who do well without too much effort. He loved reading, and from an early age he wanted to grow up to be a writer.

Things changed when Henryk was eleven years old. His father had a nervous breakdown and never worked again. Now there was never enough money and Henryk was told that he should give up his idea of being a writer. He would have to find a career that would make money for him and his family. Henryk liked helping people and thought that the best way he could help others was by becoming a doctor like his grandfather had been. When he reached medical school, he decided that the people he most wanted to help were children, so he became a children's doctor, a pediatrician.

But he still loved to write. While Henryk Goldszmit was in medical school, he wrote a play about mental illness and entered it in a literary competition. Maybe because it was about mental illness—and his father was mentally ill—Henryk chose to send the play in under a pen name. He said that Janusz Korczak wrote the play. He took the name from the hero of a Polish novel. Today, this would be a little like entering a writing contest using the name Harry Potter. His play didn't win the contest; it got only an honorable mention, but he liked writing under this name, and he used it whenever he wrote books and stories for children.

In 1901—when he was just twenty-three years old—Henryk wrote his first book. He called it *Children of the Street*. In it, he told about all the orphans and homeless children he treated in his first years as a young doctor. He told how awful their lives were, but he also told how brave these homeless children were and how important right and wrong was to them. People all over Poland were shocked to learn how many orphans and abandoned children there were. They were shocked again five years later when Henryk wrote a book called *Children of the Salon* which told about how children were raised in rich homes and how they thought money was the only important thing in life and how the children of the rich hardly ever thought about right and wrong. Was it really possible that homeless children were growing up to be better adults than children of the rich? Henryk's question still bothers us today.

From now on, he would live a double life—he was Dr. Henryk Goldszmit, a pediatrician who wrote about children and their problems; and he was also Janusz Korczak, the author of popular books for children and a champion of children's rights.

The Orphanages

In 1912, Henryk was asked if he would create a Jewish orphanage in Warsaw. It was a challenge that he was ready to accept. In those days, orphanages were generally terrible places. The food might be all right. The beds might be all right. The children might be treated all right. But orphans seldom smiled. There was no excitement, except maybe when somebody was punished for misbehaving. And orphanages were really boring. They were just waiting stations with all the orphans just hoping to be adopted. And many of them never were adopted. Goldszmit decided to make a new kind of orphanage.

He helped his orphans to organize their own government so that they could make the rules for the orphanage. When someone broke the rules, a court with child judges set their discipline. He helped the orphans edit their own newspaper—and the newspaper became such an important place for children to speak out that it was published not just for the orphanage but also as part of a large daily newspaper. He made the orphans happy to stay in the orphanage, made the school challenging, and made the graduates who left his orphanage proud that they had grown up with the doctor.

Korczak took no salary from his orphanage. He lived in a small attic room with very little furniture. And he often shared his room with some child who needed to be away from the others or who needed quiet for a while. He even took his turn doing chores like washing dishes or scrubbing the floor.

Nine years later, in 1920, Korczak opened another orphanage, this time for Catholic children. He called his orphanages, "children's republics." And he and his devoted assistant, Stefa Wilczenska, ran both orphanages.

Korczak wrote more and more now. Using his own name, Henryk Goldszmit, he wrote a popular book called *How to Love a Child*. He argued that children should have rights, and he began drafting a declaration of the rights of children. People all over Poland recognized the doctor's name. And he was only getting started.

In 1928, using the name Janusz Korczak, he wrote a children's book, *King Matt the First*. It was as popular as *Peter Pan* or *Alice in Wonderland*. In just a few years, *King Matt the First* was translated and published in twenty languages! Now more people knew him as Korczak than had ever known him any other way. If you asked who Henryk Goldszmit was, people would hesitate. But if you asked who Janusz Korczak was, they would know right away. It's a little like asking today, "Who is Ted Geisel?" A lot of people would shrug and wonder. But if you said, "Who is Dr. Seuss?" they would say, "Don't you know?" Janusz Korczak was famous. From then on, Henryk Goldszmit used the name Janusz Korczak all the time.

Was he really as popular as Dr. Seuss? The truth is, he was even as popular as Dr. Ruth! In the 1930s, before television was invented, Korczak had a regular program on Polish radio. He was "the Old Doctor," answering questions about how parents could make their children's lives better.

In the meantime, the children who graduated from his Jewish orphanage were trying to make a better life for themselves.

A bunch of them moved to Palestine to help build a new Jewish state. He went to visit them. Many were living in a new kind of settlement, the kibbutz. He liked this new way of life right away. It was very much like his orphanages, only for grownups. Everyone shared in making decisions. Everyone shared in chores and tasks. Everyone shared in work and in fun. His graduates said, "Things are not good for Jews in Poland. Stay here with us. Help us build this new life." Korczak said he would return to the kibbutz but only if he could bring the children with him. This would never be.

The End

Not long after his visit to the land of Israel, Germany invaded Poland and the tragedy began. Both of his orphanages were closed, and Korczak and 200 of the orphans were forced into the walled ghetto of Warsaw. Four hundred thousand Jews were squeezed into a small space that measured only about one thousand acres—a space just a little bigger than New York's Central Park. Before he moved the children into the Warsaw ghetto, Korczak managed to get hold of a sack of potatoes. He guarded it like a sack of gold, but during the move, one of the German soldiers took it away from him. He marched into the office of the governor of Warsaw, demanding that the potatoes be returned because they were for "his children." The governor had him arrested and Korczak was sentenced to four months in jail.

The Polish people had not forgotten their "Dr. Seuss." As soon as Korczak was released from prison, they offered to help him escape. Korczak refused. He would stay with the orphans. He told the Poles, "You do not leave a sick child in the night, and you do not leave children at a time like this."

In his diary Korczak wrote: "Our bodies may live forever as green grass or in a cloud—we just don't know. ... What we can know is this: Our children, and theirs, may go on ... I only want to be conscious when I die. I want to be able to tell the children 'Goodbye' and wish them freedom to choose their own way." He returned to his orphanage in the ghetto.

Korczak tried practicing medicine to help the Jews—children and adults—but the Germans allowed each person in the ghetto only enough food for 184 calories a day—roughly what you might get from half a candy bar or two pieces of bread—and the Jews soon began to starve to death. For nearly two years, Korczak and Stefa did what they could to keep things normal for the orphans, but conditions in the ghetto worsened day by day.

The end came on August 6, 1942. Janusz and Stefa demanded that the German police wait while they got the children ready to go. They dressed the children in their best clothes. Stefa told the orphans that they were going to a picnic some place where there would be green grass on which to sit and open fields in which to run. The children formed up in a neat row—two hundred of them five across. Korczak took the two smallest by the hand and led the way. At times, he even carried the littlest child. And they marched to the railroad station.

King Matt

Not every story—not even every story written for children—has a happy ending. In Korczak's book, *King Matt the First*, Matt's mother dies in childbirth, and Matt's father dies when Matt is only nine or ten years old. Matt becomes king, but he has to learn what can be changed in the world and what cannot be changed. Before the book begins, there is a picture of Janusz Korczak at age nine or so. Under the picture it says:

> When I was the little boy you see in the photograph, I wanted to do all the things that are in this book. But I forgot to, and now I'm old. I no longer have the time or the strength to go to war or travel to the land of the cannibals. I have included this photograph because it's important what I looked like when I truly wanted to be a king, and not when I was writing about King Matt. I think it's better to show pictures of what kings, travelers, and writers looked like before they grew up, or grew old, because otherwise it might seem that they knew everything from the start and were never young themselves. And then children will think they can't be statesmen, travelers, and writers, which wouldn't be true.
>
> Grownups should not read my book, because some of the chapters are not very nice. They'll misunderstand them and make fun of them. But if they really want to read my book, they should give it a try. After all, you can't tell grownups not to do something—they won't listen to you, and you can't make them obey.

The book concludes when the reforms that King Matt tries to make—things like sending the grownups back to school and letting the children run the country—go wrong. King Matt is taken prisoner by the army of a jealous king who sentences Matt to death. But two other kings convince the jealous king that it is not a good idea for one king to put another king to death. It might give people the idea that all kings should be put to death. So they decide that, at the very last minute, they will banish Matt forever. But they don't tell Matt. He marches through the city thinking that he is going to his execution. Korczak writes:

> It was a beautiful day. The sun was shining. Everyone had come out to see their king one last time. Many people had tears in their eyes. But Matt did not see those tears, though that would have made it easier for him to go to his death. ...
>
> He was tied to a post on the square near a freshly dug grave. But he was still calm and composed when the firing squad loaded their rifles and aimed them at him.
>
> And he was just as calm when, at the last moment, he heard his reprieve: "Death sentence commuted to exile on a desert island."

Korczak ends the book by saying, "I'll tell you what happened to Matt on that desert island just as soon as I find out."

At the train station in Warsaw, the children were told to remove their yellow stars and pile them together. One of the guards remembered, "It looked like a field of buttercups." Legend has it that one Polish guard at the station recognized Korczak. He offered to smuggle his favorite author out of the ghetto if Korczak would just load the children onto the transport and leave them. Instead, Korczak helped the children on to the train and went with them to Treblinka. Neither he nor the children were ever seen again. They were all put to death in that forest near the railroad crossing.

It's not a happy ending to the story of Janusz Korczak and his children's republic. But maybe it was not the real ending, either. I'll tell you what really happened to them just as soon as I find out.

Our Dialogue
with Buber

Many of us seriously believe that the answer to difficult issues must be either this or that. In The Proud Tower, *Barbara W. Tuchman tells us that seeing both sides is "the penalty of the thoughtful" person. Alfred Lord Balfour, more thoughtful than many a British politician, once arriving at a great house "whose staircase split in twin curves, he stood at the bottom for twenty minutes trying to work out, as he explained to a puzzled observer, a logical reason for taking one side rather than the other" (p. 51). Logic is the sticking-point. Martin Buber as a Jewish existentialist philosopher uses the bold poetry of language and life to break through the pale limitations of the either-or.*

As a young man, studying in Jerusalem, I encountered Martin Buber. It came about in this way: My classmates and I were assigned to read *I and Thou,* Buber's masterwork, and I was preparing for class with a close friend. Try as we might, there was a passage in the book that neither of us could comprehend. We argued for nearly an hour over its interpretation, at the end of which time my friend looked at me mockingly and said, "Well, Buber is here in Jerusalem. Why don't we just ask him?"

He obviously intended to put an end to our discussion, but the idea appealed to me. I realized the chances of arranging such a meeting were remote. But I decided to try.

Perhaps it was the thought of two young people from the Diaspora trying to fathom the depths of *I and Thou* that was amusing to Dr. Buber. Or perhaps it was his own guiding principle that "All real living is meeting" that turned the trick. Whatever the reason, without undue formality, and to my utter astonishment, Dr. Buber's secretary set an appointment for us with the scholar for a week later.

My friend and I sat with Martin Buber for half an hour. He first checked whether we could speak Hebrew (which we both could, though haltingly). Next, he asked about our backgrounds and where we were studying. Only then did he inquire about the problematic passage which had prompted our visit. We read the paragraph to him from our English language version of his book, and he sat back in his chair and contemplated it in silence. Then he asked what we thought it meant.

He soon realized that our Hebrew was insufficient, so he kindly asked us to use as much English as we needed to make ourselves clear. When each of us had expounded the meaning we individually gleaned from the passage, he smiled. He had only spoken Hebrew so far and he continued to do so now. He said, *Ken, ken,* literally, "Yes, yes." Now, in Hebrew parlance, doubling a word may be understood in one of two ways. The doubling may lend emphasis, so that what he said meant, "Absolutely." Or it could simply be two instances of "yes,"—one "yes" for each of us—inferring that each of us was correct. Dr. Buber went on to say that we were both on the right track. Then, in a minute's time, he explained the passage. I do not think either of us could follow his Hebrew entirely.

In fact, I have no recollection of the exact passage we disputed or of our individual interpretations. I no longer recall the words the great professor used. I remember no particular detail of the study which was so much like offices of other professors. But I see Martin Buber's eloquent eyes. I hear his comforting tone. And I recall feeling his presence somehow encompassing us, feeling that Martin Buber was concerned with us—with me—with two students he had never seen before and would, no doubt, never see again. All too soon, then, the secretary came in and our encounter was over.

A few years later, when I heard the news of Dr. Buber's death, I felt a sense of personal loss. Yet I could not bring myself to feel depressed. My memory of Dr. Buber was too vivid. Ever since, when I read a passage in his works, I can close my eyes and ask my questions and seek my understanding without fear that he would be judgmental.

And, when I think I understand the meaning of a passage correctly, I can hear again his voice, saying *Ken, ken*, "Yes. Yes." Today, one "Yes" is definitely for me, but if you will remember my story and share it, the other "Yes" is my gift to you.

The Purity of Piety
Sefer Yetzirah *and the* Hasidei Ashkenaz

An oft-told story (probably anecdotal) has it that when Abraham Lincoln first met Harriet Beecher Stowe just after the beginning of the Civil War, he said, "So this is the little lady who started this great war." He referred, of course, to the effect attributed to her runaway best-seller novel, Uncle Tom's Cabin or Life among the Lowly. *Books can be that influential, and as an author, I am awed by the way in which the ideas books contain can spread virally with intended and unintended consequences. This essay begins with a single book, its author unknown, which empowered two major formations of Jewish life and thought. As a chapter in the history of ideas, I believe it deserves to be better-known.*

The centers of Jewish life in Roman times were Judea, Babylonia, and Egypt. Outside these centers, Jews lived scattered throughout the Empire on every periphery of its slowly eroding borders. Most of these Diaspora communities began in the heyday of Rome as trading centers. Perforce, the Jews maintained contact with the folks "back home." At first, "back home" meant Judea but the authority of the Judean sages waned following their exile from Jerusalem (a result of the disastrous defeat of Bar Kochba in 135 CE). More and more, Jews in the Diaspora measured the authenticity of their Jewish lives against the rulings of the Babylonian rabbis.

In all Jewish communities, no matter how far-flung, literacy was valued. Men, and many women, could read at least enough to recite prayers and psalms and often enough to study

Bible and Talmud. Learning was deemed the highest form of religiosity. It was expected that those who were the most literate would be most observant of the niceties of Jewish law while those who had less ability or time for study would observe the broad requirements of the law without being castigated or stigmatized for any failures of practice. A system of correspondence, literally a "Questions and Answers" system, operated between distant communities and the authorities of Babylonia. Letters traveling in either direction by ship or caravan often required months in transmission. Scholarship was just one more commodity that was conveyed along the ancient trade routes until, slowly, Diaspora communities imported rabbis or developed scholars of their own.

The most prosperous of these trading communities spread out along the banks of the Rhine River. The Jews called this area *Ashkenaz* from the biblical word for "North." Jewish towns, villages, and trading posts dotted the map of what is now Germany and France. In Northern France, one particular scholar, Rashi (Rabbi Shlomo ben Isaac) of Troyes (1040-1105), emerged as the greatest educator of his age turning Jewish teaching into an art form. His simple, eloquent commentaries on the Bible and the Talmud remain a valuable introduction to Jewish studies for new students. Rashi's prestige was enormous even in his lifetime. He died just before or just after the First Crusade, but students of his academy continued his work. Collectively, they are known as the *Tosafists* ("those who add [to Rashi's work]").

The Crusades swept over and devastated *Ashkenaz* like huge tsunamis. As far as crusaders were concerned, the Jewish communities represented the infidel close at hand. Never mind that the crusaders' avowed goal was to drive Muslims from the Holy Land, they took it upon themselves to pause along the way to practice rapine on the Jews of Europe. At times, the crusaders offered Jews an opportunity to convert—though not many Jews were willing. Just as often, the crusaders burned and pillaged Jewish communities without warning. So fierce was their fanaticism that the Jews were virtually helpless against them. Martyrdom was so common in *Ashkenaz* that it came to be considered an act of ultimate devotion to God: *Kiddush HaShem*, "[dying for] the holiness of [God's] Name."

The religious conflict which pitted the Christian realm against the Muslim empire deprived the Jews of *Ashkenaz* of direct contact with their brethren living under Muslim rule in the Holy Land and also in Spain and North Africa (the lands called *Sepharad* by the Jews, from the biblical name associated with Spain). The break in easy communication occurred just as the Jews of *Sepharad* were entering a Golden Age. Jewish philosophy and poetry, sacred and secular, flourished, but little of this filtered northward to *Ashkenaz*.

These basic conditions applied as a new kind of Jewish community embracing magic and mysticism emerged between 900 and 1300 among the Jews of the Rhineland. This formative religious movement reached its height in the hundred years from 1150-1250, but scholars generally agree that the inspiration came from a book that had already been in circulation for hundreds of years. This formative tome was entitled *Sefer Yetzirah* ("The Book of Creation"). It was probably composed between 200 and 600 CE and circulated in many hand-copied editions (sometimes even purporting to be the recorded teachings of the patriarch Abraham).

Sefer Yetzirah was one of many books known to the *Merkabah* or "Chariot" mystics of the Holy Land. It seems to have been written (or edited from many sources) by a sage well-versed in the mystic study of *Ma'aseh Bereshit* ("the Work of Creation"). Still, it was a unique composition. Most *Merkabah* texts aimed at enabling mystics to achieve ecstatic states, to journey through the heavens, to propitiate the angels that guarded heaven's portals, to measure God's glory, to "descend" to the Chariot of God, and even to become angels themselves. Atypically, *Sefer Yetzirah* scrutinized God's creation and the organization of this world.

In its early formulations, *Sefer Yetzirah* circulated for several generations among the mystics of Palestine. It is mentioned at least twice in the Talmud and seems to have been considered a work suitable for sharing only among advanced initiates. Early commentaries on it divulge a slightly different purpose, viewing *Sefer Yetzirah* as a "side path" for the advanced mystic—a set of instructions for perceiving the imperceptible in the universe.

Whatever its original intention, *Sefer Yetzirah* was destined to become a masterwork of Jewish mysticism. Its logic is often vague which leads us to speculate that either its ambiguity was intentional—a deliberate attempt to confuse the uninitiated— or, alternatively, the author may have simply been uncertain or tentative. We are also faced by other conundrums. Its unknown author was either exceedingly original or else adept at consolidating the originality of others. He may have been among the inner circle of the *Merkabah* mystics, or his work may have been accomplished entirely on the fringe. And in stark contrast to his many moments of vague reasoning, at times he claims the authority of prophecy.

In the end, though, the author's ambiguity may have been the greatest contribution to the lasting popularity of *Sefer Yetzirah* for ambiguity invited explanation and examination. Learned commentaries were composed continually from at least the sixth century on. New commentaries appear to this very day. Speculations on *Sefer Yetzirah* were embedded in almost all the later schools of Jewish mysticism. For the mystics emerging in *Ashkenaz*, the teachings of *Sefer Yetzirah* were the mysteries behind the mysteries.

On the surface, *Sefer Yetzirah* deals with simple matters: the ten whole numbers and the twenty-two letters of the Hebrew alphabet. Together, these are often referred to as the "thirty-two paths." According to *Sefer Yetzirah*, all the "elements" of the created world have their origins in the ten numbers. These numbers are called the ten *sefirot*, a term which has many meanings, but which we may, for the moment, render by what may be a distant English cousin "spheres." As the author uses the term, each *sefirah* or "sphere" is a kind of stage or representation. The spheres do not, however, lead either upward or downward like the steps of a staircase. Instead, their precise relationship is amorphous. In poetic language the author writes: "their end is in their beginning and their beginning in their end, as the flame is bound to the coal—close your mouth lest it speak and your heart lest it think."[1] Commentaries differ as to whether *Sefer Yetzirah* is trying to say that the *sefirot* emanate from God, forming links in a chain beginning in the spiritual ether of the heavens and ending in the mundane material of the created world, or whether they are idealizations that only give the impression of a progression. In another place, the ten *sefirot* are personified as angels prostrating themselves in prayer before the Holy Throne. You can get a feeling for the ambiguity and the poetry of the text—and also attempt to judge the interrelationship of the *sefirot* for yourself—from this brief description:

> There are ten intangible *sefirot*: ten and not nine; ten and not eleven. Understand with wisdom, and be wise with understanding; test them and explore them ... Understand the matter fully, and set the Creator in his place. Only he is the Former and Creator. There is none other. His attributes are ten and infinite. There are ten intangible *sefirot* whose measure is ten without end ... Ten intangible *sefirot* whose appearance is like lightning, whose limits are infinite. His word is in them in their backward and forward movement, and they run at his decree like the whirlwind, and they bow down before his throne ...
>
>> One: spirit of living *Elohim* [God], blessed and blest is the name of him who lives forever ... His beginning has no end; his end has no end.
>>
>> Two: spiritual air from spirit. He engraved and hewed out in it twenty-two letters as a foundation: three mothers, seven doubles, and twelve simples. They are of one spirit.
>>
>> Three: spiritual water from spiritual air. He engraved and hewed out in it chaos and disorder, mud and mire ... and it became earth. ...
>>
>> Four: spiritual fire from spiritual water. He engraved and hewed out in it the Throne of Glory, *seraphim* and *ophanim* and *hayyot* [living creatures], and ministering angels. From the three of them he established his dwelling place ...
>
> He chose three of the simple letters, sealed them with spirit and set them into his great name, *YHV*, and sealed them through six extremities.
>
>> Five: he sealed height; he turned upwards and sealed it with *YHV*.
>>
>> Six: he sealed abyss; he turned downwards and sealed it with *YHV*.
>>
>> Seven: he sealed east; he turned forwards and sealed it with *VHY*.

> Eight: he sealed west; he turned backwards and sealed
> it with *VHY.*
> Nine: he sealed south; he turned right and sealed it
> with *VHY.*
> Ten: he sealed north; he turned left and sealed it with
> *VHY.*
> These ten intangible *sefirot* are One—spirit of living *Elohim*;
> spiritual air from spirit; spiritual water from spiritual air; spiritual
> fire from spiritual water; height; abyss; east; west; north and
> south.[2]

Having identified the ten sefirot, *Sefer Yetzirah* turns to the
twenty-two letters of the Hebrew alphabet categorizing them
and describing the role they play in creation. The idea that the
Hebrew alphabet was an essential part of the original process of
creation was not original to *Sefer Yetzirah*. It occurs outside the
circle of the *Merkabah* mystics in the Midrash:

> The Holy One, the Blessed, said "I request laborers." The Torah
> told Him: "I put at your disposal twenty-two laborers, namely
> the twenty-two letters which are in the Torah, and give to each
> one its own."[3]

The sages generally presumed that the alphabet was also
essential to all subsequent creation whether undertaken by God
or human beings. In the realm of art, for example, they assigned
the Hebrew alphabet the role we currently assign to inspiration.
Thus, the Talmud showered high praise on Bezalel, the artist
commissioned by God to create the original *menorah* (seven-
branched candelabrum), saying: "Bezalel knew how to combine
the letters by which the heavens and the earth were created."[4]

Obviously, this emphasis on the twenty-two letters rests on
the assumption that God spoke Hebrew. To the sages this was
axiomatic: Hebrew was the language of creation, the language
of heaven, God's primary language. *Sefer Yetzirah* presents a
special instance of this axiom, namely that the particles of
which Hebrew is composed—the *Alef Bet* or alphabet—are as essential to creation as the particles which comprise the language
of mathematics—the ten numbers. *Sefer Yetzirah* describes the
Hebrew letters as the physical tools of creation:

> [God] drew them, hewed them, combined them, weighed them,
> interchanged them, and through them produced the whole cre-
> ation and everything that is destined to be created.[5]

Everything created in the material world, in time and in human existence, was the result of combining and recombining the twenty-two letters of the Hebrew alphabet. In another leap of faith, most manuscripts of *Sefer Yetzirah* speak of the letters as "231 gates," a figure somehow said to represent the possible combinations of the letters when they are paired. And in yet another leap of faith, the text states that whatever letters are used in the creation of a thing, all created things are based on the letters in the name of God. At one point, *Sefer Yetzirah* suggests an etiological explanation for this: Read as a single word, the twenty-two letters of the alphabet form one of God's names, so it may be said that God's name is inherent in all things. Still, this seems too metaphorical to be what the author really intended by saying that all created things bear God's imprint. In the end, no doubt, the meaning really derives from the elemental Jewish presupposition that the spirit of God is in all things. This is another example of the kind of ambiguity in *Sefer Yetzirah* which invites commentary.

Sefer Yetzirah correlates the three "base" Hebrew letters (the *immot* or "mother letters"—*alef, mem,* and *shin*) with air, fire, and water. From these three, the text states, all the other letters came into being. The *immot* are also equivalent to the three seasons of the year (using the reckoning of seasons common to Greeks and Hebrews) and the three main elements of the body (head, torso, and stomach).

The second group consists of seven "double" letters (*bet, gimmel, dalet, kaf, pe, resh,* and *tav*). In Hebrew, each of these may be sounded in two distinct ways depending on whether it contains an added internal dot (*dagesh*). The "doubles" gave rise to the "sevens"—seven planets, the seven days of the week, the seven bodily orifices (the two eyes, the two nostrils, the two ears, and the mouth), and the seven "opposites" in human life (the common belief that each life is allotted seven "good" and seven "evil" events).

The twelve remaining letters—the *Sefer Yetzirah* calls them "simples"—account for the zodiac's twelve signs, the normal year of twelve months, and the limbs (or, perhaps, behaviors) of the body. The simple letters are aligned with the activities of the human being in the temporal world.

In this manner, *Sefer Yetzirah* describes the twenty-two letters of the alphabet, assigning to them much the same function as DNA serves in genetics. Arranging and rearranging the letters forms every necessary and desirable combination of life.

In some manuscripts, *Sefer Yetzirah* also includes a second categorization of the letters arranged according to phonetic standards. The letters are divided into labials, velars, gutturals, sibilants, and dentals based on the five ways in which the mouth and tongue form their sounds. Most scholars concur that this second division is a later addition to the text. It assumes specialized knowledge from the study of Hebrew linguistics, a study of which there was little evidence at the time the book was written.[6] Yet, even if this section were added later, it fits the book seamlessly.

In addition to the thirty-two paths, *Sefer Yetzirah* explores many other themes common to the *Merkabah* mystics. A lengthy section, for example, compares the alphabet with various parts of the four *hayyot* or "beasts" which bear the Chariot of God in Ezekiel's vision. In the end, though, we are not concerned so much with the details of the book as with the many interpretations of *Sefer Yetzirah*'s purpose.

Sefer Yetzirah can be understood as a philosophical tract, paralleling many Greek forms while borrowing and Judaizing elements of Pythagoras, Aristotle, Plato, etc. Or it may be taken as an oracular treatise, a set of pronouncements based on a Jewish-Hellenist philosophic position. In either of these cases, its purpose would be to provide a key to the innate interrelationship of language and mathematics to the orderly universe. If the book did not delve into the mystic realm, either of these explanations would suffice. Instead, they are just the beginning of the possibilities.

The mystic, for example, might consider *Sefer Yetzirah* a description of a journey into the spiritual world—commencing in the mundane world and extending through more and more fantastical realms eventuating in the basic ethers of which all things are composed. In such a reading, letters and numbers can be combined to create a mystical path—though not a straight path by any means. If *Sefer Yetzirah* is perceived of as a journey, however, its destination differs from the one normally sought by the *Merkabah* mystics. They normally wished to reach the heavens while *Sefer Yetzirah* seeks to explore the created universe.

On the other hand, the notion that all things are created by means of combining elements of language, letters, and mathematics—that creation in its essence is a verbal process—could also be taken to mean that "the thirty-two secret paths of wisdom" (the ten numbers and the twenty-two letters) and the "231 gates" (the combinations of the letters) might be intended as thaumaturgy or magical knowledge. When the sages said that Bezalel had employed combinations of letters to create the original *menorah*, they might have intended to say that Bezalel's skills went beyond mere artistry. They might have implied that the artist employed magic. Indeed, as far back as the Talmud, the sages claimed that it was literally possible to use the *Sefer Yetzirah* as a manual for magic:

> Rabbi Hanina and Rabbi Oshaia spent every Sabbath eve studying the *Sefer Yetzirah*, by means of which they created a three-year-old calf which they ate. [Sanhedrin 65b]

That is, if one knows the precise combinations, one can use language and mathematics to create even higher order living things. As part of this formulation, *Sefer Yetzirah* specifically notes that not only the ten numbers and the Hebrew alphabet must be combined in the act of creation, it is also necessary to call on God's names. This is familiar territory to the *Merkabah* mystics who were accustomed to using God's names in their magical practices. One magic technique they employed was known as "donning the Name." The magician prepared a special robe, weaving the name of God into its warp and woof, then ritually garbed himself in the garment so that he would be impregnated with God's power.[7] Whether this was done to gain esoteric knowledge—the secrets of creation, the dimensions of God, the secret names that give control over all existing things—or to gain mastery over the secrets revealed in the Torah, it was obviously an instance of ritual magic. Despite the story told of Hanina and Oshaia, *Merkabah* mystics generally claimed to abjure magic, relegating it to extraordinary circumstances.

Nevertheless, as time and space distanced the *Sefer Yetzirah* from its point of origin, the temptation to use it as a manual for ritual magic met with less resistance. Some texts of the book even include introductions that suggest specific magical practices that might form an appropriate "celebration" for the student completing a study of *Sefer Yetzirah*. So the possibility also exists that *Sefer Yetzirah* was intended as a manual for those who wished to purposely manipulate creation. And even if this were not its original intention, it became one of the purposes to which the book was put in the course of time.

The emerging mysticism of the Jews of the Rhineland was built upon *Sefer Yetzirah* utilizing its every possible purpose. Even the idea of mysticism itself was altered by this new approach.

❄

In ancient times, the term *mystic* was used to describe an initiate of the Greek mystery religions. As we use it now, it means any person who seeks direct immediate contact with the numinous. Almost every major religion harbors some form of mysticism, and no two forms are identical since each relies upon its own religious orientation. Historian Robert Seltzer states this general rule as it refers to the Jews:

> When Jewish mystics ... experienced a falling away of the mundane world, revealing an omnipresent spiritual reality, they did so in terms derived from the Jewish religious tradition.[8]

It is fair to say mystics of all ages partake of a common goal while maintaining predefined expectations of where that goal may lead. They share another important trait as well; they almost always conceive of themselves as inheritors of some secret knowledge who bear the responsibility for transmitting that knowledge to the next generation of mystics.

This poses a somewhat oxymoronic difficulty: The desire to share mystical knowledge is an imperative on one side of the equation while the desire to maintain the secrecy of mystical knowledge is equally imperative on the other side. In the end, efforts to keep secret knowledge from falling into the wrong hands—the hands of the evil or the unprepared—can sometimes be *too* successful. As times change, and, especially in the case of the Jews, as people move from place to place, the chain of transmission may at times be broken. Later generations often find themselves unable to reconstruct the mystic beliefs and practices of former ages. The secrets of the ancient Greek mystery religions, for example, were so well guarded that today we know little about them. Most mystical traditions leave few written texts.

Among Jews, however, literacy and reverence for the written word combine to create a peculiar effect. Jewish mystics have always composed vast numbers of written texts which in turn have been lovingly reproduced and circulated often with extensive commentary. This process ensured that the texts of Jewish mysticism would be handed on from generation to generation alongside verbal transmissions. In this sense, Jewish mysticism may be said to be somewhat less secretive than other mystic traditions. Yet even with these written texts, we are not always able to reconstruct the practices employed by the mystics. Nor do we always comprehend the original intent of the texts themselves. Indeed, mystic texts are often intentionally ambiguous as we have noted in the case of *Sefer Yetzirah*.

As far as we know, the practice of the *Merkabah* mystics was aimed at bodily experiences—journeys to the heavens to encounter God's throne as Ezekiel had, attempts to enter God's chariot as Elijah had, and perhaps even hopes to be transmuted to angelic form as Enoch had. By what means did the practitioners hope to achieve these bodily travels? Other cultures, as is well known, have made use of nature's pharmaceuticals for this kind of purpose. While hallucinogenic substances were known and used in ancient times, and while the *Merkabah* mystics may have utilized drinks brewed from mushrooms or preparations made from poppies, there is no direct mention of this. Even if mind-altering substances were employed, they clearly never became a central element of Jewish mystic practice. Descriptions of the sages' journeys speak instead of lengthy spates of solitude during which food and drink were taken sparingly, if at all. Prayers and incantations—employed mantra-like—were recited to transport the worldly body to ecstasy. By whatever means, the more fervent and adept the mystic, the more likely he was to be transported.

Long hours of study prepared the mystic for what would be discovered on the journey. Some aspect of the experience was expected to be unique to the individual, yet all mystics anticipated similar experiences: entering the palaces of heaven, meeting angels, persuading angels to let them pass from one heaven to another through the use of secret names and memorized formulae, and so on. Those who were most adept could expect to actually "descend" to the chariot. Some might perceive the dimensions of God's limbs. A few might not return from the journey or might return so changed in character that their lives would be remade by what they had encountered.

By the tenth century, the expectation that a Jewish mystic might bodily enter heaven had evidently receded. The texts of the *Merkabah* mystics had survived, but their practical purpose had been altered. This change seems to have taken place gradually. Toward the end of the talmudic period, the *Shi'ur Komah*— the measuring of the limbs of God's body—had become a metaphorical contemplation rather than a real encounter. In a similar fashion throughout the centuries, the teachings of the *Sefer Yetzirah* were received in metaphorical terms. This process of alteration was abetted by the proliferation of commentaries, the traditional Jewish approach to texts. Thus, as *Sefer Yetzirah* was physically transported from Palestine to Babylonia and thence to Italy, Spain, North Africa, and the Rhine, it was elaborated in each new place with the view of the scholars who were themselves being transplanted. The version of *Sefer Yetzirah* received in *Ashkenaz* seems to have come directly from Baghdad via Italy.

When it reached them, the Jews of *Ashkenaz* were under the influence of a Christianity that viewed holiness in monastic terms and a feudal government that encouraged personal rather than national loyalties. It was natural for the Jews to develop a mysticism that partook of both these characteristics—one that encouraged asceticism and reveled in the cult of personalities. By the twelfth century, these tendencies had prepared the way for three individuals—all members of the Kalonymus family—to dominate the mystical thinking of all German Jewry and to command the loyalty of a kind of loosely organized cult. All three of them celebrated *hasidut*, "piety," a concept that led to a movement in Hasmonean times but was now redefined. The first of the three was Samuel ben Kalonymus of Speyer, referred to as Samuel *HeHasid* ("the Pious"). The second, Samuel's son, was Judah *HeHasid* ("the Pious," circa 1150-1217) of Regensburg. And the third, Eleazar of Worms (1165-1230), a relative and student of Judah the Pious.

Samuel and Judah were called "the Pious" by their disciples because it was believed that they embodied the precepts of this new mystical movement. Their followers called themselves *Hasidim* ("Pious Ones") and we refer to them as *Hasidei Ashkenaz*, "The Pious Ones among the Northerners." (They should not be confused with modern *Hasidim* even though some of the ideas of *Hasidei Ashkenaz* were later adopted by modern *Hasidism*.) The term, *Hasid*, was used from early talmudic times to describe a person who went beyond the law to draw particularly close to God. For example, in the defining statement from *Pirkei Avot*, "The Sayings of the Elders":

> There are four types among people: the one who says, "What is mine is mine and what is yours is yours"—this is the common type, while some say that this is the type of Sodom; the one who says, "What is mine is yours and what is yours is mine"—this is the uneducated person; the one who says, "What is mine is yours and what is yours is yours"—this is the *Hasid*; and the one who says, "What is yours is mine and what is mine is mine"—this is the wicked person. [5:10]

"What is mine is yours and what is yours is yours"—this ultimate altruism of the *Hasid* as depicted in the Mishnah becomes only a point of departure for the concept of *Hasidism* among the Jews of the Rhineland. The mystical qualities that they combined with this altruism came from a unique brew of scholarship and superstition. First, there was the popular mysticism in the Christian society of their time. Judah the Pious, the greatest single figure of the *Hasidei Ashkenaz*, was a contemporary of St. Francis of Assisi. This is not to say that a direct relationship existed because these figures participated simultaneously in mystic movements. As one scholar aptly noted, "Mysticism was in the air, and its seeds fell on fertile soil both among Jews and Christians."[9]

Mysticism might be "in the air," but the *Hasidei Ashkenaz* had a head start. Ironically, the spread of Jewish mysticism was aided by the Christian conqueror, Charlemagne, a man who could barely write his own name. Charlemagne had fallen under the influence of Alcuin, a monk who taught the emperor a deep respect for literacy. In 787, anxious to attract scholars to his realm, Charlemagne convinced members of the outstanding Italian Kalonymus family to found an academy in the German city of Mainz. Ten years later, Charlemagne initiated a cultural exchange with the Caliph of Baghdad, Harun al-Rashid. As part of this exchange, the Caliph sent a Jewish talmudist, Rabbi Machir, who established an academy in Narbonne in the south of France. Study of Talmud in the Rhineland had its beginnings in these migrations. Close connections—particularly to the Jewish scholars of Italy—were maintained by the Jews in France and Germany who became the recipients of the renaissance of *Merkabah* mysticism. Jewish mystic texts and teachings were transmitted from Baghdad and seized the Jews of Italy around the tenth century.

By the eleventh century, some of the *Tosafists*, the immediate disciples of Rashi, practiced mystical rites based on *Merkabah* texts. In his commentary on *Sefer Yetzirah* composed in the first half of the thirteenth century, Elhanan ben Yakar of London speaks of having studied mysticism with the *Tosafists* in Northern France. One of his students, Ezra "the Prophet" of Montcontour, was known throughout *Ashkenaz* as both a visionary and a wonder-worker. It was reputed that he heard God's voice speaking to him from the clouds and that he made several ascents to heaven. At one point, this Ezra announced that the Messianic era would commence in 1226 and be fully realized by 1240 (the year 5000 in the Jewish calendar). Such predictions were atypical among the *Ashkenazim,* but then, so was Ezra the Prophet.

The *Hasidei Ashkenaz* even turned rational Jewish philosophy into mystic fodder. We know, for example, that they had access to *The Book of Philosophic Doctrines and Religious Beliefs* written by the Babylonian sage, Saadia Gaon (882-942). Saadia had written in Arabic to instruct Jews of his time who were already deficient in Hebrew, but by 1186 his work appeared in a paraphrased Hebrew translation that softened its strict philosophic reasoning by adding poetic flourish and quasi-mystical language. In fact, the Jews of the Rhineland—reading only the Hebrew paraphrase—considered Saadia among the great mystics. (A student of Eleazar of Worms even wrote a commentary on the *Sefer Yetzirah* and attributed it to Saadia Gaon probably to gain credibility.) Moreover, from the little that filtered to them of the philosophy and poetry of their co-religionists in Spain, the *Hasidei Ashkenaz* inherited Neoplatonic ideas commingled with mystic strains. To these influences, they added their own studies of early Jewish magic and huge dollops of credence in ancient German superstitions regarding witches and demons.

It is plain to see that no rational system could possibly account for these diverse influences. Many traditions co-existed, their individual importance waning and gaining from time to time. So, for example, when Eleazar of Worms in his books speaks of a "philosopher," he uses the term in the sense employed in Medieval Latin works to mean an "alchemist" or "occultist."[10] Perhaps the most remarkable thing about this strange admixture of superstitious psychology and mythological mystic tendencies—especially in light of the sufferings the Jews were undergoing as a result of the Crusades—was that (the prediction of Ezra of Montcontour notwithstanding) there was no general belief in the imminence of the Final Judgment. They simply did not believe that the world was going to end tomorrow. Instead, the *Hasidei Ashkenaz* stressed the singular splendor of the eventual End of Days and sought comfort in the knowledge that those who were martyred immediately were among the eternally blessed.

The life of the *Hasidei Ashkenaz* centered in personal cults surrounding three pivotal figures. The life of the first, Samuel the Pious, is shrouded in mystery. We know little about him save that he was born in Speyer and authored a treatise that, in his son's hands, became the early chapters of the *Sefer Hasidim* ("The Book of the Pious"). The rest must be gleaned from legends of his devotion and of his ability to work wonders. The titles he was accorded—"the Pious," "the Saint," "the Prophet"—indicate the high esteem in which Samuel was held; indeed, the *Hasidim* regarded Samuel as their founder much as George Washington is reputed to have been the father of his country. Nevertheless, the movement only reached its peak under his son, Judah.

Judah the Pious, born and raised in Speyer, relocated to Regensburg. Like his father, his contemporaries recorded few details of his life. Nevertheless, he became the subject of legend even in his lifetime. His learning extended to writing, but he insisted on authoring his books anonymously. Some of his recipes for practical magic have survived along with a brief book, *Sod HaYichud* ("The Secret of [God's] Unity"). His masterwork, *Sefer HaKavod* ("The Book of the Divine Glory"), exists today only in profuse quotations in the works of other authors. The work for which Judah is most remembered—the work which gave form to the *Hasidism* of his time and simultaneously left us the most complete picture of the everyday life of the Jews of the Rhine—was the *Sefer Hasidim*.

The third influential figure of the *Hasidei Ashkenaz* was Eleazar of Worms. Born in Mainz, his pursuit of knowledge led him to many centers of learning both in Germany and northern France. Though he later praised many of his teachers, he was above all the self-proclaimed disciple of his relative, Judah the Pious. Unlike his two predecessors, Eleazar was a prolific writer and bequeathed us a detailed and vivid picture of his life in his writings.

When Jerusalem fell to Saladin in 1187, angry Crusaders took revenge in a new outbreak of persecutions against the Jews in Europe. Eleazar was severely injured in one attack, and his wife and two children were murdered. Eleazar included accounts of these terrors in several of his books and memorialized his lost family in both story and poem. Looking back at the waves of Crusader persecution since 1096, Eleazar came to believe that *Ashkenazic* Jewry was a community bound for imminent destruction and that all chains of oral tradition would be broken by its disappearance. In the introduction to *Sefer Ha-Hochma* ("The Book of Wisdom"), which Eleazar wrote on the occasion of the death of Judah the Pious in 1217, he states that the only effective means for passing on the heritage of the *Hasidic* movement was through the written word.

It was this sense of desperation that set Eleazar apart from Samuel and Judah. They had hoped that the examples of their lives and the repetition of their oral teachings would speak for them. By contrast, in the face of the renewed depredations, Eleazar became fierce in his efforts to leave behind an accurate record of his life and learning. (In short, he was much like today's Holocaust survivors.) Inevitably, though, like Samuel and Judah, Eleazar was also destined to become a figure of legend.

Eleazar wrote in many fields. His *Sefer HaRoke'ach* ("The Herbalist's Book") became a standard text for many generations by explaining law and ritual in simple terms. His poems, composed in the unique style of the *Hasidei Ashkenaz*, are full of mystic nuance and strike an oddly modern note by including protest against God for the sufferings of the Jews and sometimes even call for revenge against the crusaders. He wrote poetry and brief commentaries on the Torah and the Talmud though most of these writings are lost to us. Fortunately, his commentary on the prayer book is extant and reveals some of the methods used by the *Hasidei Ashkenaz* to connect prayer to the Divine.

Above all these, Eleazar's masterwork in mysticism was the five-volume *Sodei Razaya*, "Secrets of Secrets." The first part, heavily influenced by *Sefer Yetzirah* and liberally citing the works of the *Merkabah* mystics, discusses the world's creation based on the twenty-two letters of the Hebrew alphabet—the secrets of the heavens, the elements, the stars, the earth, and so on. The second part, based on the work of the early mystics but relying heavily on the work of Saadia, deals with secrets of the Divine Chariot: the Holy Throne, the angels, the voice of God, how God is revealed to the prophets, and the meaning of prophecy in general. The third part examines the meaning of God's many names. The fourth part deals with the ways in which the human soul may be connected to the Divine—inspiration, dreams, life after death, and so on. The fifth part is a commentary on *Sefer Yetzirah* that, among other things, contains detailed instructions for using the magic in *Sefer Yetzirah* to create a *golem* (humanoid).

It is already possible from this brief account of the three sages and their works to see how the movement of the *Hasidei Ashkenaz* emerged. But no account would give the proper impression without some taste of the legends that came to surround them especially since it is in the legends that we perceive how closely mysticism and magic were linked in the popular mind. The following two brief examples—a cautionary tale from his childhood and a duel with other magi—are among the legends told about Samuel:

> Once upon a time Rabbi Samuel the Pious went to a mill to grind the Passover wheat for his father Rabbi Kalonymus, and while he was in the mill grinding the wheat, there was a cloudburst and the waters rose so high that the asses could not carry the flour home without getting it wet and unfitting it for the use of Passover. Rabbi Samuel was very much vexed and at first did not know what to do. Then he made use of the mystical name of God and there appeared a huge lion, bigger than a camel. He put the sack of flour on the back of the lion, sat down on the top, and thus rode through the water on the lion's back until he came home to his father's house.
>
> When his father saw him coming home on the lion, he understood that his son must have used the sacred name. So he grew very angry and said to him: "You have committed a grave sin in having created the lion by means of the mystical name, and as a punishment for this great sin you will never have any children." Rabbi Samuel was very much grieved, for he did not know that he had committed so grave a sin. Two days later he went to his father again and said to him: "Dear father, you say that I have committed a grave sin, I pray you to impose a penance upon me and I will gladly accept it." Then his father said to him: "Dear son, the penance which I ought to impose upon you would be far too heavy and you would not be able to carry it out." The son replied: "Dear father, I will do everything that you impose upon me." The father said: "My dear son, if you desire to receive atonement for the sin which you have committed, you must wander continuously for seven years, and must never stop more than one night in the same place, except on Sabbath and festivals. If you carry out this penance properly, I assure you that your sin will be forgiven, and you will have pious children." So he took the penance upon himself and wandered for seven years uninterruptedly, spending his time in study as an exile. Some say that he spent nine years as an exile so as to make up for the Sabbaths and festivals.[11]

> One day three priests from foreign lands came to see Rabbi Samuel the Pious, for they had heard that he was a very remarkable man. Informing him that they were able to perform magic with the aid of evil spirits, they said: "We have heard much of your skill and wonderworking in all the countries through which we have

passed. We therefore ask you to show us your clever tricks and we will show you our own, which are greater than yours...."

Now there lived at that time in another place a great man called Rabbi Jacob, who had in his possession a book belonging to Rabbi Samuel. So he said to the priests: "If you can conjure an evil spirit to carry a letter from me to Rabbi Jacob, asking him to send me the book, I will believe you to be great masters of the art." The priests replied: "We have come here to honor you; therefore we will show you a greater wonder than this." Then they said to him: "Come, let us go out into the open country to a secret place and there you will see a very wonderful thing. One of us will draw a circle and the other companions will conjure his soul to leave his body, take the letter from your hand, carry it to Rabbi Jacob, and bring you his answer together with your book, just as you have requested us to do. The man whose soul has left him, will not leave the spot for three days. But will remain lying still within the circle until the three days are over, then the soul will return to the body, which will become alive and healthy again."

... So they went back to the town, and on the third day the two priests said to Rabbi Samuel: "Now let us go again to the field and there you will see how the soul will re-enter the body of our companion." The pious man went with them to the field but by his art made it so that the soul, when it came back, was not able to re-enter the dead body.

When the two priests saw that the corpse would not rise again, but lay there like any other corpse, they raised a great lamentation for their companion and mourned bitterly for him. The pious man then said: "If you will acknowledge that I can do more than you, I will make the soul enter the body again as before." So, they both fell at his feet and begged him in God's name to bring their companion to life again. They were glad, they said, to acknowledge that he was a greater master than they. Then the pious man conjured the evil spirit to cause the soul to re-enter the body, and instantly the man stood up alive and gave the pious man the letter as well as the book which he had missed for a long time. The priests thanked the pious man and went their way, saying that his art was even greater than the reputation of it in foreign lands.[12]

Lengthy tales are told of how Samuel and Judah manage to avert "evil decrees" against the Jews. In these stories, the pious ones intuit that the community is about to be attacked, then perform some magical act of penance or prowess to prevent the

attack. Tales are also told of how, through their piety and for-
bearance, they cause important figures in the Christian community to respect them and even in some cases to convert to
Judaism. The following legend featuring Rabbi Judah reads like
an episode from a television mystery series and combines many
of the most recurring themes:

Story of what happened in Regensburg. Two builders worked in
the house of a Jew in the Jewish street. During their work they noticed a large quantity of silver and gold in one of the rooms. Ac-
cordingly, they plotted to get into the chamber while the Jews
were absent in the synagogue and take everything away. And so
they did. They entered the chamber and took many articles of silver and gold. Then one of the builders said to himself: "What do I
want a partner for? I can do the job myself." So he took a hammer
and when the other fellow was getting out of the hole, he
knocked him on the head, and he fell back into the chamber
dead. Then he took all the silver and the gold from the dead man
and ran away. All the while the Jews were in the synagogue.

When they returned home, the master of the house found the
dead body in his house. They were very much frightened and
wanted to remove the corpse outside the gate of the town, for
they feared that a crowd might gather, as indeed happened. For
the rumor spread in the Christian street that the Jews had murdered the Christian. Thereupon a large crowd of Christians came
running into the Jewish Street and were about to begin rioting.
Then R. Judah the Pious came along and went straight to the
mayor of the town and said to him: "Sir, what are you going to do?
Will you allow so many people to be killed for the sake of one
man, when you know well enough that we are not guilty? Two men
were working in the house, and I can prove to you that one of
them killed the other." Then the mayor said: "If you can prove
what you say, no harm will befall any of you." And he gave orders
that the people in the Street should remain quiet. Then R. Judah
said: "Close the gates, so that the murderer shall not be able to
escape." This was immediately done. Then the pious man wrote a
charm with holy names on it and placed it in the hands of the
dead man. The dead man rose up, turned around and saw the
murderer hiding behind another man. So he ran up to him and
said: "You murderer, you killed me so that you should have the
stolen property all to yourself. You struck me in the head with a
hammer and I fell back into the chamber." The murderer was
arrested, thrown into prison immediately, and condemned to

death and executed. Then the pious man said to the mayor: "You see, if I had not stopped you, you would have shed much innocent blood." The mayor "Quite true; therefore, my dear master, forgive me for such a thing. It shall not happen again. In the future I shall first try to find the true facts."

The man who had been killed had many rich friends, who offered a great deal of money to Rabbi Judah and begged him to let the man live. But Rabbi Judah had no such intention, for he said he was not allowed to do it. He took the charm away from the man who had been killed and he fell down again and lay dead like any other corpse. The mayor was very good to R. Judah after that.[13]

The legendary lives of the three central figures of *Hasidism* portray them in roles and with attributes that the community sorely needed. They are Superman in Metropolis constantly saving the day and rewarding the righteous. They can even travel "faster than a speeding bullet," for it was said of Eleazar of Worms that he rode a cloud wherever he needed to go, especially in order to be in attendance at the circumcision of each new male child throughout all of *Ashkenaz*. Before we dismiss such legends as mere wish fulfillment, however, it is important to note that ordinary individuals aspired to the kind of piety achieved by the masters in order that they too might aid the community. For it was piety, *hasidut*, that lay at the very heart of this new brand of Jewish mysticism.

The piety that the *Hasidei Ashkenaz* sought was, to them, a greater virtue than either tradition or scholarship. The true *Hasid* was a person who had renounced the things of this world, who had risen to a sublime state of equanimity of spirit, and who had set self aside before the needs of others.

To renounce the things of this world meant, in practice, to prepare oneself for *Kiddush HaShem*, martyrdom. Though it sounds deeply pessimistic, a certain practicality inheres in it, for the times were hazardous and life expectancy was directly related to the changing whims and fortunes of the church. The world seemed a dark place; hope seemed an elusive dream. Eleazar gave voice to this kind of reasoning when he compared a person with a rope. God holds one end, he said, and Satan holds the other, and the person is constantly stretched between them as they pull. In the end, he adds, God's pull is stronger.[14] *Sefer Hasidim* calls this *azivut derech eretz*, "leaving the normal life"—including averting one's eyes from persons of the opposite sex, refraining from playing with children, refraining from the keeping of pets, refraining from the use of strong language—in short, refraining from innocent pleasures of all kinds. The strength gained through such detachment helps one to prepare for the inevitability of separating from this world and oddly enough, for the anticipated splendor of the afterlife.

Equanimity is defined for the *Hasid* as the real imitation of God. It is a foregone conclusion that the fate of a person in this world is to be insulted and reviled at every turn, but the one who bears this burden is worthy of eternal bliss. The *Hasidim* were fond of quoting the verse from Isaiah which states: "I have kept silent from of old, kept still and restrained myself" [42:14]. And the verse from Psalms: "It is for Your sake that we are slain all day long, that we are regarded as sheep to be slaughtered" [44:23]. Somewhat perversely, the extreme piety which is exhibited in ignoring slander and in not responding to insult often provokes greater violence and leads more directly to martyrdom. The *Hasidim* spoke of this as the price one had to pay for devotion.

The principle of setting self aside, of altruism, was of equal importance. The *Sefer Hasidim* describes it as:

> The essence of *hasidut* is to act in all things not on but within the line of strict justice—that is to say, not to insist in one's own interest on the letter of the Torah: for it is said of God, whom the *Hasid* strives to follow [Psalms 145:17], "God is *Hasid* in all his ways."

The usual translation of *Hasid* in this verse from Psalms is "kind" or "merciful." But the translation understood by the *Hasidim* is more likely "self-abnegating" since the ideal of the *Hasid* was one who, in pursuit of aiding the community, set aside even the common strictures of Jewish law. Thus, the *Hasidim* actually claim to answer to a "higher authority" than the Torah itself, for their altruism demands that they pay heed to a law of heaven which is only minimally recognized by ordinary human beings and which even goes beyond what the sages of the Talmud recorded as the necessary obligations of the Jewish individual. This higher law is only binding on the *Hasidim* and it is taken up on a voluntary basis.

An interesting aside may be mentioned here. In his code of Jewish law, *Sefer HaRoke'ach*, Eleazar of Worms added a chapter explaining the special behavior of *Hasidim*. In doing so, he went beyond setting forth the traditional principles of Jewish law. He also showed how these principles might be "reformed." Without exaggeration, Eleazar meant to carry out an undeclared revolution in Jewish law. His revolution succeeded only partially even in its own time. Nevertheless, the tendency to reform legal thinking continued to mark German Jewry from that time forth; in fact, it was in the bosom of this community in the nineteenth century that what we now call Reform and Conservative Judaism were born.

The three elements of piety—renouncing the worldly, seeking equanimity of spirit, and subordinating self to others—combine to lead a person to a state of bliss. For the *Hasid*, even the performance of God's laws is an act of pure devotion:

> The soul is full of love of God and bound with ropes of love, in joy and lightness of heart. He is not like one who serves his master unwillingly, but even when one tries to hinder him, the love of service burns in his heart, and he is glad to fulfill the will of his Creator ... For when the soul thinks deeply about the fear of God, then the flame of heartfelt love bursts in it and the exultation of innermost joy fills the heart ... And the lover thinks not of his advantage in the world, he does not care about the pleasures of his wife or of his sons and daughters, but all this is as nothing to him, everything except that he may do the will of his Creator, do good unto others, keep sanctified the name of God ... And all the contemplation of his thoughts burns in the fire of love for Him.[15]

The *Hasidim* never considered abstaining from marriage and sexual love. Except for this, their ideals paralleled the ideals of Christian monks of the same era. They denied themselves the world to devote themselves to the passionate love of God. By the same token, their extremism was unusual in Jewish terms. The normative ideal Jew was one who carried out God's commands as found in Jewish law (*halachah*). The *Hasidim* held a rather unique view of the ideal Jew's performance of Jewish law.

For the *Hasidim*, to carry out one particular *mitzvah* or commandment with scrutiny throughout one's lifetime was considered to be the insignia of the true *Hasid*. Quoting from the paraphrase of Saadia relied upon by the Jews of the Rhine: one "who all his life devotes himself to one particular religious commandment" is to be praised, while "one who wavers from one day to another between the various commandments is not called a *Hasid*."[16] Individuals who had devoted themselves to a single commandment were not unknown in Jewish history, but for an entire community to devote itself to this as an ideal was a hitherto alien form of extremism. Among the *Hasidei Ashkenaz*, it became a truism that only by adhering to a chosen single commandment could a *Hasid* be deserving of (and capable of) all that the Kingdom of Heaven could provide including prophesy, wonderworking, and magic.

Magic, too, played an essential role in the inner workings of *Hasidism*. In his schema, Judah the Pious drew a distinction between the magician and the *Hasid*. The magician, he argued, seeks to control the forces which change the world while the *Hasid* submits fully to God and thereby induces God to work wonders on his behalf. In this sense, the *Hasid* is the true magician for his magic is not achieved through intermediaries such as demons or through tricks or sleight of hand. As we noticed in one of the legends of Samuel cited above, the true magic always resided with Samuel. The other magicians could only conjure, relying upon the limited control that non-believers confuse with true power.

In practice, however, the barrier between the magician and the *Hasid* was little more than a semi-permeable membrane. Magic is pervasive throughout the *Hasidic* system. In the legends about them, the three central figures are each portrayed as great magicians. In their writings, they transmit all kinds of magical formulae—making little or no distinction between these and their ethical teachings. True, they expect their works only to be read by the morally upright, and they expect that the magic can only be accomplished by the pure of spirit, yet the same can be said of the qualifications expected in almost all guilds of magicians in almost all cultures. For the *Hasidei Ashkenaz*, magic and mysticism were entirely intertwined, a fact which led to some amazing possibilities. For example, among the magical recipes of Eleazar of Worms is one which Gershom Scholem refers to as "the quintessential product of the spirit of

German Jewry,"[17] the recipe for the creation of the *golem*. In Eleazar's formula, the *golem* was produced through the resources found in *Sefer Yetzirah*: the manipulation of the letters of the alphabet and the names of God. Once produced, it was sustained by the ecstatic state of its human creator. As long as the ecstasy of the magician was sustained, the *golem* retained its power.

The idea of the *golem* exercised a fierce hold on the imagination of German Jewry even as the idea of Frankenstein's monster continues to intrigue us today. The notion that a human Superman could create an even more powerful non-human Super-Superman was so reassuring that it was simply mind-boggling. As later versions of the recipe attest, the *golem* eventually became a separate entity no longer reliant, even for spiritual sustenance, upon the human who brought it into being.

As the ultimate formulation of magic, the creation of the *golem* stands in a direct line with ideas which emerged in primitive human societies, continued in ancient Mesopotamia and Egypt, extended through every layer of the Bible, and denoted the work of the *Merkabah* mystics. The point in all cases—in magic, as in religion, as in mysticism—is the miracle of transformation (in this case, bringing something into being which was not there a moment before).

In addition to magical incantations to heal the sick and the wounded or to protect the weak from demons and evil spirits, the *Hasidic* mystics practiced magic through prayer in rituals that remain somewhat baffling to this day. They developed a method for counting each word and letter of the traditional prayers in order to unveil the secret powers that *Sefer Yetzirah* led them to believe were hidden in the words. Techniques later attributed to Kabbalistic circles first appear in the work of these mystic mathematicians. Relying on the fact that each Hebrew letter represents a numerical value, they used the ancient system of *gematria*—counting the value of a word or phrase and showing its equivalence to another word or phrase. Eleazar developed mystical meditations on traditional prayers which the

Hasid could evoke during the actual repetition of the words. He uses *gematria* throughout his revelation of the "Secrets of Secrets" to unravel the great mysteries of the world and its Creation, of the Divine Chariot, and of the angels. He enhances *gematria* by applying it to entire verses. For example, he sums the numerical value of the verse from Song of Songs (6:11), "I have gone down into the nut garden," and proves it equivalent to "This is the depth of the Chariot." The uninitiated might read the verse and understand its literal meaning, the better educated might understand its metaphorical meaning, but only the mystic could read the verse *and* contemplate its secret meaning. Since Hebrew is the language of God and Creation, it was reasoned that the secrets revealed using *gematria* were not at all accidental; they only awaited discovery.

The *Hasidim* also made use of a technique called *temurah*, the interchange of the letters of a word according to a set of predefined principles. The term *temurah* means "exchange," and it is the name of a tractate of the Talmud in which the use of "alternative readings" created through the transposition of letters in a word occur frequently. This transposition could result in the revelation of secrets though it was used far less frequently by the *Hasidei Ashkenaz* than *gematria* for the simple reason that the entire system of counting to reveal secrets was based on the reliability of the texts of the Bible and the prayer book. If they were indeed accurate renderings, then (so it was reasoned) the transposition of characters to reveal secrets could only be an interesting sidelight, not a source of major revelation.

More closely related to *gematria* is *notarikon*, a technique often employed by the *Hasidim*. The term *notarikon* literally means "device." In this technique, words are represented in a kind of shorthand—by one or more of their letters—according to a fixed set of rules. In fact, the term, *notarikon* derives from the use of shorthand by the *notarii*, the stenographers of the ancient Roman court system. In one kind of *notarikon*, each letter of a single word is taken to represent the first letter of an entire sentence. To use a well-known example from the Talmud, the first word of the Ten Commandments, *Anochi*, consisting of the four letters *alef, nun, kaf, yud*, meaning, "I," is taken to represent four words that make the verse, "I Myself wrote and gave [these commandments]."[18] At times, a word was broken into parts to reveal its hidden meaning as when mystics divided the first word of the Bible, "In the beginning" (*bereishit*), into two words (*bara sheit*) which then meant "created in six primordial [days]." The *Hasidei Ashkenaz* applied *notarikon* to the interpretation of prayers, Bible, and synagogal poetry (*piyyutim*). Again, the faithful understood that such hidden meanings had been implanted in the Hebrew purposefully, and they contemplated these secret truths as they recited the literal words.

The *Hasidei Ashkenaz* created "a cult of the prayer book which fondled its every phrase, counted every word, played kabbalistic games with the letters, and left a library of some seventy-three volumes of commentary [on the liturgy]."[19] In weighing the words, they discovered that Psalm 136 (recited on the Sabbath and festivals in the morning service) contains twenty-six repetitions of the phrase, "for God's mercy endures forever." Since this number corresponded exactly to the numerical value of God's four-letter name, *YHWH*, the psalm contained extraordinary holiness for them. They instituted the ritual of rising for this prayer to honor God's name. A congregational response uttered in Aramaic during the prayer called the *Kaddish*—"Let God's great name be praised for ever and ever"—contained seven words and totaled twenty-eight letters which they discovered to be the same number of words and letters contained in the Bible's first verse. This persuaded them that one who utters the response with true devotion becomes God's partner in creating the world. The examples that could be cited are vast almost beyond number.

Though such calculations may smack of sophistry to the modern mind, to the *Hasidei Ashkenaz* they were the precious truth of God's manifestation in the holy words and letters. This had the fortunate side effect of fixing the Jewish prayer ritual permanently and prohibiting any tampering with the words as the Jews of the Rhine received them. From that time forward, "any change, accidental or deliberate, would disturb the established count and would immediately reveal that an error had crept into the text."[20] In short, they considered the prayer book very nearly as sacred as the Bible itself.

Merkabah mystics had sought to reach heaven in a physical way, but the *Hasidei Ashkenaz* plotted a new sensibility that depended on the spirit rising through contemplation of the mysteries in prayer. The *Merkabah* mystics had created a new verbal system to enable them to reach the level of angels, but the *Hasidei Ashkenaz* rooted their mysticism in pious devotion to the words fixed by tradition. How did this work in practice? Even with all the texts available to us, we have scant knowledge of the mystic ritual itself; the best we can do is to infer it from an account given by one of its critics:

> They set themselves up as prophets by practicing the pronunciation of holy names, or sometimes they only direct their intention upon them without actually pronouncing the words. Then a man is seized by terror and his body sinks to the ground. The barrier in front of his soul falls, he himself steps into the center and gazes into the faraway, and only after a while, when the power of the name recedes, does he awaken and return with a confused mind to his former state. This is exactly what the magicians do who practice the exorcism of the demons. They conjure one from their midst with unclean exorcisms, in order that he may tell them what has perhaps been happening in a faraway country. The conjurer falls down on the ground where he was standing and his veins become cramped and stiff, and he is as one dead. But after a while he rises without consciousness and runs out of the house, and if one does not hold him at the door, he would break his head and his limbs. Then when he again becomes a little conscious of himself, he tells them what he has seen.[21]

Induced prophecies seem to have been as common in Jewish circles then as they were in Christian circles. Again we have a direct correlation between the way of life of the pious Jew and the Christian monk. Gershom Scholem cites the collection of "Responses from Heaven" by Jacob Halevi of Marvège that contains solutions to problems of Jewish law based on the answers to "dream questions." While many scholars discouraged the use of dream questions to legislate matters of law, the fact is that we have hundreds of magical recipes in the writings of the *Hasidei Ashkenaz* for inducing answers in dreams.

Having evidence that a combination of calculation and meditation on mystic secrets was used to achieve ecstasy in prayer, and that the ecstasy was in turn capable of revealing further secrets, does not quite complete the picture. A full correlation between the Jews and the community surrounding them required the development of another system hitherto unknown to the Jews—a systematic ritual of penitence.

❋

Penitence, the restitution the *Hasid* offered to God for insults and sins (real or imagined), ran the gamut from frequent fasting through various acts that might bring discomfort and pain to the sinner, to the ultimate self-inflicted punishment—voluntary exile from the community. *Sefer Hasidim* divides penitence into four categories. The first is refraining from committing the same sin when faced by the same set of circumstances. The second is placing restraints on the possibility of coming close to the same set of circumstances. For example, if the offense occurred in the north part of town, then in addition to abjuring the sin, the sinner might voluntarily refrain from ever entering the north part of town for any reason. The third involves inflicting a self-exile of enough duration to equal the amount of enjoyment gained through the sin. Fourth, if one transgressed a sin for which the Torah demanded death, then one must undergo tortures as bitter as death itself. As Scholem writes:

> In regard to these practices we have the evidence not only of the *Hasidic* writings, whose exhortations might be dismissed as belonging purely to the realm of theory, but also of a good many accounts of actual happenings through which the fame of the German *Hasidim* soon spread far and wide. These stories, of which there are many, leave no doubt about the spirit of fanatical earnestness which animated the zealots. To sit in the snow or in the ice for an hour daily in winter, or to expose one's body to ants and bees in summer, was judged a common practice among those who followed the new call. It is a far cry from the talmudic conception of penitence to these novel ideas and practices.[22]

Stories of the intensity of the punishments these penitents inflicted on themselves persisted for many centuries. It is told, for example, that when a scholar believed that he had accidentally washed clean a parchment containing the name of God, he punished himself by lying at the doorstep of the synagogue so that everyone entering to worship would be forced to pass over his body. When people would accidentally kick him or step on him, he rejoiced and praised God. Other mystics felt that their penitential sufferings were absolutely necessary since it was well known that the Messiah would be suffering until the time of his coming. Again, in contrast to their Christian neighbors, none of the penitential acts of the Jewish mystics, however severe, seem to have extended to abstinence in marital relations.

❀

The *Hasidei Ashkenaz* turned again and again to *Sefer Yetzirah* as a source for their philosophical thought. The idea that a wholly invisible and incorporeal God was able to emanate forth in ethers and created matter by means of numbers and letters led them to a new conception of God which, in some ways, bordered on pantheism.

> [God] is One in the cosmic ether, for He fills the whole ether and everything in the world, and nowhere is there a barrier before Him. Everything is in Him, and He sees everything, for He is entirely perception though He has no eyes, for He has the power to see the universe within His own being.[23]

In another way, the mystics drew from Saadia the idea that this unseen and omnipresent God had created a first light, a *Kavod* (the word literally means, "glory"), which can speak the words of God in God's voice. This *Kavod* was what was revealed to the prophets and mystics in its infinite variety of forms. Eleazar of Worms thus says that God does not speak but maintains silence while supporting the universe. Instead, God creates a vision of God to enable God to be revealed. This notion of a created emanation of God would have been entirely foreign to the *Merkabah* mystics. Judah the Pious wrestled with this concept in a slightly different way saying that God has both an inner and an outer glory. Human beings cannot communicate with the formless inner glory of God, but they can connect themselves to it and perceive the outer glory of God. This visible side was the God revealed to the prophets, the occupant of the *Merkabah* (the Chariot) in the vision of Ezekiel, and the body measured in the *Shi'ur Komah*. Perceiving the outer glory of God, the prophet is assured that his or her vision is the word of truth. According to Judah, demons—who can speak with human beings and might attempt to deceive the prophet—are powerless to produce the phenomena of the *Kavod*. Indeed, the perception of the *Kavod* is the true reward of the *Hasid*.

Coexisting with this notion of the *Kavod* on God's throne is the idea that one angel has been singled out or raised up to be the occupant of God's throne. This angel (the *cherub*) can take any form, human or beast. The *Hasidim* maintained that the human form of the *cherub* was, in fact, the actual image in which God created human beings. Whenever the Bible speaks of God in anthropomorphic terms, it is to this *cherub* that the reference refers. When the prophets speak of God, it is this *cherub* that they have perceived. When we call out in prayer to God the King, it is to this *cherub* that we address our call; however, the true intention of our prayers is to reach beyond this *cherub* to the hidden glory of God. It is obvious that these two perceptions—that of an inner and outer glory, and that of a *cherub*—are contradictory. Nevertheless, both were current without any noticeable sense of contradiction. In fact, the mystics of the Rhine also spoke of God's outer glory as the "Presence" or *Shekhinah* which they conceived of as an emanation of pure light, and in various places Eleazar states that prayer is specifically meant to reach the *Shekhinah*.

The *Hasidim* also believed that an ideal image of all things in the created world is spread on a curtain which surrounds God's throne on all sides but the western side, and they described this curtain as being constructed entirely of blue flame. When prophets foretell the future, they averred, it is through reading the placement of the ideal or archetypical images on the curtain.

❋

While the mystic philosophers worried about the emanations of God, the common folk depended on their ideal leaders, "the Pious Ones," to protect them from the demons that surrounded them on every side. The powerful demons discussed in the Talmud seldom worried the Jews of the Rhine. As they put it, the demons that concerned the people of Israel and Babylonia did not exist in these northern lands since "the nature of man has changed."[24]

Nevertheless, some traditionally "Jewish" demons continued to exercise an influence on the people. One such demon was *Lilith*, the demon who was consort to Adam. *Lilith*'s name actually derived from the Assyrian, *Lilitu*, and the Sumerian, *Lilla*, both feminine for "demon." The folk erroneously assumed *Lilith* to be related to the Hebrew word for "night," *lailah*. Female night demons were called by the plural, *liliot,* and were said to attack newborns and their mothers by night and to seduce men as they slept, causing nocturnal emissions which in turn became the source for hybrid demon-humans. Female night-demons were particularly potent against newborn boys until their eighth day (when they were circumcised) and girls until their

Page from *Sefer Raziel* with "angel writing"

Magical Squares: Numbers & Hebrew Letters as Numbers

twentieth day (for what reason we no longer know). A whole variety of remedies was used against *Lilith* and her demonic cohort.

New demons assailed the *Hasidei Ashkenaz*. An evil spirit called an *estrie* took the form of a woman living among the people of the community. A cross between a witch and a vampire-demon, she would attack children whenever possible but might on occasion also feast upon a fully-grown man or woman.

> A certain woman, who, it transpired, was an *estrie*, fell ill and was attended during the night by two women. When one of these fell asleep the patient suddenly arose from her bed, flung her hair wildly about her head, and made efforts to fly and to suck blood from the sleeping woman. The other attendant cried out in terror and aroused her companion; between the two of them they subdued the demon-witch and got her back into bed.[25]

The *estrie* and her close relation, the *broxa*, lived within the community to assure their proximity to a ready supply of human blood. If they were discovered, they would immediately die unless they were able to overcome and take the lifeblood of their discoverer. Yet even death was no guarantee. As Eleazar of Worms advises in his *Sefer HaRoke'ach*:

> When a *broxa* or *estrie* is being buried, one should notice whether or not her mouth is open; if it is, this is a sure sign that she will continue her vampirish activities for another year. Her mouth must be stopped up with earth and she will be rendered harmless.

More prevalent still was the sorcerer or demon who could become a wolf at will to frighten and attack human beings. This werewolf was a form of vampire that required human blood to continue its existence. Another source of fear inherited from the general society around them was the *mare*. This evil figure is described as a demon that rests on human beings while they sleep, keeping them from speaking by tightly holding their tongue and lips and causing them to breathe in fitful gasps. The *mare* is also said to be the cause of nightmares as still reflected in the use of this word in the English language (though it likely derives from the Middle French: *cauche mare*).

A recollection of the age-old worship of Teutonic goddesses seemingly became a Jewish tradition around this period. The goddess of fertility (Berchta or Perchta) was worshipped by women in rites that involved offering human hair. In time, the offering itself was replaced by the baking of braided bread, called *berchisbrod*, that resembled plaits of human hair. Jewish women along the Rhine imitated this style in preparing their loaves for the Sabbath offering, and the Sabbath *hallah* in *Ashkenaz* was called a *berches*, a word which well-suited the faithful who confused its etymology with the Hebrew word for "blessing," *berachah*. Jewish women may or may not have thought of Berchta as a goddess or demon, even while they may have sought the blessing of fertility through the braiding of the bread. In any case, whether in imitation of the ritual or of the baker's style, this tradition of braiding the Sabbath bread has subsequently spread to almost all lands where Jews live.

Judah the Pious and Eleazar of Worms write as piously about the ways of protecting oneself from demons as they do about the mystical contemplation of prayer. They recommend the use of various names of God as especially effective, and the more letters in the name the more powerful it seems to be. Against lesser demons, the four-letter name of God might suffice. The greater the evil, the more it called forth the use of a fourteen-letter name, a twenty-two-letter name (the same number of letters as the number of letters in the Hebrew alphabet), or even a mighty seventy-two-letter name of God. In addition, one was well advised to recite Psalm 91 prefaced with the last verse of Psalm 90, for this had proven efficacious as the "anti-demonic psalm." It is unclear if this was the psalm indicated as anti-demonic in the Talmud, and some scholars argued that Psalm 3 was to be preferred, but the *Hasidei Ashkenaz* generally accepted Psalm 91 as the more authentic weapon. Eleazar states that Psalm 91 is correct on the basis of the mystical names of God that it contains and because it includes 130 words (when the last phrase is repeated) indicating the number of years that Adam lived with Lilith and produced demons by her. It became the custom among the *Hasidim* to recite this psalm every night before falling asleep, and a few rabbis made it a point to recite the psalm even before taking a daytime nap. It was recited at funerals since it was well known that demons are more active when they are near the recently deceased, and it appeared in all kinds of anti-demonic magical formulae. Because the Hebrew letter *zayin* does not occur in Psalm 91, it was considered a protection against weapons since (by a play on words) the word *zayin* can be taken to mean "weapon."[26] One magical recipe suggested that release from prison involved reciting this psalm seventy-two times daily. It was further considered a potent charm against the dangers of crossing bridges. And as the learned master of German-Jewish folklore, Joshua Trachtenberg, adds:

> We have a report that during a *Rosh HaShanah* service in the city of Frankfort the *shofar* [ram's horn] refused to function; the remedy employed was to breathe the words of the *Shir shel Pega'im* ["anti-demonic psalm" = Psalm 91] three times into the wide opening of the ram's horn, whereupon its hoarse notes were restored. Satan had seated himself inside the horn and had impeded its call until dislodged by the charm![27]

With their emphasis on numbers derived from the *Sefer Yetzirah*, the *Hasidim* also placed great store in the efficacy of numbers in their magic. They were particularly fond of repetitions in threes and sevens, numbers that were already considered magical in ancient times. To these, they added a new belief in the potency of nine which probably derived from Germanic traditions. Demons were said to congregate in groups of nine. If one sees a demon, no mention must be made of the sighting for nine days; if one wishes to counteract a demon, it is best to count nine knots. One recipe for curing a person of demonic possession calls for nine pieces of wood from nine bridges at the gates of nine cities.

The custom arose for a bride to circle her groom seven times under the wedding canopy in order to scare off any demons that might be nearby (or alternately, it was explained as a means of magically tying the wedding "knot"). Conversely, a bride's hair was purposely left unbraided on her wedding day for fear that any knots might unintentionally capture unwanted demons. Imprecations against demons indicate the belief that they are susceptible to almost any suggestion of binding or knotting and easily fall prey to being tied up by words or gestures. Imagine how inconvenient it would be for a bride to loosen her hair on her wedding night only to discover that she had accidentally freed a bevy of demons to plague her and her bridegroom!

Among the *Hasidim* it was considered fortuitous to employ new things when attempting magic or working spells against demons. We sometimes hear of the necessity of having a garment woven by virgins or obtaining a new amulet from a miracle worker or scribe. A vestige of this may have come down to us in the tradition of having the bride possess something "new" on her wedding day. Of course, amulets were important on any day in any season, and letters or shapes were often worked into them, some of which were traditional even in the time of the Talmud. The *Ashkenazim* seem to have had a special affinity for the use of figures that combined lines ending in circle-tips as well as the use of the hexagram. Though it began not as a symbol of Judaism but as a symbol in magical circles known to magicians the world over, the hexagram has now become known as "the Star of David." A page from *Sefer Raziel*, first printed in the seventeenth century, illustrates the kinds of figures that were commonly used. The strange characters ending in open circles were called "angel writing" since the *Sefer Raziel* was reputed to be the dictation of the angel Raziel to an unknown scribe.

Another popular form for inscribing amulets was the so-called "magical square." In its simplest form, it consisted of a square divided into nine boxes each containing a number in such a way that the numbers total to the same sum whether they are read horizontally, vertically, or diagonally. We are not certain as to the derivation of the use of the magical square on amulets, but as we have already noted, the *Hasidim* had a special (almost religious) belief in the importance of numbers, so a square such as this has a built-in fascination. The nine-box variety was the most common, but examples also exist of magic squares that contained sixteen, twenty-five, thirty-six, or more boxes. Sometimes the numbers are represented by Hebrew letters. And the magic squares were also in widespread use among Christians. A Christian philosopher of the early sixteenth century claimed the magic squares were popular because of their astrological significance, but this is not necessarily so. For the Jews, it was probably more significant that the number at the center of the box was five which in Hebrew is represented by the letter *heh*, the same letter used in amulets to symbolize the four-letter name of God.

The amulet most cherished by the *Hasidei Ashkenaz* began its existence as a religious memorial. The *mezuzah* was affixed to the doorpost of a house where lamb's blood had protected the Jews from the angel of death at the time of the exodus from Egypt. The *mezuzah* (the word originally meant "doorpost") reminded Jews of God when entering or leaving the house. By Jewish law, the front side of the *mezuzah*'s parchment contains two passages from Deuteronomy (6:4-9 and 11:13-21) and nothing else. No laws governed the reverse side of the parchment, however, and in Babylonia the custom arose of inscribing it with the three-letter name of God, *Shaddai*, "Almighty." The three letters could be interpreted by *notarikon* as the phrase, *Sh'mor delatot Yisrael*, "Guardian of the doors of Israel." A hole was generally made in the *mezuzah* case to allow the word *Shaddai* to be seen after the tiny scroll was rolled and placed inside. This practice, condemned by many rabbis as turning the *mezuzah* into an amulet, spread among Jews living in Christian and in Muslim countries principally because the name *Shaddai* was considered especially effective against demons.

This was evidently not protection enough for the *Hasidei Ashkenaz* who took the *mezuzah* very seriously, investing it with all the product of their combined piety and superstition. Certain hours of certain days were set aside as being the most auspicious times for writing the scroll. According to one sage, "It is to be written only on Monday, in the fifth hour, over which the Sun and the angel Raphael preside, or on Thursday, in the fourth hour, presided over by Venus and the angel Anael."[28] Not only did this apply to the writing of the scroll for the *mezuzah* but also for the scrolls contained in the *tefillin* ("phylacteries") for the head and the hands, and for amulets in general.

To the two passages from Deuteronomy, on the front of the parchment (where, according to law, nothing more was to be written), the *Hasidim* added verses that speak of protection, names of angels, and mystical figures. On the back, they added the mystical fourteen-letter name of God, *Kozu Bemuchsaz Kozu*, made up by replacing each letter of *YHWH Eloheinu YHWH*, "...the Lord, Our God, the Lord..." (three words of the *Shema* prayer) in a simple cipher code with corresponding letters of the alphabet. The scribes, acting as amulet-makers, embellished the parchment as they saw fit. Few rules applied, but commonly the names of seven or more angels, several names of God, the words of Psalm 121:5 ("God is your guardian, God is your protection at your right hand."), the pentagram, and other mystical signs were added to the front of the parchment with more mystical figures added to the two names of God on the back. There is no mistaking the fact that the *mezuzah* had become the amulet of choice to protect every *Hasid*'s home.

The *tefillin*—small boxes placed on the head and the arms by means of leather straps—had been used as amulets since talmudic times. In fact, the Greek name for them, phylacteries, comes from the same root as the word "prophylactic" and literally means "devices for protection." If there were any doubt that they were also amulets, the intricate knots and the clever ways of looping the leather straps (almost certainly devised by the *Hasidei Ashkenaz*) should convince the most skeptical. The straps are wound seven times around the forearm, and the winding of the straps around the hand and fingers form the three letters of the word *Shaddai*. Though there were always scholars who contested the validity of the *tefillin* as Jewish objects, this view was almost never expressed by the *Hasidei Ashkenaz*; on the contrary, the wearing of them was considered *de rigueur* all along the Rhine.

We could continue to cite multiple examples of the ways in which the *Hasidim* used magic in the context of their everyday lives and relied upon their spiritual guides, the pious rabbis, to help them in magical ways. Certainly, when it came to medicine, the practice of magic was the then current equivalent of the doctor's "little black bag." But books already exist on the subject of folk medicine and, in any case, it duplicates ground we have already covered. Suffice it to say that magic, like demons, suffused the air.

Though it seems that their lives were infused with magic and superstition, our examination arrives at this quintessential point: The most important form of magic known to the *Hasidei Ashkenaz* was the very piety which was prescribed by their mystical beliefs. Considering the dangers they faced from sudden and unpredictable eruptions of violence against them, they took pride in creating a Judaism uniquely fitted for their community. There is magic in the fact that Judaism was even then so extensible as to be donned like a homemade cloak fitting the needs of its pious adherents. So it was that the highest form of transformation that the *Hasidei Ashkenaz* could conceive was the transformation of the best of them into spiritual beings.

> A certain righteous and pious Jew was about to die when a man came to him with a story that his wife had been rendered barren by sorcery, and requested that so soon as the righteous one enter heaven he repair to the throne of God and beg Him to release her from the spell. The sage promised to do so. Within the year the spell was removed and she bore a child.[29]

The piety of the righteous was the greatest protection of all. When every folk remedy failed, and every amulet proved less than adequate, and every magical recipe had been tried in vain, the *Hasid* could rely on Samuel and Judah and Eleazar and their many disciples. Religious faith, faith in magic, and faith in mysticism went hand in hand.

❋ *Endnotes*

1 Scholem, Gershom, *Major Trends in Jewish Mysticism* (New York: Schocken Books, 1941), p. 76. The heart was considered the center of wisdom in ancient Jewish literature, while the center of emotion was located in the liver.

2 Cohn-Sherbok, Dan, *Jewish Mysticism: An Anthology* (Oxford: One World, 1995), pp. 61-62.

3 Scholem, Gershom, *Kabbalah* (New York: Meridian, 1974), p. 27. From *Midrash Tanhuma*, in Ephraim Urbach, *Kovetz Al Yad*, 6 (1966), p. 20.

4 Berachot 55a.

5 Scholem, *Major Trends in Jewish Mysticism*, p.76.

6 Scholem, *Kabbalah*, p. 25.

7 Scholem, *Major Trends in Jewish Mysticism*, p. 77.

8 Seltzer, Robert, *Jewish People, Jewish Thought: The Jewish Experience in History* (New York: Macmillan Publishing, Co., Inc., 1980), p. 419.

9 M. Guedemann, quoted in Scholem, *Major Trends in Jewish Mysticism*, p. 84.

10 Scholem, *Major Trends in Jewish Mysticism*, p. 86.

11 *Ma'aseh Book*, edited and translated by Moses Gaster, (Philadelphia: Jewish Publication Society of America, 1934), pp. 323-325.

12 *Ma'aseh Book*, pp. 320-323.

13 *Ma'aseh Book*, pp. 358-360.

14 Scholem, *Major Trends in Jewish Mysticism*, p. 92.

15 Eleazar of Worms, *Sefer ha-Roke'ach*.

16 Scholem, *Major Trends in Jewish Mysticism*, p. 97.

17 Scholem, *Major Trends in Jewish Mysticism*, p. 99.

18 Shabbat 105a.

19 Lowenthal, Marvin, *The Jews of Germany* (Philadelphia: Jewish Publication Society of America, 1936), p. 109.

20 Millgram, Abraham, *Jewish Worship* (Philadelphia: Jewish Publication Society of America, 1971), p. 484.

21 Taku, Moses, *Ketav Tamim*, cited in Scholem, *Major Trends in Jewish Mysticism*, pp. 102-103.

22 Scholem, *Major Trends in Jewish Mysticism*, p. 105.

23 from the commentary on *Sefer Yetzirah* ascribed to Saadia, quoted in Scholem, *Major Trends in Jewish Mysticism*, p. 109.

24 Trachtenberg, Joshua, *Jewish Magic and Superstition: A Study in Folk Religion* (New York: Behrman's Jewish Book House, Inc., 1939), p. 36.

25 Trachtenberg, Joshua, *Jewish Magic and Superstition: A Study in Folk Religion*, pp. 38-39.

26 The word *zayin* (and the basis for the shape of the letter) either derives from the Hebrew for "hook" or for "penis." The kind of hook intended was that used primarily in the cultivation of trees while the shape of the letter in Hebrew clearly resembles the human penis. There is a kind of rotund, folkloristic humor in comparing these to weapons.

27 Trachtenberg, Joshua, *Jewish Magic and Superstition: A Study in Folk Religion*, p. 113.

28 This oft-quoted opinion was cited as the work of a tenth-century gaon, Sherira, but we have evidence of it only in the works of the *Hasidei Ashkenaz*, and it seems to have been ascribed to Sherira in the same way that the commentary of *Sefer Yetzirah* was ascribed to Saadia.

29 Trachtenberg, Joshua, *Jewish Magic and Superstition: A Study in Folk Religion*, p. 154.

A Taste of Honey

Rituals passed down for many generations tend to erode or "lose their edge," to be romanticized or to defy logical understanding and finally to be abandoned as no longer "relevant." Also, some stages of life, like early childhood, have little by way of memorialization or special customs. It seemed, therefore, intriguing to seek the origins of one extremely popular early childhood ritual.

As it is commonly retold, Jews used to sweeten a youngster's first study of the Hebrew alphabet by spreading honey on the open page of a book and inducing the child to lick the honey from the page.[1]

It sounds quaint and romantic, but it also demands closer scrutiny. Honey combined with printer's ink is hardly a delicacy. Licking honey from paper seems a bit nasty, and inducing a child to do this might be more difficult than it appears. In earlier times, books were rare—or at least expensive—and the idea of applying a sticky substance to the pages of a book had to be off-putting.

In fact, a conflicting tradition is more often reported. We are told that in the East European *cheder* (the "schoolhouse"—often a single room attached to the synagogue or the rabbi's house) the child's first study of the letters was "sweetened" when the instructor would rain candies or coins "from above" on the open pages of the prayer book from which the child was reciting.[2] Both the legend of the spreading of the honey and the tradition of pouring down candies and coins have at base the same pedagogic purpose—that is, so it seems at first. But the legend regarding honey, traced to two early Jewish sources of the twelfth century, turns out to be a small part of a much larger and more elaborate ritual. According to these sources, the honey was spread on the hard surface of a child's slate. If a pun may be forgiven, taken this way the whole affair seems much more palatable.

Studying the twelfth-century sources, one finds not only the origin of the quaint custom of having a child lick honey but a whole series of new questions—questions which raise serious doubts that the custom was ever "pedagogic."

The first source is found in the book *Sefer HaRoke'ach* ("The Herbalist's Book") by Rabbi Eleazar of Worms (1165-c.1230).

It was a custom of our fathers that children were brought to study on *Shavuot* (Pentecost), for on it the Torah was given. A hint with regard to this: They covered the youth that he might not see a gentile or a dog on the day they would teach him the holy letters: [*No one else shall come up with you, and no one else shall be seen anywhere on the mountain;*] *neither shall the flocks and the herds graze at the foot of this mountain* (Ex. 34:3). At the first rays of dawn on the day of Pentecost, they brought the youths, since: [*On the third day,*] *as morning dawned, there was thunder and lightning,* [*and a dense cloud upon the mountain*] ... (Ex. 19:16). And they hid him beneath the overcoat from their house to the synagogue or to the house of the rabbi, and they—those that brought him to study—placed him in the rabbi's bosom, for it is said: [*Did I conceive all this people, did I bear them, that You should say to me, Carry them in your bosom*] as a nursing-father carries the sucking child, [*to the land that You have promised on oath to their fathers?*] (Num. 11:12). *I have pampered Ephraim, taking them in My arms;* [*but they knew not that I healed them.*] (Hosea 11:3).

And they bring the slate upon which is written [the letters] *alef, bet, gimel, dalet* [and] *tav, shin, resh, kuf. Moses commanded us a law* ... (Deut. 33:4), "The Torah shall be my faith," *And the Lord called unto Moses* (Lev. 1:1). And the rabbi reads each letter, letter by letter, from *alef, bet,* and the infant repeats after him, and each one of *tav, shin, resh, kuf* [representing the Hebrew alphabet recited backward from the end to the beginning], and the infant repeats after him, and in the same way "The Torah shall be ...," and in the same way "And the Lord called ..."

And he places on the slate a bit of honey, and the infant with his tongue licks the honey that is upon the letters. And afterwards they bring the cake that has been baked in honey, and upon it is written: *The Eternal God gave me the tongue of them that are taught, to know how to speak timely words to the weary; Morning by morning, He rouses my ear to hear as disciples. The Eternal God opened my ears, and I did not disobey, I did not run away* (Is. 50:4-5). And the rabbi reads each phrase of these verses and the young person repeats after him.

And following that, they bring a hard-boiled egg, the shell peeled from it, and upon it is written: *And He said unto me: "Son of man, feed your stomach and fill your belly with this scroll that I give you." I ate it, and it tasted as sweet as honey to me* (Ezek. 3:3). And the rabbi reads each phrase and the infant repeats it after him, and the youth is fed the egg and the cake, for this is good for the opening of the understanding—and let no man change this custom.[3]

Much more elaborate is the description of a similar ceremony given in the *Machzor Vitry* ("Holy Day Prayer Book of Vitry"), written by a student of Rashi, Rabbi Simcha of Vitry (died c. 1105):

When a man enrolls his son in the religious school, they write for [the student] the letters [of the alphabet] on the slate, and they bathe him and dress him in clean clothing and they knead for him three loaves of semolina with honey—and a virgin kneads the dough—and they cook him three eggs, and bring him apples and other fruits and they later provide one wise and important man to accompany him to the school and they hide the child beneath [the man's] wing and take the child up to the synagogue, and they feed him the honey-cakes and the eggs and the fruit, and they read him the letters and afterward they cover the letters with honey and say to him, "Lick it," and then they return him to his mother still covered.

And when they begin teaching him, in the beginning they entice him and finally flog him on his back; begin his instruction with the Priestly Laws [The Book of Leviticus], and accustom him to shaking his body as he studies, and when he comes to the "Perpetual Statute" [Lev. 3:17: *It is a perpetual statute throughout the ages, in all your settlements: you must not eat any fat or any blood.*], read it as it is chanted by the congregational prayer leader, and make him a feast according to it.

Know that the whole business is as if he were being brought near to Mount Sinai ... To teach you that you shall behave toward your son when you enter him into religious school in this manner, to cover him and to raise him up, just as Moses behaved in this manner unto Israel ... *And they took their places at the foot of the mountain* (Ex. 19:17), as if they were hidden beneath the mountain

... And why do you bathe and clothe him in clean clothes? It is the way in which the Torah was given ... [Ex. 19:14: *And they washed their clothes.*] And why are the loaves kneaded in milk and honey? Because, as it is said, *And He made them suck honey from the crag* (Deut. 32:13).

And what is the origin of the tradition for opening the understanding? That it is said, *Honey and milk shall be under your tongue* (Song of Songs 4:11). And why can no other except a virgin knead the cake? ... A young girl shall come, one who is pure, and she shall knead for the young one—in that he is pure. And for what reason do they bring him three hard-boiled eggs as has been seen? Not to fulfill the necessities of any *mitzvah*, but as a ritual implement for the *mitzvah*, for it is required to eat it without its peel [and] it is necessary that there be full compliance. And why eggs? Because the knowledge of the infant is much like that of the egg ... [that is, both are beginners].

And why does the wise man hide him beneath his wing? It is the decent and humble way ... Or another thing, that no evil shall befall him and no notoriety among those who pass along the road, that no evil eye shall rule him, and no disaster ...

And why do they cover the letters in honey and say to him, "Lick"? This is like the concept explained in Ezekiel [3:3]: *I ate it, and it tasted as sweet as honey to me*, as if to say, the letters comfort him to lick and thus the Torah will be a comfort to him to study and to teach ....

And what is the explanation for beginning with Leviticus? Thus it is taught: Rabbi Jose said, "Infants begin with the book of Leviticus, as God said, 'Let the pure come and busy themselves with purity and I shall come upon them as if they had offered up a sacrifice to me'" (*Leviticus Rabbah* 280:8). And why accustom him to tremble with his body as he studies? For thus it was as the Torah was given: *And all the people who were in the camp trembled* ... And what is the explanation for concluding with the passage, *You must not eat any fat or any blood?* [Lev. 3:17]. For the infants who have little milk and little blood, thus said God, "I will come upon them as if they had come closer to me ..." And for this reason, read this verse in song, as if giving song and sacrifice to the Eternal, when performing this *mitzvah* ... And for this reason it is necessary to make a feast [in order to properly fulfill the *mitzvah* which has just been read with regard to eating neither blood nor fat]. And having this feast is made necessary by the blessing and saying: "God will open your eyes through God's Torah ..."[4]

Both sources indicate that the honey-licking is far more than an old-time romantic conceit. It is, instead, one element of a highly developed, tightly regulated procedure meant to be followed precisely as prescribed. "And let no man change this custom," Rabbi Eleazar warns—the ominous threat of danger, as if what is being said and the actions being directed are so vital to the welfare of the youth and his future that any deviation will result in some kind of reversal.

Clearly the rituals described are highly valued by medieval Jewish society. Unlike what might be expected from the contemporary Jews of neighboring Spain, there is no attempt in either of our sources to deal with the philosophy of this practice or to reconcile Jewish modes with Greek modes. And just as our modern romantic version of the custom is watered-down and quaint, the version the Jews of the northern countries possessed was an entirely pragmatic formulation.[5] Quaint to us; dire to them.

What was it about the mentality of medieval society, Jewry in particular, and specifically of Jewish communities away from the centers of Jewish study and philosophy in Spain and Provence, that gave rise to this cluster of rituals for a child's first day of school?

While the world of Islam was enjoying its most creative period, the Middle Ages in the rest of Europe saw an upsurge of dependence on superstition and mythical thought. The Crusades are an example of the powerful influence religious mythology had over the medieval mind. In the so-called Children's Crusade (1212), perhaps thirty thousand children banded together—it seemed spontaneously—marching and singing as one great human body. Asked where they were going, they replied, "To God."[6] Early accounts were sparse and less glamorous, and the reputed numbers seemed to grow with the growing popularity of the legend. Similarly, Frederick II (1194-1250), crowned Emperor of the Romans by the Pope in 1220, was reputed by the common folk to be the Messiah incarnate; even his death could not end his influence. The current eschatological reasoning was that he was merely hiding, waiting for the proper moment to again "reveal" himself.

> All the social classes depended on their mythological traditions. Knights, artisans, clerks, and peasants accept an "origin myth" for their condition and endeavor to imitate an exemplary model. These mythologies have various sources. The Arthurian cycle and the Grail theme incorporate, under a varnish of Christianity, a number of Celtic beliefs, especially those having to do with the Other World. The knights try to follow the example of Lancelot or Parsifal. The trouvères elaborate a whole mythology of woman and Love, making use of Christian elements but going beyond or contradicting Church doctrine.[7]

Amidst this burgeoning reliance upon mythological interpretations of the world-order, the Jews found sympathetic harmonies in their native mystic tradition which had grown up parallel to the legalistic rabbinic teachings. Drawing upon this strain of Jewish esoterica, religious life among the Jews was all too similar to that of their Christian neighbors:

> The Jewish atmosphere, as well as the Christian, was filled with demons and monsters. Birds grew spontaneously in the air on trees, and the Sea of Galilee flowed into the ocean. Jews ... took omens from dreams like the rest of the world. The mystical movements of the middle ages were also the source of the admission into Jewish life of a good deal of ignorant superstition. Jews knew of men who had no shadows, of evil spirits lurking in caverns, they feared the evil-eye, believed in witches and ghouls who devoured children, trusted to spells and incantations. In all this the Jews were in the same position as the Christians.[8]

Nor did this preoccupation with mythologies, beneficent and demonic, affect only the psyche of individual Jews. It also manifested in Jewish communal life throughout the Middle Ages until the half-understood principles of Kabbalah became the sure-footed bases of superstitious behaviors among the Jewish masses.

The systemization of demonology was an effective and dangerous factor in the development of the Kabbalah. There had been demons since ancient times, of course, and the Jewish masses outside the scholarly academies recognized them.

> It would be hard to find many religious customs and rituals that owed their existence or development to philosophical ideas. But

the number of rites owing their origin, or at least the concrete form in which they imposed themselves, to Kabbalistic consideration is legion. In this descent from the heights of theosophical speculation to the depths of popular thought and action, the ideas of the Kabbalists undoubtedly lost much of their radiance. In their concrete embodiment, they often became crude.[9]

Unlike the Jewish philosophers of Spain, who treated the demonic dimension as a pseudo-problem, the Kabbalists found in it one chief motive for investigating the relation between the upper and lower worlds. They confronted the problem head on and "related their endeavors in a central point with the popular faith and with all those aspects of Jewish life in which these fears found their expression."[10]

The philosophers of the Middle Ages could not easily accept this eruption of myth in their midst, yet it was this very eruption which gave the Kabbalah the shape which we now recognize as distinctive. The common Jewish masses of the period understood far more readily the impulses of the Kabbalists than the contemplative simple dignity of the philosophers. The Kabbalists spoke to their world providing at once the Jewish doctrine of myth in religious thinking and the rituals and amulets which protected the Jews from this demonic creation.[11]

What took place within the medieval Jewish world was the culmination of a long process of folk religion already evident in biblical times. Over time, Jewish mythology had been historicized while still preserving bits of its original allegorical meaning. And while the rabbis of the Talmud had understood the Bible as both history and allegory, to the comparatively unenlightened Jews of the Middle Ages, the allegory became a surer reality than their mundane existence. The rituals, developed to recapture historical moments of Israel's greatness, were granted new authority by appeal to the allegorical interpretations of Midrash and Talmud.

Treating a similar process in the formation of the Bible, Von Rad noted that a single historical event, such as "the constitution of Israel at Mount Sinai through Yahweh and his servant Moses, when it becomes effective in the order of the people, does not have to remain in the sphere of remembrance through oral tradition or written narrative, but can be submitted to ritual renewal in a cult in the same manner as the cosmological order of the neighboring empires."[12]

And, coincidentally, it is the Mount Sinai myth which the Jews tried to recapture through the Shavuot ritual described in *Sefer HaRoke'ach* and the *Machzor Vitry*. To the Jews of the Middle Ages, what happened at Mount Sinai could be repeated by invoking the power of the myth. By recalling through re-enactment the myth of the giving of Torah, the Torah could once again be "given" and "received."

A "primitive" could say: I am what I am today because a series of events occurred before I existed. But he would at once have to add: events that took place in *mythical times* and therefore make up a *sacred history* ....

This also implies that one is no longer living in chronological time, but in the primordial Time, the Time when the event *first took place*. This is why we can use the term "strong time" of myth; it is the prodigious, "sacred" time when something *new, strong,* and *significant* was manifested. To re-experience that time, to re-enact it as often as possible, to witness again the spectacle of the divine works, to meet with the Supernaturals and relearn their creative lesson is the desire that runs like a pattern through all the ritual reiterations of myths.[13]

And equally important with the re-experiencing of sacred Time through the myth is the acquiring of magical power by which the known world can be manipulated or controlled. Such was the wont of the masses of the Jews: to know the proper incantation to rid oneself of the evil eye, to know the proper way of avoiding the succubus or incubus, to know how to overcome Satan in all his manifestations as sorcerer or Gentile, and to control a world running out of control and endangering one's very life.

We have lost much of this sense today. Our minds are too rigorous to admit to the possibility that "openings" exist between the world of reality and the world of myth. Re-enactments of rituals have far different meanings for us today than for our medieval ancestors. To us, x ritually represents y; to them, it was always $x=y$. For example, when Jews today pray the daily morning service (x), it represents a replacement for the daily morning sacrifice in the ancient Temple (y). To Jews in the Middle Ages, in their living world of myth, the morning service (x) *was* the morning sacrifice (y). This is a small but powerful distinction.

> "Living" a myth, then, implies a genuinely "religious" experience, since it differs from the ordinary experience of everyday life. The "religiousness" of this experience is due to the fact that as one re-enacts fabulous, exalting, significant events, one again ceases to exist in the everyday world and enters a transfigured, auroral world impregnated with the Supernaturals' presence. What is involved is not a commemoration of mythical events but a reiteration of them. The protagonists of the myth are made present, one becomes their contemporary.[14]

Mircea Eliade in his study, *Myth and Reality*, points out five functions of myth for the believer. First, that myth provides a history of the acts of what he terms "the Supernaturals," that is, the ancestors and the divine. Second, that because myth is sacred, it provides a *true* history. Third, that myth relates how a thing came into existence and fourth, thus grants control over the thing, control which can be experienced ritually, either by ceremonially recounting the myth or by performing the ritual for which it is the justification. Fifth, "that in one way or another one 'lives' the myth, in the sense that one is seized by the sacred, exalting power of the events recollected or re-enacted."[15]

So we have seen that the medieval world of the Jews along the Rhine was "truly" populated by demonic forces, that there was widespread belief that through knowledge of the "origin" of these forces one could learn to control and manipulate them, that ritual granted knowledge which in turn became the power to control one's destiny, and that the deep-seated reality of mythology made for a world of "experiences" which could quite literally place one "at the foot of Mount Sinai."

❉

Taken within this context, the two accounts of the honey ritual (that is, the Shavuot ritual) call for a re-examination.

Three times the *Sefer HaRoke'ach* calls upon verses which remind us of the experience of the Children of Israel at Mount Sinai. In speaking of how the child must be "covered" as he is taken from the home to the synagogue or the house of the rabbi, he reminds us of the verse which commanded Moses to enter the mountain alone (Ex. 34:3)—*neither shall the flocks or herds of the Israelites graze at the foot of this mountain.* In instructing us to bring the child "at the first rays of dawn," he invokes the biblical account of the giving of the Torah: *[A]s morning dawned, there was thunder, and lightning ...* (Ex. 19:16). But most conclusively, he draws a direct connection by instructing that the child be brought first on Shavuot, "for on it the Torah was given."

Similarly, Rabbi Simcha Vitry invokes the historical event of Sinai. In his version, the child must be covered on the way to synagogue because *the Israelites took their places at the foot of the mountain* (Ex. 19:17) "as if they were hidden beneath the mountain." The students must be bathed and wear clean clothes because "it is the way in which the Torah was given." And the child must be made to shake his body while studying because *the people who were in the camp trembled ...* (Ex. 19:16).

Thus, the ritual of Shavuot, connected in earlier times primarily with harvest, was first historicized in talmudic times becoming the time of the giving of the Torah. Its pastoral meaning was paramount while Jews lived in the land of Israel; its historical meaning found expression in the medieval ritual of passing Torah yearly to a new generation.

> The Jewish rites developed in the Talmud still reveal an intimate bond with the life of man in nature ... In the Diaspora of the early Middle Ages this contact with the earth was gradually lost. The rites based on it became obsolete, because the corresponding ordinances of the Torah were held to be "dependent on the Land," that is, applicable in Palestine and without validity elsewhere. Thus the ritual of the Jews in the Diaspora took on its char-

acteristic paradoxical form, in which the natural year is replaced by history ... A nature ritual is transformed into a historical ritual that no longer reflects the cycle of the natural year, but replaces it by historical reminiscence, which became the principal basis of the liturgical year.[16]

It might at this point be enough to say that Shavuot was chosen for this ritual because "on it the Torah was given." But to stop by making this simple connection, which Rabbi Eleazar has made for us so neatly, would be to miss the full import of this ritual and the rich and diverse associations from which it derived its power over the medieval mind. In the words of the *Zohar*, the monumental Jewish work of medieval Jewry:

If the law simply consisted of ordinary expressions and narratives: the words of Esau, Hagar, Laban, the ass of Balaam, or of Balaam himself, why should it be called the law of truth, the perfect law, the true witness of God? Each word contains a sublime source; each narrative points not only to the single instance in question, but also to generals.[17]

If there were no more to be learned from these medieval rituals than that they were connected with the re-enactment of Sinai, then why the dire warning: "And let no man change this custom?" No, we must infer that these rituals somehow provide a deeper draught for those who are prepared to drink of it, an "opening" into the world of myth which was so unequivocally real to medieval Jews. Once more, in the words of the Zohar:

Those who have more understanding do not look at the garment but at the body beneath it whilst the wisest, the servants of the Heavenly King, those who dwell at Mount Sinai, look at nothing else but the soul, which breathes in the Torah.[18]

From the point of view of historians of religion or anthropologists, what we are dealing with in this mythico-historical Shavuot ritual is a rite of passage. The term was innovated by anthropologist Arnold van Gennep in his classic work, *The Rites of Passage*. He divides these rites characteristically into three distinguishable segments: separation, transition, and reincorporation. The initiate is first separated from his or her old status often by being physically isolated. The initiate then undergoes a period of transition during which unaccustomed behavior patterns must be followed. And finally, the initiate is returned to normal life in his new status by ritual observances that carry with them the assurance that the new position is socially accepted.[19]

The parallels are close. The child (our initiate—always male in this instance, at least as far as we can tell) is taken from his home, and symbolically from his parents, by a "wise and important man" and is physically isolated by being hidden beneath an overcoat on the way to the place where the ritual is to occur. His period of transition is marked by a number of actions to which he is unaccustomed; repeating the letters of the alphabet forward and backward, reciting verses from the Bible in mimicry of the rabbi, licking honey from a slate, eating inscribed pieces of cake and hard-boiled eggs, and being made to shake his body back and forth through a ritual flogging. He is then given a feast by the community which thereby shows its acceptance of his new position as "student of Torah" and returned to his parents' home still covered.

Rene Guenon, in another study of initiation, refers to these three stages as "potentiality," "virtuality," and "actuality." This description makes the process clearly one of progression in which each stage leads to the next. Further, he describes the inner purposes to which the three stages are directed.

> (1) *Qualification* constituted by various possibilities inherent in the individual's own nature and which are the *materia prima* on which the initiatic work will have to operate; (2) *transmission*, by means of attachment to a traditional organization, of a spiritual influence conferring the "enlightenment" which will allow the being in question to make order in his inherent possibilities and develop them; (3) the *inner work* by which, with the help of "auxiliary" elements or "supports" from the outside, according to need and particularly in the first stages, this development will gradually be realized, so that the being may pass, step by step, through the different degrees of the initiatic hierarchy that will lead him toward the final aim of "Deliverance" or "Supreme Identity."[20]

The child is started in school at five years of age, having reached the point at which, according to the Talmud (*Avot*), he is ready to be instructed. He is now "qualified" for instruction in

Torah. Taken from his parents by means of a "support" (the "wise and important man" who serves as his initiatory "guide"), he is ready for the "transmission" of spiritual influence which is guaranteed to develop his inherent potentiality to be a scholar in Israel. He will receive the Torah as it was received by the Children of Israel standing at the foot of Mount Sinai, thus achieving "gradually" his "Deliverance" or "Supreme Identity" with the Jewish people.

So the Shavuot ritual, including the taste of honey, is one of initiation. It remains to be seen what purpose all the elaborate preparations serve. Why go so far beyond the yearly communal celebration of Shavuot?

❀

There is one more element accounting for the meticulous arrangements and the danger which lurks in failure: the intent to open the individual to sacred Time. This is accomplished through the recitation of verses from the Bible, the verses recalling the origin on which the mythic ritual is founded.

> These myths are told to the neophytes during their initiation. Or rather, they are "performed," that is, re-enacted ... We see, then, that the "story" narrated by the myth constitutes a "knowledge" which is esoteric, not only because it is secret and handed on during the course of an initiation but also because the "knowledge" is accompanied by a magico-religious power.[21]

One may wonder to what extent the participants in the ritual realized that they were effecting a form of "sympathetic magic" by their actions, but one can readily see that Eleazar of Worms, for one, was conscious of the necessity of carrying out each element as perfectly as possible.

This is a primary necessity in the performance of all magical acts. The operator must succeed in carrying out each operation precisely as it has been carried out in the past for the formula to be properly realized. Each letter must be read perfectly by the rabbi, each verse intoned precisely—even to the singing of the named verse from Leviticus just as the congregational prayer leader would sing while reading from the Torah scroll.

If the procedure succeeded, the general experience of historical Israel, as it stood at Mount Sinai to hear the Torah in God's own voice, could become the specific experience of the child entering upon study of the Torah for the first time.

> The "inner nature of things" is one way of describing the most primitive and widespread subject of magical activity. It is universally believed that all things are endowed with occult virtues and powers, that they possess mutually sympathetic or antipathetic qualities, and that it is possible to "step up" magical currents from the particular to the general, and down again from the general to the particular, by the simple manipulation of natural objects, which is the commonest form that magic takes.[22]

It is the calling down of the experience of revelation which is the real content of the initiation rite, and that content is nothing more or less than magical. The Shavuot ritual is a common application of the kind of magic with which Kabbalah is entirely conversant.

Take, as a first example, the use of biblical verses. Trachtenberg, in *Jewish Magic and Superstition*, points out that "Medieval Jewish magic depended for its effects mainly upon the spoken word."[23]

> The Kabbalists made quite a to-do over certain portions of the Pentateuch to which they attributed a very deep mystical significance ... Most efficacious of all, in this respect, were the portions of the Torah which describe the sacrificial offerings; regular study of them in their mystical sense, which constitutes an effective substitute for the actual sacrifices, produces wondrous results.[24]

Note that the child's study begins with the Book of Leviticus, the book which describes in detail the sacrifices and the laws regarding them. Also, the verses recited are associated with both the ritual and its corresponding ancient event.

> The verses chosen for magical use were of two sorts: those which because they contained the name of God or spoke of His power and His mighty deeds had come to be regarded as themselves possessed of power; and those which seemed to have a more or less direct bearing (allowing for mystical interpretations) upon the immediate situation in which they were to be employed.[25]

Study was considered a prophylactic protecting scholars from the demonic powers. Hence, the introduction of the student to study through a magical, mythical formula was intended as insurance against the demonic powers abroad in the world.

Magic elements sometimes encroached on pedagogy as upon all other phases of medieval life ... Study, as such ... was considered the most effective defense against the demonic powers. Although Rashi voiced a widespread belief that "scholars require superior protection, for demons are more envious of scholars than of other men" (*Commentary* on Ber. 62a), it was generally agreed that they were entirely immune from attack during study periods.[26]

Both the verses chosen, and the importance laid upon the value of study, indicate that the ritual is thought to have magical efficacy. But there is no need to make the case so weakly. Examples abound which can be tied more substantively to the ritual itself.

Both sources cite biblical verses to account for hiding the child on the way to the synagogue. Rabbi Simcha drops a further hint that this may be a form of protection from "notoriety" and the "evil eye." The evil eye was a constant danger.

Any act or condition that in itself may excite the envy of the spirits is subject to the evil eye; taking a census or even estimating the size of a crowd, possession of wealth, performing an act which is normally a source of pride or joy—all evoke its pernicious effects. A father leading his child to school for the first time took the precaution to screen him with his cloak.[27]

Another magical element is the use of hard-boiled eggs in the ritual. Though the obvious explanation is that both the egg and the initiate are "beginners," there is the underlying dimension of the egg as the symbol of a microcosm, the "cosmic egg" of myth:

The image of the cosmic egg is known to many mythologies; it appears in the Greek Orphic, Egyptian, Finnish, Buddhistic, and Japanese ... Not uncommonly the cosmic egg bursts to disclose, swelling from within, an awesome figure in human form. This is the anthropomorphic personification of the power of generation, the Mighty Living One, as it is called in the cabala.[28]

Can this association of the Kabbalists have escaped the *cognoscenti*, those who knew the underlying roots of the ritual?

Perhaps. But there is also the use of a virgin to knead the cakes of semolina and honey. Why should a virgin be specified?

> Of ... magical import was the insistence upon the use of new things, which is universally encountered ... The apprentice sorcerer was instructed to place his decoction in a new cup or bowl ... the circle was to be inscribed with a new sword ... virgin earth was to be used to mold an image... amulets were to be written on virgin parchment ... the first action performed at the beginning of a week, or month, or year, were portentous for the ensuing period. Such instances can easily be multiplied many times. New things, first actions, are innocent and virginal ....[29]

But the most substantive connection, the one which drives home the point beyond any reasonable doubt, is the use of sympathetic magic to replicate the experience of Ezekiel who was commanded by God to fill his belly with the scroll which God proffered him.

> The many methods of transferring the word to the body, of bringing it into physical union with the person in whose behalf it is to operate, reveal the very human propensity to assist the supernatural with material reinforcements. This means of applying magic is best exemplified in the field of medicine, where the spells or the mystical names were frequently consumed just as though they were so many cathartics to expel the disease-demons. The same procedure was favored in charms to obtain understanding and wisdom, and to sharpen the memory. The injunction is frequently encountered to write the names, or the biblical verses, or the spell upon a cake (the preparation of which was often quite elaborate), or upon a hard-boiled egg that had been shelled, and to devour it. According to a Geonic account, "all the scholars of Israel and their pupils" used to eat cakes and eggs so inscribed, "and therefore they are successful"; it has been suggested that the name of the famous poet Eleazar Kalir was derived from the *collyrum*, or cake, which his father fed him as a boy, and to which he owed his accomplishments. During the Middle Ages such delicacies were proffered to school children when they began their studies "to open their minds." Magic cakes were also prepared for a bride, to ensure fecundity, and were administered on various occasions for good luck.[30]

So the student, like Ezekiel, performs a magical operation to induce knowledge—not the knowledge which will form the remainder of his studies through all the years of his life—but the esoteric knowledge, the magical link of the lower and upper worlds, the knowledge which places him at the foot of Mount Sinai at the moment in which God speaks to all the Children of Israel, those that were present, and all those yet to be born. Through the use of sympathetic magic, the opening to the world beyond is symbolically accomplished. And to the Jew of the northern communities in the twelfth century, *symbolically* is *actually*; the myth is the reality.

Do we deduce then a magical significance to the licking of the honey from the slate? Indeed.

> The words of the Torah are compared with water, wine, oil, honey, and milk ... But because oil is half bitter and half sweet, therefore the Torah is also compared with honey; as honey is sweet, so are the words of the Torah (Ps. 19:11).[31]

And is Israel not the land flowing with milk and honey?

Moreover, we easily imagine what happens as a young child licks the honey dripped over the letters of the alphabet on the slate. Surely the letters disappear as if by magic. Simultaneously, the writing on the slate and the sweetness of the Torah and the taste of the honey become one, to remain so indelibly and forever. And since the symbolic is actual, the formula cannot fail as it seizes the child's imagination in the moment of its performance. It is the climax of the ritual, the axial moment in which reality and sacred Time merge once and forever, again and again.

Armed with an understanding of the medieval formula, modern inquiries based on psychology, anthropology, history of religions, or sociology pale. They are useful in categorization, neatly naming all they encounter. Labeling, cubby-holing, though, is a nominalist practice and today's scholars are often more nominalist than their medieval precursors. By calling a behavior pattern an Oedipal Complex, we imagine we have cured it; by naming six stages of moral development, we imagine we have a true understanding of all children's ethical behavior. Ironically, we often forget the lesson taught by the father of the nominalists, William of Ockham (died c. 1349). Ockham separated philosophy from theology with one brief stroke of the pen by pointing out that reason has no competence in matters of faith.

Though we have been examining two sources in the history of early medieval Jewish education, the truth is we are not dealing with pedagogy. After all, this study is about magic, myth, and faith; as long as the ritual was performed flawlessly, and no one changed the custom, it worked in every sense. Given what we paradoxically call *suspension of belief*, it might even work today.

In any case, there is a sense in which it indeed still operates. The beginning of a child's study, the first day of school, is analogous today to what it was in medieval times. It is perhaps a shame that we do not take more seriously or ritualize that milestone event in a child's life.

The medieval Jews realized, as we seldom do, that the child's moment of separation from the home and initiation to the school were momentous and possibly traumatic. Ours is a weaning process—the slow lengthening of the hours of schooling from grade to grade, the change from tables and chairs to desks, the transformation of children moving from classroom to classroom instead of teachers arriving to the child's classroom. The Shavuot ritual instead provided the child with a symbolic breakage, a purposeful spiriting away of the child from its parents and a spiritual acceptance of the child by the community.

> Ancient history and the rituals of contemporary primitive societies have provided us with a wealth of material about myths and rites of initiation, whereby young men and women are weaned away from their parents and forcibly made members of their clan or tribe. But in making this break with the childhood world, the original parent archetype will be injured, and the damage must be made good by a healing process of assimilation into the life of the group ... Thus the group fulfills the claims of the injured archetype and becomes a kind of second parent to which the young are first symbolically sacrificed, only to re-emerge into a new life.[32]

The removal of the child from the bosom of his parents and the placement of the child in the "rabbi's bosom" signifies this transfer. And the two verses accompanying the explanation reveal much of the sensibilities of the medieval Jew to this significant moment. The rabbi must hold the child *as a nursing-father carries the sucking child* ... (Num. 11:12). The child's nourishment in this new incarnation will be the nourishment of study. For that reason, the rabbi (literally, "teacher") becomes the ultimate father-figure in human form.

And beyond the rabbi a father-figure in a form less human—the One who nourishes us all with teaching. "And I," said the Eternal, "*I have pampered Ephraim, taking them in My arms* ..." (Hosea 11:3).

We have devised a modern ritual in the form of Consecration when children in their first year of schooling, usually on the holiday of *Simchat Torah* (literally, "Rejoicing in the Torah"), are called to the Torah to be blessed, and a miniature printed Torah scroll is given to each child as a memento of the occasion. It seems too little in light of what we have seen here. It does not closely identify the sweetness of life with the sweetness of study. It fails to pinpoint the teacher as a symbol of parent and role model. And it does not point beyond—it does not "open behind" to reveal God as the ultimate Parent-Teacher and the community of Israel as the ideal Family.

Kabbalah claims that a human being is an embodiment of the universe, a microcosm, or a little world by himself as the sages express it, that: *Adam olam katan bifnei atzmo*, "A person is a small Universe in himself."[33] The cosmic egg of Jewish mysticism opens to reveal "the Mighty Living One." By contrast, today we are each left to our own devices when it comes to establishing our identities irrevocably with that of our people and our God. But how many are sufficient unto the task?

> In his life-form the individual is necessarily only a fraction and distortion of the total image of man. He is limited either as a male or as a female; at any given period of his life he is again limited as child, youth, mature adult, or ancient; furthermore, in his life role he is necessarily specialized as craftsman, tradesman, servant, or thief, priest, leader, wife, nun, or harlot; he cannot be all. Hence, the totality—the fullness of man—is not in the separate member, but in the body of the society as a whole; the individual can be only an organ ....
>
> The tribal ceremonies of birth, initiation, marriage, burial, installation, and so-forth, serve to translate the individual's life-crises and life-deeds into classic, impersonal forms. They dis-

close him to himself, not as this personality or that, but as the warrior, the bride, the widow, the priest, the chieftain; at the same time rehearsing for the rest of the community the old lesson of the archetypal stages ... Generations of individuals pass, like anonymous cells from a living body; but the sustaining, timeless form remains. By an enlargement of vision to embrace this super-individual, each discovers himself enhanced, enriched, supported, and magnified. His role, however unimpressive, is seen to be intrinsic to the beautiful festival image of man—the image, potential yet necessarily inhibited, within himself.

Social duties continue the lesson of the festival into normal, everyday existence, and the individual is validated still.[34]

Every initiation is the compacting of the cumulative experience of the people into the specific life-form of the person. The apogee of that experience for the Jewish people is the giving of the Torah at Mount Sinai—and particularly that moment when the gathered nation stood and heard as one the voice of God. Like all moments in the realm of sacred Time, it is eternal. The moment awaits each of us and is available to all of us as we enter wholeheartedly the covenant between Israel and the Divine. Can any magic be as powerful as the seizure of self, the shattering of the mirror of reality into a thousand-thousand crystalline fragments, each a reflection of the One beyond? Can any sweetness equal the half-remembered taste of honey that lingers forever on the tongue?

❊ Endnotes

1 For popular versions of this legend used today in teaching, see Jacob Benlazar, "The Legend of the Honey," *Bar Mitzvah Treasury*, ed. Azriel Eisenberg (New York: Behrman House, Inc., 1952), pp. 164-165; and Francine Prose, *Stories from Our Living Past*, ed. Jules Harlow (New York: Behrman House, Inc., 1974), pp. 31-33.

2 Mark Zborowski and Elizabeth Herzog, *Life is With People: The Culture of the Shtetl* (New York: Schocken Books, 1952), p. 88.

3 Simcha Asaf, *Sources for the History of Jewish Education: From the Beginning of the Middle Ages to the Period of the Haskalah.* (Hebrew, Tel Aviv: D'vir Publishing House, 1954), p. 3.

4 Asaf, pp. 2-3.

5 *Encyclopedia Judaica*, Vol. 6 (Jerusalem: Keter Publishing House, Ltd., 1971), p. 407.

6 Mircea Eliade, *Myth and Reality* (New York: Harper & Row, 1963), p. 177.

[7] Eliade, p. 174.

[8] Israel Abrahams, *Jewish Life in the Middle Ages* (New York: Atheneum, 1969), p. 367.

[9] Gershom Scholem, *On the Kabbalah and Its Symbolism* (New York: Schocken Books, 1960), pp. 99-100.

[10] Scholem, p. 99.

[11] Scholem, p. 98.

[12] Eliade, p. 49.

[13] Eliade, pp. 13, 19.

[14] Eliade, p. 19.

[15] Eliade, pp. 18-19.

[16] Scholem, pp. 120-121.

[17] *Zohar* III, 140b. It is somewhat anachronistic to quote the *Zohar* since it was quite unknown to the Jewish communities of Rabbi Eleazar and Rabbi Simcha Vitry. Yet this work of *Sephardic* Jewry grew from the same mystic traditions which had influenced *Ashkenazic* Jewry, and its summaries of the importance of mystic and mythical traditions are to be preferred here even over modern scholars who might be cited.

[18] *Zohar* III, 152a.

[19] Arnold Van, Gennep, *The Rites of Passage* (Chicago: University of Chicago Press, 1960).

[20] Rene Guenon, *Aperçus sur L'Initiation* (Paris: Études Traditionelles, 1953) in *Parabola: Myth and the Quest for Meaning*, Volume I, Issue 3 (Summer 1976), p. 47.

[21] Eliade, pp. 14-15.

[22] Joshua Trachtenberg, *Jewish Magic and Superstition* (New York: Behrman's Jewish Book House, 1939), p. 21.

[23] Trachtenberg, p. 120.

[24] Trachtenberg, p. 106.

[25] Trachtenberg, p. 108.

[26] Salo Wittmayer Baron, *The Jewish Community: Its History and Structure to the American Revolution*, Vol. III (Philadelphia: Jewish Publication Society of America, 1942), p. 169.

[27] Trachtenberg, p. 55.

[28] Joseph Campbell, *The Hero with a Thousand Faces* (Princeton: Princeton University Press, 1949), pp. 276-277.

[29] Trachtenberg, pp. 121-122.

[30] Trachtenberg, pp. 122-123.

[31] *Song of Songs Rabbah* 1:2,3.

[32] Carl G. Jung, *Man and His Symbols* (Garden City: Doubleday and Company, Inc., 1964), p. 129.

[33] Levi I. Krakovsky, The Omnipotent Light Revealed (New York: Yesod Publishers, 1939), p. 46.

[34] Campbell, pp. 382-383.

"Addiction"
& Other Sermons

Surviving Addiction

I served as a congregational rabbi for five years. I witnessed too much in that brief period of the evils suffered by addicts and the evils addicts inflict on others. The following is slightly revised but basically the Yom Kippur sermon I delivered at Congregation Jewish Community North in Spring, TX, on October 9, 2008. The subject matter, unfortunately, remains vital.

Hello, my name is Seymour and I am an addict. (Right here, you are supposed to answer with "Hello, Seymour.")

I confess that I am addicted to loving other people as myself. I am addicted to not standing idly by while someone else bleeds. I am addicted to choosing life. I am addicted to being my brothers' keeper, and my sisters', and my aunts' and my uncles', and my children's, and my parents', and my cousins' fourth-removed. I am addicted to saving lives, feeding the hungry, clothing the naked, giving support to the widow and orphan, raising up the fallen, bringing the stranger into my home, and treating animals with kindness—right down to my dog who just chewed off a corner of a book and is currently regurgitating on my Oriental carpet. I am addicted to studying and teaching, to praying and preaching because these are marks of a Jew, and we are taught that being Jewish is not a selfish affair, rather "All Israelites are responsible for one another."[1] My name is Seymour, and I am addicted to loving other people as I love myself.

And I am not making fun of addiction. No matter what shape or creed, no matter what color or substance addiction takes, addiction is always ominous. Maybe you are addicted to aspirin or pain killers or nasal sprays or having your nails done. Maybe you are addicted to sleeping in front of the television in your favorite chair. People today are addicted to Sony Play-

Station, Microsoft Xbox, and Nintendo Switch—addicted to removing themselves from their families by ducking into earphones and cuddling up with iPads. People are addicted to email, eBay, Facebook, LinkedIn, Twitter, Instagram, and IM. Some are addicted to online adventures in the virtual universe of "Minecraft" or "Angry Birds." Indeed, there are so many virtual addictions that it seems amazing that people also manage to be addicted to gambling, heroin, methadone, ecstasy, cocaine, amphetamines, nicotine, morphine, alcohol, surfing the net, cell phones, texting, and work.

In fact, anything you seize that seizes you back, anything that envelopes you and demands more and more of your time and effort, anything that exhausts you and removes you from family and friends can destroy your world and destroy the world of everyone around you.

Addiction used to be defined as "physical dependence," a term coined in 1906 to refer to opium addicts. But we have grown accustomed to using *addiction* in another sense, as psychological dependence. Addiction may sometimes, or perhaps most of the time, be typified by both physical and psychological aspects. Some forms of substance abuse, drug abuse, computer abuse, phone abuse, and problem gambling may be hereditary. Some say addictions are overpowering because they are wired into the pleasure centers of the brain. And some say that addictions are a social problem. To those who live with an addict, points of origination are of little consequence. The destruction and devastation are the same no matter the underlying cause.

Even being addicted to being a saint can be destructive. In talmudic times, two persons were appointed to collect the charity fund that was distributed to the poor just before the Sabbath. But whenever the charity collectors caught sight of Rabbi Eleazar ben Birtah, they would hide themselves from him. He was addicted to giving *tzedakah*, so much so that his whole family suffered.[2] What good is it for a person to give so much that they themselves fall on the support of the community? To be addicted to giving too much and too often is just as harmful as being addicted to giving not at all.

> An old man was once walking along on a cold winter's day when he saw a snake freezing to death at the side of the road. He took

pity on the snake and decided to save its life. He picked it up, held it close for warmth, and rubbed the snake to restore its circulation. But as life flowed back, the snake slowly wound itself around the old man. When the old man was in its grip, the snake said, "Thanks for your help. Now I am hungry and it's time for me to eat you."

The old man asked, "Is this how you repay me for saving your life?"

The snake said, "It is written in the Torah that, ever since the Garden of Eden, God commanded snakes to strike at men."

The old man protested. "It is unfair. At least let us ask for three opinions."

The snake knew the old man could not escape, so he said, "Go ahead, ask."

The first passerby was a donkey. The old man told him the situation and asked what he thought was fair. The donkey said, "Men push me, pull me, and beat me from dawn to dusk. They deserve nothing less than death."

The snake hissed out a wicked laugh, even as an ox happened by. The old man put it to the ox and the ox replied, "In this world, good is always repaid with evil. I hurt no one and every day humans yoke me to the plow and work me until I am nearly dead. What difference does it make to me if the snake eats you? Fair is a nice idea, but the world is never fair."

The snake said, "I am hungry. Let's get on with it."

The old man said, "You promised I could ask three!" And, just then, a young man came up the road. The old man told his story again, but the young man turned to the snake and asked, "Are you ready for me to judge this case?"

The snake already had two out of three opinions on his side. He said, "Certainly."

The young man said to the snake, "You have quoted the Torah to prove that snakes should destroy people, but the Torah also demands that when two stand before the court, both must be equal in standing. Therefore, before I render my verdict, you must unwind from the old man and stand side by side as his equal."

The snake reluctantly uncoiled from the old man, but stayed very close, within striking distance, so as not to lose his dinner. The young man went on: "Here is my ruling. It is written in the Torah that, ever since the Garden of Eden, the snake shall attack man and also that man shall bruise the head of the snake."

With that, he handed his walking stick to the old man who quickly raised it up and killed the snake. The young man said, "I

am Solomon, son of King David, and I say that is what you should
have done when you first saw the snake."

That is the folktale.[3] Now, let us imagine that the snake is
an addicted person. Whenever the addict is kept from her habit,
it is as if she were freezing. It always seems that without the object of the addiction, the addict is about to perish. So some poor
soul, possibly a husband or a wife, a child or a parent, takes pity
on the addict and tries to warm the addict by giving the addict
what he or she needs. In return for this help, the addict senses
weakness and sets out to exploit the one who helped. In socio-
logical terms, we call that person an "enabler," one who enables
the addiction to continue through pity or through a sense of responsibility or through guilt. We hear about "tough love," the
idea that enablers must learn to say "No" and must shun the addict and must separate their lives from the life of the addict. All
that is easier said than done.

But is there an especially Jewish way of approaching this
complex relationship between the addict and the enabler? For
the addict, *loving your neighbor as yourself* means first feed my
addiction, then please understand that I think so little of myself
that I have little or no regard for you. For the enabler, *loving
your neighbor as yourself* means not turning the addict out into
the cold but instead reaching out to help thereby showing the
weakness the addict preys upon. Can the solution really be as
simple as Solomon suggests? Can it be a positive Jewish demand to destroy the addict, or at least to stand by and allow the
addict to destroy him or herself?

We do not know why Cain killed Abel. The Bible only hints
that they had an argument of some kind. The rabbis say the motive was jealousy. But it may also be a story about addiction and
enabling. Whatever Cain did, his younger brother Abel under-
cut him. Abel was addicted to getting center stage. Abel became the favorite in his family by playing the role of the weaker
brother. His mother and father coddled him, and even God
seemed to prefer him. Cain brought a sacrifice to God, so Abel
brought one, too. But it seemed to Cain that God paid attention
only to Abel's sacrifice. Finally, Cain had enough of this. When
would his younger brother relent and let Cain gain even just a
little affection? One day in the field... well, you know the rest. It
was probably manslaughter, not intentional murder, but the re-

sult was the same. Cain finally gained his parents' attention and finally received God's attention, too. It was not the best possible outcome, but it was inevitable that someone would bring down the stick on the head of the snake at some time or other.

Addiction is a reality in our world, and so many of us live with addiction and with enabling addiction every day that we must confront it one way or the other. In his book, *Friedman's Fables*, rabbi psychologist Edwin H. Friedman tells the story of two men on a bridge. In the middle of the bridge, one man says, "Please hold this," and hands the other man the end of a rope. As soon as the second man has the rope in his hands, the first man jumps off the bridge and dangles from the rope's end.

Now the man on top of the bridge struggles just to hold on to the rope in his hands. He looks around, but there is nowhere on the bridge to fasten the rope and alone he does not have enough strength to pull the dangling man back up on the bridge.

He leans over the side and asks, "What are you doing? Don't you know that I am not strong enough to hold you?"

The man down below says, "Look, friend, my life is in your hands. Don't let go. If it will be easier, why not tie the rope around your waist?"

So the man on the bridge ties the rope around his waist. Still he cannot get enough traction to pull the dangling man to safety. He leans over again and says, "Friend, I cannot raise you up, but you could climb the rope and save yourself."

But the dangling man answers, "My life is in your hands now. I am your responsibility. Just don't let go and I will be alright."

How do you think the story should end? This is the challenge that faces us with addiction. If we just stand on the bridge with the rope around our waist, we become enablers. We make it possible for the addiction to continue and for the addict to dangle precariously above the precipice. Judaism demands that we choose life, but can we choose life for ourselves alone? Can we consider letting go of the rope and abandoning the addict to certain destruction? And if we are the addict, the strange truth is that we see nothing wrong in dangling above the chasm that represents our impending destruction. So long as there is one person still holding us, still enabling us to feel connected, there seems to be no problem at all. How should the story end? In Friedman's version, the fable ends like this:

["Listen carefully," the man on the bridge said,] "because I mean what I am about to say. I will not accept the position of choice for your life, only for my own; the position of choice for your own life I hereby give back to you."

"What do you mean?" the other asked, afraid.

"I mean, simply, it's up to you. You decide which way this ends. I will become the counterweight. You do the pulling and bring yourself up. I will even tug a little from here." He began unwinding the rope from around his waist and braced himself anew against the side.

"You cannot mean what you say," the other shrieked. "You would not be so selfish. I am your responsibility. What could be so important that you would let someone die? Do not do this to me."

[The man on the bridge] waited a moment. There was no change in the tension of the rope.

"I accept your choice," he said, at last, and freed his hands.

With the sobering image of the rope slipping between the fingers and out of the hands of the man on the bridge, Rabbi Friedman concludes.[4] His outcome has the virtue, at the very least, of placing the responsibility where it belongs.

All the same, his ending is too bleak and severe for me. Remember: I am addicted to choosing life. But what ending can we conceive that would be better? Let it not be the ending of the snake story or the story of Cain and Abel. It seems the coward's way out for the enabler to deliberately kill the addict or to deliberately allow the addict to self-destruct.

If there is an answer more in line with Jewish ethics, I believe it begins earlier. Particularly on Yom Kippur—but in many other instances throughout the Jewish calendar—we seek atonement not only for our personal sins but for the collective sins of our community.

Idolatry is one of the cardinal sins in which both individuals and communities share the blame. Addicts are like idolaters because they worship above all the object of their addiction. And a society that enables addicts provides the context for such idolatry to take place. The Jewish response is taking responsibility not just for ourselves but for our society—and for the addicts that our society enables. What the enabler needs to realize is that he or she is never alone in being responsible. It is imperative for the whole community to ease the burden of addiction.

I believe a more satisfying—to me, a more "Jewish"—solution to Friedman's fable might be summed up in nine words: *never be alone on the bridge with an addict.* No matter how the addict is related to you, whether friend or family, when he or she wants to hand you one end of the rope, *you* must turn away and seek help. The addict may refuse counseling, but *you* must go for counseling. When the addict says, "My life is in your hands," you must be prepared to say, "There are resources for us. We can find help."

Never be alone on the bridge with an addict. Believe me, friends, once you reach that bridge, you are helpless on your own. Yet you have access to resources. Judaism does not call on us to become saviors of other people; it only reminds us that we are capable of distancing ourselves from our own compulsive behavior and moving toward more positive propulsive behavior. In this life, as on Yom Kippur, you can only change the behavior of one person—yourself. You yourself can seek help; you yourself can learn to stop being an enabler. With competent professional counsel, with good friends, with a good community, you yourself may just possibly rescue yourself, your family may just possibly survive intact, you may be able to salvage your friendships and, with the mercy of God, you may get help for yourself and for the addict from all of us instead of collusion from one of us.

✿ *Endnotes*

1   B. Talmud, *Shavuot* 39a.

2   B. Talmud, *Ta'anit* 24a.

3   *Tanchuma Buber*, Introduction, p. 157; with many medieval variants, especially in Sephardic folklore.

4   Friedman, Edwin H., *Friedman's Fables* (New York: The Guilford Press, 1960), pp. 9-13.

✿
Tzohar: The Secret Light
A Rosh HaShanah Sermon

Many of the sermons a rabbi gives are tied to a specific moment in time. It may be a national event or a local occasion, but it tends to give a sermon a limited shelf-life. Though I admire fine sermons, I find sermon collections a difficult genre. I am including only a handful of sermons in this retrospective of my writing, and I hope these few have some lasting value. This one speaks to inspired activism.

On the day that the Six-Day War broke out in June of 1967, a twenty-five-year-old woman in Toronto withdrew her entire savings from her bank. This savings account was set up twelve years before, starting with the money given to her by family and friends for her Bat Mitzvah. She was conscientious and frugal, never extravagant. She didn't care much for fashions and fads, so every week for twelve years she deposited a portion of her income into that savings account. By 1967, the amount was substantial. On June 6, 1967, she withdrew it all in cash and walked to the office of the Consulate of the State of Israel in Toronto, where she placed her entire life savings on the desk of the receptionist. "This is a contribution for the State of Israel," she said.

The receptionist stared at the cash on her desk, bills and change, then looked up in total amazement at the young woman standing before her. The receptionist was unsure of what to do next. Finally, she asked, "Wouldn't you like to give this directly to the Consul?" The young woman said, "I am sure the Consul is very busy with the war and all." The receptionist said, "Let's take this to our administrative assistant. He can write you a receipt for the money." The young woman said, "I don't need a receipt. Just give the money to the State of Israel." The receptionist counted the money and placed it in an envelope. On the front of the envelope, she wrote the amount of the donation. Then she looked up to ask the young woman for her name and address, but the young woman was gone.

❀

In April 1945, one writer and one photographer—two American reporters—were the first civilian outsiders to enter a Nazi death camp. One of them would go on to help shape an entire generation of American Jews.

His name was Meyer Levin and his career began in 1923 when, at the age of eighteen, he joined the staff of *The Chicago Daily News*. This was a tumultuous time in Chicago. The city was overrun by gangsters. Newspapers were published like broadsides, issuing special editions several times a week, sometimes more than once a day. In 1924, the election for mayor of suburban Cicero was the most crooked in all of Chicago history. Dishonest voters were paid to literally "Vote Early and Vote Often," and honest voters were threatened by thugs at every precinct. Al Capone engineered these elections, and his candidate was elected mayor by a wide margin. Within a week, the new mayor tried to make himself popular by promising to drive the mobsters out of Cicero. It was probably an empty promise, but it did not sit well with Scarface. Capone personally threw the mayor down a flight of stairs at City Hall. *The Chicago Daily News* printed a special edition. But violence did not scare young Meyer. He had grown up in the "Bloody Nineteen Ward," the most corrupt and violent part of Chicago.

It was good that he was prepared for violence, too, because in that same year of 1924 two teenagers from wealthy Jewish families brutally murdered fourteen-year-old Bobby Franks. Meyer was assigned to report the trial of Nathan Leopold and Richard Loeb. He was taking notes as Clarence Darrow delivered the twelve-hour closing argument that saved the lives of his clients.

While reporting for the *News*, Meyer was also writing for a national Jewish monthly called *The Menorah Journal*. And in 1929 he published his first novel, *The Reporter*. This set the pattern of his life. He first lived a story, then told it. He was ever an activist, a commentator, and a storyteller in that order.

He traveled to Palestine to live on a kibbutz. Meyer admired this experiment in creating a new kind of Jewish community. In 1931, he wrote *Yehuda*, the first novel describing kibbutz life. He returned to work on the new *Esquire Magazine*, and he wrote *The Old Bunch* (1937), a novel about twelve young Chicago Jews flirting unsuccessfully with assimilation. It struck a chord that made it wildly successful, the growing-up novel for his generation. In 1937, when ten steel mill strikers were shot down, Meyer led a citizen's campaign against police brutality, reported the story for the *News*, and wrote a powerful novel about it called *Citizens* (1940).

He kept shifting back and forth—being a Jewish author writing about American society and then being an American writer exploring Jewish themes. Then his life changed radically; he was suddenly a war correspondent on the front lines in the Spanish Civil War and then in World War II. He was a first-hand witness to the Battle of the Bulge. He reported the battles, but he also sent back dispatches on American army discrimination against Black soldiers.

In 1945, he was part of a reporting team with photographer Eric Schwab. Schwab was worried about his mother who lived in the small town called Terezin. He had not heard from her in several months. The two of them joined a jeep convoy headed that way. On April 4, 1945, an emaciated skeleton of a man led them into Ohrdruf, one of the smaller outposts of the concentration camp of Bergen-Belsen. It was through Eric's photos and Meyer's dispatches that the world heard about and saw the camps for the first time. Their reporting drew Eisenhower to Ohrdruf where the Supreme Commander was so outraged that he forced his own troops to go through the camp to bear witness and then had his soldiers gather Germans from every surrounding town forcing them to march through the camp to witness the horrors first-hand.

After that, Meyer rushed to each new camp as it was identified sometimes arriving even before the army. He kept sending reports home, but he also took the names of survivors and organized relief for them. One time, he met a Jewish woman who had been badly used by the Nazis—kept alive and fed, only to be brutalized and raped. Other survivors were too weak to travel, but this woman was only crushed in spirit. He helped her into the jeep and took her to where he and the other American reporters were being housed, a local mansion that had recently been the Nazi headquarters. She was still dressed in rags, so he led her to a closet containing a profusion of dresses, shoes, hats, stockings, and nightgowns—all left behind by the Nazis. He told her to take whatever she needed, but she looked at him as if he were a visitor from some strange planet. She shook her head and spoke four unforgettable words: "That would be stealing." She was a victim by chance; she refused to become a perpetrator by choice.

As the concentration camps were freed, Meyer turned to the plight of the refugees. He fell in with the Haganah to rescue Jews by taking them across Europe to waiting boats that would smuggle them into Palestine. With unbelievable energy, he wrote and filmed a docudrama about the rescue directing his "actors" even as the rescue was actually taking place. Meyer's film, *The Illegals*, revealed the bravery of the Haganah and the refugees and starred a French actress who would soon be his wife. Film was a new form of reporting for him. In Palestine, he made another docudrama about a young Holocaust survivor searching for his father. It was called *In My Father's House*, and it helped promote the cause of reuniting Holocaust survivors.

In 1951, his wife asked him to read a book just published in Paris, the diary that a young Dutch girl kept before her death in the Holocaust. Immediately understanding its power, he sent it to his publishers in the United States, and he met with Otto Frank, father of Anne, asking for permission to write a stage play based on Anne's diary. The play, as he wrote it, stressed Anne's struggle to find her Jewish identity. The producers rejected his version. They produced a play with scarce mention of Judaism and no search for identity. For Meyer, this was a Jewish tragedy. For thirty years, he struggled in the press and in the courts. One jury awarded him a verdict for the appropriation of his ideas, but his play never saw floodlights on Broadway. Instead, it became an underground classic—copied, circulated, studied, and staged in small venues around the world.

He took his energies back into fiction starting with a book he had been planning for nearly thirty years. *Compulsion* was the thinly veiled story of the Leopold-Loeb trial and he brought to it a new technique born in the filming of his docudramas. It was nonfiction fiction. As Hollywood was planning the movie version, Meyer wrote a trilogy of novels about the Holocaust, and to preserve the memory of the Jews of Europe, he wrote three textbooks for children in religious schools—*The Story of the Synagogue, The Story of the Jewish Way of Life,* and *God and the Story of Judaism.* In the 1970s, Meyer was writing two huge novels that would describe the history of the State of Israel.

He was nearly seventy years old, bright, driven, gifted, and still a Jewish and humanitarian activist. That was the Meyer Levin I met, the Meyer who became my friend. He split his time between homes in New York, Paris, and Israel. When he was in New York, he would stop by our Jewish publishing house. One time, I told him I was on my way to exhibit books at the General Assembly of the Council of Jewish Federations in Montreal. He was also anxious to go, he said, but every hotel room was already booked. So I invited Meyer to become my roommate for five days. He thought it might be an imposition, but I thought of it as an exciting opportunity for me. How right I was!

Toward the end of the nineteenth century, western Jews first became aware of the black Jews of Ethiopia, the tribes of Beta Israel. The history of their beginnings was lost in myth. They believed that they were the descendants of the biblical Queen of Sheba who converted to Judaism on her return from visiting King Solomon. Whether or not that were true, they were certainly Jews practicing an ancient Torah-based Judaism right down to the fringes on the four corners of their garments.

In the mid-twentieth century, the Beta Israel were suffering persecution and neglect. Ethiopia had become dangerously anti-Semitic, and many of the small tribal groups were persecuted and starving. Meyer Levin wanted to be at the General Assembly because the Federations had invited an elder of Beta Israel as a featured speaker. Meyer knew this elder personally. At his own expense, he had traveled to Ethiopia in the 1960s and filmed a documentary showing the primitive and harsh living conditions of the Beta Israel. The first I knew about any of this was when Meyer arrived at our hotel room with a can of 35 mm film under his arm determined to screen his documentary for the General Assembly. Together we collared every important delegate and financier we could emphasizing the need to rescue the black Jews of Ethiopia. He showed his film several times.

Unbeknownst to us, the State of Israel had been quietly transporting a few hundred Ethiopian Jews each year, but the raising of consciousness at the Montreal General Assembly jumpstarted an effort that culminated in 1984 when the State of Israel conducted Operation Moses, an emergency exodus of 14,000 Ethiopian Jews, followed in 1991 with Operation Solomon, another large transport of 20,000 Beta Israel. Nevertheless, even as I speak to you tonight, there are still whole villages of Ethiopian Jews living on the edge of starvation and waiting to be rescued.

The last time I saw Meyer Levin was in New York City in 1980. I was driving my car down Broadway, and I spotted him walking on the sidewalk. I stopped and gave him a ride. He was on his way to speak to a Jewish group about the growing pockets of poverty in the State of Israel. He was still driven by activism, still writing novels, and still concerned with justice for his people. He died in the summer of 1981 just as his last book was being published. You can trust me when I tell you that he was not only a memorable person to know, but his memory will always be a blessing for the Jewish people.

An anonymous young woman who empties her bank account to save the State of Israel and a short, stocky giant of a man who lives, struggles, and reports every essential cause of his generation—together they hold the key to the secret of being Jewish. Just one more story should make it all clear.

Like all good stories, this one begins at the beginning when God spoke the first words of Creation, "Let there be light." And there was a light—but a light unlike the sun or the moon or the stars. By this first extraordinary light, you could see from one end of the world to the other. God did not create the sun, moon, and stars until the fourth day, but as soon as these luminaries were fixed in the firmament, God condensed and folded the first light of Creation and hid it inside a gemstone called the *Tzohar*. All other gems become brilliant by reflecting light, but the *Tzohar* glows from within, bringing light to everything around it.

Legend says that an angel named Raziel gave the *Tzohar* gem to Adam and Eve after they left Eden. Now this is something to keep in mind because the name of that angel, *Razi-El*, means "God's secret." When he was dying, Adam gave the *Tzohar* to his third son, Seth. In turn, Seth passed the *Tzohar* on to the righteous Enoch. In his time, Enoch was a master of wisdom. Some say that it was the *Tzohar* that brought him his wisdom. True or not, Enoch expanded his consciousness to the point that he never died. Like pure energy, he was transported to heaven where in his wisdom he was transformed into an angel and became God's scribe.

Before departing this world, Enoch entrusted the *Tzohar* to his son, Methuselah, the man who lived longer than any other human has ever lived. Could it be that his long life was because he possessed the *Tzohar*? True or not, Methuselah was still living when the world became so corrupt that God determined to bring on the Flood.

God knew that the rain clouds would hide the sun and the moon for forty days and forty nights. But Noah and his family would need light to care for the animals on the Ark. So God commanded Noah, saying, "Work the *Tzohar* into the Ark" [Gen. 6:16], but Noah had never heard the word *Tzohar* before. "What is the *Tzohar*?" he asked, and God explained, "It is the light of all Creation. For you, it will glow dimly by day and brightly by night, so that you will know day from night. By its light, you shall do My work on the Ark" [Gen. Rabbah 31:11]. That night, the angel Raziel appeared to Noah in his dreams, saying, "Fetch the *Tzohar* from Methuselah, for the time has come for him to die."

The very next day, Noah went to see old man Methuselah. Methuselah greeted him warmly and said, "I have been waiting for you to come. I have lived long by the light of this wondrous gem, but now I am relieved to be gathered to the bosom of my fathers and mothers." And Methuselah gave the *Tzohar* to Noah who hung it in the Ark.

After the Flood, when the Ark rested on Mount Ararat, Noah planted grapes and made wine. All this time Noah had been doing God's work, but now he imbibed so much wine that he fell into a drunken stupor. For ten generations, the *Tzohar* had passed from one righteous person to another, but at the moment of Noah's sin the *Tzohar* vanished from the Ark and was lost for the next ten generations. Those were the generations of idolatry, of the makers of idols, of those who pursued created things instead of the God of Creation.

It fell to Abraham to seek the mystery of God. Abraham thought, "How can I discover the true God while I remain among these idol worshipers?" So he took himself to a cave on the mountain of Ararat for he knew it was a holy place, the place where the Ark came to rest. All day, alone in that cave, Abraham pondered the universe and prayed for understanding. When night fell, the light of the *Tzohar* jewel filled the cave, and suddenly Abraham realized that there was just One God who had created all things. Then Abraham heard the voice of God commanding him to go forth from his land and from his birthplace, to walk in God's ways, and to go where God directed his steps.

The *Tzohar* lit his way from that day on, and he passed it on to his beloved son, Isaac, and Isaac passed it on to Jacob, who always kept it by his side. It was the *Tzohar* that lit Jacob's dream, so that he could see the stairway connecting earth and heaven. It was the *Tzohar* that gave Jacob hope as he lived outside the Promised Land working for his wily father-in-law, Laban, and gaining wives and children, followers, and flocks.

Some say it was the angel Raziel who appeared to Jacob on the night he returned to the Promised Land. Raziel said, "Only the worthy, only the righteous, can possess the *Tzohar*. You must give it up because you are nothing but a trickster. You deceived your brother Esau to steal his birthright, and you deceived your father Isaac to steal his blessing. Now I have come to remove the *Tzohar* from your hands." But Jacob refused to relinquish the precious gem of his family. All night, he wrestled with the angel. Jacob would not give up, even when the angel wounded him. Finally, Raziel begged Jacob, saying, "Let me go, for the dawn comes and every morning every angel must be in heaven to sing God's praises." Jacob answered, saying, "I will release you only if you give me your blessing." Then Raziel said, "I bless you with your new name, Israel, meaning, 'the one who struggles with God and prevails.'" So Jacob released the angel and Raziel was gone. Of course, as everyone knows, the wrestling match was a draw; neither Jacob nor the angel won. But, if so, why did the angel give Jacob such a name as Israel, "the one who struggles with God and prevails?" It is because through his wrestling, Jacob did win. He kept the *Tzohar* in this world though the angel had wanted to take it from him.

One day, Joseph told his father and his brothers that he had a dream in which the sun and moon and stars bowed down to him. The brothers thought this meant that Joseph would one day force them to bow down, but Jacob understood that Joseph had dreamt about the *Tzohar*, for the sun, the moon, and stars all bow to the primal light of the *Tzohar*. Jacob called Joseph aside, dressed him in the colors of the rainbow, and gave him the precious jewel making him vow never to mention the gem to anyone.

Thus, the *Tzohar*'s light was with Joseph when he was thrown into the pit, when he was sold into slavery, when he was thrown into the dungeon in Egypt, and when he told Pharaoh the meaning of his dreams. Even when Joseph ruled Egypt, the *Tzohar* never departed from him. When Joseph was old and dying, he made his children, his brothers, and all their children take an oath: "When you return to the Promised Land, promise that you will take my body up and let me be buried there with my ancestors."

In the years of slavery in Egypt, the *Tzohar* remained hidden in Joseph's coffin. But before leaving Egypt, Moses went to fetch the coffin to fulfill the oath to return Joseph to the Holy Land and bury him there. When he arrived at the coffin, the angel Raziel appeared, saying, "Moses, open the lid and remove the glowing jewel, the *Tzohar*, the gem that holds the true light of Creation. As long as you do God's work, it will protect you and guide your way in the world."

When he saw the wondrous light of the *Tzohar*, the humble Moses was at once afraid that owning it might make him proud. But Raziel reassured him, saying, "Do not hesitate to take the *Tzohar*, for this is all part of God's design."

Moses took hold of the gem, and its light gave him strength. Whenever the people complained, whenever they sinned, and even when they were forced to do battle, Moses found the will to go on in the *Tzohar*. It was with him when he went up to Mount Sinai. It brought him consolation when he found the people worshiping the Golden Calf. It always brought comfort and faith.

Moses still had the *Tzohar* when God told him it was time for him to die. Moses asked God, "Why remove this *Tzohar* from the world with me? Why bury it in my grave where no one will ever find it? Its light brings faith and wisdom and inner joy. If it has done so much for me, would it not do as much for Your people, the Children of Israel? If only every one of them could have a *Tzohar*, could feel its warmth, and live by its light, would it not protect them from sin and urge them to do Your work in the world?"

God whispered to Moses, "Such was always my design. Before you, the righteous who possessed the *Tzohar* only used its light. You are the first to see its inner truth. Therefore, the secret of the *Tzohar* will bear your name forever."

Suddenly, the gem stirred in Moses' hands. Lo and behold! The light unfolded itself, expanding until it became a scroll of light. God said, "In your hands I place My *Torah*—it will bear your name as the Five Books of Moses. You will give it to the Jewish people before you die. Whoever studies it will discover its inner secret as you have. The Torah is the *Tzohar*, it is the jewel that shines its light from within, radiating warmth and wisdom and peace to all who treasure it."

Now you know how the light of the Torah entered the world as a gemstone to illumine the path of righteousness and guide each and every one of us to use the best that is in us to bring wisdom and light to our lives. This is the *Tzohar*, the secret light that glowed in the heart of the young woman who gave her life savings to save Israel and glowed in the soul of Meyer Levin as he wrestled against every injustice of his generation and struggled to bring peace and wisdom to his people of Israel, to the new State of Israel, and to the world.

There is only one more secret to reveal about the *Tzohar*. When King Solomon was about to build the Temple, the angel Raziel appeared to him in a dream, saying, "Hang a light above the Holy Ark that protects the scrolls of the Torah and always keep that light alive. It will be for you a *Ner Tamid*, an 'Eternal Light' like the one that Moses kept in the Tabernacle above the ark in the wilderness. Every time the people of Israel see the Eternal Light, they will remember the secret that the Torah is the *Tzohar*—it is the light of creation by which you can see from one end of the world to the other."

To this very day, wherever that light hangs—in Jerusalem; in Moscow; in Toronto; in London; in Cracow; in Berlin; in Tel Aviv; in Sydney; in New York City; and wherever Jews live—it points to the *Tzohar*, the jewel that has made the world a brighter place since the time of creation, the Five Books of Moses, our Torah. Know this my friends: You do not belong to a synagogue because the synagogue does this for you, or it does that for you. You belong to a synagogue because you are a Jew and you possess the secret of the *Tzohar*. You must do everything in your power to keep the *Tzohar* from leaving this world, to ensure that the Torah passes on from your generation to the next, to ensure that God's light will never depart from us. That is the secret that ties the people of Israel and the land of Israel together with the God of Israel.

❀

Real Magic

A Rather
Unorthodox Sermon

*This sermon suggested itself in early 2007. A congre-
gant complained that the "new" synagogue with its
"new" prayer book and its "new" music and its "new"
ways did not seem to have as much appeal as the synagogue she remembered from her youth. Had she been
speaking with another friend, she might have added
"new" rabbi, too. I understood her issue. I wrote this sermon to reassure her and to remind myself about the real
magic.*

$\mathbf{A}$t the burning bush, God commanded Moses to throw his
shepherd's staff to the ground. When he did, the staff became a
living snake. Moses was so startled that he fled, but God instructed Moses to come back and take that serpent by the tail.

Now, I do not know about you, but I would have thought at
least twice about approaching that snake and laying hold of its
tail. Only faith and fear could possibly propel Moses to grab that
hissing danger. Moses had to trust God completely. Even more,
Moses' fear of God had to be greater than his fear of snakes; otherwise, he could never have acted as he did. He grabbed the serpent by the tail and, thank God, it became his staff again.

Umberto Cassuto, the greatest Jewish Bible commentator
of the twentieth century, tells us that this little episode was no
simple magic trick. God explains its purpose: "Then the Eternal
said to Moses, 'Put out your hand and grasp it by the tail ... that
[the Israelites] may believe that the Eternal, the God of their fathers, the God of Abraham, the God of Isaac, and the God of Jacob, did appear to you'" (Exodus 4:4-5). In short, the magic was

designed to convince the elders of the Israelites to place their trust in Moses.

Snake charming was common throughout the ancient world. Many a charming gal or guy could induce a hypnotic state in a cobra, so that it could be carried like a rod or walking stick and then magically returned to its normal hissing self. Inducing this hypnotic state required motions of the hands and music or chanting which was intended to cast a spell over the snake. It took time and patience even with a well-trained snake. As Cassuto pointed out, what God had Moses do was exactly the opposite. It was far more miraculous to take a rod made of wood, cast it to the ground with no utterance at all—no spell, no incantation, no music, no chanting—and have the wood instantly transform into a seething serpent, then watch as the living serpent metamorphosed into a wooden staff again. That was a real miracle. No wonder the Torah called it "the rod of God" (Exodus 4:20).

Yet, there was one more element of this metamorphosis, this transformation, that should startle readers of the episode. God instructed Moses to grab the snake by its tail! No one ever grabs a snake by its tail! The only way to avoid being bitten is to grab the snake right behind its head. To grab the tail is either stupid or an act of blind faith. That may have been the precise message God wanted to deliver to the Israelites! You can trust Moses; you can summon up your faith in God the way Moses has placed his faith in God.

Something else happens when Moses and Aaron go before Pharaoh as representatives of God Almighty. When Pharaoh asks for their qualifications, Moses has Aaron cast down his rod, and it instantly transforms, not into a snake, but into a crocodile! Old translations call it a serpent, but they are mistaken. At the burning bush, the rod became a *nachash*, the Hebrew for "snake." A snake was entirely appropriate in the wilderness where snakes are fearsome creatures. But in Egypt, the king of the Nile, the most feared of all reptiles, was not the snake but the crocodile. The Hebrew word for crocodile is *tannin* which literally means "dragon," but in the context of Egypt always means the ferocious crocodile.

In Egypt, snake charmers have always been a dime a dozen. But the priests of Egypt were skilled at the much more difficult challenge of charming crocodiles, and Pharaoh called upon them to show their wonders. As the verses read in the Torah, "Then Pharaoh, for his part, summoned the wise men and the sorcerers; and the Egyptian magicians, in turn, did the same with their spells; each cast down his rod, and they turned into crocodiles" (Exodus 7:11-12). Notice that the Torah says the magicians turned their staffs into crocodiles with their spells. They brought crocodiles trained to undergo hypnosis and stiffen, then to return to their natural state as writhing serpents. Now imagine the scene as you never have before. The Torah states it very simply: "each [magician] cast down his rod, and they turned into crocodiles, but Aaron's rod swallowed their rods." Summon up your courage and imagine Pharaoh's throne room as Aaron's crocodile snapped its jaws time and again, mauling and killing every other crocodile in a frenzied, bloody orgy of gorging. Crocodiles do not swallow their victims like snakes do; instead, they eat their way through their victims with powerful jaws and jagged teeth. That is what Pharaoh and all his magicians witnessed. And when the bloody scene was complete, Aaron nonchalantly reached out for the tail and grabbed the crocodile that had just consumed beast after beast, and the huge reptile with its swollen belly was suddenly transformed back into Aaron's rod. So the Bible says.

The magicians of Pharaoh had to be wondering what the next trick was going to be and how they were supposed to match it. They had to wonder because in ancient Egypt wisdom was measured in magic. The priest with the biggest magic was the wisest in Pharaoh's eyes, and right off the bat that seemed to be Aaron and not the magicians. But Pharaoh himself was a jaded fellow. He had seen many a magic trick in his time, so he probably thought, "These guys just have a better *shtick*! They have more zing in their act. They have probably played Vegas. So what? Let them come back next week. In the meantime, my boys will figure out how to make our crocodiles do the eating." Or, as the Torah puts it, "Yet Pharaoh's heart stiffened and he did not heed [Moses and Aaron], just as Adonai had predicted" (Exodus 7:13).

In Egypt, wisdom, medicine, and magic were the roles of the priesthood. Pharaoh's advisors are always referred to as his "wise men and sorcerers"—one and the same. The representatives of the gods of Egypt were expected to work miracles. Religion was expected to produce miracles, especially the greatest miracle of all, the triumph of life over death. In ancient Egypt, people expected their religion to work even that wonder for them.

That's still what people expect from religion. Times have not changed people all that much, and people have not changed through all these times. When the rabbi comes to visit the sick, it is not a nice guy or gal that the sick person expects; it is a healer. When the rabbi sits with the dying, it is not a nice guy or gal that the dying person anticipates; it is the person who is supposed to save them from death or at least guide them safely to the next life. Rabbis do not come with magic spells, but the sick person or the dying person hears the Hebrew prayers as if they were spells and incantations.

You do not need to be sick or dying to need religion. You come to religion because you want miracles and wonders for your everyday life, too. You expect sacred things to happen, and you are disappointed when they do not. If the rabbi's sermon is a dud, or if the prayers do not move you, you go home wondering why you should return. You expect to be moved; no, you come to synagogue with the prayer that you will somehow be *transformed*. In other words, you come like a stick of wood seeking to be thrown to the ground spiritually so that you will metamorphose into something very much more alive. You may leave as a stick of wood again, but you will be different; you will carry away the inner knowledge that there is a serpent in you, a writhing, hissing *self* inside you that is alive with feelings.

You want that kind of knowledge in your gut, and believe me, it is something you cannot get from watching television or playing a video game or going to the movies. Yes, they sometimes evoke magic, but you know they are only casting a spell. Even the best programs or films, the ones that move you every time you see them, are manipulative. If you take just one step back, you can discover how they are working their magic. It is magic that requires hundreds of thousands, sometimes millions, of dollars to create. But if you want, you can always see just how it was created. Not here in the synagogue. First, we do not have hundreds of thousands of dollars for each performance. But we do not need all that money because we have the real stuff, the real magic, the kind of magic that only God can produce. Even the worst rabbi in the poorest synagogue can bring about moments of magic that Hollywood could never hope to equal.

A prayer is chanted for healing. What magic can compare to that? A baby is brought up to the ark to be blessed and named. Nine adults spend a year to prepare a *bar* or *bat mitzvah* that none of them received as a child. A Confirmation class commits to carrying on the covenant of Israel. What magic compares to these? What drama can hope to equal the carrying of the Torah, the opening of the Torah, the reading of the Torah, or even the recital of the Adoration? And when you are in mourning, what other power in the world is equal to the awesome rush of the words of the Mourner's *Kaddish*? You do not need a great rabbi to make these things sacred. You barely need a rabbi at all. The connections are in your soul.

You come to the synagogue like the rod of God, stiff and wooden as you enter. But it is not the rabbi or cantor that works the miracles here. It is you transforming yourself by entering into age-old rituals. Life can pour into you here in the synagogue. Outside the synagogue, life all too often has a way of sweeping you up and tearing out your soul. Inside the synagogue, religion has a way of lifting you up and restoring your soul.

You want magic here and I do not blame you. I only ask that you think of the magic here in a different way. Outside, magicians wonder how to produce an effect on you. They begin with the live crocodile and try to hypnotize it. Inside the synagogue, we begin with deadened, wooden souls and give them over to God. The spark of God that is in you suddenly lights up and joins the sparks of God all around you to produce an inner flame that warms everyone on a normal day and fires everyone up on an exceptional day. What has changed is not something on the outside, but something on the inside. What has been transformed is not a stick of wood, it is you yourself. Here in the synagogue, the God that is all around us touches the God that is within us. That is the only real magic that has ever existed and the only real wisdom that has ever triumphed.

Comfort from a Leaf

How should we feel about dying? In Jewish tradition, we face this question at major holy days throughout the year. A special prayer service is set aside as a Yizkor *or "Memorial." Taking its theme from the fables about Moses spun by the ancient rabbis, this was the message I delivered during the Yom Kippur Yizkor service on October 13, 2005.*

To everything there is a season, and a time to every purpose under the heaven. A time for giving birth and a time for dying... — Eccl. 3:1-2

The time was drawing near for Moses to die, but Moses was not at all reconciled to the idea of death.

When God first informed Moses that he must die without entering the Promised Land, Moses reasoned that so long as the course of his days had not yet been run, everything was still in his power. But now, in sight of the Promised Land and with not much time remaining, he sought help in appealing for God's mercy. Because he was Moses, he first approached Heaven and Earth, the Sun and the Moon, the Stars and the Planets, the Mountains and the Rivers. But all of these turned a deaf ear to his prayers for all of them knew full well that, in the wisdom of God, their days were also numbered. Even Mount Sinai refused to beseech God on Moses' behalf, for it had been greatly shaken and disturbed by all that had happened on its shoulders.

Moses had no choice. He was not a proud person; up to now, he had been entirely humble. Yet now he knew he needed help.

So Moses implored human beings to intercede for him before God.

He went first to his disciple, Joshua, saying, "My son, remember that I taught you Torah day and night—and not just what is written in the Torah but all that the wise will derive from the written word throughout the ages. In return, pray for me that I not be taken in death but allowed to enter the Promised Land with you."

He went to Eleazar, son of Aaron, saying, "My son, when your father sinned by casting the Golden Calf, I prayed for him and he was saved from death. Now, raise your voice to God and pray for me that I may be saved from death."

He went to Caleb and the seventy elders of Israel, and to all the judges he had appointed over the people, and to the chieftains of the twelve tribes, saying, "My children, recall that when the people sinned, I prayed for them that they not be put to death. In return, I adjure you now to pray for me that I not be taken in death."

All tried to pray for Moses, but none were able for God sent Samael, the very angel of death, to prevent their prayers from reaching heaven.

Now, Moses came before the people of Israel, reminding them that God had wanted to destroy them utterly and to replace them with a new people formed of the sons of Moses. "Without my intercession," Moses reminded them, "there would no longer be the Twelve Tribes of Jacob, the children of Israel; there would be instead the Children of Moses and the Tribes of Moses. So pray for me now that God should not put me to death, but that I should be allowed to enter the Promised Land with you."

The people put on sackcloth and painted themselves with ashes. They tore their garments and wept bitter tears. They cried out to God on behalf of Moses for thirty days, fasting and wailing, and imploring and beseeching. But God had sent the angel, Samael, to stand in the way of their prayers, so that not a single prayer of all those offered was heard in heaven. For God had decreed that Moses would die and not live. And God had sealed the decree with God's own pledge.

When Moses saw that neither creation nor humanity could aid him, he sought out the most powerful of all angels, the Angel of the Face, saying, "Pray for me, that God may take pity upon me, and that I may not die." But the angel replied: "Why, Moses, do you exert yourself in vain? I was standing behind the curtain drawn before God, and I clearly heard that this prayer is in vain. The decree is settled, and the shape of it is recorded and sealed." Moses now placed his hand upon his forehead and wept bitterly, asking, "To whom shall I now turn to implore God's mercy on my behalf?"

God was growing impatient with Moses. Moses had witnessed God carry out many decrees harsher even than forbidding him to cross over to the Promised Land. But God was placated as soon as Moses raised his voice in God's own words:

Adonai, Adonai, God full of compassion and gracious, slow to anger, and generous in mercy and truth; keeping mercy for thousands, forgiving iniquity and transgression and sin. (Ex. 34:6-7)

Then God spoke kindly to Moses, saying, "Behold, I have registered two vows. One is that you must die, and the other is that the people of Israel must perish. You yourself implored me to cancel My vow against the Israelites, but I cannot cancel both vows. Therefore, decide for yourself: If you choose to live, Israel shall be destroyed."

"Master of the world!" Moses cried in agony, "You approach me artfully; You seize the rope at both ends, so that I myself must now say, 'Rather let Moses and a thousand of his kind perish, than a single soul out of Israel!' But will not all children of earth exclaim, 'Behold the reward of Moses, the servant of God! The feet that trod God's heavens, the face that beheld God's Presence, and the hands that received God's Torah—all this, and now Moses is like all others, covered with dust!'"

But God answered: "Think again. In truth, people will affirm: 'If a man like Moses, who ascended into heaven, who was a peer of the angels, with whom God spoke face to face, and to whom God gave the Torah—if such a man cannot change God's decree, how much less can an ordinary mortal of flesh and blood, who appears before God without having excelled in good deeds or studied God's ways, resist God's will?'"

"Yet, tell me," God said, "why should you be so much aggrieved at the thought of death?"

At first, Moses answered, "I am afraid of the sword of the Angel of Death."

God replied. "If this is your reason, then speak no more about this matter, for I will not deliver you into the hands of the angel of death. I will draw the breath from your body myself with a kiss—for you are My beloved, and this I do for all I love and all who place their faith in Me."

But Moses would not yield. He asked, "Shall my mother, Yocheved, to whom my life brought so much grief, suffer sorrow after my death also?"

God said, "It is of no use to worry about those who may be left behind when you die. For death is decreed for all Creation. So was it in My mind even before I created the world; and so is it for all born.

"This you must understand, Moses," God added. "Every generation has its learned, every generation has its leaders, every generation has its guides. In your time, it was your duty to guide the people, but the new generation requires your disciple, Joshua. What was destined for you remains destined for him. Your dreams become his destiny, and his dreams become the destiny of those who will follow him."

Moses bowed his head. Death seemed not sweeter because he understood God's plan. Somehow, God's plan meant that he was to be disappointed, that he would not enter the Promised Land though he had given his every breath and his life and limb to bring his people to its edge. Does the candle know when its flame will soon be quenched? No, but human beings are cursed with knowing. Most humans sense when their light will soon be extinguished, and those who stay behind always know when the light of another has been extinguished.

Then what is the point of it all? If goals cannot be reached and dreams cannot be realized, what good is striving and working? How much effort should a person expend if the ultimate truth is that no amount of effort is ever enough?

Just as that thought passed through his mind, a leaf fell from a tree nearby, and Moses watched as it turned over and over in the air falling gently to settle on the ground. Here was a miracle. The tree stood proud and tall above him and other leaves suspended from other branches glistened in the sunlight bringing life to the tree even while one of their companions had fallen. Moses thought, "All of these leaves will fall, one by one, or the wind will tear them off in little groups—sometimes not just the leaves, but even twigs and branches—and yet the tree will stand and grow. It will bear seed, and its seeds will be carried like dreams on the breeze. Some of the seeds will fall in streams and on rocks where they cannot grow, but a few will take root and new trees will sprout. If this tree falls, its children standing around it on every side will carry on, and there will still be a forest. Life itself will not be denied though many deaths must occur."

People speak of living on in other people's memories when they die. But death is more than this. The longer and stronger a person grows, the more his or her life engenders life all around. Ideas live on; messages are received along with genes and genomes. Goodness enters the world through people and remains in the world when the people themselves pass out of it. Dreams are bequeathed from generation to generation, some bearing fruit in the children of the dreamer and some bearing fruit only after many generations have passed.

Moses knew that he was privileged in this. Privileged to have seen the tree, privileged to have seen the bush, privileged to have dreamed the dream of the Promised Land, especially privileged to have come so close—so close that he could look out from the hill where he stood and see the Promised Land itself and know that his children and his people would soon cross over into it. Moses knew that life was a privilege.

> Moses went and spoke these things to all Israel. He said to them: I am now one hundred and twenty years old, I can no longer come and go. Moreover, *Adonai* has said to me, "You shall not go across yonder Jordan." ... Joshua is the one who shall cross before you, as *Adonai* has spoken.... *Hazak v'amatz*, be strong and resolute.... (Deut. 31:1-6)

Then Moses spoke to Joshua in the sight of all the people of Israel, with the same words, "Be strong and resolute."

> *Hazak v'amatz*, be strong and resolute, for it is you who shall go with this people into the land that Adonai swore to their fathers to give them.... (Deut. 31:7)

And these are the words that we use to this very day when we charge new leaders for our people, *Hazak v'amatz*, "Be strong and resolute." When a leader is removed, when a person we loved has died, when we realize that it is up to us to carry on the dreams of those who came before us, more than anything else, we need to hear those words. We must be strong, and we must be resolute.

It is impossible not to mourn at all, for then we would forget the meaning of our lives. But if we mourn overmuch, we forfeit the purpose of our lives. We need to trust that, like the leaf, when the end comes it will be a gentle place to which we are carried on a breeze that has in it the breath of God. And that other leaves will carry on, for their own sake, for the sake of the trees, for the sake of the forest... for the sake of the dream.

"Every Bush Is Burning"
& Other Essays in Education

❋
Tzimtzum
A Personal Stance

*Everyone teaches, but some of us do it formally, purpose-
fully, intentionally. Our human search for immortality
includes the desire to impart some of what we think and
some of what we know to those we care about. For this
reason, teachers have ever been compared to nurturing
parents. This essay explores how we know when to step
back and allow the growth we have engendered as
teachers to blossom into independence for our students.*

In his essay, "*Tzimtzum*: A Mystic Model for Contemporary
Leadership," Eugene B. Borowitz (1924-2016) argued that too
much contemporary leadership rests on relationships of power.
Even seemingly pure relationships often contain a political
structure, so "our hope of accomplishment in most fields rests
largely on how power is organized there or what can be done to
change that arrangement."

Seeking a more effective model, Borowitz suggested the
teachings of the influential mystic, Isaac Luria of Tsfat (1534-
1572). Like Borowitz himself, Luria was both a creative philosopher and a practical leader within his circle. Luria spoke of God
as "creator" and human beings as "co-creators." Before Luria,
Jewish tradition celebrated creation as God-directed. God expressed the will to create ("Let there be light ..."), and the word
brought the intention into existence ("And there was light.").
Luria stepped back from this obvious beginning by asking a revolutionary question which, once he posed it, seemed entirely
obvious. "If God is everywhere, what space remains for God's
creation? How can there be any place outside God for God to
create in?"

Luria's question draws forth an immediate rebuke from our
modern minds. It is a too-literal view of God and the universe,

an anthropomorphic conception and obviously unscientific. Borowitz assisted us by reframing the issue as a religio-philosophical conundrum. *If God is a fundamental being and fully realized, how can there be a secondary being, that is, any being only partially realized?*

Luria answered his question by making the bold assertion that creation began with an act of *tzimtzum*, "contraction." God voluntarily contracted (withdrew) from a portion of reality in order to make room for God's creation. "By this act," Borowitz observed, God "leaves a void in which ... creatures can come into being." By necessity, something of God had to remain behind for creation to be supported. Luria pictured this as an essence, like the residue of oil or perfume that lingers even after we have emptied the bottle.

Withdrawal was the necessary prelude to creation, but it was followed by a positive externalized movement in which God sent forth a beam of light into the void. From this first light, all creation as we know it eventually took shape.

Creation, for Luria, is this two-fold process—the act of contraction leads to the act of expansion. Moreover, it is a constant rhythmic movement, for God continues the work of Creation each day reliably. In this sense, all existence pulsates to the divine regression and egression. "Here," Borowitz comments, "Luria's sense of time and the opportune moves in a mystic realm no fine-tuned atomic instrument can ever hope to clock."

But the act of withdrawal was not merely serendipitous. The cost of a creating space in which God was present in only a residual fashion, in Luria's metaphor, was "a cosmic catastrophe." Luria described how the divine beam of created light entered the void and proceeded through various transformations. In the end, it produced "vessels" to contain the light. But God's light proved too powerful for some of these lesser vessels. They shattered and, as a result, creation became something less than perfect. Evil came into existence in a cosmos which God conceived as good.

The *shevirah*, the "shattering" of the vessels, was no reason for pessimism in Luria's doctrine. Luria sees the meaning of human existence in this "catastrophe." Creation may be flawed but not entirely. God's presence, however slight, remains in the world, so the creation cannot merely be chaos. Instead, we see all around us the "shells" or "husks" of what God envisions—these are the shards of the vessels from which the kernels of God's light have escaped. Something of God's power, some little spark, still inhabits each shard. Luria thus speaks of all creation containing divine sparks. By lifting up or "redeeming" these sparks—by restoring them to their proper place in God's spiritual order—all things may become what they were intended to be. The act of restoring the sparks is termed *tikkun*, "repair."

> What astonishes us here is Luria's bold insistence that *tikkun* is primarily humanity's work, not God's. In everything one faces, in every situation one finds oneself in, one should realize that there is a fallen spark of God's light waiting to be returned to its designated spiritual place. Hence, as people do good moment by moment and give their acts of goodness a proper, inner, mystic intention ... the shattered creation is brought into repair. The ailing cosmos is healed. The Messiah is brought near.

Jews do this work of *tikkun* through the practice of Jewish law and through concentrating proper intention in the performance of the Jewish virtues. Luria argued that if enough people spent enough time restoring creation to its perfect form, God would send the Messiah. In Borowitz's eloquent terms,

> If people, by their acts, restored the creation to what God had hoped it would be, then all the benefits of [God's] gracious goodness would be available to them.

A Model for Jewish Education

God's contraction-creation can be translated into human terms. Borowitz posits a model for leadership in general, but I propose it as a model for Jewish education in particular, a model for teachers in our classrooms. In our age of power posturing, we tend to look up to the "creative" teachers whose actions mold classrooms and bend students to their will. But *tzimtzum* presents a counterintuitive alternative. Just as God's power must first be withdrawn to make room for creation, so, too, the educator or teacher who wishes to initiate learning must first withdraw from power.

Consider the normal classroom. There are goals to be accomplished, courses of study to be covered. Nevertheless, the teacher's methodology makes a great deal of difference. Students resent feeling that a teacher is using them only to accomplish the teacher's purposes. Students appreciate teachers who convey the feeling that they genuinely respect students even as they labor together toward common ends. Thus, the ability to practice *tzimtzum* in the classroom shifts the teaching environment from accomplishment-directed to person-fostering.

> Leaders, by their power, have a greater field of presence than most people do. When they move into a room, they seem to fill the space around them. We say they radiate power. Hence, the greater the people we meet, the more reduced we feel ... So, in the presence of the mighty we are silent and respectful ... Who we are is defined by what they think of us.

What Borowitz observes of leadership in general is also true of classroom teachers. Teachers sometimes are so busy doing things for their students that they forget to leave room for the students to do things for themselves. Teachers tend to talk too much. Students report that when teachers stop talking for a moment and ask for questions or honest comments, "We don't believe them. We know if we stay quiet ... they will start talking again."

The *tzimtzum*/contraction approach for the classroom does not call for a complete shift from dominance to abandonment. Withdrawing to make room for student growth should not become a teacher's excuse for indolence, for refusing to plan, for not providing resources, or for not making proper demands on the class. The contraction must be accompanied by a suitable infusion, a "letting in" of light.

> Leadership in the Lurianic style is particularly difficult, then, because it requires a continuing alternation of the application of our power. Now we hold back; now we act. To do either in the right way is difficult enough. To develop a sense when to stop one and do the other and then reverse that in due turn, is to involve one in endless inner conflict.

Even if a teacher has made a lifetime study of a subject, it is important to listen to what students have to say. If the teacher does not allow minor inconsistencies to pass by unchallenged—

if the teacher constantly interrupts the student—the student's sense of self-worth may inadvertently be destroyed. On the other hand, the teacher can only tolerate a certain degree of incompetence. A student who is misinforming the class or making major misstatements that may falsify following information must be interrupted. "Danger lurks equally in action and inaction," Borowitz concludes.

> And with all this, we cannot help but realize that our judgment to intervene may only be a power-grab while our decision to stay silent may really mean we are unwilling to take the responsibility for interrupting.

This sheds light on the complex nature of the *tzimtzum* model for teaching. It may cause anxiety in the teacher. After all, in the normal course of things, most teachers tend to retreat—that is, to emulate the ways in which their teachers taught them. And few teachers of the past used a model anything like this.

There also remains the possibility that through teaching in the Lurianic model, the accomplishments will be blemished and imperfect like the shattered vessels of creation. It is only logical that *tzimtzum* should lead to *shevirah*. Here, we must trust that people can grow toward perfection if we only allow them room. We must trust our students to do the work of *tikkun*, to restore our teachings in the course of time. It may be instructive to note that Luria himself used to emphasize to his students that they were all a part of one organism "and therefore needed to care and pray for each other." And as for his own method of teaching, Luria proceeded by "hints and allusions." He did not talk too much.

Seeking a Jewish Point of Departure

Since the early 1970s, I have made *tzimtzum* a regular part of my classroom methodology. In the course of time, it has become practical and effective. David Ausubel's experiments, demonstrating that short lectures punctuated by other forms of classroom activity is a highly effective technique, taught me that not speaking to the entire class for long periods of time did not mean I was not teaching. I found that Ausubel's distinction between meaningful learning and rote learning and the use of advance organizers also fit nicely with the *tzimtzum* method.

Jacob Kounin's work in "preventive" classroom discipline taught me that being in front of the class was not the same thing as controlling the class; Benjamin Bloom's work in questioning taught me that the quality of the answers was directly related to the quality of the questions and not to their quantity—and so on, through a myriad of well-developed and well-documented theories and insights which I attempted to pass along in my teacher seminars and in my book for Jewish teachers, *Managing the Jewish Classroom: How to Transform Yourself into a Master Teacher.*

What I sought most of all—and what proved most elusive— was a Jewish point of departure, something that distinguished Jewish teaching in particular from other models of teaching. In the Lurianic model as interpreted by Borowitz, I found a grounding for a Jewish methodology and a hint of where a Jewish philosophy of teaching might begin. I am, of course, aware that this is only one step toward a true philosophy of Jewish education.

In *Managing the Jewish Classroom*, I provided some insight into the work of one of the great theoreticians of modern Jewish education, Franz Rosenzweig (1886-1929). As a young man, Rosenzweig wrestled with my problem. Where should a philosophy of Jewish education begin? He never fully answered; instead, he settled on rethinking the issue of a Jewish curriculum for his time and place. In a letter to his philosopher friend, Hermann Cohen, Rosenzweig wrote:

> We are concerned with [the student's] introduction into the "Jewish sphere" which is independent from, and even opposed to, his non-Jewish surroundings. Those Jews with whom we are dealing have abandoned the Jewish character of the home … and, therefore, for them, that "Jewish sphere" exists only in the synagogue.… Within [the synagogue's] narrow sphere everything desirable is included. To talk only of the literary documents: [Bible,] talmudic and rabbinic writings … the works of the philosophers—but all this notwithstanding, the prayer book will forever remain the handbook and the signpost of historical Judaism. He to whom the prayer book is not sealed more than understands the "essence of Judaism"; he possesses it as a portion of his inner

life; he possesses a "Jewish world." He may possess a Jewish world, but he is surrounded by another one, the non-Jewish world. This fact cannot be changed, nor does the majority of those with whom we are concerned wish to change it; nevertheless, they wish to renew that Jewish world. ... [O]f the language of Hebrew prayer we may state categorically: it cannot be translated. Therefore the transmission of literary documents will never suffice; the classroom must remain the anteroom leading to the synagogue and of participation in its service. An understanding of public worship and participation in its expression will make possible what is necessary for the continuation of Judaism: a Jewish world.

Rosenzweig was speaking of the German-Jewish community at the time of the First World War. His letter was actually composed in the trenches as he served in the German military. His assumption was profound in its time but must be recast for modern Jewish educators to fully appreciate it.

Circumstances have changed drastically. The prayer book no longer represents the "essence of Judaism." But we can replace the prayer book with factors which do tie us inextricably to our "Jewish world," namely, our combined heritage of synagogue and Federation life; our common concern for the State of Israel; our common ethics; and our mission to explain to ourselves and to the world the meaning of the Holocaust. In these elements, we may begin to shape a new Jewish curriculum for our time and place as Rosenzweig did for his. In these elements are a beginning for a philosophy of Jewish education in today's Diaspora.

But even these do not completely satisfy our needs. To them, we could profitably add the definition supplied by another modern Jewish educator, Rav Abraham Isaac Kook (1865-1935) of Israel. In his book, *Orot HaTorah*, Kook wrote:

The goal of Jewish education is to mold the child according to the fullest possible potentialities of his natural dispositions and inclinations. If *halakhah* [Jewish law] is not the child's strength, then try to interest him in *aggadah* [Jewish "lore"]. If he persists that this too is not according to his abilities—do not force the literary tradition upon him, for it will corrupt him if he rejects it instinctively. If the child leans toward the sciences or "general wisdom" [meaning any useful field of liberal education], good! Develop this side of his personality—but encourage him to set a permanent time to study Torah daily, for Torah is becoming with productive pursuits.

Rosenzweig and Kook both begin their prescriptions for Jewish education with the student. Rosenzweig asks, "What is the common ground that students share as a starting point?" In his time, he answers, "the prayer book." From that point he postulates the future survival of Judaism. Kook asks, "What sparks the inborn interests of the student?" He answers, "Whatever it be, it can include a regular time for Jewish studies, for Torah (his way of saying, "all Jewish study") complements and deepens all other pursuits. These three then—Luria, Kook, and Rosenzweig—all bear a significant and timely message for today's Jewish education.

More Mystical Insight

In *Managing the Jewish Classroom*, I spoke of the fragility of teaching. A good example may be had from before the Second World War. As Nazism was on the rise in Germany and Fascism in Europe, a congress of Freudian analysts posed itself the following dilemma: "Since our skills are devoted to helping a person become more fully adept at what he or she is about, should we help a Fascist to become a better Fascist?" The discussion was complex, but the answer was a disappointing "Yes." There could hardly be a better example of the secular desert at work. In the end, the devotion of the analysts was not to morality, and not even to concern for the outcomes of their teachings, but to their methodologies, their theories. They abandoned responsibility for what was being accomplished preferring to concentrate on the ways they had created to accomplish it.

Jewish educators often reach outside the Jewish community for "new" methodologies. This effort is commendable, but the downside must also be considered for when the focus of Jewish education is turned to finding ways to use theories and means to fit religious concerns to external methods, the focus of Jewish education is frequently perverted. Ultimately, the wasteland of secularism invades the spiritual framework of our schools.

Instead, I believe we must focus on how we can utilize these methods to serve our purposes. The schema into which they fit must first be a Jewish schema. As Rosenzweig points out, it must emanate from what Jews still view as their common heritage. As Kook points out, our heritage must take precedence over the secular forces, even for students who will never entirely embrace it.

Tzimtzum is a part of the answer. It respects the student. And the Jewish mystical tradition may hold yet another useful insight. Jewish mystics teach that the soul is divided into three principal components: *nefesh, ruach,* and *neshamah.* The *nefesh* is that segment of the soul which we share with the animal and vegetable world. The *ruach* is that segment which distinguishes good from evil and which is inhabited by the two inclinations— the inclination to do good and the inclination to do evil. The *neshamah,* however, emanates directly from its Creator. It is the part of the human soul which recognizes the Divine Will.

In my book, *When a Jew Seeks Wisdom,* I offered a functional definition of *neshamah* as "religious awareness"— religious awareness being the ability to discover the sacred in the ordinary world, the ability to see what is possible in what already exists, and the ability to sense the right action even when a law or *mitzvah* cannot be found to set a definitive precedent.

Reb Zusya of Hanipol, a leading *Hasidic* teacher, was afflicted with blindness toward the end of his life. As we would expect whenever tragedy strikes, the human begins to doubt and to question. "Would a merciful God allow this to happen?" "Why does God not put an end to the suffering of the righteous?" Such questions tend to be on the levels of *nefesh* and *ruach.* Overcoming tragedy without jeopardizing faith requires a deeper strength. In this spirit, Reb Zusya assigned himself the difficult task of finding a blessing where there seemed only a curse. Using his religious awareness to overcome the lesser forces of his soul, he offered up the prayer, "Thank You, O Lord, for making me blind so that I might perceive the inner light."

There is no law commanding one to thank God for personal tragedy. A law such as that would be both cruel and bitter. And there is no commandment requiring us to accept whatever happens without anger, disappointment, or discouragement. But what Reb Zusya realized through his *neshamah* is that no physical blindness is as destructive as spiritual blindness—the blindness of the heart.

Because religious awareness is within that segment of the soul directly attuned to the Divine, we read in Proverbs (20:27), "The *neshamah* of the human is the lamp of the Lord, searching all the inward parts."

Jewish Education

Our understanding of Jewish education extends from these points. Educating a student Jewishly is more than the education of the *nefesh* and the *ruach* in their concern with how the world operates and the distinctions between good and evil. Jewish education also includes the training of the *neshamah*, the development of religious awareness.

Judaism is rich with occasions for the exercise of religious awareness, applications which exist in the everyday boundaries of time, space, and mind. The ceremonies of Jewish life, for example, and the rituals of Jewish celebration are prime occasions. Not only is the birth of each Jewish child fundamentally tied to the coming of the Messiah, but the wedding ceremony itself is called *kiddushin*, or "making holy." One senses the special attention of the community present in such public religious events just as one senses continually the benign Presence close at hand.

In the Passover *Haggadah,* we are reminded of the verse from Exodus (13:8): "It is because of what the Lord did for me when I came forth out of Egypt." Understanding oneself as the emanation of all selves throughout history is exercise par excellence for the *neshamah*. And most brilliantly of all, the Sabbath shines as an example, a space in time made holy once each week, a foretaste of the World to Come. These are gifts of our Jewish heritage, opportunities for bringing light into the chaos of everyday existence.

We can train our students to exercise religious awareness in many ways: in prayer, in action, in interaction, in poetry, in art, in drama, in sculpture, in photography, and in design. Through time, Jews have constructed a path which turns constantly upon itself, in which each action stirs the religious awareness to another action. One good deed draws another in its wake.

A stunning example is this: We may study the Mishnah in the course of any Jewish curriculum, but there is a custom of studying the Mishnah together in memory of the departed. Religious awareness leads to this and derives the practice from the fact that the Hebrew word *mishnah* is equivalent to the Hebrew word *neshamah*—both are constructed of the same letters merely rearranged! The added dimension of knowing this is similarly equivalent to the added dimension of not only experiencing a rainbow but having the religious awareness to connect it with God's covenant.

Some Implications

Perhaps I have gone too far afield. This is not a philosophy of Jewish education, though it may hint at the direction in which such a philosophy can proceed. The classroom should not be considered an adjunct to the synagogue, the welfare federation, or any other institution. It is only an adjunct to perceiving the world Jewishly, to gaining a consistent and continuous religious awareness. It is a place for honing the *neshamah* of each and every student. Every Jew, indeed every human being, has the necessary resources: *nefesh, ruach,* and *neshamah.* Many train only their *nefesh* and their *ruach* and still manage to live useful lives, but the lucky ones, the ones who encounter a master Jewish teacher, may also discover the value of religious awareness. For them, the world is never a secular desert. It is a meeting ground for the human and the Divine. It is a place filled with holy sparks awaiting redemption. It is a place where human discussions are held "for the sake of Heaven." It is a place where blessings are recited for a glorious sunset.

Every time you teach, you can bear this message. Every soul you touch, you can ignite. The power is yours to perform redemption if only you can withdraw yourself enough to make room for others to grow. And the real beauty of this understanding of Jewish teaching is that you will be learning as well. We are all a part of one organism. Is it too much to hope that we can pray for, care for, and teach one another?

❋

What Makes Our Students Tick?

Teachers' Day Keynote September 7, 1999

Throughout my career in Jewish education, I have been convinced of two needs—the need for relevance and the need for rapport. What we teach must be relevant to the individuals we are teaching no matter how young or how old our students may be, and nothing we teach can be deemed relevant by our students if they do not feel personally open to us as their teachers. As I like to say, "We can never teach a textbook or a subject matter or a curriculum; we can only teach students."

Today is a day of study. We began with the traditional prayer for studying together, praising God for consecrating us and calling us *la'asok b'divray Torah*, "to immerse ourselves in learning."

Just as this prayer is an expression of faith, I would like to follow it with another expression of faith: I say to you today that Jewish education in North America is not old and gasping for its last breath; Jewish education in North America is in its infancy. This is a matter of faith as well as a matter of fact. This is the good news. We have entered a new age, and anyone who teaches today's Jewish children must be aware that they are different from the Jewish children of the past.

Of course, most of us heard the bad news first. Since 1990, we have been worrying about the results of the Jewish Population Study which seemed to say that American Jewry is disappearing like a cartoon character being erased from the feet up by its artist. This is 1999, and we are still discussing our predicted demise. By now, though, I find it difficult to trust these statistics. From what I see, we have not disappeared, nor are we on the verge of disappearing.

Thanks to the Jewish Federation of North Jersey, I have this precious time to share a few words with you. I want to talk about the population study, about my belief that North American Jewish education is improving, and about a revolutionary proposal I can make for your students. But first, a story.

A man was walking with his daughter along the road when his daughter looked up at him and asked, "Daddy, why does sunshine look yellow?"

Her father answered, "That's a very good question, my child, a very good question. I don't know the answer, but the question is excellent."

They walked a little while longer, and the girl looked up at her father again and asked, "Daddy, what makes the sky blue?"

Her father answered, "I really don't know. But that's a wonderful question."

They went on walking, and pretty soon the daughter asked, "Daddy, why is grass green?"

Again, the father said, "That's a very good question, my child. I don't know the answer, but the question is very good."

Now the little girl sensed that she was causing her father some discomfort, so she looked up and said, "Daddy, I'm sorry that I am asking such hard questions."

The father replied, "Tut, tut, my child, that's quite all right. If you don't ask questions, you will never learn."

Gathering Facts

The people who ran the National Jewish Population Survey began by gathering facts, but facts are not answers. It is a lot easier to gather data than it is to analyze it. I am not an expert in either of these fields—neither a data-gatherer nor a data-analyzer—but I *am* a healthy skeptic who has been around awhile, and I have studied some of the critiques of the last few years.

Two main findings are striking to us. One, the study says that American Jews are not affiliating with the Jewish community in the percentages they customarily did. If this were true, it would certainly be a more important point than the second which speaks of intermarriage becoming a way of life. But the study itself indicates in other ways that affiliation is somewhat elastic.

The study maintains that at any given moment (for example, at the moment the population study was conducted) only fifty percent of the American Jewish community is affiliated with a synagogue or federation. Compared to the past, that is disappointing; however, if we look at the rest of the data, we find that over the course of the family's life cycle, nearly eighty percent of Jewish families affiliate at one time or another with the synagogue or the federation, and the picture is much more positive if we look at it this way. It means that people *do* come into the synagogue—perhaps to ensure that their children will receive an official Bar or Bat Mitzvah, perhaps because one of their children is soon to be married, perhaps because of a death in the family, perhaps because they are troubled or inspired. It is the same with federations. People give and participate in federations at some points in their family life and not at others. At any given time, some fifty percent of Jews are affiliated. Yet over the long haul, through federation and synagogue, we have the opportunity of working with nearly eighty percent of the American Jewish community.

I explained this to a Christian friend of mine who is a deacon in the Methodist Church, and he was overwhelmed. He told me that if eighty percent of the Christian community in America would attend churches, even on a rotating basis, the churches would be swamped. In fact, the Christian community never sees fifty percent of its total population! Yet we could hardly say that Christianity in America is disappearing!

So, we may not be disappearing in terms of affiliation, and that leaves only the disturbing statistics regarding intermarriage. Of course, intermarriage has a real impact on our community. Not only does it change the composition of our synagogues, it changes the terms in which we can teach in our classrooms. Still, it hardly spells the end of the Jewish people. Historically, we have gone through many periods in which intermarriage was very nearly a way of life, yet the disappearance of Jewish communities has rarely been traced to intermarriage alone.

The data which was gathered regarding intermarriage may also be skewed. In counting intermarriages, the National Jewish Population Study seems to have counted a marriage between two Jews as one marriage, but if the two Jews married non-Jewish partners, they counted that as two marriages. You can see how that might exponentially affect the figures pretty quickly. In actuality, the way it should have been done was to count a marriage between two Jews as two Jewish choices and to count two intermarriages as two more Jewish choices. This would bring the count of actual intermarriage down significantly. In the end, it is safe to say that we are more likely to lose our understanding of Judaism than we are to lose our Jews.

Now we turn to the subject of the day: Jewish education. What did the Jewish Population Study say about Jewish education? It calls Jewish education a sham, a pose, and a waste. It says that children coming out of Jewish day schools are just a little more likely to identify Jewishly many years later than those who studied in Jewish supplementary schools. It says that all Jewish schools are equally ineffective.

While this may be based on solid data, one must ask if the data is being interpreted correctly.

Consider the variables that creep into longitudinal studies such as this one. Is it the school that fails or the society that fails after the child leaves the school? Where should the long-term blame be placed? On parents who do not practice Jewish ritual in their homes? On families that do not attend the synagogue even when their children are in the school? On teachers? On rabbis? Who fails in the system? Or is the whole system rotten? Or are we just doing everything wrong?

Let's ask the question in another way: "What makes Jewish education effective?" *Why* does Jewish education work when it *does* work? Is affiliation with a synagogue what makes Jewish education effective? Is giving to the federation what makes Jewish education effective? If so, as we have seen, nearly eighty percent of our population does one of these things at some period in their lives. Then shouldn't we say that Jewish education *is* effective?

If, as it appears, we are a community in which people come and go as their needs demand, perhaps no one is really failing. It only looks that way when we cut into a moment in time the way you might slice a pie. Then you could say, there is half a pie here and half a pie there, when indeed, except for that small piece which happened to be eaten by the general society, almost all of the pie remains.

That's almost all I have to say about the Jewish Population study. We are close to the year 2000; we have not disappeared yet, nor does it look like we are going to disappear. The study is nearly a decade old, but we are thousands of years old and still going. But there is one positive thing to say. I believe it is healthy for us to *think* that we are about to disappear. Jews have used this strategy for millennia to urge themselves to exert extra effort in the cause of survival. And if the Jewish Population Study has caused the Jewish community in America to place education at the top of its agenda, I think that is very healthy, indeed! We are just beginning to see some dollars for Jewish education, and that is not bad. As my friend and teacher, Rabbi Levi Olan, always reminded me—we Jews should be "short-term pessimists and long-term optimists."

The North American Jewish Experience

I began by saying that Jewish education is still in its infancy, and I want to take up this theme once more. I think the whole North American Jewish experience is just about to take shape. Before World War II, nearly all the great world leaders of Judaism came out of the well-established communities of Eastern Europe. Conversely, the American Jewish community was known only for one great Jewish attribute—it had developed a tradition of *tzedakah* which was unparalleled anywhere in the Jewish world. Even in the world of the *shtetl*, often cited for its giving—where the beggar could have the *hutzpah* to say when a man gave less than usual on a Friday afternoon, "So you had a bad week, why should I?"—there was less giving than in America. After all, the rabbis in Europe were supported by the state, but in most of North America, the establishment of the synagogue and the payment of the rabbis has always been the job of individual Jews relying on their commitment to *tzedakah*. And so, with the rest of community giving, whether it was through the *landsman-*

schaften—coalitions of migrant communities for self-help, the free loan societies, the B'nai B'rith, or the emergent Federations, North American Jews were always known for giving.

The Holocaust was the first of three great events to interrupt and change the nature of the American Jewish community. It destroyed those age-old communities of Europe and eliminated the traditional status of being Jewish as a church or state definition. Except for the unfortunate Jews still trapped in the Soviet Union or in Arab countries, Jews suddenly had the necessity to self-identify, to define themselves as Jews if they chose to do so. That was one major effect of the Holocaust.

Another major effect of the Holocaust was that, in one brief instant, the leaders of world Jewry suddenly ceased to exist. We can look backward in anger at what the North American Jewish community failed to do to save the Jews of Europe, but we must understand their failure in the context of the times. At the time, few world leaders of Judaism existed outside of Europe. American Jewish leaders had always deferred to their European counterparts when it came to international affairs. Now, caught without strategy or experience, they developed new capabilities quickly.

We sometimes forget to credit the Jews of North America with what is perhaps their greatest accomplishment: Within twenty years after the war, with the money and work of American Jewry and with help from the Jews of Israel, all the Jews of Europe who could be moved were relocated to safe havens. This enormous task was accomplished even while the Jews of America were rebuilding their individual lives at home which was no small undertaking in itself. Thus, since World War II, American Jewry has emerged as the leading community of the Diaspora taking over international affairs as the Europeans had done before them. Of course, American Jews do this in their own style and in their own way, and largely through the means they best understand—through *tzedakah*.

Things have also changed drastically due to a third event, the establishment of the State of Israel. I will not go into all the delicate features of the relationship between North America's Jews and Israel, but I will point out that every action of Israel as a political unit has immediate reverberations for the Jewish community in America.

So the last fifty years or so have been a time of adjustment to conditions which occurred during or shortly after World War II. We have had to redefine world Judaism; rescue the Jews of Russia, Africa, and the Arab countries; and come to grips with the State of Israel. At this moment, however, none of these problems provides meaning for our continued existence. Now it is time to move on. It is time for us to define a Jewish future for ourselves, for North American Jewry. Every movement—Orthodox, Conservative, Reconstructionist, and Reform—feels this need. All of us are talking theology, identity, and spirituality. We are not turning inward; we are just attempting to discover what Judaism means to us now and in our future.

There was a time when we spoke of Jewish theology in terms of what God does for us. We said that God was so all-pervasive that God had to literally contract to make space for the world and for humanity to exist. Our tradition calls this contraction *tzimtzum*. If there was a time when God filled all space and had to do *tzimtzum* to allow us to exist, the tables have surely been turned. Today, every Jewish individual in North America must do *tzimtzum* to make space for God to exist. We need to create room enough in our lives for an absolute being, a commanding being, to exist. This is a matter of individual choice—no matter whether you are Orthodox, Conservative, Reconstructionist, or Reform.

As Jewish communities go, we are in our infancy. The first two hundred years have been a tough but exciting beginning. Now we must determine what unique contribution, if any, our community can make to the long history of Judaism as a whole. I have nothing against Holocaust museums, for example, but I would far rather see us pledge to create one Jewish teacher for each victim of the Holocaust than one museum for each city. If our need is for a Jewish future, our need is for effective teachers and effective education.

Jewish Education

What Jewish education really means is that you are on the front line working day by day to recreate Jewish life. Yet there is no blueprint by which to work. Today's students are different. They are far removed from the Holocaust. They do not automatically feel the need to give *tzedakah*. They view Israel as a possible place to spend a pleasant vacation.

You need a plan, and no one seems to be able to give it to you. It certainly does not exist in any national curriculum. These curricula are flawed from the outset, and they have lost much of their relevance by the time they reach Detroit, or Cleveland, or Denver, or Montreal, or any of the other cities. They are ineffective even along the Western or Eastern seaboards! Most of the curricula available today are packaged patterns for recreating our past when what we really need are blueprints for creating our future.

It is obvious that the National Jewish Population Study was right, but for the wrong reasons. As teachers we know, deep in our hearts, that the schools as they now exist do not work! To borrow a phrase from Dr. Jon Woocher, we have taken a "vaccination" approach to Jewish education. We say, "let me give you this vaccination shot now, and later you will stay Jewish and marry Jewish and raise Jewish children." We have tried to see Jewish schooling as a way of creating a Jewish adult. This approach renders our classrooms useless.

It is useless to say to today's nine-year-old, "You need to study Hebrew because Hebrew will open the riches of Judaism for you later," or "You need to study Hebrew because later you will need it for your Bar or Bat Mitzvah." The nine-year-old wants to know, "How does Hebrew help me *now*?"

The truth is that what the centralized curricula have given us is *subjects* to teach while what we are really teaching are *children*! What we need to teach a nine-year-old is how to live a nine-year-old's Jewish life. A thirteen-year-old needs to learn how to live a Jewish life as a thirteen-year-old. A seventeen-year-old needs to learn to live a Jewish life at seventeen. A thirty-year-old needs to learn how to live a Jewish life as a thirty-year-old. And a seventy-five-year-old person needs to learn to live a Jewish life at seventy-five.

School alone cannot accomplish this task, so we must stop thinking of the religious school as the central address for Jewish education. Then how should we see it? The religious school is the place where we connect with young Jews and their families. We must stop thinking of the religious school as a place for "vaccinating" our students for a Jewish future, and we must be-gin showing them how they and their families can live a Jewish life now. We must stop thinking of a religious school as a place that *ends* at a specific grade because there *is* no end to Jewish learning. Jewish education continues to exist whether it is training five-year-olds or seventy-five-year-olds. We must reach out to every age level with programs that fulfill the require-ments of each.

Religious schools will remain, but they are only a part of my ideal Jewish apprenticeship. The other parts are so important that they need to be incorporated into the education of every Jewish child and every Jewish adult. They are the youth group (with its adult concomitants—the *havurot* and synagogue com-mittees, the brotherhood, and women's organization), camp-ing (with its adult concomitant—the retreat weekend), and trips to Israel. The schools are essential to the success of the camps, the youth groups, and the Israel trips, but the youth groups, the camps, and the Israel trips are equally as important as the schools. All together, these four elements are the Jewish ap-prenticeship of which I am speaking; take away any one of these elements and the other three become significantly weaker.

My revolution in Jewish education is really nothing more than an awakening to what is already working when it works. Family education is a term we use for almost any combination of these parts. What family education always seems to come down to is some conglomeration of retreat weekend or school-bound experience or Israel program—a mixture of adult and children's programs bound to satisfy few of the participants. What a shame we don't use this to open our apprenticeship to the real world! Here is a chance for us to say that everyone needs to understand Judaism on his or her own level. What does it mean to a busi-nessperson, what does it mean to a single parent, what does it mean to someone married to a non-Jew, what does it mean to a girl about to become a Bat Mitzvah, what does it mean to a man getting ready for his wedding, what does it mean to someone studying for conversion, and so on, and so on, and so on... To re-ally deal with a family, we must deal with each member of the family in a unique way, constantly asking the question—what does this mean to *you*? This is not a new question. This is what the Passover *Haggadah* demands of us. Each of us must imagine what it means to us to come out of Egypt. We must extend that question to every subject we teach in the classroom.

We very much need to hold teacher workshops and seminars like this one, but it is incumbent upon us to remember that these are just tools for reaching our real goal. And we need to define our ultimate goal as something much more significant than mere schooling. We need to forget schooling and concentrate on making and keeping contact, much the way a master does with an apprentice. We are charged with training Jews to live their everyday lives as Jews, and in that pursuit, we need to spend more time speaking to our students about their everyday lives, explaining how Judaism—learned through sources, through history, through Bible, through customs and ceremonies, through arts and crafts, through media, etc.—impacts their lives every day.

You and I know, because we are educators, that students remember what is important to them to remember. They retain what is important to them to retain. We also know that the decision of what to learn and what to retain is a personal decision, made individually by each and every child. When you teach a value, you try to connect that value to something in the child's everyday world. You cannot simply say, "Learn this now, so you can use this later." That "vaccination" approach clearly does not work. You must be proactive. "Learn this now because you need this now, because it will make this moment better—and here is how it applies to you *now*." If you can do this with every subject you teach, if you can tie in what you are teaching in religious school this week, or in the day school this day, to the life of the child as he or she comes out of the classroom today, then what you are teaching will stick.

Some of you do this much of the time. Many of you do this some of the time. In fact, we all must get better at doing this *all* of the time. The next time you are going to say to a student, "Learn this because you will need it later," think again. Imagine a way in which the student could use it now. And if you can't imagine a way in which it is immediately useful to your student, ask the student; students can often provide just the answer that we are looking for. Ask them. After all, it's their life, their identity, their Judaism which is really at stake.

Teach Now

This is my message to you as Jewish teachers. You cannot teach your students what Jews will need to know in the future because none of us can see the future. We haven't got the kind of prophecy in our midst that can tell us what the future holds. But we do make contact with Jews, and we can teach them to make room for God in their everyday lives. If we do that—if we make every Jewish lesson relevant to the student—and if we encourage every student to join our youth groups, use our camps, go on our weekends, and take our trips to Israel—we cannot help but succeed. If we stop thinking of schools as the quintessential educator and start thinking of our educational enterprise as something much larger, as an apprenticeship for Jewish living, then we can succeed even with four walls around us.

Now I have to say something to you directly. An apprenticeship is no good if the master is not setting the right example for the apprentice. If you teach Jewish prayer, but never go to synagogue yourself, your teaching is less effective. The model you are setting falls far short of the mark. If you teach Jewish practice, but do not practice Jewishly, then the apprentice learns as much by what you do not do as by what you do.

The magic of making contact is that we invite people to become part of our community, but if we ourselves are not in the community, then why should others join? The teacher is the key to creating the community. The Talmud tells how Rabbi Judah the Prince sent two rabbis out to all the small towns. In each town, they would ask, "Show us the guardians of your city." The people would show them the Jews who stood guard at the gates of the town. Then they would say, "These are not the guardians of your community. Show us your teachers. They are the true guardians." *You* are the guardians of your community.

Yours is a great responsibility. Sure, you are a good person. Sure, you live a moral life. But this is not enough. You must be *in* the community, a part of the synagogue, a contributor to the federation, a part of the celebrations—a full participant in everyday Jewish existence. Otherwise, the contact you make is artificial. Your students sense the difference, they grasp the difference, and they behave according to the way you behave. Your students' parents know the difference, they feel the difference, and they also look to you for a model. In Jewish teaching, the contact you make with the home is as important as the contact you make with the student. Every Jewish teacher should have two parts to every lesson plan—the part that takes place within the classroom and the part that goes home with the students to help their families get involved. And every Jewish teacher should be proud to be a Jewish role model.

Success

I count Jewish education today as a great success today. It is successful precisely because of things we cannot measure. We are not there with our population studies when a stressed-out Jewish college student considers taking his or her life in desperation. We are not there with our population studies when that student suddenly recalls how important life is, how the Nazis and all our other enemies tried to rob us of life to destroy us. We are not there with our population studies when that student considers how Hillel was saved by his teachers from freezing on the roof and warmed by the light of a forbidden fire on the Sabbath. When that student decides *not* to commit suicide, we do not get his or her name so that we can say that Jewish education succeeded. When another young person decides not to pilfer from a store or become part of a gang, we are not there. When someone decides not to be complicit in fraternity or sorority cruelties against others, we are not there. When a former student of ours becomes a lawyer and decides to defend the poor because of what he or she learned in our schools, we are not there.

In all cases, we are not there, and the person who *is* may not even realize that his or her decision has anything to do with his or her Jewish education. Yet it does. It matters. Jewish education changes lives. It transforms people in ways that we may never fully comprehend.

Any day now, in any one of your classes, the future Messiah may be sitting and listening. After all, someone is going to have to teach the Messiah. The budding Messiah may be the tough boy in the last row who never seems to pay attention. Or she may be the little girl in the second row who spends all her time doodling. You and I cannot know which student the Messiah will be. Yet every one of our students must be treated as if he or she were the Messiah because every one of them has the potential for changing the world.

Someone taught Hebrew to a little boy named David Green in Russia, and he became David Ben-Gurion, the first prime minister of the state of Israel. Someone taught Bible to a little girl in Baltimore, and she became Henrietta Szold, a founder of Hadassah and the leader of Youth Aliyah Child Rescue in Jerusalem. Someone taught Jewish history to a little girl in Milwaukee, and she grew up to be Golda Meir, fourth prime minister of Israel. Someone taught the Jewish value of life to a young boy in New York, and he grew up to become Dr. Jonas Salk, developer of the polio vaccine. Every day, you and I teach Judaism to young people who will eventually grow up to change the world.

Let's abandon the idea of the school because it does not work, and instead let's work on the piece of that idea which actually does work—the apprenticeship, the experience of Jewish living, the study of materials that are relevant now, that change us now, that transform us now, that make us identify with our Judaism today and every day from the day we are born to the day we die. Let's transform the school, the youth group, the camps, and our instructional trips to Israel into one great apprenticeship of Jewish experience. If we do that, we will create a new Judaism which is uniquely North American and authentically Jewish, and we will make an important contribution to that great experiment in living in God's image which is the history of our people.

It is my prayer for you and for me that all of us will find the wisdom to make a space in our lives, a *tzimtzum*, to make room for God inside of us.

✤
Lucy & the First Amendment

*A large audience attended the discussion on March 13,
1997, at Congregation Emanu-El on New York's Fifth
Avenue. The event was entitled "Congress, Court, and
Classroom." I was invited to participate on a panel of
three speakers in my capacity as Director of the Department of Education of the Union of American Hebrew
Congregations (now the Union for Reform Judaism). I
am not surprised that so many years later the topic and
my response both remain relevant.*

**Congress shall make no law respecting an establishment
of religion, or prohibiting the free exercise thereof ...**

I like to think of the First Amendment to the Constitution of
the United States as a kind of Old Faithful of the legal system.
Routinely, it throws up a spewing fountain of opinion, resolutions, ink, and invective. It guarantees a separation of church
and state in simple, straightforward language. It is clear in intent and clear in purpose. Nevertheless, it is perennially debated. There are surely valid reasons for this debate: Pressure is
brought for tax credits or some form of equity payments to subsidize those who send their children to parochial schools as opposed to public schools. Claims are made that whole districts
are restricted from having public school prayers even though
their entire population is of one denomination. And so on.

Recently, however, with the rise of the religious right, a
new wrinkle has appeared. The argument has been advanced
that the First Amendment is contrary to the Christian origins of

our Constitution. James Dobson of Focus on the Family says that "the Constitution was designed to perpetuate a Christian order,"[1] and Pat Robertson claims that the wall of separation between church and state is "a lie of the Left," and that our original Christian government has been subverted by a cabal of twentieth century liberals and free thinkers. "If Christian people work together," says Robertson, "they can succeed in winning back control of the institutions that have been taken from them over the past seventy years."[2]

This would have been news to our founding fathers. John Adams, for example, wrote in 1786, that the architects of American government never "had interviews with the gods or were in any degree under the inspiration of Heaven."[3] James Madison, in the well-known *Federalist Papers, No. 10,* argued that zealous pursuit of religious opinions, far from leading people to "cooperate for their common good," usually causes them "to vex and oppress each other." And one of the most common criticisms of the Constitution during its ratification phase was that it showed a "cold indifference towards religion" and had no reference to a deity.[4]

None of the founding fathers, and none of their critics, intimated that the church and the state were synonymous. Yet that is the very claim being made now by the religious right. I suppose that it would be naïve of me to be surprised by such a claim. After all, there are those who claim that the Holocaust never happened and would wish us to teach this "truth" in our schools. And there are those who claim that the research of science is flawed since the Bible clearly states that the world was created in six days, and they would wish us to teach this "truth" in our schools.

Some years ago, when I was a lecturer in the adult extension courses at Hebrew Union College-Jewish Institute of Religion in New York City, I was assigned to teach a course in the history of the Bible. In my class was an eccentric student we shall call Lucy. She came each session burdened by shopping bags filled with books. While I was lecturing, Lucy would reach in her bags for one book or another to examine it and sometimes make a quick note in it. I asked other teachers about her, and many said that Lucy had taken their courses, too, and that she always carried books to class and always spent time annotating them. They explained that Lucy had a theory, and she was making the round of teachers at our rabbinical college just to prove her theory. I asked them what the theory was, but they smiled and said, "Ask Lucy." So, one evening I did. I asked Lucy if she wanted to share her theory with the class. She said, "I'd love to," and she proceeded.

Lucy told the class that she believed the world was created around the time of George Washington. In fact, George Washington was not just "the Father of our country," but George and Martha Washington were the real Adam and Eve. Lucy thought that most of the Bible—the Old Testament part—was actually written by Benjamin Franklin. The rest—the New Testament part—was written by Thomas Jefferson. Lucy said that if you looked very closely at everything in the history of the United States, you could easily see that everything we learned from the Founding Fathers and Founding Mothers of our country was secretly someplace in the Bible. Lucy ended by saying that she could prove everything that she believed.

I think of Lucy more often these days. As I hear theories of why the First Amendment must be changed or repealed, how the United States should find the courage to become a theocracy, how our founding fathers were closet Christians merely pretending to be deists, I find that there is really only one thing about Lucy that surprises me: With such a fabulous theory as hers, I wonder why she failed to break through as a national star. There should have been a ready market for her ideas, perhaps in the *National Enquirer* or in appearances on late night television. Lucy, like the folks of the religious right, was a "true believer." Nothing could change her mind. She attended class to the end of the term, continued to sift through her shopping bags in response to remarks and discussions, and refused to be confused by evidence.

Like the religious right claiming that we live in a Christian country, Lucy started with a theory and built her world around her theory. I like to think that I avoid that method. I like to start by listening, reading, and checking and building what I believe—my theory—on evidence. I like to think that when facts conflict with my theory, it is my theory that gives way.

After all, we have plenty of evidence of what happened in history. We have evidence that the Holocaust happened. We have evidence that the world was not created in six twenty-four-hour days. We have evidence that the world is not flat. And we have evidence that the Founding Fathers crafted, and the thirteen colonies approved, a radically godless document intentionally freeing politics from its age-old linkage with religion—despite the fact that many of the colonies had religious beginnings and continued to have state constitutions demanding religious adherence of one kind or another.

Of course, we have every right and every reason to teach respect for religion. Not just for one religion, but for all religions. Not just in public schools, but in all schools. But respect for, and practice of, are separate matters in the United States. Separate by design, separate by intention. I say this as a religious educator, knowing that if mine were the majority religion, I would still say this, for the glory of our system is that there is a place for me and a place for Lucy, even if Lucy would wish otherwise.

❀ Notes

1 James Dobson in Isaac Kramnick and R. Laurence Moore, *The Godless Constitution: The Case against Religious Correctness*, New York and London: W. W. Norton and Company, 1997, pp. 22-23.

2 http://www.cc.org/commentary

3 John Adams, *The Works of John Adams, Second President of the United States*, Vol. 4, Boston: Charles C. Little and James Brown, 1851, p. 292.

4 See Isaac Kramnick and R. Laurence Moore, *op. cit.*, p. 28.

✳

The Educational Imperative

A Report

For more than twenty-five years, every summer I attended—and helped shepherd—the foremost venue for teacher education ever assembled for the North American Jewish community. Three conferences beginning in 1976 proved that there was a thirst among teachers and educators to come together to teach one another—a thirst that knew none of the usual bounds of this or that movement, this or that branch of Jewish religion. There was also a need for a formal structure to continue this work, and it had to come from the folks themselves. If there were to be a continuation, teachers had to advocate for themselves. After the fourth conference, I was commissioned to write this report which was published in abbreviated form in the American Jewish Committee's magazine Present Tense *and in full in the independent journal* Response.

No doubt every Jewish organization should include in its conference budget an item for a professional anthropologist. It is difficult to know what really happened at a conference since one is most keenly aware only of what happened to oneself. It might, therefore, be enlightening to read a general account of conference behavior. That is, of course, if an anthropologist could make head or tail of it.

Certainly, the few pages below about "what really happened" at the Fourth Annual Conference on Alternatives in Jewish Education held at Rutgers University, August 23-28, 1979, will not suffice as a complete report. Still, it may serve to balance an impression which just a glance at the 166-page program book or the Conference resolutions may give.

The People

First and foremost, they came. People were still frantically registering as the Shabbat curtain fell a full day and a half after the beginning of the conference. It seems that over one thousand people gathered at Rutgers University over the course of these five days.

Some educators came looking for jobs complaining that the best jobs were being taken by rabbis untrained in matters educational. Rabbis who had staked out education as their specialty (and there are now quite a few) complained that there were not enough educational jobs to go around.

Some came because they could feel the winds of change blowing past them. The leaders of the Conference referred to them collectively as the "establishment," agencies dealing with Jewish education. They came to see if the message which had been going around were actually true: *voluntarism was beginning to have an impact on organized Jewish education.* Teachers were literally paying their own way to this conference coming from as far away as Texas, California, and Great Britain. The leaders of educational agencies may have felt that they would soon be faced with lay leaders in Jewish education, and they had to see it first-hand.

The establishment came for another reason, too. The hardest and most long-fought battle which Jewish education in America has faced is the battle among Reform, Orthodox, Conservative, Reconstructionist, Secular, and Zionist Jews about what the words "Jewish" and "education" mean when spoken in the same breath. Somehow, that did not seem a concern of this [new] Coalition on Alternatives in Jewish Education (CAJE). The one thousand people who gathered came from every shade and nuance of Jewish lifestyle, and they were intent on working together.

By far the greatest majority came to be part of a happening in Jewish life. The "Woodstock" of Jewish Education had occurred two years before at the Second Conference on Alternatives in Jewish Education in Rochester, New York. About 700 attended that conference. Although the layout of the university campus was very spread out making it inconvenient for people to attend sessions, people still found themselves suddenly involved in a few intensive days of Jewish activity after a summer of Jewish starvation. Soon the word got out that the Rochester conference of 700 had been an "intimate" experience. (Naturally, those who had attended the much smaller first conference held in Providence, Rhode Island, at Brown University in 1976 when only 350 people showed up, felt that the Rochester conference was "too large.") It was clear from the outset that the people registering for the Fourth Annual Conference were here to be "intimately" involved with 999 of their closest friends in Jewish education.

Expectations of Intimacy

Most of those who came treated the Conference as a one-time phenomenon. Many arrived on Friday just to "share" Shabbat. One CAJE leader wryly observed of the ten *minyanim*—ranging from an Orthodox *minyan* to a *minyan* for women only—that the Reform *minyan* was like being at a Conservative synagogue for Shabbat, the Conservative *minyan* was like attending an Orthodox *shul*, and so on.

It was a day replete with activities. Beginning Friday evening with programs following prayer, one could choose between such diverse offerings as "Dietary Preparations for the Messiah" and "Creating a Jewish Agenda for the 1980s." Text study classes after Saturday lunch ranged from "Toward a Jewish Interpretation of Dreams" to "Exploring Jewish Philosophers and Their Views of Education." Entertainments and further study sessions Saturday afternoon included sessions on "Earthy Ecstasy" and "The Gospel Tradition."

If there were a "happening" at this Conference, Shabbat was it. As a happening, it had been a bit weaker in the past, probably because it was less carefully orchestrated. This time, however, it reached its climax when the entire group gathered in a square outside the Commons Building for a *Havdalah* Service followed by dancing and singing.

In addition to the size of the Conference body, the programmatic content of the remainder of the Conference served to keep intimacy at bay. In planning the programs for the first two conferences, there had been an attempt to find program leaders who were willing to share what they knew and to learn what others had to teach. Everyone who led a session was expected to attend sessions led by others. Therefore, the program had been dominated by newer, less-established leaders and by recognized presenters and teacher-trainers who came as volunteers and became true participants. Little distance was felt between teacher and leader, between participant and expert.

The organizers of the Rutgers Conference became lax in stressing the importance of the teach-study model of the earlier conferences. Therefore, some better-known teacher trainers and textbook authors came only to present their own sessions and then left. They may have been, by count, no more than ten percent of those leading sessions, yet they were a noticeable ten percent.

One of the reasons that people at Rutgers may have felt a slipping away of the "intimacy" gained during Shabbat, then, was that these leaders who spoke in the course of some 158 Modules (sessions lasting three, six, or nine hours) and 139 "Lehrhauses" (one and a half hour sessions named for the famous adult education project undertaken in Germany between the wars) were beginning to feel more distant from them. Inevitably, even within a small community like that of Jewish education in America, some distance accrues between those who are "published" and their peers.

A Composite Portrait of the Leadership

Sitting at a meal in the huge dining hall or sitting in one of the sessions teaching everything from how to make puppets to how to prepare a Torah text for presentation, one began to sense that this *was* a special gathering. Participants' backgrounds varied—the most-Orthodox and the most-liberal often sat side by side discussing issues and testing opinions. Old and young studied together without self-consciousness. For many who attend other conventions of Jewish educators and rabbis during the year, this was a conference where the tie and dress could be shunned in favor of jeans and tee-shirts.

People heard about the conference in every way imaginable: official mailings to schools, synagogues, and educational institutions; contact with people who had been to a previous conference; or by word of mouth.

And the whole thing was brought together by a very small group with a predominantly volunteer staff living in borrowed space. In fact, almost all who worked to draw this conference together were also working in full-time professional capacities.

Many of the original CAJE leaders were graduates of the Jewish student movement organization called Network. Most of them, even by the time of the Providence conference in 1976, had separated themselves from this beginning and developed a new premise: they were entering the field of Jewish education, and they wanted to change it and make it better, not only individually but collectively.

Money was not their strong suit. Instead, they volunteered their time and skills, and they expected anyone who wished to be a part of their circle to do likewise. Even at the Rutgers Conference, no session leader was paid (though a few were given small travel subsidies) and no CAJE leader was paid, yet hundreds of people volunteered to lead sessions.

Education is generally a low priority item in Jewish fiscal spending, and despite the fact that our participants were not rich, a quick glance at those who made donations which helped to subsidize the costs of the Conference shows that 80% of these donations were made by the participants themselves—this in addition to registration fees and travel expenses.

Leaders and participants alike responded to the educational imperative set forth by past conferences: *If each would give according to his or her ability, they would all benefit; and if they benefitted, Jewish education would benefit.*

In contradistinction to this message, CAJE leaders have tried for five years to convince one Federation after another, one local Board or Bureau of Jewish Education after another that the need is there. They have been forced to raise funds with little recognition from above, and in a way which, by its very nature, had to cause the established educational institutions of the Jewish community to feel that CAJE was a pariah group competing for the same funds which are the very lifeblood of these established agencies.

Things, however, grew more and more complex. With each new success, with more teachers and laypeople at each succeeding conference, the CAJE leaders grew frazzled. The amount of money needed to subsidize each conference grew in proportion to the number attending. CAJE leaders found themselves increasingly in the role of fundraisers and less in the role of educators. They found that every year greater demands were being made both on their time and on their personal resources. They were themselves confronting serious moments in their personal careers as professionals in Jewish education. (CAJE leaders are mainly drawn from college, day school, and religious school faculties, and from among principals and administrators of Jewish schools and heads of important departments of Jewish education.)

Even as external politics were becoming more problematic, so, too, were internal politics. The Coalition had opened an office on the west coast prior to the Irvine Conference and had opened an office on the east coast prior to the Rutgers Conference. Now, looking forward to a fifth Conference in Santa Barbara, California, in 1980, there was a need to continue the West Coast office. At the same time, for fundraising purposes, it seemed impossible to discontinue the East Coast office.

West Coast leaders expressed concern that most of the funds raised should be sent to the West for the next conference, but certainly the East had a claim on these monies as well. For a while it seemed there might be a split into two separate entities; however, one thing which held them together was the prospect of a 1981 conference somewhere in the Midwest. In being held together in this tenuous way, they were much like a couple on the verge of separation which imprudently seeks to have a child in hopes of saving their relationship.

The Politics of an Experience

Two leadership cadres had emerged, one on each coast. As both recognized that the issues were growing larger and not smaller, they called a Policy Conference in June 1978. After three days of meetings, three basic premises were hammered out. One, the group would remain as one Coalition. Two, they were not ready to join any other existing national agency for Jewish education though they were willing to cooperate with other agencies. Three, they were anxious to nurture new leadership by encouraging volunteers to take on new jobs within the movement—jobs which would continue throughout the entire year thereby binding one convention to the next.

This last idea was a significant departure, since it called upon professionals in Jewish education to become volunteers in their own field. It was also a new direction since it stressed voluntarism above fundraising. The concept was simple. Instead of passing resolutions condemning this or calling for that, CAJE would recognize official task forces of volunteers willing to actively work for select causes. Each task force would be a mini network of teachers spread across the continent, corresponding by mail, reporting at board meetings, and forming the backbone of the board of directors of the organization.

The entire membership was solicited by mail a week before the conference, and proposals for task forces were quickly returned to the conference office. On Thursday evening of the conference, the proposals became the basis for a preliminary task force meeting. Rooms were assigned to the various interest groups and people coming in were informed that joining a task force meant committing themselves to work on this task for the coming year.

Again, the idea was met with enthusiasm. One of the outstanding phenomena of the conference was the constant announcement at meals of task forces eating together in various sections of the dining hall or calling meetings late into the evenings. By the time of the first plenary session, twenty-one different groups of volunteers had submitted task force resolutions calling on the Coalition to recognize them as official projects and to support their efforts.

In the end, every task force was accepted, most by unanimous vote. They included Task Forces on Coordinating Services for Soviet Jewish Educators; Special Needs Education; Teaching by, for, and about the Aging and the Aged; Research in Jewish Education; Teacher Training; Improving the Quality of

Intermediate Hebrew Instruction; Peace; Women in Jewish Education; and a host of other topics.

Ironically, almost all these projects are also considered to be concerns of one or another of established agencies which deal with Jewish education. Representatives of these agencies at the conference spent much time warning CAJE leaders that the Task Forces would "step on the toes" of the establishment, thereby causing CAJE great embarrassment and making fund-raising even more difficult.

The CAJE leaders tried to explain that these were not competitive but cooperative forces. Yet both sides realized that the line between competition and cooperation on any Task Force ultimately depended on its success.

The Meaning of "Coalition"

The CAJE conference harbored conflict from start to finish. Two events, central to the Rutgers gathering, serve to illustrate how conflict emerged and how it was resolved.

One Shabbat afternoon session was the most controversial of all the conference activities. It was ostensibly a forum entitled, "Israel and Jewish Educators: Critical Options for the 1980s." Regrettably, however, it turned into a debate between the presenters—who tried to deal with West Bank settlement, Palestinians, and Israel's relations with the Diaspora—and outspoken members of the audience who both reasoned and heckled, espousing the most traditional political views of Israel and her foreign relations. The net result was dissatisfying—an experience which convinced many that the session was totally aimed at politics in general and at leftist politics in particular—and that it was out of place in the context of a Conference on Alternatives in Jewish Education.

A plenary session resolution subsequently deemed all direct political activity "inappropriate" and banned it from future conferences. The debate which preceded this decision was heated, yet the consensus which won out spoke not to the issues of the debate but to the intent of the Coalition. The majority agreed that there are some issues which must be considered "beyond the pale" if any Coalition is to exist.

These issues are evidently a question for issue-by-issue review. Israel and her foreign and domestic policy were clearly one of them. Another was highlighted during debate on a resolution calling for a task force on Women in Jewish Education. Just to set the scene, the plenary sessions took place in the dining hall which is built in the fashion of two large rectangular rooms converging at a 90° angle. The far corner of this angle held a stage from which speakers could be seen and heard in both wings of the hall. The Eastern CAJE leaders seemed to gravitate toward the front, near the stage, and somewhat to the left of it. The Western leaders stayed further back, almost dead center in the small end of the angle. The Orthodox tended to group together to the right of the stage and in fair proximity to one of the standing microphones set up for comments from the floor. The rest of the members sat in small groups, some with their task forces, some with friends, some with an eye to political advantage.

As the resolution on creating a task force on Women in Jewish Education was read by its sponsors, the groups visibly tightened. The sponsors were calling for a task force that would critique curriculum, determine whether proper role models were being set in Jewish textbooks, and enhance professional opportunities for women in Jewish education. The Orthodox faction took clear exception to these ideas. Even before the reading of the resolution was complete, several Orthodox women were standing at the microphone ready to refute it. Their arguments were sound. "Who is to determine what is a 'proper' role model?" "Are we truly going to constitute a censoring committee for textbooks?" "Is there only one position which can be taken within these issues?"

The debate lasted until a motion was made to table the resolution. In many cases, tabling spells the end of a resolution, and it seemed as though this might be the case. Then one of the Orthodox women came to the microphone and asked if task force membership were open to anyone in CAJE, if anyone interested in any task force could automatically join. The answer was a simple yes. Anyone could join any task force. This rule was considered to be the elemental check and balance system for keeping task forces "kosher."

What followed was remarkable. Even as other resolutions were being discussed, a small contingent of Orthodox women sought out the sponsors of the resolution and sat with them in the back of the dining hall ironing out a new text acceptable to all. They brought this new resolution to the attention of the chairperson who allowed them to present it. Now the original sponsors stood side by side at the microphone with the Orthodox women who had opposed them from the floor. The new resolution, greatly moderated, still called for significant action to determine how women fit into various kinds of role models and how women could best be integrated into the professional realms of Jewish education. It was passed by acclamation.

There was a clear sense in the momentary pause that followed that something significant had happened. The educational imperative had held again; the participants had expressed a greater need for Coalition than for conflict.

The Educational Havurah

During the plenary sessions, entertainment of all kinds was also scheduled. This conflictive scheduling was prompted by the experience of CAJE leaders who found that only about one-third of the members were genuinely interested in political activities of the organization. Reading the program book and seeing the variety and number of entertainments offered up against the plenary sessions, one might be tempted to conclude that being political was considered by the conference planners as just another way of having fun.

The plenary sessions, though, gave one a very different impression. The inner leadership made it clear that work makes one a *haver*, an inner circle member. Their emphasis on commitment and their valuation of people in terms of the devotion which they brought to their tasks recalled the kibbutz days of the Second Aliyah. There were more than a few young A.D. Gordons in action at these sessions.

There is little doubt that CAJE is no longer the counter-culture movement that it once was. Its cultural status, if not its political and financial future within the Jewish community, is established. Its members and leaders are increasingly the establishment's professional leadership. In a sense, they have only to grow older and more powerful before they can demand prerogatives which are now held by more entrenched professionals. There is also little doubt that an attempt at reconciliation which might emanate from the present educational establishment would be warmly received by the CAJE leaders.

The Rutgers Conference gives the impression that the educational imperative is truly operative in American Jewish life. The teachers themselves wish to be educated and come willingly. Likewise, the leaders themselves see the conference as an opportunity for learning and growth and so share their professional talents freely—talents for which they are normally well paid. For the sake of continuing their Coalition, factions set aside differences of religious and political leanings and concentrate on what they can practically do in their classrooms to help their students.

The Educational Imperative

To this day, the effects of the Rutgers Conference reverberate in religious and day school classrooms, in adult education classes, in youth groups and movements, in camps and camp retreats. There is an expressed and implied commitment to the ever-heightening quality of Jewish education—a commitment that rises above the cries that there is not enough money for Jewish education to survive.

This is the educational imperative represented by the voluntary nature of the political and cultural leadership of the Fourth Annual CAJE Conference: that people are willing to work for their own betterment so that this generation may pass on what it knows and the next generation may know more.

A Brief History of CAJE

The Conference and the Coalition

This "history" does not cover the end of CAJE. Sadly, CAJE's elected leaders chose to expand ambitious programs by hiring more and more professionals. Simultaneously, conferences became more difficult to schedule and more expensive to run. Colleges—the best venues—were now using their campuses year-round. At the same time, communal allocations for Jewish education were being curtailed—even long-established boards and bureaus of Jewish education fell before insufficient funding. CAJE, like other noble endeavors, became a victim of its own success. Yet the need for a national Jewish teacher in-service cooperative is more imperative today than even when CAJE was founded. Perhaps this history will help some young visionary to begin anew.

Welcome to a history of CAJE, one of American Judaism's proudest successes. CAJE is one acronym that shares two personalities: First and foremost, CAJE stands for the **Conference on Alternatives in Jewish Education**, the annual opportunity to take the pulse of Jewish teaching and to be immersed in Jewish living. Friends, colleagues, teachers, students, and disciples came together at CAJE Conferences to form a *yeshivah* in the best sense: a "dwelling-place" of Jewish learning.

But CAJE was more than just an annual Conference. The CAJE acronym also stands for the **Coalition for the Advancement of Jewish Education**. Between Conferences—and through special Conference programs—our Coalition provided advocacy, benefits, resources, training, and networking for the nearly 4,000 members who form the backbone and marrow, the heart and spirit of Jewish education in North America.

How CAJE Began

In the late 1960s and early 1970s, the North American continent was in turmoil, and its Jewish community was no exception. "Counter-culture" and "alternatives" were buzzwords of choice. In particular, college students demanded, and were given, a greater voice in the Jewish community. The Federations provided funds to create the "North American Jewish Students Network," and that Network organized a "Conference on Alternatives in Jewish Education." On August 29, 1976, nearly 350 Jews attended the first CAJE at Brown University. No one was sure what to expect. The organizers' motivation was to tap the voice of youth to unbalance and energize the *status quo*. In the jargon of its time, CAJE was born to be an "anti-establishment" movement.

Yet even from the outset, the CAJE Conference was a phenomenon that constantly confounded and amazed its founders. It was not only youth that answered the call of youth, it was the entire Jewish educational community. Never before had any Jewish conference gathered such a diverse collection of North American Jews: teachers, administrators, principals, consultants, lay leaders, college students, professors, camp counselors, part-timers, full-timers, Reform, Orthodox, Conservative, Reconstructionist, *Hasid*, Yiddishist, secularist, humanist, Zionist, and others who bore multiple identities. In age, the first *CAJEniks* ranged from thirteen to seventy. We were drawn to Providence at the end of a hot summer because we "heard" of CAJE. As yet, there was no Internet, and few, if any, of us had e-mail. We "heard" about CAJE because the Jewish world—especially the Jewish educational world—then, as now, is small and intensely intertwined.

It was a small, devoted group of folks who formed the Boston organizing committee that planned the first CAJE Conference. Their talents shone through in the basic CAJE forums they designed: the *Module* (an intensive, university-like, minicourse) and the *Lehrhaus* (a ninety-minute presentation).

These forms were distinctive to CAJE conferencing from the beginning right through the twenty-eighth annual Conference. So the first CAJE Conference became an opportunity for educators and lay people alike to share strategies, games, ideas, workshops, curricula, budgets, approaches, philosophies, projects, crafts, *simchas*, and *tsores*. At the same time, the first Conference was also an historical event. At the closing session, the assembly voted to adopt the *Brown Agenda*, a document full of high-flown, 70s-type rhetoric meant to fulfill its "anti-establishment" purpose. Even more far-reaching, the group also demanded that a second Conference be held, and a board was elected to organize CAJE 2.

The Early Years

The newly elected board managed to convene a second CAJE Conference in 1977 at Rochester Institute of Technology in Rochester, NY. Again, the principal form of advertising was word-of-mouth. This time, nearly 700 Jews attended. In my review of the Rochester Conference, published in the American Jewish Committee's *Present Tense* magazine, I dubbed this "the Jewish Woodstock." At RIT, *CAJEniks* voted to form a permanent organization calling it the "Coalition for *Alternatives* in Jewish Education." Our first statement of purpose said that the new CAJE was formed "to firm the link that ties one generation of Jews to the other..." (Some years later, the rest of the Jewish community would also speak of Jewish education as "continuity.") In that first statement, we also reaffirmed our belief "that we can somehow touch those important to us—our students." So the four -letter acronym, *CAJE*, suddenly stood for both an annual Conference and a movement. We voted to hold Conferences bi-annually.

Nevertheless, in 1978, our California colleagues called for a laid-back, "local" CAJE Conference at University of California, Irvine. The result was predictable: The Irvine gathering turned into a national conference. In fact, that year, a borrowed Los Angeles office conducted all CAJE's national business. The Irvine Conference became CAJE 3, and the precedent of annual conferencing was firmly established.

From the beginning, each Conference differed, each experimenting with new ideas. *Media Centers* were introduced to debut audiovisual resources, and *Teacher Centers* encouraged more hands-on creativity. *Computer Centers* explored new Jewish uses for technology.

In the first years of CAJE conferencing, evenings were devoted mainly to political and philosophic plenary sessions. By the third Conference, however, the plenary sessions gave way to "hands-on" Jewish entertainment, folk dancing, and homegrown songfests—all meant to give us more resources to bring back to our classrooms.

Prior to the fourth Conference, a select group of CAJE leaders and planners met to envision a future direction for CAJE—to consolidate what we had learned and how we might continue to grow. In 1979, the CAJE Conference met at Rutgers University. The number of sessions now topped 300; the Conference attendance topped 1,000! There were marathon plenary sessions (in the middle of the day) based on the work of the select group to discuss the future of CAJE. We adopted a formal CAJE constitution. We divided the country into CAJE regions, deciding to meet alternately in the various regions. We set up Task Forces (which later became *Networks*) to allow people with similar interests to keep in touch year-round.

Definitely great successes, but these early Conferences invariably left us with debts. Fortunately, CAJE was blessed with benefactors. In time, CAJE received grants from all but a very few Federations, from many boards and bureaus of Jewish education, from membership dues, from individuals, from foundations, from the Jewish National Fund, and from several departments of the World Zionist Organization. In fact, we owe the WZO (now JAFI, the Jewish Agency for Israel) special thanks since it provided the seed money for our first Conference and faithfully continued to support us thereafter. Nor should we fail to single out Sam and Florence Melton of Columbus, OH, educational visionaries who led the way in helping CAJE grow. Today, recognizing our roster of devoted supporters requires pages and pages. Their names are listed in each CAJE Conference Program Book.

The Organizing Years

During the early 80s, CAJE shuffled its office between the two coasts. It was clear that the organization needed year-long tending. We managed to establish the first *Israel-America Jewish Educational Dialogue*; published *Mekasher*, a computerized listing of CAJE resource people; and hired our first full-time Executive Director, Dr. Eliot G. Spack. Finally, we established one official office in New York.

Meanwhile, the Coalition board sought ways to change the face of American Jewish education between conferences. CAJE members (on behalf of the Coalition) served as "guest-editors" of an issue of *Sh'ma* magazine devoted to Jewish education. We developed our *CAJE Newsletter* and issued the *CAJE Crisis Curriculum* series. When anti-Semitism surfaced in 1981, we joined the Simon Wiesenthal Center in co-sponsoring a Teach-In in Los Angeles. We co-sponsored *Mini-CAJE* Conferences, teacher workshops, and teacher days in cooperation with many local boards and bureaus of Jewish education.

In 1982, we topped all previous attendance records when nearly 1,800 people attended CAJE 7 at Brandeis. The program book reached a whopping 208 pages! There were highly specialized Pre-Conferences (which later gave way to *CAJE Network Pre-Conferences*). CAJE 7 was also the last Conference to witness electioneering. At prior Conferences, prodigious energy (and reams upon reams of multi-colored paper) had been devoted to campaigning for CAJE elections. Cleaning up the campus after a CAJE Conference was a major headache, and the election process deflected attention from in-service workshops and sessions. The Coalition Board finally formalized a plan to do elections by mail.

All CAJE Conferences included family-oriented programming with educational content and in some cases, mini-schools for children, family Shabbat observance, and more. At Stanford University in 1984, we experimented with a "community day." Local artisans, artists, authors, and craftspeople offered original works for sale. This was in addition to the *CAJE Exhibit Hall* (later called *CAJE Expo*), which housed the best that the Jewish commercial world had to offer from the first Conference to the last.

During the 80s, CAJE offered a membership benefits package including life and health insurance even for part-time teachers. CAJE's *Newsletter* made regular appearances, and in the 90s it evolved into the *CAJE Jewish Education News* (*JEN*). After a preview of the movie, *The Chosen*, at CAJE 6, we prepared the *Leader's Guide* that was distributed nationally with the movie's release. For a while, the Coalition issued *CAJE Marketplace* to help teachers and educators find new positions; later, we offered this service at conferences and on the CAJE web site. CAJE issued *Model Teaching Units*, and for those with questions or problems, we provided automatic membership in *The CAJE Curriculum Bank* (later located on the web as the *CAJE Curriculum Response Service*).

Maturing and Changing

CAJE 10 began with Theodore Bikel leading an evening of folk songs dedicated to the *Refusenik* teachers of the Soviet Union. Tapes of the concert were smuggled into the Soviet Union and featured on Radio Free Europe. That year, CBS filmed a segment on CAJE for the nationally syndicated television series, *For Our Times*, and the Council of Jewish Federations awarded CAJE the coveted *Schroder Award for Excellence in Jewish Programming*.

In 1983, the first *Bikurim* ("First Fruits") magazine shared the work of the *CAJE Curriculum Bank*. (*Bikurim* was later replaced by "Hot Sheets.") In 1986, the Coalition received national recognition for its prophetic *CAJE Crisis Curriculum*, "Disaster in Chernobyl."

Times were changing, however. CAJE was no longer a "counterculture" movement. Either CAJE had caught up with the "establishment," or it had caught up with us. At the 1987 Conference, we officially changed our organizational name to the *Coalition for the Advancement of Jewish Education*. Of course, the Conference remained the *Conference on Alternatives in Jewish Education*. The initials CAJE continued to serve for both the Conference and the Coalition.

Coordinated by the CAJE board, many *CAJEniks* attended the 1988 March on Washington when Jews from all over Amer-

ica demonstrated solidarity with Soviet Jewry. Within a week after the March, CAJE again showed its devotion to the cause of
Soviet Jewry by issuing a *CAJE Crisis Curriculum* entitled "The
Gathering," providing lesson plans and activities for schools,
camps, and youth groups.

CAJE and the World

We are flattered that Jewish communities outside North America have seen fit to form CAJE-like conferences of their own.
Great Britain has *LIMMUD* (with a British flavor, naturally).
The Jewish community of Brazil organized a conference called
Mifgash and Argentinian Jews called their conference *Havaya*.
A continental European conference was organized by the Educational Council for European Jewry. In 2002, an event modeled on CAJE and called *Etrog* was held in the Ukraine. And, of
course, in Israel we have formed close partnerships with JAFI
and *Histadrut HaMorim*, the Israeli Teachers' Union.

CAJE celebrated its *bar/bat mitzvah* year and Israel's forti-
eth anniversary in 1988 by convening in Jerusalem. I served as
the Conference Chairperson as 1000 *CAJEniks* met with nearly
1000 Israeli educators, joined by 200 educators from all corners
of the world. Opening night in the amphitheater of the Hebrew
University with the moon as her backdrop, our own Debbie
Friedman (who debuted her famous *Alef-Bet* song at CAJE 4)
performed, celebrating the coming of age of American Jewish
music. New formats emerged: the *Beit Midrash* (small-group
text study), the *Kallah* (lectures by outstanding Jewish thinkers), and the *Havayot* (off-campus sessions and field trips co-
sponsored by Israel's finest educational organizations). One
evening, the Israel Museum opened exclusively for CAJE for an
Erev Tarbut Yisrael ("Israel Culture Night"). With an *intifada*
keeping many tourists away, we were proud to be Israel's largest
Jewish gathering that year. One of the CAJE 13 program chairs,
Dr. Deborah Weissman, won an Israeli prize for her work on the
Conference, and CAJE received the *Israeli Shazar Prize* from
the President of Israel. In America, *Moment* magazine awarded
the 1988 Conference organizers a collective *Community Service Award* for the impact of the CAJE Israel Conference on the

American Jewish community. Just prior to the Israel Conference, we held CAJE Institutes in San Diego and Milwaukee, each focused on a theme. All told, at home and abroad, in its thirteenth year CAJE sponsored in-service workshops for more than 3,200 Jewish educators!

Experimenting

The Conference and the Coalition both continued their experimentation with new ways of presenting knowledge through the 90s. The Conference Program Book continued to swell sometimes reaching over 400 pages and listing upwards of 600 sessions. The Coalition extended its *Teen Experience for High School* and added a *College Experience*—programs to encourage young people to view Jewish education as a promising profession. CAJE's *Open University* offered continuing education credits to CAJE participants. We introduced *Think Tanks*, in-depth Talmud sessions, and a *Demonstration School.*

Coalition-sponsored publications dealt with current issues such as family education; continuity; feeding the hungry; ways of dealing with anti-Semitism; mainstreaming in Special Education; terrorism; the Jewish crisis in Argentina; the effects of the *intifada* on Israel and Israel education; AIDS; the celebration of 500 years of the Sephardic Jewish heritage; and more. *JEN* grew into a major forum for articles on Jewish education, and CAJE put out the *CAJE Page* to provide more informal information for *CAJEniks.*

Some Conferences tried thematic afternoons, like the "picnic" at CAJE 19 called *Focus Israel. American Zionist Movement Song Competition Finals* were held at CAJE. We even extended the evening programs by including outstanding Israeli performers like *NOA* (Achinoam Nini). A *Session Surfer* made its appearance in this period to make session-planning easier for *CAJEniks.*

In 1996, prior to CAJE 21, the Coalition experimented with a unique text-study event at the Concord Resort Hotel in the Catskills. Designed as a small-group experience, the success of the Concord event afforded new possibilities for CAJE's future between Conferences.

CAJE 21, held at the Hebrew University, was the second time the CAJE Board appointed me to be Conference Chairperson. Fitting for our return to Jerusalem, we built a truly *international* CAJE Conference. It was chockablock with partnerships: CAJE and the Ministry of Education of the State of Israel joined to create an *Intensive Mifgash* program involving Jewish educators from every continent. CAJE and the *Histadrut HaMorim* (Israel's Teachers' Union) together celebrated Jewish teachers of the world in a closing evening of fireworks featuring the world-renowned Israeli actor and singer Yehoram Gaon. CAJE and the Jewish National Fund together celebrated "Jerusalem 3000" in an international inauguration of a new *Gan Yaldei Yisrael* ("Israeli Youth Garden"). CAJE repeated the *Havayot* joining with nearly sixty diverse Israeli educational groups and institutions. CAJE partnered with Israel's finest ongoing adult learning programs to create an outstanding *Beit Midrash*.

As the 90s came to a close, the *CAJE Expo* added a *Judaic Crafts Exhibit*. CAJE Conferences included special *tzedakah* programming, enabling CAJEniks to transform teaching and learning into action. Jewish web surfing became the latest "hands-on" approach to education. At CAJE 25, in the year 2000, the Conference planners experimented with *Kivunim*, "pathways," offering eleven choices of "specializations" for participants. And the Coalition commissioned *Hanukat CAJE* (soon renamed The CAJE Advocacy Commission) as a self-renewal process.

The Twenty-First Century

With a new century beginning, CAJE sponsored a resolution passed by the General Assembly of the United Jewish Communities calling on North American Jewry to address the personnel crisis facing our schools. To vitalize this endeavor, our CAJE Advocacy Commission, with the help of the Covenant Foundation, established *Project Kavod* to recognize the years of devotion represented by veteran Jewish educators.

In 2003, CAJE convened its first-ever spin-off, a CAJE Conference for Early Childhood and Day School Educators. Not only did this Conference draw 700 educators to Hofstra University in

June, but with funding provided by six dedicated contributors, CAJE established an Early Childhood Department in our national office. In 2004, and again in 2005, the Conference for Early Childhood and Day School Educators was successfully repeated.

The CAJE Achievements

As with the new Early Childhood Department, generous foundations and individuals supported many projects of the Coalition. The Coalition established an *Endowment Program* to ensure its continuing growth. At the same time, the old "mini-grant program" for creative and innovative efforts evolved into a far more significant grants program promising new alternatives for the future of Jewish education in North America. All this and more—the Spack Fellowship, the Dornstein Memorial Writing Contest, the Schusterman College Program, the Newman Film/Media Program—involved CAJE in advancing the Jewish educational agenda.

Thirty years after its launch, CAJE supported the CAJE Conference, the CAJE Early Childhood/Day School Conference, publications, advocacy, and other fine programs. Anyone at all involved in Jewish education received some benefit from CAJE. In return, the most essential support for CAJE came from its members. Dues helped, but beyond that there was willingness to work for the organization, to stand for office, to sit on the board, or even to become an officer of CAJE. Jewish education had experienced significant changes since 1976, and CAJE was an essential element of many of these changes.

For the years of its existence, CAJE was a national teacher's *yeshivah*. Educators came to seek community, Jewish continuity, spiritual growth, family, friends, sustenance, knowledge, a setting in which *klal yisrael* ("Jewish unity") and *ahavat hinnam* ("open-hearted acceptance") were like gems in the crown of Torah. Most of all, those of us who worked to make CAJE special, those of us who attended conferences and worked between conferences because CAJE was special, and those of us who made contributions to keep CAJE afloat were doing it for a singularly simple reason—"to firm the link that ties one generation of Jews to the other...."—for our students.

Every Bush Is Burning

Teaching Judaism as a Spiritual Religion

This essay appeared as an article in the Spring 2014 issue of the CCAR Journal: The Reform Jewish Quarterly, a distinguished publication in which to leave a permanent record for future generations. Of course, I am a more practical sort. I was thinking that this proposed program for spiritual education might be discovered (and possibly put into use) by present-day colleagues. It may yet be if you will emulate Moses and turn aside to take a closer look.

What young people need is not religious tranquilizers, religion as a diversion, religion as entertainment, but spiritual audacity, intellectual guts, power of defiance. — Abraham Joshua Heschel[1]

Heschel forces us to confront the experiential, to go beyond what is found in most Jewish educational settings today. Just rephrase his criteria as questions: Are we teaching defiance? Does our instruction lead to intellectual guts or spiritual audacity?

For the most part, present curriculum tends to the mechanical. It conveys the facts and data of organized religion, but it seldom conveys the liveliness and vitality of Jewish tradition. Heschel hints at this shortcoming in his use of the term "spiritual." Spirituality once denoted a quality reserved for the church, the synagogue, and the clergy, but it has more recently connoted a concern for, and sensitivity to, religious values and moral attitudes. The distinction can be sharpened by a whimsical example.

Picture our present curriculum as concentrating on the form of Adam lying lifeless in the mud—we examine every aspect of the figure from head to proverbial toe, and exclaim, "Isn't it marvelous?" Yet our review of the outward form is not nearly so astounding as what transpires when God's breath fills the lifeless nostrils so that Adam springs from the mud, male and female in one being, free to choose between good and evil. Through that infusion of life, of experience, we comprehend what made the lifeless figure worth examining. Without the inspiration, the breath, the living being of spirituality, our curriculum remains dispassionate.

The debate on how to teach spirituality, therefore, transcends how best to apply modern technology in the classroom. Modern technology may be useful, or it may add an additional layer of separation to an already clinical examination. To paraphrase John F. Kennedy, the challenge is not only to question what Jewish tradition can bring to the learner but what the learner can bring to Jewish tradition. Alternatively, we can ask ourselves in what spiritual actions can the learner immediately participate in ways that are both consonant with, and derived from, Jewish tradition.

There is, of course, one well-known theory of Jewish education that assumes the teaching of spirituality can rely on action alone. This theory proposes that if we teach students to put on *t'fillin* or to light Sabbath candles, they will soon come to know Jewish spirituality. To this end, we are inundated with books about God and texts explaining how to do acts of *tzedakah* and loving kindness in the hope that if learners discuss God, practice ritual, and do good deeds, they will emerge as spiritual Jews. While there may be some truth in this, it is a short path that represents a long route. Rather, I propose a long route that I believe reaches our desired end more surely and perhaps with even greater rapidity.

This path is equally experiential, rooted in discovering the spiritual elements of Judaism as they are contained in our people's history—again, not in the facts of that history but rather in the conceptions we impose on those facts, conceptions that impinge on the everyday experiences of our learners. This curriculum includes organized religion—history, culture, custom, and language—the essence of what our people have built out of tradition and spirituality. These essentials are where most of us, teachers and learners alike, safe and secure. Yet this new approach to curriculum transcends what is organized and refined to include the wild and God-crazy path of the prophets, mystics, and visionaries—the willingness to assume God's presence, listen for God's voice, and venture where God sends us. It is a spiritual curriculum in Heschel's sense, a curriculum focused on "awareness," "guts," and "audacity." Without claiming to be comprehensive, I have identified five major conceptions readily accessible to our teachers and students beginning with the traditional God-readiness embodied in the Hebrew word *hineini* ("I am present").

God-Readiness

God-readiness, the tradition of being present and responsive to God's call, extends back to our very beginnings. The underlying theme is that of being awakened, even as Jacob is awakened after dreaming the dream of the staircase connecting heaven and earth. In this moment, Jacob reacts with wonder, saying, "Surely God is present in this place, and I did not know it!"

Tradition avows that opportunities for religious awakening are around us everywhere and at any time. Spiritual education must ready our students to be open to the call of God. Jews need to learn when to say *hineini* and what *hineini* means when we say it. We internalize this learning by studying how *hineini* is used in our faith history.

Hineini is the key to the story of the binding of Isaac. God calls to Abraham, and Abraham answers, "*Hineini.*" Isaac speaks to Abraham on the way up the mountain, and Abraham answers, "*Hineini.*" The angel speaks to Abraham at the moment of truth, and Abraham answers, "*Hineini.*" *Hineini* is the word of spiritual readiness: readiness to hear what God wishes us to hear and readiness to hear what others say to us. *Hineini* is the word of presence. It infers, "I am present now, this instant, even if being present now means that the rest of my life will be changed forever."

Jacob speaks the word *hineini* when he hears the voice of God's angel telling him that God is protecting him. Jacob answers *hineini* when God tells him that it is necessary for him to go down into Egypt. "I hear, and I am comforted," Jacob replies. "... I am present to be commanded."

Moses speaks the word *hineini* at the Burning Bush, and his life is transformed. Samuel is sleeping near the tabernacle when God calls him; he answers *hineini*, and his life is transformed. Isaiah hears God ask, "Who shall I send?" and he answers, "*Hineini*, send me."

The examples I have drawn from the literal use of the word *hineini* in tradition only hint at the way in which we as teachers and as students may find God-readiness in our own lives. In choosing to teach, for example, Jews encounter an inner God-readiness, speak the word *hineini* whether aloud or in silence, and actualize a Jewish choice. In the same way, whenever we choose, or feel impelled to choose, to do what is right and what is just, we are expressing God-readiness. The spiritual curriculum does not have to arrange for the *hineini* moments in our lives; it only has to make it explicit to us that our finest decisions and aspirations arise out of a willingness that links us with the Jewish chain of tradition in such a way that each impulse to do what is good prepares us for another.

The God-readiness section of our curriculum recounts moments from our faith history to prepare our students for those critical moments when they realize that they have themselves encountered a new quest, that they have been commanded to follow a new path, that they have been ordered to make some spiritual commitment. At any moment, each of them must be ready to say, "*Hineini*. Here I am. I am a Jew. I am fully present. I am ready to respond."

Partnership

The second part of our curriculum of spiritual awareness is partnership. This is *tikkun olam* (repairing the world), but it is much more than that, too. In Genesis, we are told that we are created to rule over the world the way that God rules over the heavens. It might be said that Moses subsequently taught us ways to rule over ourselves to help prepare us for ruling over the world. The Rabbis spoke of us as God's presence in the world. Since we are

God's creation, they said, we must somehow be necessary to carry out God's plan. But it was the mystic, Isaac Luria, who redefined our partnership with God, so it is Luria's teachings that undergird this element of our curriculum.

Luria radically transformed the meaning of creation in Jewish tradition through his daring account. Though it is informative in its full and complex form, I draw attention here to just two main points that are immediately applicable to Jews today. For one, Luria taught that, out of necessity and out of mercy, God made space for human beings, for the world, and for the universe by performing *tzimtzum* (the act of "contraction"). In emulation of God, whenever we make ourselves just a little smaller, we make room for others to grow just a little larger. If we can think just a little less of ourselves, we are able to think just a little more of others. Jewish spiritual awareness depends on our acts of *tzimtzum*.

Luria also provided us with a key for responding to evil in our world. Evil, he taught, is that which must be repaired and that which must be restored. It is the *k'lipot* (the "broken shards," the mistakes) that are made and the harms that are done. Luria believed that we inevitably find these shards strewn along our path. No one lives who does not experience pain and suffering, but the pain and the suffering can be offered up as our sacrifice and redeemed as our healing. Until we understand this, the world makes little sense.

Tikkun olam is not just doing *tzedakah*, although that is certainly part of it; it is also accepting responsibility. We have been chosen to be partners in healing the world. "Healing" may mean saving the whales, or it may mean saving our community. It may mean speaking kindly to those who would choose to hate us, or it may mean helping our neighbors plant a new tree in their garden. It is any and every opportunity to place a smile on someone else's lips or ease someone else's burdens. Surely, it means taking care of the widow and the orphan, sharing whatever wealth we may have with those who have less, and being responsible for others whether they are Jews or not. Maimonides was correct in saying that *tzedakah* must begin with those who are close, and that it is often most difficult to give to people who are kinfolk; however, Luria is even more spiritually attuned since he makes no distinction at all. *K'lipot* are where we find them—the shattered pieces in God's world lie all around us. All of God's world, not just the Jewish neighborhood, needs repair.

To the extent that we act as God's partner in creation, our lives are filled with the meaning of creating a world of peace. Even our prayers take on new significance as we feel ourselves partners in whatever task we ask God to help us accomplish. If there is one God, then the proof of it is that the world is not just a Jewish world but a world that Jews share with others. We hope that they will practice *tzimtzum*, that they will make a place for us in their world. In return, we must never stop practicing *tzimtzum*, making a place for them in our world. We must practice *tzimtzum* especially by having patience for those Jews who fail to understand this simple lesson, those who mistakenly place Jews above all others. The partnership is not just between us and God but between us and all God's creatures, too.

Alerting Our Senses

The third section in our new curriculum of spiritual awareness is alerting our senses. Here, students can often teach us even more than we teach them because some lucky folk find this the most natural thing in the world. These are the people among us who stand transfixed by a sunset or who daydream wonders as they sit at their desks. Yet all of us need to learn that there are things that we cannot see, hear, or feel with our external senses; love, fear, desire, awe, and anger are all very real. Jews who are religiously alert comprehend these as ways of balancing organized religion with spirituality. We sometimes hear people refer to this comprehension as "listening with the heart."

The story of Elijah is the basic faith history of "alerting the senses." It is Elijah who stands at Horeb as God passes by. First there was a great and mighty wind splitting mountains and shattering rocks, but God was not in the wind. Then there was an earthquake, but God was not in the earthquake. After the earthquake, there was fire, but God was not in the fire. But after the fire, there was a still, small voice. Before Elijah, God was pictured as thundering forth from the mountain so that the people following Moses were afraid even to hear the word of God directly. But through Elijah it is revealed that everyone hears the word of God directly. It may not be loud or come in earthquakes or tornados or fires, but if you listen closely, that still small voice is speaking.

In fact, the less God seems to be in a place, the more power-ful God's presence may be. During the Holocaust years, when Jews celebrated Passover in the ghettos and reached out to help one another in the concentration camps, and, later, when the Refusenik Jews of Soviet Russia made Chanukah menorahs out of potatoes and saved their rations of fats to burn as candles, their senses were alert to the still, small voice.

Our job as educators is to help our students alert their senses, to help them to hear the unspoken sounds within their hearts, to help them to see the unseen places in the corners of our dreams, and to help them to stay alert to the still, small voice. Then, like Tevye the Dairyman, we can commence a con-versation with God that is an ongoing dialogue with our heart. The Jew who can do that can learn to hear his or her dreams. The object of Jewish camping, of sending Jews on missions to Is-rael, of sending Jews to Europe to stand on the site of former concentration and death camps, of visiting Holocaust muse-ums, of bringing Jews to Washington to confront and experi-ence advocacy of Jewish issues firsthand—all fall into this category of raising our spiritual sensibilities. But so, too, do more easily accomplished local experiences, for the small voice of spiritual awareness is present in preparing to visit and actu-ally visiting with the elderly, in planting trees, in making get-well cards for those students suffering prolonged absence. None of these are new as Jewish learning, what is new is that we contextualize them, actualize them, perceive them as instants of Jewish awareness. It is the difference between knowing that it is right to write a check to Federation and feeling that it is a privilege and a blessing to be able to write that check.

Bearing Witness

The fourth element of our spiritual curriculum is an old and venerated part of Jewish tradition—one that was also passed on to Christianity and to Islam. Today, we hear it more from the lips of Christians and Muslims than from Jewish lips, and this should embarrass us—not because we thought of it first, for the odds are that it was an ancient idea even before Jews became a people—but because it is an idea that is essential to anyone who seeks awareness. This part of the spiritual curriculum is called bearing witness.

To bear witness is to share our experience of God, to talk about God, and to be willing to open ourselves to others to enhance our encounter with God. It was through spiritual actions that Abraham conveyed the Presence of God, and those who came into close contact with him were captured by that awareness. Likewise, a long string of Jewish texts states that sages should be judged as much by their actions as by their wisdom. While it is undoubtedly true that the Jewish tradition demands that we study and prepare ourselves for the acquisition of wisdom, it is equally true that the Jewish tradition recognizes that wisdom can be found even by those who possess little factual knowledge. Our image of godliness is drawn from those who act wisely not necessarily from those who can turn an elegant phrase.

In this manner, the Midrash avers that "visiting a sage is like visiting the Presence [of God]" (*B'reishit Rabbah* 63:6). A sage can act in ways that give us a glimpse of God. As we act in godlike ways, we bear witness to God and more of God is revealed to the world.

"In every action," said the Berditschever, "a person must regard his body as the Holy of Holies, a part of the supreme power on earth which is part of the manifestation of the Deity ... Whenever a person lifts his hands to do a deed, let him consider his hands the messengers of God."[2]

Our hands are powerful tools. If we choose to use them to do evil, we know that people will point to the evil we do and maintain it as proof that God does not punish the evildoer; God does not act justly; God is unfair; or even that God does not exist. But when we choose to use our strength to do that which is just and that which is right, when we act in godlike ways, we bring evidence of God's existence into the world. God's mercy in this world is in our acts of loving kindness. God's justice in this world is in our honesty and our integrity. It is only through the actions of those who behave spiritually that God is magnified at all. In Isaiah we read:

You are My witnesses, said God, and My servant whom I have cho-
sen; that you may know and believe Me, and understand that I am
the One; before Me there was no god formed, neither shall there
be after Me (Isa. 43:12). [Rabbi Simeon bar Yochai commented:]
When you are My witnesses, I am God, but when you are not My
witnesses, I am not God. Similarly, you say, *Unto You I lift up mine*
eyes, O You that art my enthroned one in the heavens (Ps. 123:1). If
not for me, You would not be enthroned in the heavens. (*Sifrei*
D'varim 346)

This is the great mutuality, the common need that persists
in the spiritual union between God and us. It requires moral
courage, or as Heschel phrased it, "audacity," to be willing to
say aloud that our deeds express our belief in the divine imperative. Here again, the training involved is not a matter of a particular kind of Jewish action or a particular *mitzvah* but rather a
raising of our consciousness and the consciousness of our students to expressing our beliefs out loud to family, friends,
neighbors, and community. As we bear witness to God, we keep
God's Presence fresh in the hearts and minds of others and
fresh in our own minds and hearts, as well.

Mutual Respect

Arising from the first four segments of our spiritual curriculum
comes a fifth. It, too, is grounded in our shared Jewish tradition, specifically in the Genesis faith history when Abraham
meets Melchizedek, the king of Shalem. We are told that
Melchizedek is the priest of *El Elyon* (the "God on High").

Abraham immediately recognizes Melchizedek as a priest
of the one God. Abraham willingly receives the blessing of
Melchizedek and gives the king/priest a tenth of everything
that Abraham won in his war against the evil kings. This thematic story underlies the teaching of mutual respect.

We must let our students in on what is too often kept a secret, and that is that we are aware of the truth of *many* faith traditions. The Jewish people are the property of God, but God is
not the property of the Jewish people. God is revealed to all peo-
ples in different ways. We should revere God-fever wherever we
encounter it whether it is to our taste or not. We should respect
the Mormons and the *Hasidim*, the Christians and the Mus-

lims—Arab or Black. We can respect them even when we do not agree with their interpretations of God or with their actions. We need to remember that their interpretations and actions are human and imperfect as are our own interpretations and our own actions.

When we encounter the Melchizedeks of our time, we should recognize them as "god-folk." We should revere the faith of Mother Theresa even as we revere the weeping of Rachel. We should hear the words of Martin Luther King, Jr. with the same reverence that we hear the words of Abraham Joshua Heschel. (By the way, Heschel did just that when he marched beside Dr. King to Selma, Alabama, and this, too, is a story of our faith history.)

We should give the same credence to the work of Albert Schweitzer and the Dalai Lama as we do to the work of Maimonides. We need to teach that faith heroes are those who are called and answer the call no matter what religion they may happen to be. Our faith history demands that we be "a light unto the nations," but it does not leave us off the hook. We must also be willing to gather the light of other nations and see it all as the light of the one God. This takes intellectual guts; it is spiritual awareness, and it is embedded in the finest expressions of our tradition.

In the curriculum of mutual respect, we must enable our students to revere the work of others and to find models for our own behavior in those who have excelled in healing people and in restoring the world. Our way remains the Jewish path, but it is not the singular path to God; it is only the path that we as a people have chosen. If non-Jews also light the way along our path, that is no reason for us to believe that our path is any less effective and appropriate than theirs. It is, on the contrary, a reason to rejoice in the fact that we are on the right road and a reason to welcome the models of those who happen to be on paths that join with ours.

In the end of days, it is written, all will worship at God's holy mountain (Isa. 2:2). It is not written that only Jews will get there. Our spiritual curriculum can prepare us with the mutual respect that is essential if we are ever to enjoy that promised time of peace in this world.

The Spiritual Curriculum

These are the five segments of our curriculum of spiritual awareness: (1) *God-Readiness*, knowing how to answer with your whole
self when God calls; (2) *Partnership*, making space for God and
others, even as God makes space for you and knowing we are
partners in the work of repairing and restoring the shattered
shards of evil in the world; (3) *Alerting our Senses*, learning to
hear and use the still, small voice as a compass to guide you on
your path; (4) *Bearing Witness*, acting and sharing in the world
in such a way that you not only *study* Torah, but *become* Torah,
so that your words and your deeds become proofs of God's presence; and (5) *Mutual Respect*, knowing that all who are searching for God are on the same road or at least on a road that often
intersects with yours—and knowing, too, that all seekers of God
may provide you clues and omens that may inform your quest.

Judaism is concerned with spirituality even as it is concerned with ritual and commandment. In the life history of our
eponymous ancestor Jacob, the stranger who wrestles with him
blesses him by naming him Israel because, as the stranger says,
"You have struggled with beings both human and divine." Before there can be a community that wrestles with God, an "Israel," there must first be individuals who are not afraid of facing
their "stranger." The risk we take in entering the spiritual fray
is actually discovering that we are wrestling with God, and that
we are being commanded by God to wrestle with human beings.
As Martin Buber put it, "God does not want to be believed in, to
be debated and defended by us, but simply to be realized
through us."[3] God-wrestling leads to world building. The true
repair of the world is not undertaken by the passive and the sub-
missive but by the one who seizes freedom, responds to the
command of the Voice, and becomes Torah.

The finest Jewish educators are not the ones who teach
what Judaism is today but the ones who seize on what Judaism
has always been and will always be—the spiritual Judaism that is
shared by priest and prophet, the spiritual awareness that can
be awakened in each of us.

The Torah makes a special point of saying that not only did
Moses see the Burning Bush, not only did he encounter a bush
alive with fire and unconsumed, but he also took the time and

made the effort to turn aside from his path to witness it more closely. Only then did God speak to him from behind the bush. This "turning aside to witness" is the kind of audacity that a spiritual curriculum could imbue in our every learner. For in truth, as soon as we become spiritually aware, religiously alive, a larger truth is revealed to us: God is addressing us every moment of every day. No matter where we look, if our inner eye is open and our inner being is prepared, every bush is burning.

❀ *Notes*

1 Abraham Heschel, *Insecurity of Freedom* (New York: Farrar, Straus and Giroux, 1959), 53.

2 Louis I. Newman, *Hasidic Anthology* (New York: Schocken Books, 1963), 254-55.

3 Martin Buber, "Jewish Religiosity," in *On Judaism*, ed. Nahum N. Glatzer (New York: Schocken Books, 1967), 94.

❊
Publications

When my first book was published, author's copies hot off the press were delivered to my office at Behrman House, Inc. I happened to be sitting just then with Rabbi Eugene Borowitz who had done much editorially to improve my manuscript (so much, in fact, that his notes in green ink on the first draft were nearly as verbose as the first draft itself). Now, he held a copy of the new book high in the air and pronounced his judgment: "Congratulations, Seymour, a real achievement! Just know that the next one will be just as difficult." In this, as in so many other things, his observation was inerrant.

I feel blessed that I have been able to pursue my several different lives in the literary world of Jewish America. I dreamt of being a writer and I have written. In college, I discovered I had a talent for helping others to strengthen their voice. Ever since, I have been privileged to serve as editor to many fine authors. Being an editor was instrumental in shaping my career in publishing.

Simultaneously, I remained active in teaching and teacher training. For a decade, I wrote and compiled computer programs and served as a computer consultant for small businesses. For nearly a decade (one thing overlapping another), I wrote direct mail marketing pieces to raise funds for nonprofit organizations involved in rescuing Refuseniks trapped and oppressed in the Soviet Union; rescuing Ethiopian Jews from prejudice, poverty, and hunger; and feeding and housing poor and elderly Jews stranded in inner cities here in North America. There is a brief chronological biography at the end of this collection that gives a factual timetable of my career but I am delighted to report that no factual timeline could possibly capture the richness of spirit and energy that I have been afforded by my peers, by my friends and family, and by the good God above.

Books by Seymour Rossel

The Essential Jewish Stories, Second Revised Edition (Rossel Books, 2018)

The Wise Folk of Chelm (Rossel Books, 2013)

The Holocaust: An End to Innocence (Rossel Books, 2012)

The Essential Jewish Stories (KTAV, 2011)

Bible Dreams: The Spiritual Quest, Second Revised Edition (Rossel Books, 2010)

The Torah: Portion by Portion (Torah Aura Productions, 2007)

The Storybook Haggadah (Pitspopany Press, 2006)

Bible Dreams: The Spiritual Quest (SPI Books, 2003)

The Holocaust: On-line Resource (web-based, for *www.rossel.net*, 2000)

Basic-Judaism-on-the-Web (web-based, for *www.rossel.net*, 2000)

Managing the Jewish Classroom: How to Transform Yourself into a Master Teacher (Torah Aura, 1987; revised 1998)

Sefer Ha-Aggadah: The Book of Legends for Young Readers, Volume 2 (UAHC Press, 1998)

Sefer Ha-Aggadah: The Book of Legends for Young Readers, Volume 1 (UAHC Press, 1996)

Facilitator's Guide to The Jewish Condition by Alexander M. Schindler (UAHC Press, 1995)

A Congregation of Learners: Transforming the Synagogue into a Learning Community, co-edited with Isa Aron and Sara Lee (UAHC Press, 1995)

Let Freedom Ring: The Jews of America (Behrman House, 1995)

A Thousand and One Chickens (UAHC Press, 1995)

A Spiritual Journey: The Bar and Bat Mitzvah Handbook (Behrman House, 1993)

The Sephardic Jewish Heritage: A Quincentenary Celebration (Board of Jewish Education of Greater New York, 1992)

The Holocaust: The World and the Jews, 1933-1945 (Behrman House, 1992)

Teacher's Guide to The Holocaust: The World and the Jews, 1933-1945 (Behrman House, 1992)

The Holocaust: The Fire That Raged (Franklin Watts, 1989)

A Child's Bible: Lessons from Prophets and Writings (Behrman House, 1989)

Teacher's Guide to A Child's Bible: Lessons from Prophets and Writings (Behrman House, 1989)

A Child's Bible: Lessons from the Torah (Behrman House, 1987)

Teacher's Guide to A Child's Bible: Lessons from the Torah (Behrman House, 1987)

Israel: Covenant People, Covenant Land (UAHC Press, 1985; revised 1998)

Journey through Jewish History, Volume 2 (Behrman House, 1983)

Mitzvah: The Teacher's Guide (Rossel Books, 1982)

Journey through Jewish History, Volume 1 (Behrman House, 1981)

The Holocaust (Franklin Watts, 1981)

Family: A First Book (Franklin Watts, 1980)

Judaism: A First Book (Franklin Watts, 1976)

When a Jew Seeks Wisdom: The Sayings of the Fathers (Behrman House, 1975)

When a Jew Prays (Behrman House, 1973)

Lessons from Our Living Past, contributor (Behrman House, 1972)

Articles by Seymour Rossel

"Teaching Judaism as a Spiritual Religion: Every Bush is Burning," *CCAR Journal: The Reform Jewish Quarterly,* Spring, 2014

"Isaac: God's Special Child," *www.rossel.net,* January, 2011

"Make Us Holy as God Is Holy," Interview, *Jewish Herald Voice,* Houston, May, 2008

"A Passover Message," Mazon, *http://www.mazon.org,* April 2007

"The Way of Creation," *Sh'ma*, 36/626, December 2005

"The Dead Sea Scrolls and Us," *Jewish Herald Voice*, Houston, November 2004

"Thank You, Teacher," *Reform Judaism*, Spring 1995

"Managing for Performance: What Research into Teaching Can Do for Us," *Compass Magazine*, Winter-Spring 1994

"Lifelong Learning: The Art of Being Jewish," *Compass Magazine*, Fall 1993

"Transforming Jewish Education," *Compass Magazine*, Spring, 1993

"Why Be Good?" *Keeping Posted*, November 1988

"Plight and Demonstration" in *The Gathering*, CAJE, 1988

"Disaster in Chernobyl—A Teaching Unit" *CAJE Crisis Curriculum*, 1987

"Holocaust," *The Encyclopedia Americana*, 1984

"The Covenant," *Keeping Posted*, Special Issue, March, 1984

"Kibbutz," *The Encyclopedia Americana*, 1983

"Isaac Leib Peretz," *The Encyclopedia Americana*, 1983

"Jewish Folk Tales for Grown-Ups," weekly column in *The Baltimore Jewish Times*, 1981-82

"The Educational Imperative," *Response Magazine*, Winter 1979/1980

"Report from New Brunswick," *Present Tense Magazine*, Fall 1980

"Publishing Holocaust Literature," *Judaica Book News*, Spring, 1979

"Clarifying Jewish Values Clarification," *Alternatives*, Fall 1977

"Laurence Kohlberg and the Teaching of Jewish Ethics," *Jewish Education*, Summer/Fall 1977

"Why Choose to Be Good?" *Keeping Posted*, January 1976

"On Teaching Jewish Ethics," *Response Magazine*, Spring 1976

Short Fiction by Seymour Rossel

"Who Will Be My Surety" in *The Shavuot Anthology* ed. by
Philip Goodman (Philadelphia: Jewish Publication
Society, 1974)

"The Demonstration" in *Growing Up in America* ed. by R. A.
Rosenbaum (New York: Doubleday, 1969)

Musical Compositions by Seymour Rossel

"Adon Olam" in *Ura! Hasidic Style Songs* ed. by Velvel
Pasternak (New York: Tara Publications, 1975)

"Halleluhu: Psalm 150" in *Ura! Hasidic Style Songs* edited by
Velvel Pasternak (New York: Tara Publications, 1975)

Computer Programs by Seymour Rossel

CONFER: The CAJE Conference Program, New York, NY, 1987
(revised 1998, 2003, 2004)

SSAD-pBASE for the Solomon Schechter Academy of Dallas,
1997

pBASE: The Religious School Principal's Database, Rossel
Books (1989 & distributed by Behrman House from
1992)

Series Edited by Seymour Rossel

Studies in Contemporary Judaism, Association for Progressive
Judaism

The Studies in Reform Judaism Series, Rossel Books

The Limited Editions Series, Rossel Books

The Jewish Legacy Series, Behrman House

The Jewish Concepts and Issues Series, Behrman House

The Living Past Series, Behrman House

Books and Publications Edited by Seymour Rossel

Altshuler, David A. *Hitler's War Against the Jews: A Young Reader's Version of The War Against the Jews by Lucy S. Dawidowicz* (New York: Behrman House, 1978)

---. *The Jews of Washington* (Chappaqua, NY: Rossel Books, 1985)

Axelrad, Alex. *Meditations of a Maverick Rabbi* (Chappaqua, NY: Rossel Books, 1985)

Beilin, Yossi. *His Brother's Keeper* (New York, NY: Schocken Books, 2000)

Blaser, Elissa. *Exodus: The Russian Jewry Simulation Game* (New York: Behrman House, 1974)

Blecher, Arthur C. *Stories from Our Living Past / Teacher's Guide* (New York: Behrman House, 1974)

Borowitz, Eugene B. *Choices in Modern Jewish Thought: A Partisan Guide* (New York: Behrman House, 1983)

---. *Contemporary Christologies: A Jewish Response* (New York: Paulist Press, 1980)

---. *Reform Judaism Today, Book I: Reform in the Process of Change* (New York: Behrman House, 1978)

---. *Reform Judaism Today, Book II: What We Believe* (New York: Behrman House, 1977)

---. *Reform Judaism Today, Book III: How We Live* (New York: Behrman House, 1978)

---. ed., *Reform Judaism Today, Book IV: Leaders Guide by Joel Soffin* (New York: Behrman House, 1979)

Bridger, David S. *The New Jewish Encyclopedia* (Revised Edition) (New York: Behrman House, 1976)

Cherry, Kelly. *Lessons from Our Living Past / Teacher's Guide* (New York: Behrman House, 1972)

Chesler, Evan R. *The Russian Jewry Reader* (New York: Behrman House, 1974)

Diesendruck, Zevi. *The Ideal Social Order in Judaism*, Studies in Reform Judaism (Houston: Rossel Books, 2005)

Elon, Amos. *Understanding Israel: A Social Studies Approach with Educational Materials by Morris J. Sugarman* (New York: Behrman House, 1976)

Frankel, Max and Judy Hoffman. *I Live in Israel* (New York: Behrman House, 1979)

Ganz, Yaffa. *Our Jerusalem* (New York: Behrman House, 1979)

Gelb, Ludwig. *My Third Escape* (Dallas, TX: Rossel Books, 1993)

Gold, Manuel. *Renegade Rabbi* (Dallas, TX: Rossel Books, 2019)

Goldstein, Albert S. *The Ever-Present Presence: Selected Writings of Albert S. Goldstein* (New York, NY: Association for Progressive Judaism, 2006)

Grobman, Alex and Daniel Landes. *Genocide: Critical Issues of the Holocaust* (Chappaqua, NY: Rossel Books, 1983)

--- *et al. The Simon Wiesenthal Center Annual, Volume I* (Chappaqua, NY: Rossel Books, 1984)

Harkabi, Yehoshafat. *The Bar Kokhba Syndrome* (Chappaqua, NY: Rossel Books, 1983)

Harlow, Jules, ed. *Exploring Our Living Past* (New York: Behrman House, 1972)

---. *Lessons from Our Living Past* (New York: Behrman House, 1972)

Jacobs, Louis. *A Jewish Theology* (New York: Behrman House, 1974)

Kaplan, Mordechai M., *et al. The New Haggadah,* Revised Edition (New York: Behrman House, 1978)

Kaunfer, Alvan and Marcia Kaunfer. *Dilemma: A Jewish Community Simulation Game* (New York: Behrman House, 1973)

Karkowsky, Nancy. *The Holocaust / A Discussion Guide* (New York: Behrman House, 1976)

Karp, Laura. *Stories from Our Living Past / Workbooks 1 & 2* (New York: Behrman House, 1974)

---. *When a Jew Prays / Students' Encounter Book* (New York: Behrman House, 1975)

---. *When a Jew Seeks Wisdom / Students' Encounter Book* (New York: Behrman House, 1976)

Katz, Betsy Dolgin. *Reinventing Adult Jewish Learning* (New York, Ktav Publishing, 2012)

---, *Jerusalem 3000: Or Hadash—Let a New Light Shine* (New York: UAHC Press, 1995)

Kitman, Carol and Ann Hurwitz. *One Mezuzah: A Jewish Counting Book* (Chappaqua, NY: Rossel Books, 1984)

Klein, Gerda Weissman. *A Passion for Sharing: The Life of Edith Rosenwald Stern* (Chappaqua, NY: Rossel Books, 1984)

---. *Promise of a New Spring: The Holocaust and Renewal* (Chappaqua, NY: Rossel Books, 1982)

Kraft, Stephen. *A Child's Introduction to Torah / Workbooks 1 & 2* (New York: Behrman House, 1973)

Kushner, Lawrence D. *The River of Light* (Chappaqua, NY: Rossel Books, 1981)

---. *The Way into Jewish Mysticism* (Woodstock, VT: Jewish Lights Publishing, 2001)

Lipstein, Morissa. *Lessons from Our Living Past / Workbooks 1 & 2* (New York: Behrman House, 1972)

Long, Frances. *The Jews of America / Student Inquiry Book* (New York: Behrman House, 1975)

---. *The Jews of Israel / Student Inquiry Book* (New York: Behrman House, 1976)

Neusner, Jacob. *Learn Mishnah* (New York: Behrman House, 1978)

---. *Learn Talmud* (New York: Behrman House, 1979)

---. *Making God's Word Work: A Guide to the Mishnah* (New York: Continuum, 2004)

---. *Meet Our Sages* (New York: Behrman House, 1980).

---. *Mitzvah* (Chappaqua, NY: Rossel Books, 1982)

---. *Our Sages, God, and Israel: Selections from the Talmud of the Land of Israel* (Chappaqua, NY: Rossel Books, 1985)

---. *Torah from Our Sages: Pirkei Avot* (Chappaqua, NY: Rossel Books, 1984)

---. *Tzedakah: Can Jewish Philanthropy Buy Jewish Survival?* (Chappaqua, NY: Rossel Books, 1982)

Newman, Shirley. *A Child's Introduction to the Early Prophets* (New York: Behrman House, 1975)

---. *Introduction to Kings, Later Prophets and Writings* (New York: Behrman House, 1980)

Priesand, Sally. *Judaism and the New Woman* (New York: Behrman House, 1975)

Prose, Francine. *Stories from Our Living Past*, ed. by Jules Harlow & Seymour Rossel (New York: Behrman House, 1974)

Rabin, Y. *Jewish Lights: A Substitute Teacher's Kit* (Chappaqua, NY: Rossel Books, 1984)

Rivkin, Ellis. *The Unity Principle: The Shaping of Jewish History*, (Behrman House, 2002)

Romm, Leonard. *The Swastika on the Synagogue Door* (Chappaqua, NY: Rossel Books, 1984)

Rosenthal, Gilbert S. *The Many Faces of Judaism* (New York: Behrman House, 1979)

Schein, Jeff and Jacob J. Staub. *Creative Jewish Education: A Reconstructionist Perspective* (Chappaqua, NY: Rossel Books, 1985)

Schick, Eleanor. *When a Jew Celebrates / Students' Encounter Book* (New York: Behrman House, 1973)

Schwartz, Howard. *Rooms of the Soul: A Novel Told in Hasidic Tales* (Chappaqua, NY: Rossel Books, 1984, revised 2020)

Siegel, Seymour and David Bamberger. *When a Jew Prays / Teacher's Guide* (New York: Behrman House, 1973)

--- and David A. Altshuler. *When a Jew Seeks Wisdom / Teacher's Guide* (New York: Behrman House, 1975)

Slonimsky, Henry. *Judaism and the Religion of the Future, Studies in Reform Judaism* (Houston: Rossel Books, 2005)

Staff of Park Synagogue. *Jewish Awareness Worksheets, Volumes 1 & 2* (New York: Behrman House, 1977)

Steinsaltz, Adin. *A Guide to Jewish Prayer* (New York: Schocken Books, 2000)

Stern, Chaim. *Gates of Freedom: A Passover Haggadah* (New York: Behrman House, 1997)

---. *Paths of Faith: Siddur Netivot Emunah—The New Jewish Prayer Book for Synagogue and Home* (SPI Books, 2003)

Strassfeld, Michael. *A Book of Life : Embracing Judaism as a Spiritual Practice* (New York: Schocken, 2002)

Sugarman, Morris J. *The Rabbis' Bible: The Torah / Student Activity Book* (New York: Behrman House, 1979)

---. *The Rabbis' Bible: The Later Prophets / Teacher's Guide* (New York: Behrman House, 1975)

---. *Understanding Israel / Student Activity Book* (New York: Behrman House, 1977)

---. *Understanding Israel / Teacher's Guide* (New York: Behrman House, 1977)

Wurtzel, Yehudah. *Lights: A Fable About Hanukkah* (Chappaqua, NY: Rossel Books, 1984)

Zimmerman, Sheldon. *The New Family Prayer Book: Minhag LaMishpachah*, illustrated by Sharon L. Wechter (New York: Ktav Publishing, 2012)

---. *The Family Prayerbook: The Fall Holy Days* (Dallas, TX: Rossel Books, 1989)

---. *The Family Prayerbook: Shabbat* (Dallas, TX: Rossel Books, 1992)

---. *The Family Prayerbook: The Spring Holy Days* (Dallas, TX: Rossel Books, 1990)

❀.
About the Author

This whole book, of course, is "About the Author." Nevertheless, I was urged to add a brief overview of my careers to date by way of a biographical statement.

Rabbi Seymour Rossel has authored many books and edited a great many more, working with some of the most distinguished Jewish authors of our times. Seymour is currently the CEO of Rossel Counseling and Consulting, Inc., and the Publisher of Rossel Books. He serves as a lecturer on the faculty of the Women's Institute of Houston and is popularly known as a weaver of words and an accomplished storyteller.

In the course of his career Seymour was Director of the Union for Reform Judaism's Press and Department of Education; Director of the Joint Commission on Reform Jewish Education; Dean of the School of Education of Hebrew Union College-Jewish Institute of Religion, NY; President of Rossel Books; Executive Vice-President of Behrman House, Inc.; Expert on Adult Education for the United States Holocaust Memorial Council, and Headmaster of Solomon Schechter Academy of Dallas, TX. He was the first Director of Education of the newly-formed Temple Shalom of Dallas, TX, and he was Director of Education of Temple Beth El of Chappaqua, NY. Seymour's work with the Coalition for the Advancement of Jewish Education culminated in his begin chosen as Chairperson for the Coalition's two international conferences on Jewish education: CAJE 13 (1988) and CAJE 21 (1996), both convened at the Hebrew University on Mount Scopus in Jerusalem. He served as Rabbi of Congregation Jewish Community North of Spring, TX.

As speaker, author, and editor, Seymour is listed in *Who's Who in the Eastern States*, *Contemporary Authors*, *The International Authors and Writers Who's Who*, as well as *Who's Who in World Jewry*. He holds the Israel Bonds' *Bonei HaNegev* award for excellence in Jewish Education and was honored by being made an ex-officio member of the Central Conference of American Rabbis.

Seymour is well known for his appearances as scholar-in-residence; teacher, board, and congregational workshop leader; and guest lecturer for Jewish synagogues and communities throughout North America.

Seymour and his wife Sharon L. Wechter live with their two bichon frise friends, Yofi and Shiri, relishing the time they spend with children and grandchildren. Seymour continues writing and publishing because, as he notes, he simply can't summon the will to stop.

Made in the USA
Monee, IL
11 September 2022